Nothing But Memories

Derek Fee

For Aine

All secrets are deep. All secrets become dark. That's in the nature of secrets.

Cory Doctorow, *Someone Comes to Town, Someone Leaves Town*

CHAPTER 1

Jim Patterson looked around the bar of `The Auld Sash' on the Woodvale Road and let his glance fall across the faces of the regular after-work drinking crowd. 'The Auld Sash' was a typical West Belfast working class pub with the regulation dark brown tobacco stained ceiling and dirt ingrained linoleum floor added to a selection of faces which would not have been out of place in the saloon scene of 'A Fistful of Dollars'. Every time Patterson entered this dingy hole he pulled himself up to his full height with pride at his position of a 'regular'. It was only within the confines of the 'Auld Sash' that he felt truly at home. Here, he could sit over a pint of Guinness and listen to the other patrons as they sounded off on the latest happening in sport, their conquests with the members of the opposite sex or their opinions on the politics of Northern Ireland. Although peace had been declared, the denizens of the 'Auld Sash' longed for the days when they could dish out various types of murder and mayhem on the Catholic residents of the province. The regulars of the 'Auld Sash' had status in Protestant West Belfast principally because the tavern had been home to one of the most ruthless gangs of Loyalist paramilitaries. There, amid their cronies they could boast of their crimes in the certain knowledge that not a single word would be passed to the Security Forces. No regular of the 'Auld Sash' had ever been known to grass on a comrade. No matter how obscene or heinous the crime, 'mum' was the word.

Patterson himself had no truck with violence. He would have shat himself if anyone had proposed that he join the paramilitaries but his otherwise boring life was enhanced in the eyes of those he encountered by his acceptance among the drinkers at the 'Auld Sash'. Jim Patterson was the quintessential voyeur who lived through the exploits of the patrons of The Auld Sash. He also had enough good sense to have the opposite of a photographic memory. Whatever Patterson heard within the confines of the 'Auld Sash', he allowed to stimulate him then he instantly forgot.

He sat, as usual, alone, a copy of the `Sun' newspaper stretched on the bar beside his half empty pint glass. He raised his glass to his lips and flicked the newspaper to page three for what must have been the fiftieth time. Four bare breasts dominated the page. His eyes scanned the headline-`Double Dollop of Delicious Dollies'. The twenty-first equivalent of news for the masses, two semi-nude girls cupping their ample bosoms in their small hands, stared back at him. Not a word on Iraq or Afghanistan. Just sex and the bizarre activities of so-called celebrities. He took a slug of his Guinness and let his eyes fall again on the 'double dollop'. The girls had huge breasts and inviting smiles. Patterson ran his tongue around his lips licking the remnants of the Guinness froth from his lank blond moustache. He wondered what it would be like to cup a pair of those breasts in his bare hands. The thought caused a smile to run along his thin lips. He was almost thirty years old and he had yet to savour the delights that he daily examined in the pages of the tabloids. He flicked the newspaper over so that the back page was facing upwards.

From one of the corners of the pub Joe Case watched the man he was about to kill go through his daily routine with the newspaper and the pint of Guinness. A man of habit our Mister Patterson, Case thought as he watched his intended victim stare into his newspaper. You could set your clock by Patterson if you had a mind to. If it was six o'clock, then you could be sure that Patterson was in the `Auld Sash' having his evening pint. Case leaned back in his seat and sucked hungrily on his pint of Guinness. He had been watching Patterson for three days. Shadowing the creep had been a breeze. The dossier he had received on the little tosser had been thin but accurate. Patterson's was a life in which there were no unexpected turnings. It was a 'bed to work' existence with the regular evening drinks at the 'Auld Sash'. Case had followed when Patterson left for work in the morning and was ensconced in his corner of the pub by the time Patterson arrived in the evening. Being a true professional, he knew that there had been no rush to finish the job. The mark suspected nothing and in any case hurrying would only increase his chances of screwing-up. And Case certainly wasn't going to screw-up. Just that fair haired weed at the bar and three more like him and he could slip away from the God-forsaken kip that was Belfast.

The fact that Patterson was a frequenter of the `Auld Sash' had thrown Case at first. The pub was a known haunt of the local members of the Ulster Defence Association and its sister hard-line group the Ulster Volunteer Force. More than one of the pot-bellied patrons now standing at the bar had been guests of Her Majesty for their excesses in `culling' the growing Catholic population and sometimes for the excesses in culling each other. But all that was over now. Back then in the 'Troubles' there was a smattering of politics on the side of the paramilitaries now it was just plain gang warfare. There were now as many reformed murderers in Ulster as there were in Bosnia. And only the bleeding heart liberals were talking 'war crimes tribunal' or 'truth and reconciliation'. A load of bollox, Case thought. The Protestant politicians still liked to talk about representing the 'majority' but demographics and Pope Benedict were working against them. Everybody knew that the Catholics bred like rabbits. Case looked over the rim of his pint glass at Patterson's slight figure. If the little bastard had been a member of the UVF, it would have put a right royal screw on his plans for him. But his luck was in. It hadn't taken long to learn that Patterson was just a hanger-on. A pussy. Rubbing shoulders with the hard men of Protestant Belfast probably gave him a hard-on. But that would all be over soon.

Case glanced at his watch. The large red digital display blinked out the figures 7:50. In exactly ten more minutes Patterson would wrap up his newspaper and drop it into his pocket, drain the last of his Guinness and begin to make his way back to his garret in Leopold Street where a plate of microwaved crap awaited him. It wasn't a long walk but it was the last that Patterson would ever take. Case looked up towards the window of the pub. Even through the grime on the glass pane and the filthy net curtain, he could see the water streaming down the outside of the window. Filthy bloody night, he thought to himself. There won't be many people on the streets on a night like this. A fine night to get this little job out of the way.

Case turned back towards the bar in time to see Patterson fold his newspaper and drop it into his pocket, then pick up his pint glass and drain the contents.

Showtime. Just like clockwork, old son, Case said to himself. He watched Patterson push open the pub door before standing up, hunching his black donkey jacket around his broad shoulders and following.

A sheet of icy cold rain blew directly into Case's face as he pushed open the door to the street. The warm dry interior of the pub was in direct contrast to the cold wet surroundings of the Woodvale Road. Patterson was twenty yards ahead of him hugging the walls of the terraced houses which lined the street. A quick glance in both directions was enough to assure Case that the streets were empty. Even the citizens of Belfast, inured as they were to living in one of Europe's dreariest cities, couldn't face the dismal streets with cold rain streaming down.

Case fell into step behind Patterson staying close to the wall. He moved quickly and silently on his rubber-soled running shoes so as to close the distance between him and the man in front.

As Patterson turned the corner, a wintry breeze pierced his cheap anorak and chilled his whole body. He could feel the water seeping through the cloth of his trousers causing the bottoms to stick uncomfortably to his shins. He cursed the rain and the cold. But most of all he cursed the winter and he cursed Belfast. He thought of the application form for emigration to Australia sitting on the mantelpiece of his tiny bedsit. Why not, he thought pushing himself closer to the red-bricked wall in a vain attempt to mitigate the impact of the rain. There was nothing to lose. No family, no friends, just a grubby bedsit and a life on the edge of redundancy. Things couldn't be any worse on the other side of the world. At least the sun shone in Australia. Patterson was vaguely aware of the sound of footsteps behind him. Not the clip of leather but the sucking sound of rubber. He turned and recognised one of the men he'd noticed sitting in the corner of the `Auld Sash' hurrying along behind him.

Case was about twenty feet from Patterson when he removed the Browning automatic from the inside pocket of his donkey jacket.

The distance between the two men closed. Fifteen feet, then ten. Case glanced around one last time. The rain soaked street was still deserted. He slipped the safety catch to off and pointed the gun at the back of Patterson's head.

Patterson heard the soft click of the safety release above the spiting sounds of the rain. He was about to turn again and look at the source of the sound when an explosion went off in his ear and a sharp blow struck the back of his head flinging him forward. He was dead before his body hit the wet pavement in front of him.

Case stood over the fallen man and clinically pumped two further bullets into the already shattered head. He replaced the gun in the pocket of his jacket and hurried into the darkness of one of the adjoining streets.

CHAPTER 2

Detective Chief Inspector Ian Wilson of the Criminal Investigation Division of the newly constituted Police Service of Northern Ireland eased his bulk into the rear of the police car. "No siren," he said and then dropped into silence. It was three hours beyond the end of his shift and he had been thinking of a glass of hot whiskey in front of his television set when the call had come in about the body in the Shankill. He glanced to his side at the neatly packed blue plastic suit that sat on the seat beside him. How many times had he donned a suit like that in the past twenty years. Too many, he thought. The Peace Process had returned Northern Ireland to some kind of normality. Not so many gratuitous murders these days. Terrorism and sectarian murders may be a thing of the past but the feuds between the UDA and the UFF had ensured that the body count hadn't diminished. That meant that Wilson and his team in the Belfast Murder Squad were under constant pressure to solve murders where there was bugger all chance of finding the culprits. Add to the terrorist body count the occasional 'straight' murder and you were looking at the most experienced set of murder detectives in the United Kingdom. Wilson looked out at the rain-soaked streets of Belfast. A couple of years ago he would have seen them as glum and threatening. But Belfast had taken on a new character since the official end of hostilities. There was a gaiety about every day life which most of the inhabitants of Ulster had almost forgotten existed. He was sure that the Victorian side-streets had not changed physically. The cramped brick buildings which had been built to house the shipyard workers at the end of the nineteenth century maintained their dour utilitarian outlook but the air that

12

surrounded them contained a new element - hope. Wilson too had hoped for an end to the death and destruction. His complete career in the Royal Ulster Constabulary and now the Police Service of Northern Ireland had been spent at the pit face of the 'Irish Problem'. He had viewed at the closest possible proximity the torn and broken bodies which were the fruit of the three hundred year old tribal conflict between the Catholic and Protestant communities in Northern Ireland. A spasm gripped his stomach as he realised that he was on his way to view yet another body in circumstances which were suspiciously similar to those which had obtained during the almost thirty years of conflict. He ripped open the pack that contained his blue plastic suit and shook it out. The car swung around the corner beyond 'The Auld Sash' bar and came to an immediate stop. Wilson slipped off his overcoat and immediately shivered. I'm too old for this, he thought as he slipped his feet into the blue leggings. He struggled into the upper part of the one piece suit, zipped it up and sat back.

"We're there, boss," the young policeman at the wheel said glancing over his shoulder.

"Ay, that we are," Wilson replied pushing himself up from his slouching position. His hand moved slowly towards the handle of the door and he pushed it as though it resisted the pressure of his hand. The door swung open and he climbed slowly out of the rear of the car.

"Filthy night, boss," a policeman approached the car and held the door wide so that Wilson could exit with ease. The constable wore a black waterproof poncho over his uniform.

Wilson pulled the white plastic gloves out of his pocket and slipped them mechanically on his hands as he looked ahead. The earlier heavy rain had turned into a light mist that the Irish call a soft rain. It was the most insidious kind of rain. A grey spray of tiny droplets barely containing any liquid. However, its softness was an illusion. If you stood about in rain like this for any period of time it would drench you to the skin. Wilson surveyed the scene in the street. It was one he had looked upon too many times in his career. Two mobile units had arrived as soon as the call had been received that a body had been found. They had immediately sealed off the area with crime scene tape. Because of the rain they had already erected a yellow plastic canopy over the body to protect whatever evidence remained at the crime scene and the two ark lights that had been set up on either side of the plastic cover cast a ghostly light over the proceedings. A generator hummed in the distance. Moving about under the tent he could see the shadowy figures of the SOCOs in their blue plastic overalls.

"No sign of the Doc," he said glancing along the street. Other than the police activity, the street was completely empty. The inhabitants of the Shankill had decided to ignore the death in their midst.

"He's due any minute," the policeman said.

Wilson glanced at his watch and looked through the front window of one of the terraced houses. Through the meshed curtain he could just discern the green of a football pitch and he remembered that Manchester United were playing in the Champion's League. The citizens of Belfast were obviously much more interested in the fortunes of their favourite team. Dead bodies had been two a penny in Belfast for much too long to cause a stir among the local population. He made his way slowly towards the canopy and signed the attendance sheet before slipping under the crime scene tape.

"What do we have, Billy?" Wilson asked the larger of two uniformed policemen standing outside the canopy.

"Some poor bastard with half a head," the Constable replied. "SOCOs inside looking for evidence. We touched nothing and as far as we can tell neither did anybody else."

"No last words by any chance?" Wilson asked more in hope than anything else.

The police constable named Billy turned his eyes skywards. "Wait until you see the body. Somebody wanted to make sure that this guy died and that he stayed dead. My guess is that he didn't even get the chance to say 'Ah shit.' never mind tell some passer-by the name of the man that nailed him."

He pulled aside the yellow plastic sheet of the tent and revealed to Wilson the corpse lying prone on the wet pavement. Two members of the forensics team were taking photographs of the body and the surrounding area.

"Hello lads," Wilson said entering the tent. "Filthy night. What have we got?"

The man taking the photographs turned to face him. "So far we've got fuck all." He nodded towards three shell casings each circled with white chalk. "That's the limit of it. If there was any other evidence, which I doubt, then it was washed away long before we arrived. No muddy footprints. No hairs. No strands from the jacket. No blood under the victim's fingernails. We've got nothing other than one very dead citizen and three shell casings."

"Mind if I take a look," Wilson didn't wait for an answer before moving to the body. Christ Almighty, he thought as he looked down at the corpse. As far as he could tell, the first shot had been from the rear and it had removed the top of the man's head sending slivers of brain and cranial blood in streams across the pavement and the wall of the adjacent house. The poor bastard would have died instantly. Wilson patted his pockets instinctively. His mind and every pore in his body cried out for nicotine. He

15

hadn't smoked in a year but if by chance his searching fingers had come upon a packet, his resistance would have immediately crumbled. He pushed the thought from his mind and knelt beside the body.

'Pencil?' he said to the SOCO closest to him holding out his hand. A short stub was dropped into his open palm. The three copper shells had been ejected onto the pavement. The killer was so confident that he wouldn't be caught that he didn't mind leaving the police a few shreds of evidence. He picked up one of the shells with the pencil and lifted it towards his face. It looked like a nine millimetre. Ballistics would be able to tell him whether it had been fired from a known pistol.

'Bag,' Wilson said. The SOCO produced a plastic bag and opened it. Wilson dropped the shell into the open bag. He picked up the second and third shells and repeated the process. As the last shell hit the bottom of the bag the SOCO immediately zipped it closed All the weapons in Northern Ireland had supposedly been 'de-commissioned' but only a fool would believe that there weren't still caches of arms hidden for the day that might come again. There were enough pictures of balaclava wearing fools brandishing all manner of weapons to show that there were still a healthy number of guns on the street. You don't convince people who have spent generations learning hate to immediately embrace their former enemies. There had been a lot of hot air spouted in the pursuit of peace and reconciliation but it would take more than the ending of hostilities and the establishment of a devolved assembly in Stormont to wipe away the years of mistrust. Wilson took the sealed plastic bag and dropped it into his pocket. At least there was one nine millimetre pistol which had not been handed in.

"Let's find out who this poor bugger is," he said pulling at the fingers on the gloves. He bent carefully over the body and slipped his fingers into the side pocket of the black jacket the corpse was wearing. Empty. He repeated the procedure on the other side and pulled out a cinema stub, a used bus ticket and a Bic pen whose clear plastic had been chewed through at the top. He carefully transferred the useless tickets and the pen to evidence bags. He moved on carefully to the trousers pockets. His fingers moved reluctantly. There was an element of violation in examining the contents of a person's pockets. Even if that person had recently become a corpse. Wilson pulled out the contents of the right hand trouser pocket. There were a half dozen pound coins and some small change. The left hand pocket produced nothing. Wilson dropped the coins into an evidence bag. He moved the body slightly and saw the copy of the tabloid newspaper staring up at him. Rain had soaked the pages and they began to disintegrate as he turned the body. The two smiling girls with the large breasts evaporated as the paper fell to pieces. Wilson let the body return to its original position and stood up. So far not a scrap to identify the corpse. It was likely that something would be found somewhere on the body that would yield a name and an address but Wilson would have to wait until the body had been transferred to the morgue to carry out a detailed search. The canopy moved above his head and he turned to look at the bland round face of Detective Sergeant George Whitehouse.

"Boss," Whitehouse said in mock surprise. "I thought that you'd be at home with your feet up before the fire by now."

"The call came in as I was about to head home," Wilson said wearily. He looked down into his sergeant's face. The two men were the Mutt and Jeff of the PSNI.

17

Wilson was muscular and stood at well over six-feet while Whitehouse was built closer to the ground at something just over five and a half feet. The face that Wilson stared into was that of a Prussian pikeman and could have been taken directly off his forefather who had lined up along the Boyne in 1690 to fight for King William against the Papists. Woodhouse's jowls gave him the appearance of a bulldog but the rest of the face was without feature. The nose was neither to large or too small and his eyes were blue but without the depth and liveliness normally associated with that colour. Whitehouse had a build which was normally called 'brick shithouse' – he was almost as broad as he was tall and looked like it would take a tropical hurricane to topple him. His paunch hung over the belt of his trousers a testament to his liking for Guinness and the lifetime lack of exercise. His blue plastic suit was XXL and was still bursting at the seems. Wilson had often surmised that George's family name certainly hadn't started out as Whitehouse. But who was going to quibble about a bit of foreign ancestry. George Whitehouse was as British as the Queen of England. On second thoughts he was probably just a little bit more British.

"I thought that I'd save you the trouble of rousting me," Wilson said returning to his examination of the body.

Whitehouse bent to examine the corpse. "Somebody surely wanted this poor sod dead," he said standing up. "Anyone who thought that those rats had given up is whistling up a gum tree. Fucking murderin' IRA bastards."

"Let's not jump to any rash conclusions, shall we George," Wilson peeled off the surgical rubber gloves. In Whitehouse's book every murderer was an 'IRA bastard'. "So far all we've got is a dead body and the fact that somebody put three shots into his head." He handed

18

Whitehouse one of the plastic evidence bags. "This is all I got out of his pockets."

"Five will get you ten that the stiff is a Prod," Whitehouse glanced quickly at the contents of the evidence bag before dropping it into his pocket. "We're right in the middle of Prod territory here." He followed Wilson out from underneath the canopy. "Didn't one of their people say one time that they weren't gone away. Well he got it right. I knew the bastards couldn't stay away from killing for very long."

"Look out, George," Wilson said running his fingers through his sodden hair. "Your prejudice is beginning to show. I don't want any rushes to judgement on this one and I certainly don't want one of my officers shooting his mouth off as to who might be responsible until we're a lot further along on this investigation. Do I make myself clear?" Why me? Wilson was thinking. Why did it have to happen on my patch? Something inside him told him that there was a shit load of trouble associated with this case and that most of that shit would be dumped on him if he failed to come up with a perpetrator quickly. Just when he was thinking that he would be back to good old solvable murder cases along comes a heap of crap like this. Somewhere in the back of his mind he remembered one of his lecturers at police college telling the class that eighty percent of murders were committed by a family member or a close friend. In those far off days before the 'Troubles' began in earnest, a detective might have one or two unsolved cases in his complete career. For some reason, usually the difficulty in establishing a motive or because the perpetrator was known but couldn't be brought to justice, those cases might stay open until the day the detective retired. Right now Wilson had worked on more than two dozen unsolved homicides and he was reckoned to have one of the best conviction records in the PSNI. The usual motive for sectarian murder was simply - religion. The perpetrator was generally totally unknown to his victim who was usually picked at random and there were always half a dozen witnesses who were ready to stand up and swear that the prime suspect was miles way when the deed was done.

"Yes, boss, I've got that." Whitehouse said through clenched lips. "But I'm still willing to lay odds that it turns out to be our Taig friends."

Wilson wiped the rain from his face. "I'll grant you that this looks like an execution. And I don't mind telling you that I'm shit scared of this case already. Most of the terrorists you and I know would need a machine gun to be sure of a kill. This one smells like a professional hit. Given the delicate political situation we have at this moment in time there's going to be a lot of heads looking over our shoulders on this one. So let's play it cool. No mentions of the IRA until we have something concrete. And I mean very concrete."

"The bastards'll never admit it. No claim, no blame. That the game they're playin'."

Wilson sighed. Whitehouse had been his second-in-command for the past five years and he was well aware of his sergeant's dislike for the terrorists of the IRA. Wilson himself hated all murderers whichever side of the religious divide they came from. But Whitehouse was a firm believer that the only way to solve the IRA problem was to shoot six hundred Republicans overnight. Whitehouse was in good company. However, the Peace Process was rapidly turning yesterday's terrorist into to-day's politician. It had happened all over the world so why should Northern Ireland be any different. Nelson Mandela, Robert Mugabe, Jomo Kenyatta, Yassar Arafat, the list went on and on. Now the names of the most prominent IRA and UVF men would have to be added to it. That might stick in the throat of men like Whitehouse but there was little or nothing that they would be able to do about it. Wilson could feel the rain penetrating the neck of his suit. The top of his jacket would be getting a soaking but his vanity precluded him from putting on the hood which hung over his upper back. He would have to get out of this weather soon or he would be in the same condition as the poor man under the canopy.

"I want to cover all the possibilities on this one," Wilson said. "Whoever pulled the trigger knew what he was doing and he definitely didn't want the victim to survive. My guess is that the second and third shots was for insurance but any fool could see that the first bullet had done its business. That means it could be drugs or some kind of vendetta which carried over from the past. I want to know everything there is to know about that man on the pavement. I want to know his name, where he lived and whether he was 'connected' with some paramilitary outfit. I want his relatives and friends questioned. And I want every house on this road canvassed. If anyone saw or heard anything I want to know about it. Use the uniforms. Did you call in Eric?"

"He should be on his way," Whitehouse said.

"When he arrives put him in charge of taking the statements."

A smile creased Whitehouse's thick lips. "He'll have his work cut out. You know where you are, boss. This is three wise monkey country. Nobody here will have seen or heard anything. And if they did, they certainly won't be telling us about it. As for SOCO,' he nodded at the ghosts in their blue suits. 'Those poor buggers will be out all night looking for clues and they'll probably come up with nothing."

"That's Eric's problem. As far as SOCO is concerned they work on the theory that someone passing through an area always leaves a trace. Let's not be too pessimistic. You stick with getting the information on the dead man. We'll set up an incident room in the Squad-Room at the Station. I'll be Senior Investigating Officer, you'll be my number two and we'll make Eric office manager. We'll hand out the rest of the work later. Make sure SOCO develop the photos of the corpse tonight and have them on my desk first thing tomorrow morning. If our friend did leave any trace when he passed through I want to know pronto." He pulled another evidence bag containing the shells from his pocket. "Get these over to ballistics. Looks like a nine millimetre and I want to know whether the gun has been used anywhere in the Province."

"Is that all," Whitehouse said lifting his head from the notepad on which he had been writing.

"For now," Wilson said smiling.

A door opened behind his back and an elderly woman stuck her head out.

"I knew it wasn't over," she said looking directly at Wilson and Whitehouse. "Them murderin' bastards will never give up the gun."

"We'll be taking statements shortly," Wilson said. "If you saw or heard anything we might catch the murderer quicker."

"Faith, I'll be no help to you. I'm almost blind and I'm as deaf as a post but if I was a man I'd get myself over to the Falls and I'd string up the Taig bastards by their balls."

She banged the door closed before Wilson could make any reply.

He saw that Whitehouse was smiling to himself. "Looks like they're going to have to teach people how to spell reconciliation before they can expect them to know what it's about."

The smile faded from Whitehouse's face. "There's a lot of people like that old woman about. It won't end that easily."

Wilson ignored the remark. He didn't want to believe that it wasn't over. The general population was tired of war without end and so was he. "Nobody thought to bring a couple of umbrellas, I suppose," he said to Whitehouse.

"I was at a Lodge meetin' when my bloody bleeper went off," Whitehouse said. "I barely got a chance to pick up this bloody suit." He squirmed as though he just remembered how uncomfortable he was in the suit.

Wilson had a bizarre mental picture of Whitehouse's mobile phone going off in a roomful of grown men dressed in regalia and with their left trouser legs rolled up. He was aware that most of his colleagues were members of Masonic Lodges and the Orange Order. Although he had been born a Protestant he had never been attracted by either the Masons or the Orange Lodge. Not that he hadn't received invitations. As soon as he had joined the Royal Ulster Constabulary he had been inundated with funny handshakes and invitations of membership. But something inside stopped him from accepting. Maybe it was that old line of Groucho Marx – I don't want to be a member of any club that would have me as a member- that preyed on his mind. He knew that his decision not to join either organisation had hampered his career such as it was but that was life. He owed nobody and nobody owned him.

"I'm out of here," Wilson said. "Before I get my death of cold." He turned to Whitehouse. "You stay with the stiff. The Doc should be here in a minute but I don't expect the pathology to tell us anything. Let's have an

23

autopsy done as soon as they can organise it at the Royal Infirmary. And don't forget. Keep that big gob of yours shut on this one."

"Roger," Whitehouse said and started back towards the canopy.

Wilson walked to the police car and pulled off his plastic suit. He put on his overcoat and slid into the back seat. He'd been right about his jacket. The neck was soaked and he felt uncomfortable. A chill ran down his back but he wasn't sure it was from the effects of the rain. He didn't like what he had just seen. It was obviously a professional hit. He could hope that it was something to do with drugs but the corpse didn't look like he had two pennies to rub together. No, this one looked like a return to the past and that didn't auger well for a quick resolution. And there would be pressure. The peace between the two communities was new and fragile. Both sides were scared out of there wits of breaking it. The people of Ulster would not forgive those who had taken their hope away. The dead body on the pavement was innocuous enough, even as a victim. But if that body signified a return to violence there would be hell to pay. And right in the middle of this huge shit pit stood Detective Chief Inspector Ian Wilson.

CHAPTER 3

Wilson opened the door of his neat semi-detached house in Malwood Park and tossed his heavy overcoat over the bottom of the banisters. Two white envelopes sat on the mat just inside the door masking the letters W and C of the word WELCOME which was still barely visible on the worn brown weave. He thought the positioning of the envelopes appropriate since his welcome in the house had always been unclear during the period Susan had been the mistress of it. He picked up the letters noticing that both had on the front the dreaded rectangular plasticated slot for his address. A major decision faced him. Did he really need the kind of aggravation that these letters were about to bring him? Deciding that he didn't, he tossed the envelopes on the tablet of the hall stand. He'd open them in the morning. Maybe.

The house in Malwood Park was, like many aspects of his life, a carry-over. His job in the PSNI wasn't the well thought out career decision which marked the current entrants. He was a copper because his father was a copper and what was good enough for his father would certainly be good enough for him. There could be no thoughts of University or even Teachers Training College. The pay and prospects in the old RUC were more than any young man could want. But good and all as they were, his wife had wanted more. Susan wanted the house in Malwood Park even when he knew in his heart and soul that he couldn't afford to give it to her. He'd listened to the admonishments of his parents and he bore the puerile gibes of his colleagues but he'd bought Susan the house she coveted. They lived among the bankers and the stockbrokers in the ritziest area of Belfast and somehow they'd struggled through the first few years of the mortgage with Susan's salary making up the shortfall.

He climbed the stairs slowly heaving with the effort of pushing his large frame up the wooden steps. God, but he was cold and tired. And wet, but mostly tired. He went into the bathroom and started to peel off his clothes. His shirt stuck to his back and he was forced to open the buttons before he could remove it. Every piece of clothing felt like it had been penetrated by the insidious cold wetness. He dumped the clothes in a heap in the corner of the bathroom and stood naked before the full length mirror. Where was the young giant of the RUC rugby team gone? He was twenty, no nearer thirty pounds overweight but his six feet four frame carried the excess easily. It was the face which looked back at him from the mirror which struck him most. The face bore the vicissitudes of life more than the body. The once lively blue eyes were dull and dead, hooded by heavy eyelids. His lantern jaw seemed to hang off the end of his long face and his once prominent cheekbones were beginning to be obscured by creeping folds of soft white flesh.

You need six months in the country, my boy, he spoke to his image as to some long lost friend but in his own mind he doubted whether six months would be enough to revitalise that dead face.

He stepped into the shower and turned the water to full heat feeling the hot droplets sting and redden his skin. Gradually he felt the warm stream wash away the cold.

When he'd finished showering and drying himself, he walked into the back bedroom. He had moved out of the room he and Susan had shared for the ten years of their marriage the week after she died. It had been a week of sleeplessness. He had lain in their bed each night with his eyes jammed shut waiting for sleep that never came. His

26

mind refused to permit him to glance towards the foot of the bed where he fully expected to see a ghostly apparition of Susan standing over him reprovingly. If there was a life beyond death, Susan would know the depth of his betrayal of her. The sleepless nights finally convinced him that he should leave the room to her ghost. The cleaning lady maintained the room as a mausoleum for his dead partner. He put on his bathrobe and went into the kitchen. Food was normally something he pushed down his throat in the police canteen. He took no pleasure in eating. The fridge was as bare as usual and green mould was beginning to consume a block of cheddar which dominated the empty space around it. He removed the mouldy cheese and a beer from the fridge. After carefully cutting away the mould, somebody had told him that it was carcinogenic, he cut several slices of cheese and put them between two pieces of stale bread. It was time to switch off his mind and switch on the television. He carried his beer and his makeshift cheese sandwich into his living room and switched on the BBC. He prayed for something light hearted to appear. As the screen brightened the news reader sat staring directly at him presenting the evening news. He half listened to the catalogue of the days atrocities from the Occupied Territories, Sierra Leone and the Congo. The cheese sandwich tasted like sawdust and he had to occasionally dislodge clumps of bread from the top of his palette with slugs of beer. Bloodied and torn bodies continued to roll across the television screen making no impact on the already immunised audience. The newscaster had commented that some of the images might cause distress. Wilson wondered to whom. He glanced at his watch and prayed for the last ten minutes of the programme to accelerate.

"On the home front," the news reader continued over a picture of Stormont Castle. "The Alliance Party has renewed its demand for the setting up of a South African style 'Truth and Reconciliation Commission'. Lord Alderdice said that the Commission should have the widest possible remit to examine some of the atrocities carried out during the 'Troubles'. He believes that without the severest examination of the actions of all the parties now involved in the political re-construction of the Province, the process of healing the wounds of sectarian strife will not be fully attained. The Unionist majority and Sinn Fein have expressed themselves as being sceptical to such a development. A spokesman for the Unionist Coalition said that the members of his Party believed that there was little to be gained from raking over the events of the past. The proposed Truth and Reconciliation Commission might in fact be counter-productive and lead to a return to conflict." The picture changed to the wet Belfast street which Wilson had left some time before. "In Belfast this evening, a man has been murdered." The camera panned across the scene of the shooting catching the PSNI officers in their flak jackets cradling their machine guns. Deep red cranial blood still stained the rain washed path. The corpse had been removed before the arrival of the television crew but the cameraman made up for the deficiency of a body by the close-up of the bloody footpath. The face of a well-known politician appeared on the screen mouthing the usual anodyne crap about 'heinous crimes and a population under threat, will this butchery never end etc.'. He had seen the same face wheeled on time after time. Perhaps only one tape existed which the television station played for every murder. He looked for the legend 'library pictures' on the screen but didn't find it. "The PSNI Press Office has stressed," the newscaster continued. "That there is absolutely no evidence to suggest that the murder was motivated by sectarianism. A team of crack Murder Squad detectives has already been assigned to the case and every avenue of enquiry would be explored."

Wilson raised his beer and toasted the screen as the news reader smoothly moved to the next story. God bless the good old Press Office. Thirty odd years of practice had made them experts at passing the right message. Now was the time to assuage the fears of the man in the street. Don't panic, folks. There certainly wasn't a vicious sectarian killer on the loose. Don't worry. The bad old days will never come again. It was his misses what done it. Blew his head off and then gave him another one for good measure. In a pig's arse, he thought. Somebody had wanted that poor bastard dead and the man who had pulled the trigger knew what he was about. This wasn't a random sectarian kill.

He didn't even get his ten minutes, he thought. The first sectarian killing rated ten minutes, the five hundredth ten seconds. He picked up the remote control and was about to press the off button when the weather map appeared on the screen. The satellite picture showed banks of dirty black clouds spreading from Newfoundland to Ireland. They were in for a prolonged period of `typical' Irish weather. He flicked the 'off' button on the remote control and watched the screen go progressively blank. There would be no solace from television. He picked up a Stephen King novel from the coffee table and started towards the bedroom. He needed a good belt of unreality.

CHAPTER 4

Case watched the same newscast on his small television and laughed out loud. He filled himself another glass of Bushmills and toasted the newsreader.

"Thanks mate," he said and drained the glass, "you've just proved that you can fool all of the people all of the time."

He poured himself another glass of the golden coloured liquid and drank it in one swallow. The bottle of Bushmills had become part of his `after-kill' ritual. Tomorrow morning he'd feel dreadful but, at that moment, having succeeded yet again, he needed to let off steam. What he would really like to have done was to pick up some brasser in Royal Avenue and screw her brains out. But that would involve a risk. And Case wasn't taking any risks.

Only three more, he thought as he downed another whiskey. It was so easy. Belfast had changed since Case had served with the Paras there. There was a time when the streets were littered with the bodies of those caught up in the 'Troubles'. Then there had been the killings when the turf battles had broken out. Now the 'Troubles' were a thing of the past and the Loyalist and Republican gangs were either involved in real politics or in criminal activities. The guy he had offed might be considered as the result of a drugs turf war rather than a sectarian killing. That's why Case was going to have to muddy the waters. What the politicians and the people feared most was a return to the bad old days. He needed time to complete his mission and he didn't need the fuzz up his arse while he was at it. So the obvious ploy was to make them think it was sectarian. That would send them on a wild goose chase and he would be out of Belfast before you could say Jack Robinson. By the time they copped on he would be on a beach somewhere.

He wondered what his old pals in the SAS would say if they saw him now. "Bastards," he chanted again and again as though he were standing on the terrace of a football ground. Too bloody violent for them, was he? Well there were people who were willing to pay good money for the kind of violence he had perfected. He took another slug of the whiskey. "Bloody bitch, bloody bitch, bloody bitch." He chanted at the television screen. He'd loved the Regiment and she'd had him drummed out. He emptied his glass and then re-filled it. He should have killed the slag. He remembered the pleasure he had derived from beating her and her lover to a pulp.

"Should have killed them both," he said drunkenly. "Should have killed both the slags."

Wonder where his bitch of an ex-wife was now, he thought. Probably giving her best in some knocking shop or other. He laughed out loud at the thought. It was about all she was good for. Wherever she was he didn't give a bollocks. When this job was finished he'd have twenty grand of spending money in his back pocket. Then maybe off to Spain. Rent a villa on the Costa and live easy for a while. Until the money runs out. Then back to work again. Since he started working for the spooks there had been continuous work on offer. It almost made up for being dumped out of the SAS. He needed the buzz. If he hadn't been picked up by the spooks he would have gone back to villainy or maybe he would have joined the Oakley Brigade in Iraq. He'd already put his name on the list for Blackwater. The buzz was everything, he thought re-filling his glass. Without the buzz he'd put a bullet through his head.

The Bushmills was beginning to bite. His eyes started to glaze over. Gotta report to the boss to-morrow, he thought, as he slowly sank into unconsciousness.

CHAPTER 5

The rain of the previous night had turned into a light mist by morning. 'Soft rain' meant that the population of the island would spend the day gazing at a constant cover of clouds which would only vary in colour between light grey and black.

Wilson had slept poorly for all his tiredness. His legs moved leadenly as he entered the PSNI station which was responsible for what had been the most dangerous fifteen square miles of city in the United Kingdom - Belfast `C' Division operating out of Tennent Street. During Wilson's ten years in Belfast, the station had been constantly under construction until it came to resemble a fortress. It still had a long way to go before it reached the totally armoured state of its sister stations in the Springfield Road and Andersonstown and although efforts were being made to create a 'softer' image to go with the new name, the impression of a fort was still unmistakable. No amount of remodelling was going to change its' character: it would always be an alien body nestling among a hostile population. Wilson wore a blue anorak over his somewhat faded suit. The Desk-Sergeant gave him a cursory nod as he passed through the public section of the station and made his way to the rear of the building where the spartan accommodations of the Criminal Investigation Division were located.

He sometimes forgot that he had been entering this building every working day for the past ten years. If the RUC, or the PSNI as it was now called, had been father and wife to him, then the building at Tennent Street was the womb. As soon as he entered through the tall grimy oak front door, he felt at home. There among the stench of sweat and cigarette smoke, cursing and swearing detectives and screaming miscreants, he had found his true element.

His small office was roughly the size of the broom cupboard at his house in Malwood Park. Four pieces of furniture dominated the room; the ancient wooden desk which he had salvaged from the wreckers took up at least fifty percent of the floor space, a dilapidated swivel chair stood facing the desk and what little space remained was taken up by a steel filing cabinet and a battered coat-stand. The floor space directly in front of his desk was covered with stacks of files which stood like mini 'Leaning Towers of Pisa', swaying in defiance of the laws of gravity. The office had been cut out of a much larger room by the erection of a glass partition. Beyond the glass in the remnants of the large Victorian room stood the six desks inhabited by the other members of the Criminal Investigation Division. Wilson oversaw them from his glass-walled cubby hole. He often wondered what thoughts ran through the heads of the members of the public who were unfortunate enough to experience the sight he gazed on every day. Raised on a diet of pristine police stations in `Z Cars' and other police soaps, the dirt and grime of a building which the Office of Public Works should have long ago condemned generally came as a surprise.

He tossed his anorak and suit jacket on the battered wooden coat-stand and sat in his chair. The base of the chair creaked under his weight. As usual, a copy of the Belfast Newsletter lay draped over the top of the computer keyboard which had pride of place directly in front of his chair. He wondered casually whether last night's victim had made the paper. If he had, it would be page ten at best. Killings in Northern Ireland still did not constitute real news. Headlines of general interest such as `Vicar Elopes With Fourteen Year Old Schoolgirl' formed the daily staple of news for the Province's readers. Death, whether by tens in Iraq or thousands in a tsunami, was too real to be confused with `news'. He flipped the paper over to the sports section and gradually moved from the rear of the paper towards the front page. The six line story was on page eight. The text was interchangeable with that of any hundred similar stories which had been run over the past twenty-five years. An unidentified man found shot in a Belfast street. Police to release the name of the dead man when the relatives have been notified. Thankfully the newspapers had refrained from speculating on whether the man was the victim of a sectarian killing. At least that was an advance. Nobody wanted to raise the spectre of a return to the past. With a bit of luck there might not even be a follow up story. 'You're full of shit," he said to himself as he scanned the paper for any further mention of the killing. Maybe Whitehouse was right. Thirty years of violence had bred a new type of individual, the psychopath couldn't give up killing even when the so-called 'war' was over. All of the main groups and most of the splinter organisations had accepted the political compromise which had finally stopped the violence. But that didn't mean that there wasn't some twisted individual out there with a gun who was willing to continue the war all on his own.

"Mornin', boss," Whitehouse stood at the door of Wilson's office. Nobody ever tried to enter the office, there just wasn't enough room. "You're about early."

Wilson looked up from his newspaper and sighed audibly. "Good morning to you George. Some day you're going to surprise me and say something subtle but I think I'm going to have to wait a bit yet." He shifted his eyes to the newspaper "I see that our client of last night made page eight of the 'Telegraph'. Sign of the times. What did you get on him?"

"His name was James Patterson," Whitehouse leaned against the door-jam. "Address in Leopold Street. He was some class of a lackey in the office over at Mackies. Then got laid off. No previous with us. I've already checked him out with our intelligence people in Castlereagh and with Military Intelligence in Holywood. Nobody's got a dicky bird on him. He's as pure as the driven snow as far as we're concerned. A right anonymous wee bugger if there ever was one."

Wilson's mouth creased into a smile. "You mean to tell me that the standard press statement was true this time."

Whitehouse nodded.

"Any chance that he was a 'sleeper'?" Wilson asked.

"Your guess is as good as anybody's on that one," Whitehouse replied. "Tryin' to keep an eye on the active ones is hard enough without attemptin' to rope in the fools who think they'd like to become part of the action."

"What about the next of kin? Have they been informed?"

"That's the easy part. There are no next of kin. The poor bugger was an orphan. Just like the song says `no mommy's kisses, no daddy's smiles'." Whitehouse paused but Wilson didn't react. "Not only was this guy nobody's child," Whitehouse continued. "But he was nobody's brother or nephew. We can't find a living soul who's related to him. This guy could have landed from Mars yesterday there's so little on him. It wouldn't surprise me to find that he hadn't a friend in the world either."

Wilson thought about the small body with the half head lying Christ like on the wet Belfast street. Nobody owned him, nobody loved him and nobody befriended him. But some bastard took away the only thing he had-his life. Something stank to high heaven in a society where the gun culture had taken over. Maybe it was inevitable after Ulster had seen so much useless death that had basically gone unpunished. You could rub shoulders in your local pub or greasy spoon with someone who had dropped a woman continually on her head until it had cracked open like an eggshell. Or maybe you could have a quiet drink with someone who had set a bomb that had maimed women and children. Wilson didn't agree with amnesty. He wanted to put the psychopaths where they belonged - behind bars. Only brain-dead politicians would put some of the idiots he'd banged up back on the streets. One thing he was sure of, whoever had killed Patterson wasn't new to it. He done it before. Probably many times before. And if he or she turned out to be someone that the pols had released as some kind of political compromise there would be hell to pay. He'd see to that.

"We can expect a quiet funeral, then," he said lost in his thoughts.

"The way things look the state will have to bury the poor bastard."

"That's going to screw up the media no end," Wilson said. "No grieving relations to be interviewed and no bigwig Loyalist pols carrying the Union Jack draped coffin. No luck with the house-to-house enquiries?" Wilson asked.

"Wise up. The uniforms could have your life for keeping them out half the night for nothing. Patterson was let go by Mackies last year. I sent a constable around there to see if anyone there could throw any light on him. Like I said last night, the poor sod happened to be in the wrong place at the wrong time. It looks like we can chalk another one up to the Fenian murderers." Whitehouse placed a single sheet of paper on the desk in front of his superior. "It's all in there," he said as he laid the paper on top of the monitor of the computer. "The pathologist examined the body last night. Nothing new. The autopsy won't give us anything new. Three shots, the last two were a waste, the first shot killed Patterson instantly. Ballistics ran a quick check on the shells. Standard nine millimetre. Could have been fired from something like a Browning."

"Is that certain?"

"No. It's just an educated guess."

"Do we have any 'players' on the street with this kind of M.O.?" Wilson asked picking up the file.

"Not that I know of," Whitehouse thought for a minute. "It took some fuckin' balls for a Taig to march into Protestant West Belfast to do this one."

"Let's not make too many leaps in the dark concerning our perp," Wilson was annoyed that he had used the word 'perp'. He hated the American cop shows with their super-cool hero living in a luxurious converted warehouse apartment. Their snappy dialogue was full of words like 'perp' and now it was beginning to influence him. He looked at the paunch hanging over Whitehouse's belt. Nothing could be further from the super-cool image of the cop show. But Whitehouse was a damn good policeman despite the fact that he was also a bigot. He glanced at the photographs of the deceased which had already been included in the file. It had been a neat clinical job.

"Are you finished with the paper?" Whitehouse's request cut across Wilson's thoughts. "There were a few football matches in England last night."

Life goes on, Wilson thought folding the newspaper and tossing it to his colleague. The death of James Patterson hadn't even been sufficiently novel to keep Whitehouse's attention.

"Read it later," Wilson pulled his anorak from the coat stand. "Don't ask me why but something about this one bothers the hell out of me. The killer wanted to make sure

38

that Patterson was well and truly dead. If Patterson wasn't a 'player' then there's got to be another reason. I want to see where this character lived." Wilson squeezed past Whitehouse into the body of the squad-room. "We'll take your car."

Whitehouse pulled up outside the house which had been Patterson's home. Leopold Street was typical of the urban blight which the well-meaning Victorian Belfast City Fathers would inflict on the future generations. The dilapidated red-bricked labourer's cottages stood side by side the length of the road. But areas like this were on the up in 'new' Belfast. 'Yuppiedom' had arrived in Belfast along with the Peace Agreement. The upwardly mobile young professionals wanted to live in the city. They wanted to ape their London and New York equivalents by gentrifying the old Victorian streets. The architects and interior designers were doing a roaring trade and the price of property was beginning to reflect the new optimism. The red-brick front of Patterson's abode was almost black from a century's deposit of city grime. Gentrification had yet to arrive. As the car stopped Wilson glanced around looking for the property vultures. They could always be found in areas like this. He saw no one. Perhaps the rain was keeping them away.

"The place is in four bedsits," Whitehouse said as the policemen approached the front door. "The house is in the name of Arthur Patel," he screwed his face up at the name. "He owns a couple of properties around the city. Rents the dumps out to students, young female office workers or single males like Patterson. I called the number of the rental agency first thing this morning. Mr. Patel prefers to live in London where he won't be bothered by asshole Paddies.

39

His office has no idea who Patterson was or where he came from. Mr. Patel doesn't take what you might call a fatherly interest in his tenants. They give him money and he gives them a dump to live in. Blood suckin' bastard."

"Careful, George," Wilson stood before the front door which bore the scars of many a battle with somebody's hobnailed boots. "Your racism is likely to overcome your bigotry."

Four bells had been crudely stuffed into a hole gauged in a brick beside the door. Each bell had a name written in faded ink beneath it.

Whitehouse removed a plastic bag from his pocket and tipped a plastic key ring holding three keys into the palm of his hand. He slipped a Yale key into the lock and turned. The key moved smoothly in the lock and the door swung open.

The hallway was dark and the steel grey walls hadn't seen a lick of paint in the past twenty years. Wilson pushed the light switch behind the door but the hallway remained unlit. Both men looked simultaneously at the ceiling where an empty light socket hung suspended from a mesh of bare wires.

"Mr. Patel must be very energy conscious," Wilson said as he moved into the hallway. "This should be fun."

There were two doors on the ground floor. Whitehouse moved to the nearest one and tried the other two keys from Patterson's key ring. Neither key made any impression on the stout lock. He went through the same procedure with the second door and the lock turned when the first key was inserted.

"Bingo," Whitehouse said as he pushed in the door and entered Patterson's bedsit. Both men fished in their pockets and removed surgical gloves which they slipped onto their hands before entering the room.

As Whitehouse passed through the door he flicked the light switch and a faint yellow glow illuminated the dark room.

Patterson's home consisted of one room approximately 15 feet by 12 feet. Within that 180 square foot space he had lived, ate and slept. The lower half of a set of steel bunk beds was pushed against the side of the room opposite the door its four redundant posts jutting the air at each corner. A sink unit had been set into one of the side walls and a two ring gas burner sat on a roughly constructed shelf. A gas bottle poked its head out from underneath the sink. A relatively new microwave sat beside the two-ring burner. The floor was covered in cheap linoleum whose original colours might be guessed at but would never again be revealed. A coin operated electricity meter stood on the floor just inside the door. A series of shelves holding books and videos had been set above the bed. The only other piece of furniture was a battered wooden chest of drawers on which stood an equally battered 19 inch television/video combination. A plastic bowl with the coagulated remains of a cornflake breakfast sat on top of the television set.

"Somehow or other I don't think Patterson was expecting a visit from 'Home and Garden'," Wilson said moving around the room. Somebody might have done the poor bastard a favour taking him away from all this, he thought.

Wilson moved aimlessly around the room trying to get a feel for what appeared to be a pathetic existence. Why the hell did somebody want to take away what little life had bestowed on Patterson? The bad feeling that started the previous night was gaining momentum in his mind. This guy was a nobody who had nothing. No family, no friends. That meant no immediate suspects. Nowadays it was drugs and prostitution that were the root causes of murder along with the traditional and occasional family altercation. This bedsit didn't look like the pad of a drug runner or a pimp so that line of enquiry would probably lead nowhere. That left a sectarian motive and that made Wilson nervous.

"Holy God, look at this soddin' filth."

Wilson turned and saw Whitehouse examining the contents of the shelves above the bed.

"This boy was sick. He needed his head examined," Whitehouse held out a magazine.

Wilson crossed to the bed and took the magazine which Whitehouse proffered. He needed only a glance to understand Whitehouse's remark. The cover depicted a young man being fellated by a second young man. Wilson flicked quickly through the well thumbed pages. The photos were exclusively of males and went way beyond the limits of the Obscene Publications Act. Patterson was a connoisseur. This kind of filth wasn't available on the top shelf of the local newsagent. It had to be sought out. Wilson took a second glance around the room. People with this kind of interest generally found what they were looking for on the internet. Magazines were old technology for the porn gang. No computer. Patterson had been low tech or maybe just old fashioned.

"Our man doesn't go only the one way," Whitehouse said passing a bundle of magazines depicting hard core heterosexual sex to Wilson. He picked up a handful of videos and looked at the boxes. "If these videos are of Bambi then she's got two legs and she doesn't object to opening them."

"Nothing political I suppose," Wilson said tossing the magazines on the bed.

Whitehouse raised his eyebrows and smiled. "None of our pols have the equipment to appear in stuff like this."

"Very drole, George. Where does that leave us?" Wilson wondered aloud. He was well aware that there was an active gay community in Belfast. The boys in vice would have to be consulted. He stretched up and pulled a tattered copybook from the shelf. It was the kind of small lined book that children generally used for their homework. The name 'James Patterson' was written in careful adolescent writing on the cover.

"Holy Jesus!," Wilson exclaimed as he flicked through the first few pages of the copybook. Patterson couldn't draw to save his life but his simplistic sketches were not difficult to decipher. The pages were littered with crude drawings depicting what appeared to be young boys and grown men taking part in various permutations of homosexual acts centred on sodomy and fellatio. Beside each drawing were descriptions of the acts written in barely literate English. James Patterson was one seriously disturbed individual.

"This adds a new dimension to the enquiry," Wilson said. "Let's give this place a proper going over." He opened the chest of drawers. "Look for letters, indications of friends, relatives, anything to give us a lead on this bloke. Someone has to know the bugger. You can't go through life without leaving a footprint. We need to find that footprint." He pulled open the top drawer of the chest of drawers. It was half full of grey faded underwear and cheap tee-shirts. Charity shop gear, he thought. The drawers beneath it were equally unproductive.

This is eerie, Wilson thought as he closed the final drawer of the small chest. No letters, no indication of the presence of any other individual in the room besides Patterson. He had been momentarily seduced by the hypothesis of a sexual motive for the murder but there were gaps in that theory. Sex murders were crimes of passion.

43

Blood and gore. Slashed throats and severed penises. Patterson had been killed with the minimum of fuss by a cold-blooded murderer. Sex couldn't be ruled out as a motive but if there was a sex killer on the loose he sure as hell knew his business.

"Not a sausage," Whitehouse said and smiled. "It'd be pretty difficult to conceal something in this dump."

Wilson looked around the room. Every drawer had been emptied and searched; every cushion lifted; the inside of every book and magazine examined.

"Find any tracks on Patterson's arms?" Wilson asked.

Whitehouse frowned. "None mentioned. Lots of scratches and scars but no tracks. I can ask the pathologist. What are you thinkin'?"

"If this Patterson character was a rent boy there should be signs of more money about." He picked up the Social Security book from the table beside the bed. "He draws the brew religiously every week. Seventy-five pounds. The rent on this hole is covered so his has ten quid a day to look after himself. He might just about manage as long as he has no bad habits. But if he were a user then he might have been forced onto the game. That might explain the reading material. I want Patterson checked out with vice as soon as we get back to the Station. I also want to know whether any rent boys have been reporting threats of physical violence."

"That's par for the course for those guys," Whitehouse said writing in his notebook. "I still say he was the wrong man in the wrong place. He's probably a perv all right but that's not what got him killed."

"That's what I like about you, George." Wilson picked up the copybook which he had thrown on the bed. "You keep an open mind right through the investigation."

44

He looked at the drawings again. What in heaven's name had possessed Patterson's mind when he had scribbled his crude drawings and penned his inarticulate descriptions of the acts they depicted? They would probably never know. "I want SOCO to go over this place with a fine tooth comb. If we've missed anything I want to know about it post haste. Fingerprints, dried semen, blood, anything. And I want all the inhabitants of this dump and the neighbours questioned. I want to know whether they think Patterson might have been on the game. I want to know whether he brought friends home. I want to know everything there is to know about this man."

"I don't envy SOCO," Whitehouse' said tossing a handful of videos onto a shelf. "This place looks like it hasn't been cleaned since the Great Flood so we've probable got the grime of ages to process. But you're the boss." His tone left no doubt about what he thought of the usefulness of the exercise.

"Let's get back to the Station," Wilson said dropping the copybook into an evidence bag and stuffing it into his pocket.

CHAPTER 6

The two men passed the journey back to Tennent Street in silence. Wilson was lost in thought. The information they had gleaned concerning the private life of James Patterson might have been germane to his death but might also have been the greatest red-herring that the killer could have hoped for. In Northern Ireland what you saw was seldom what you got so the news on Patterson complicated rather than simplified the investigation.

"Chief Inspector," the Desk-Sergeant signalled to Wilson as soon as he entered the station. "Sorry to bother you, sir. The Super wants to see you, pronto."

"I'll give him a call," Wilson started towards his office.

"I think he meant now and in person, sir," the Desk-Sergeant said before Wilson left the entrance hall.

Wilson sighed and started to mount the steps towards the office of Superintendent Joseph Worthington. He supposed that such a call was inevitable but it was just a little too soon in the investigation. What the hell could he report within the first 12 hours of a murder which seemed to have no apparent motive and no clue as to who the murderer might be.

"You wanted to see me," Wilson said as he entered Worthington's office.

The Superintendent looked away from his computer screen. "I fucking hate this thing," he said nodding at the computer screen. "It used to be meetings, meetings, meetings now it's just e-mails, e-mails, e-mails. Every bugger in the PSNI thinks that I need to know what they're up to and that's not counting the number of questionnaires I have to fill out for our friends in Human Relations."

"That's the problem of management but that's also why they pay you the big bucks," Wilson stood in front of the Superintendent's desk.

"So what the hell have you been up to now?" Worthington said taking off his reading glasses.

"We're looking into last night's murder in Woodvale. Nothing so far but it's early days."

"Nothing else? You haven't been pissing anyone off recently?"

"Not that I know of. Why? Has someone been complaining."

Worthing smiled. "Ian, you are the most insufferably insolent sod in the PSNI. I don't know one member of management that you haven't pissed off. Every day I come to this office I ask myself why it's me that has to deal with guys like you. The Deputy Chief Constable has been on to me this morning and he wants to see you immediately. I doubt it's about the investigation of last night's killing. Not screwing his secretary are we?"

"Not likely, the poor girl was made for spite."

"From what I hear that's never been an issue with you before. Some people say that you're trying to work you way through the entire female population of the PSNI. But I suppose that's only pub talk."

Wilson smiled. "I've only scratched the surface. The DCC didn't give any idea of what might be on his tiny mind."

It was Worthington's turn to sigh. "That's what I mean when I say insolent sod. He didn't say why he wanted to see you but I want you to concentrate on not pissing the man off. He gets pissed off with you, he takes it out on me. So please keep a civil tongue in your mouth difficult as that might be for you. Now piss off and let me get on with clearing my inbox. He wants you there now. Not in two hours, so get on it."

"Shit!" Wilson ran his hand through his curly grey hair as he left Worthington's office. A trip to PSNI Headquarters to meet Deputy Chief Constable Roy Jennings was not Wilson's idea of fun.

"Tell Eric where I am," Wilson said to the Duty Sergeant turning towards the door to the Station. "And tell him I want an up-dated file on the Patterson murder on my desk by the time I get back."

The Headquarters of the Police Service of Northern Ireland is housed in an impressive brick building in the Belfast suburb of Castlereagh directly fronting the more famous Castlereagh Detention Centre. Wilson flashed his warrant card to the constable on duty at the door and immediately took the lift to the top floor.

The outer office of the Deputy Chief Constable was at least four times the size of Wilson's cubby hole and looked like a suite in the Sheraton Somewhere.

"He'll be with you shortly, Inspector Wilson," the Secretary looked up from her desk into Wilson face.

"That will just make my day" Wilson said tossing his anorak over the arms of a steel coat stand. He sat in an easy chair and looked at the DCC's Secretary. He had been overcritical in telling his Super that she was pulchritudinously challenged. She was dressed in civilian clothes with a skirt that rode just above the knee. Her blond hair was shorter than the last time he had seen her and she had added several pounds to her Rubenesque figure. He might not toss her out of bed after all. She had already turned to her computer and was studiously ignoring him. Wilson's reputation for scoring with the women constables had been considerable. He had bedded quite a few during his career and none of them had been an unwilling participant even when they knew that he was a 'screw them and leave them' individual. There was a copy of the Belfast Telegraph sitting on a low table in front of him but he didn't bother to pick it up. He was still wondering why Deputy Chief Constable Roy Jennings wanted to see him when the door opened and his jaw dropped. Out of the inner office came a women who was stunningly beautiful and who he had known intimately, in the biblical sense. Katherine McCann was one of those women who had improved with age. She wore a black pin-striped suit with a skirt just above the knee. The dark colour of her clothes set off her blond hair which fell just to the collar of her white blouse. She stood erect on high heels with an air of confidence totally consistent with her standing as a Queen's Council.

Wilson pulled himself together and stood up. The look on Kate McCann's face didn't exactly please him. She looked like she had just discovered something nasty on the sole of her shoe.

"Kate," Wilson said when his voice finally started to work. "I didn't know that you were back in Belfast."

"It's my home, Ian." She maintained the look of distaste.

Wilson started to move but his feet seemed to be stuck in concrete. He felt that he should move to kiss her or at least shake hands but it seemed that there was a force-field between them repelling any intimacy. Kate had been different from all the others. She hadn't been just another conquest. Sure, he had gained huge kudos among the rank and file when it had got out that he was bedding one of Belfast's leading barristers and a beautiful woman at that. Kate McCann was the kind of woman that could get under your skin. Sometimes in those quiet hours of the morning, when sleep would not come, his thoughts had strayed to Kate. Thinking of her gave him a warm feeling. Then the guilt would set in. Why hadn't he pictured his wife during those dark hours?

"You had business with the big man," Wilson nodded towards the inner office.

"I'm still trying to get a Truth and Reconciliation Commission going. I'm doing the rounds of anyone who can make that happen." Her tone was only a degree warmer.

The Secretary was watching them closely.

"We should talk," Wilson said quietly.

"What about? ancient history?" she replied tartly.

"I didn't know that you were back," Wilson moved towards her but she did not reciprocate.

"I'm not back. London is still home but something has to be done here to wash Northern Ireland clean from the stain of the 'Troubles'. A whole bunch of old guys on television saying they were sorry for what they did before they set up their political parties just won't do. We're going to have to find out who did what, to who and at whose behest. That's why I'm back, Ian. And that's the only reason."

"Can we get together?" Wilson knew that he sounded pathetic but there was unfinished business between him and Kate. He had the feeling that she might think so too. "Maybe dinner or even a drink if that what's on."

"No," there was a hint of a tremor in her voice. "The past is another country and I no longer live there. There would be no point."

"How can I contact you?" Wilson said ashamed at the pleading tone in his voice.

"You can't," she clutched a crocodile briefcase to her chest and made for the door to leave.

He was going to move to block her path but he saw the Secretary staring at him from behind her desk. "We're not done."

"Oh yes we are," she said as she strode out of the office.

"He'll see you now," the Secretary said coldly.

Wilson heard her but he continued to look at the door through which Kate McCann had just exited.

Wilson ran his hand unconsciously through his hair and then despised himself for the involuntary nervous gesture. He turned and pulling himself to his full height he walked to the door to the DCC's office and pushed it open without knocking.

Wilson almost smiled as he entered Jennings' office. He knew that the DCC hated the sight of him. Jennings had been nicknamed 'the vulture' at the police academy because of his long scrawny neck and his prominent nose. That was twenty years ago and as he had aged he had come to resemble even closer the scavenger of the desert. It had always been a bone of contention between Wilson and his wife that Jennings and himself had been in the same class. While he had travelled the traditional route from constable to detective constable and on to detective sergeant before reaching the exalted heights of detective inspector, Jennings had chosen a less arduous route to becoming his boss. Postings in training and personnel had been followed by a stint in public relations. Wilson had long ago realised that elevation within the ranks of the police force owed more to the ability to lick arse than the ability to solve crimes.

At the moment Wilson entered, Deputy Chief Constable Roy Jennings sat hunched over his desk examining papers with the same intensity as a vulture examines its next meal. Jennings glanced up briefly revealing a face was straight out of a Marcel Marceau mime class. The deathly white colour began at the neck of his shirt and continued through his eyebrows and over the crown of his bald pate. The lips were thin and closely held together as though composed in death by some uncreative mortician. The only feature which demonstrated that the person behind the face was alive were the piercing dark eyes which darted in Wilson's direction before returning to the papers which lay before him.

"Bloody woman," Jennings muttered as he motioned at a chair in front of his desk. "Truth and reconciliation be damned." He looked up and saw Wilson still standing. "Do I have to order you to sit down? I'll be with you in a moment."

The Deputy Chief Constable continued to shuffle the papers on his desk as Wilson sat in the chair which he indicated. This was going to be an exercise in power and Wilson was going to have to grin and bear it. As soon as Wilson eased himself into the chair and looked across the desk, he realised that the visitor's chair was pitched several inches lower than the DCC's which meant that no matter how tall the visitor was, Jennings always looked down on them. Kate McCann must have sat in this very seat during her meeting with Jennings getting the full blast of his power and position. Wilson looked at the desk directly in front of him. Kate's visiting card sat on the edge of the wooden desk a mobile number scrawled in blue biro on the bottom. Wilson had an almost photographic memory for faces and names but numbers weren't his thing. He stared at the figures trying to impress them on his brain.

"Good to see you, Ian," the clear dark eyes finally raised and focused directly on Wilson.

"Good to see you too, Roy," Wilson took pleasure in Jennings' wince at the use of his first name. Wilson noticed that the Oxford accent which Jennings had tried so hard to cultivate had deepened since their last meeting. There was hardly a trace left of the bog Northern Irish accent he had entered the police college with.

"Yes, well I'm sure you've got a very busy caseload so I won't take up too much of your time," Jennings bundled up the papers he had been examining. "I understand you're dealing with that business last night in the Woodvale Road."

"I am," Wilson said. He could smell what was coming.

"I don't have to tell you how delicate the matter is," Jennings stared into Wilson's eyes. "The Chief Constable has been up half the night taking phone calls from politicians of all hues who are wetting themselves that this murder could put us back on the road to perdition. It would be useful to have the matter cleared up as quickly as possible "

"I'm aware of the overtones," Wilson said returning the stare "I don't think we should second guess the situation at this juncture. All we have is a corpse who doesn't appear to have any political connections. In fact the man appears to be a complete nobody. At a guess I'd say that politics and sectarianism has nothing to do with the murder but it's early days. We still don't know very much about the dead man. When we find out more about him maybe we'll have a line of enquiry."

"Time is a luxury you may not have on this investigation," Jennings said.

"I'm aware of the constraints," Wilson replied. "Every man in the squad will be working full time on this until we get a breakthrough. But you know we're not exactly over-staffed."

"You people in the Murder Squad are always bleating about how understaffed you are," Jennings smiled. "You'll be pleased to hear that we're going to give you an additional officer."

Jennings paused to allow Wilson to react but the Chief Inspector sat impassively before him.

What the hell is this conniving bastard up to? Wilson thought as he watched the DCC press his palms together in imitation of the praying mantis.

"The person we intend to put in your unit has just been assigned to Belfast from Strabane," Jennings continued. He glanced at the file in his hand. "A Constable McElvaney."

Now it was Wilson's turn to wince. He sat upright in his chair.

"We've known each other too long for this kind of bullshit, Roy." Again the wince from the DCC. "I suppose that this McElvaney character is a Catholic."

"You suppose right," Jennings replied pursing his lips so tightly that they disappeared completely. "Constable McElvaney is a member of the PSNI and as such one of your colleagues."

"You can keep that rubbish for your interviews with the media. My squad is one hundred percent Protestant. You drop a Catholic in the middle of them and I'll have six transfer requests on my desk before the week's out. That is if Constable McElvaney is still interested in a career in the PSNI at the end of his first week."

"There's no need to over-react, Chief Inspector."

Wilson noted that they were no longer on first name terms.

54

"However," Jennings continued. "I am counting on you to ensure that the Constable's career in the PSNI continues for a lot longer that one week. I don't have to tell you that there's been a lot of adverse publicity about the composition of the Force. The Police Service of Northern Ireland is not simply a new name, it is a new concept. I don't have to tell you that following the Patten Report the Chief Constable himself has decided that we must make greater efforts to integrate Catholics at every level of the Force. And that means into every station in the country whether it finds itself in the middle of a Protestant enclave or not. It's a new world out there, Wilson, whether we like it or not. Contrary to what some people think we're not exactly the Rainbow Nation but a lot of changes are going to have to be made and accepted."

"What the hell does the Chief Constable know about this Province?" Wilson spat out the words. "He's an Englishman sent here to impose civilised English morals on a force which doesn't easily take to civilisation. The culture of this Force is Protestant whether we like it or not and that means for a lot of our 'colleagues' Catholics just aren't welcome on board whatever the directives from the top say. We all know that it's got to change but this is shoving it down people's throats before they have a chance to digest it. The Chief Constable should haul his fat arse and his knighthood back to where he came from and leave us to fight crime the way we're supposed to. I'll tell you one thing, Roy. If you put this fellow into my squad," Wilson leaned forward and put his two large hands on the desk for emphasis. "You're prepared to screw up whatever chance we have of bringing to justice any of the well-known psychopaths running around this town just to appear modern to the politicians."

Jennings met the hard look in Wilson's eye. "Firstly I don't appreciate the tone of your voice but I'm willing to overlook that for the moment. Secondly I think that you are particularly suited to look after this officer."

"Why me?" Wilson had to restrain himself from standing up, "Do you really want to get at me that badly?"

Jennings ignored the questions. "You've never been a member of the Orange Lodge, have you, Wilson?"

Things were certainly disintegrating, Wilson noted the progression from Ian to Chief Inspector and then to Wilson.

"I never saw the need." Wilson was used to having this old chestnut pushed into his face. He glanced down again at Kate's card. The mobile number had already erased itself from his mind. To hell with Jennings he would have to manufacture a situation where he could get his hands on that card. "But that doesn't mean that I've volunteered to wet-nurse some…", the word `Taig' was about to issue from Wilson's lips but he cut it off, "Catholic officer" Christ, he thought, I'm beginning to sound like Whitehouse.

"McElvaney doesn't need to be wet-nursed," Jennings said coldly. He tapped the file on his desk. "First class record in uniform and passed first in the class at detective training. You are not being sold a cripple."

"In that case maybe you'd like to propose this guy for membership in your local Lodge," Wilson said sarcastically.

Jennings was about to reply when the door opened and the Secretary entered carrying a tray holding two cups, a tea pot and a small plate of biscuits. She laid the tray on a small side table beside Jennings while studiously avoiding his visitor.

56

Wilson took his chance as Jennings turned sideways and palmed Kate's visiting card. He slipped it quickly from his palm to his pocket.

Jennings lifted up one of the cups and handed it back to her. "Chief Inspector Wilson won't be staying for tea," there was a tone of finality in his voice. He picked up a blue folder from his desk. "This is McElvaney's file. Return it to my secretary when you're finished with it."

Wilson took the folder from the Chief Inspector's hands without comment.

"Constable McElvaney is downstairs in the cafeteria," Jennings started to pour his tea. "I suggest that you go there and introduce yourself. Then you can both return to your squad-room and get back to work." The Deputy Chief Constable poured a stream of milk into his tea and stirred the mixture to a light brown consistency.

"I can't be responsible for the repercussions," Wilson pushed the chair back and stood up.

"That's just it, Chief Inspector," Jennings sipped on his tea. "I'm going to hold you personally responsible. And by the way. Be especially kind to Constable McElvaney. You may end up working for a Catholic one day."

As he passed through the outer office he glanced at Jennings' secretary. She had a smug smile on her face.

"It doesn't suit you," Wilson said as he turned the handle of the door to the office.

"What doesn't suit me?" she asked.

"Being that fucking poodle's poodle," Wilson said as he exited the office.

CHAPTER 7

Wilson took a quick look around the cafeteria at Castelreagh. His glance encountered several tables of four or five uniformed officers chewing the fat. He continued to look around the room and saw that the only single person seated at a table was an attractive female with a head of frizzy red hair. Where the hell had this guy McElvaney got to? He flicked open the file and gazed at the coloured picture stapled to the right-hand corner of the first page. The colour drained from his face and he looked again at the single female who was returning his look.

Holy shit, he thought. A woman **and** a Catholic. The woman sitting at the table was dressed in civilian clothes as would befit her position as a detective constable. She wore a light blue blouse which set off her pale complexion. Her ensemble was completed by a dark blue trouser suit. Her demeanour and dress was more that of a management consultant than a police officer. Wilson walked slowly towards the table at the back of the room. "Constable McElvaney, I presume?" he said standing in front of the young woman. "I'm DCI Wilson."

"Sir," Constable McElvaney stood to attention.

Wilson looked into her deep green eyes. "Sit down please." He looked at the cup on the table. "I see you're having tea." Christ what do I sound like, he thought. This is worse than a schoolboy on his first date.

The young woman sat. "It could be worse, sir," she said as she took her seat.

"Worse?" Wilson said wondering in his mind how things could possibly be worse.

"Well, I could be black. That would be a full-house. Catholic, a woman and black."

58

Wilson started to smile. "It was a bit of a shock," he said taking the seat directly across from hers and opening her personnel file on the table before him.

"I could see that from here, sir," she said returning his smile. He noticed that her teeth were almost perfectly white and the smile lit up her otherwise pale freckled face. "Your face dropped so much I thought that you might have thought that you were on Candid Camera. Can I get you a tea or a coffee, sir?"

"No thank you. I think that I'm going to need something much stronger than tea or coffee. But perhaps later." You bastard Jennings, he thought to himself. He knew that the DCC hated him but this was way out of order. This was a possible career finishing tactic on the part of the DCC. Introducing a catholic officer into his all-protestant squad was one thing but introducing a female catholic was a horse of a totally different colour.

"Moira McElvaney," Wilson started reading from the personnel file. He castigated himself for not opening the file before entering the cafeteria and that wily old fox Jennings had been damn careful not to indicate the sex of his new officer. The colour photo was of the passport variety and it did not do its subject justice. "Nice bunch of A levels," he said scanning the page.

"But not good enough to read law," she sipped her tea.

"Bachelor of Arts in Sociology," he said without responding.

"I was going to change the world."

"Stint with Concern in Africa. Then social welfare officer and now PSNI." He looked into her eyes. "I'm tempted to ask what's a nice girl like you doing in a place like this."

"You were gracious enough to skip over the failed marriage," she said returning his gaze. "Just to get it out of the way. I married young. I didn't realise that I was marrying a wimp until I lived with him and we parted amicably. No children, thank God."

"You're rather up-front as they say," he turned the pages in the file to her superiors' reports on her.

"If we are going to work together then I think it's important that you should know what you've got, sir." He had kind eyes, she thought. His face was rugged and lived in. He would have been considered a handsome devil when he had been younger. She might even have fancied him herself. As the thought struck her she felt her face flush and she fought to push any sexual thoughts from her mind. When they had told her that she was being posted to Tennent Street her reaction had not been so far removed from Wilson's. Shock horror was the order of the day. But when they told her she would be working directly with the legendary Ian Wilson her courage had returned a little. Her instructors at the training college had used several of Wilson's cases to illustrate correct police procedure. It had been her dream to work with someone like him. Now she found herself seated directly before him and staring back into blue eyes that seemed to reach right into the back of his head. He was a lot bigger than she had expected. She's known that he had been a big-wheel rugby player but he seemed enormous to her. She was reminded of a large black bear. He certainly didn't seem to be the sort of guy to get into a hassle with. She found him instantly likeable unlike most of her previous bosses.

Wilson glanced at the appraisals written by her superiors. They were uniformly excellent. "Social work didn't suit either?" he asked.

"Social work wasn't my bag. I didn't have the required level of empathy to deal with the under-age mother who gets off on beating her child just because it interfered with the continuation of her social life or because it cried too much when it was hungry. So I really wanted to be a lawyer but when you don't have the grades you don't have the grades. Maybe I should have studied more and watched less of Kavanagh QC. So next best thing - join the police force. A couple of years on the beat in Strabane, exam to become one of the elite and three months college and here I am, sir."

"You're sure about this?" he asked. Please say no, he thought. She was obviously intelligent. Her superiors had graded her at the highest level and she was undeniably good-looking. What the hell had gotten into her red-haired head? He wanted to scream at her to go get a life. There would be no offers to her to join the Masons or the Orange Order. She could of course attempt to move up by offering her body to her superiors and he was sure that there would certainly be some takers but in the end loyalty to the Lodges would be the primary force in deciding promotions.

"As sure as I can be," she finished off her cup of tea. "It's a job and a damn good one at the moment. The PSNI looks like it might amount to something and it might just be the right horse to ride at the moment."

"What about Law School?" he asked.

"Too late or it can wait," she laughed. "If I didn't know better I'd say that you were trying to ditch me. We studied some of your cases at Police College. You're kind of famous in a certain way. And there's a group of officers who'd look up to you as a sort of hero." Was it her imagination or did she see colour rising in his cheeks. This man was a legend among the younger officers and he could still be embarrassed. "You don't strike me as the kind of man who'd walk away from a challenge and taking me on is quite a challenge. But I think that I can learn a lot from working with you and you can be a ground-breaker for others like me."

"Good God," he laughed. "You're beginning to talk like you're the Chief Constable already. What a politician you could turn out to be. That's a hell of a gauntlet you've thrown down. If I wasn't so world-weary and cynical, I'd think myself less of a man if I walked away and told the assholes upstairs that I wouldn't take you." Maybe that's what Jennings and gang were hoping for. He turns down the new copper and they cashier him for refusing an order. Quite Machiavellian but also quite possible.

"So where do we go from here, sir?" she asked.

He stood up and extended his hand. "Welcome to 'C' Division Murder Squad. I suppose we should go and introduce you to your new colleagues."

CHAPTER 8

Wilson was still wondering why he was the fall guy when they reached Tennent Street. Was Jennings trying to set him up for the coup de grace or did he genuinely believe that only Wilson could provide a sanctuary for a Catholic officer, and a woman at that, in West Belfast? Although he prided himself on the ability to read the criminal mind he had never fancied himself at trying to read people as complex as DCC Roy Jennings. He considered that to be way beyond his modest capabilities and most times he didn't give a curse what people like Jennings thought. Right now with a peculiar murder case on his table he was staring down the barrel of the proverbial gun. A murder investigation was a funny animal and injecting a cause of contention into his squad at this particular moment could lead to motivational problems. He didn't need that.

"Okay, let's go meet the rest of the team," Wilson said as they rendezvoused in the reception area of the station. The phrase 'into the Valley of Death rode the six hundred' flashed through his mind. "Don't expect to be greeted with open arms."

"I've learned in the last two years to expect precious little, sir" Moira looked directly into Wilson's face, "You give me the chance and I'll show you what I can do."

Wilson started out the door. "As far as I'm concerned you're a member of my team, and that means what it always has. You get a thousand percent support from me whatever the situation. I suppose that I'm an anomaly for Northern Ireland. I was born religiously neutral."

The animated conversation in the squad room died as Wilson stood in the doorway with Moira standing directly behind him.

"Gentlemen," Wilson could see from their silent faces that word had already reached them. Mark up another success for the Tennent Street bush telegraph. "You'll be pleased to hear," he continued, "that our sterling efforts have been recognised and that the Deputy Chief Constable himself has decided to boost our ranks. This young lady, and here I emphasise the word lady," Wilson stood aside to reveal Moira completely, "will be joining us as of to-day. I'm sure you'll all make Constable Moira McElvaney welcome."

Five pairs of eyes glared in the direction of the doorway. If Wilson had been introducing a new Protestant colleague, there might have been a rush to be the first to pump the new man or woman's hand. And with those handshakes an important number of messages would be passed. This time nobody moved.

"Such enthusiasm," Wilson forced a smile. "Well Constable," Wilson took Moira's elbow and led her into the room. "That wizened old reprobate on the left is my number one man, DS George Whitehouse,"

Whitehouse remained stock still refusing to acknowledge the introduction.

"Moving clockwise," Wilson continued ignoring the intended insult to Moira, "we have Eric Taylor, Ronald McIver, Harry Graham and Peter Davidson."

Wilson had expected Whitehouse's reaction but he had wondered how the others would react. He stared hard at Eric Taylor.

Taylor cleared his throat and moved forward. "Welcome to the Squad," he said extending his hand towards Moira. "I suppose that'll be the end of the dirty joke sessions."

"Only if the jokes are lousy," Moira pumped his hand.

Peter Davidson looked sideways at Whitehouse and then followed Taylor's example.

Two in, three out, Wilson thought. It could have been worse but it could have been a damn sight better. The atmosphere was bound to be charged for a couple of days but then it would work itself out. He could never see Whitehouse condescending to drink with his new colleague but as long as they could work together Wilson wouldn't care about their social arrangements.

"You're in luck joining us at this point in time," Wilson said turning to face Moira. "You are currently standing in the Incident Room for the investigation into the death of one James Patterson." He nodded to a whiteboard on which a series of stark black and white photographs of the Patterson murder scene were affixed. "Patterson was shot in the head last night by an assailant or assailants unknown. You are going to have the pleasure of assisting the best Murder Squad in Great Britain in bringing the perpetrator or perpetrators of this crime to justice. Eric, update on the enquiry please."

"Nothing, boss," Taylor began. "Whoever did the shooting didn't leave a trace behind. Not so much as a hair from his head was found at the sight. The SOCOs swept up a load of shite at the scene but nothing that appears to tie in to the killing. The pathologist has finished with the body. The autopsy showed up nothing new and the body is being transferred to the morgue. The basics you know. Only interesting item is that Patterson appears to have been into self mutilation. The pathologist found scars on his arms which were consistent with self-inflicted cuts from a razor blade. If we don't need the body for any further tests, they want to get him in the ground straight away. Since he hasn't any money to speak of the state will have to cough up for the pine box. Nothing exceptional on our victim. He was born, he lived and he died. There's no news on the gun. That's where we stand for the moment."

"Thanks, Eric," Wilson turned to his Detective Sergeant who appeared to be sulking at the rear of the office. "George, any news on whether our boy was a 'player'?"

Whitehouse stared straight ahead his lips clenched tight.

"DS Whitehouse," the smile had faded from Wilson's face. "I asked you a question. Answer it."

Whitehouse pulled in air noisily through his nose. "No, Sir," he said barely opening his mouth. "There's no criminal record. And he's not on the terrorist database. So it seems that he doesn't have any connection with a paramilitary organisation. But we're still checking."

Wilson turned to Davidson.

"Did you check his movements?"

Davidson shot a sideways glance at Whitehouse before answering. "Shortly before the killing he was in The Auld Sash on the Woodvale Road. It appears that he dropped in regular as clockwork for an evening pint."

"There's a mob that hangs out in The Auld Sash, isn't there?" Wilson said. "Maybe he was part of it. You're the expert on this kind of thing, George. Who do the mob from The Auld Sash belong to? UVF, UFF, LFF?"

Whitehouse stared at Moira. "I have no idea, boss. I didn't even know that a mob hung out there."

Wilson sighed. So it was going to be like that, was it. He really didn't need the additional aggravation. If Whitehouse was going to continue acting coy around McElvaney, then the investigation might be compromised. He wasn't going to let that happen.

"Eric," he said. 'Any news from the lab boys on Patterson's bed sit?"

"Nothing, boss." Again the sideways glance at Whitehouse. "No sign of visitors. No fingerprints other than the dead man's. I checked with vice and they've never run across Patterson. It all a big zero."

"Nothing from the neighbours either," McIver offered without being asked. "Patterson was a solitary bloke. Kept himself to himself. Nobody remembers him having a visitor of either sex. The only sound they ever heard from his room was the television or radio. The walls of that house are so thin that you could hear a budgie shit in the room next door. Sorry, boss, but we seem to be drawing blanks all over."

"Okay, boys," Wilson said. "I want the bloke who topped this Patterson character and I want him yesterday. I want every shred of evidence looked at again and again until we find something that links this guy to politics or religion or sex or whatever the hell reason got him killed."

"Wrong place, wrong time," Whitehouse said through clenched lips.

"We're all aware of your theory, George. Now can it. Moira will be the 'receiver' on this case." He turned towards her. "In case you don't know the jargon that means that you've got the shit job of sifting everything that comes in relating to this case. And I mean everything. Neither George or myself will have time to go over all the bits and pieces that come via the public but we need to see what's important. It's your job to know what's important and what's not. So get working on the statements that Eric collected last night, review the pathology evidence and go through the photographs. I want you operational as soon as possible."

"Thank you, sir," Moira said enthusiastically.

Wilson turned and walked towards his glass walled den. In the reflection of the glass, he saw Whitehouse glaring at Moira who was installing herself at the only empty desk in the room.

"George, you, in my office now," Wilson said from the door of his office.

Whitehouse moved reluctantly after his chief.

"Come in and close the door," Wilson took his place behind the desk.

Whitehouse squeezed into the tiny office and searched for a clear space to plant his feet. The only clear floor stood on either side of a pile of documents rising like a stalactite towards the ceiling. Whitehouse put one foot on either side of the documents and pulled the door closed behind him.

"Now," Wilson began raising his eyes slowly from the desk until he was staring into Whitehouse's scowling face. "I'm depending on you to make sure that there's no nastiness out there."

"A woman and a bloody Taig," red lines stood out on Whitehouse's normally pale face. "We've made it our business to put people from her side behind bars."

"You're a good copper, George, but sometimes you're a right cretin. The only side that woman is on is ours. I need this kind of shit from you like I need a hole in the head. McElvaney is an experiment and experiments have a time limit. So, if everybody relaxes, we can get over this hump together. This Patterson business is starting to give me a pain in my gut. I'm beginning to get one of my flashes and it says that whoever whacked Patterson isn't finished. That means that if we don't find out who did it then we could be looking at a complete resumption of hostilities. I don't want that on my conscience."

"We already know who did it," Whitehouse said. "Some Fenian bastard did it. Forget about the motive. Hunt out every IRA bollocks and give them to me for a couple of days. I'll give you your murderer."

Wilson leaned back in his chair. "Let's try to use normal police procedure on this one," he said sharply. "I've just been with the DCC and he has handed Moira McElvaney to me. That means that I'm responsible for her and that I'm going to make damn sure that nobody fucks around with her on my watch." His voice hardened. "Do I make myself clear. If there's so much as one ounce of intimidation, I'll come down like a ton of bricks on whoever is responsible. I've heard said that some of our colleagues sympathise with the aims of the Loyalist paramilitaries and I've even heard that some of them were responsible in the not so distant past for leaking details of suspected IRA men to the death squads. If I ever located such a man I'd fry his arse in hell. McElvaney is off limits."

Whitehouse didn't reply. The red streaks on his face were beginning to coalesce and purple patches began to appear. His shoulders slumped. His eyes became glassy. "This isn't my RUC," he said simply.

"It isn't even the RUC anymore, George. We're now the Police Service of Northern Ireland. It's all change at the station and we have to be prepared to change with the times." Whitehouse looked like his favourite dog had just died. The man was certainly a bigot and possibly a misogynist but now his whole safe world was collapsing around his ears. And he certainly would not like it.

"Boss," Whitehouse squeezed the word out of his throat. "Maybe I don't fit into this new Service. I joined up because I sincerely felt that our way of life was under threat from the Fenians. They were the terrorists. They bombed and shot their way to the table and now they're going to feast on our bones."

"Don't be so bloody melodramatic" Wilson was developing what he called his 'evening headache' and it was only early afternoon. First Jennings, then McElvaney and now Whitehouse. He was a policeman not a bloody psychologist. "You joined up for the same reason that most of us joined. It was a bloody good job and it gave you a good living."

"Aye but now it's all going to change," the colour in Whitehouse's face had returned to normal. His jowls appeared to hang lower on his cheeks. "New name, new uniform, new shield. They've kicked out too much at the same time. I used to be proud of where I worked. Now we're going to be handed over little by little to the Taigs. It's a bloody insult to all the brave men who died to hold back the tide of terrorism. The war in Ulster isn't over. It's only suspended. The Taigs won't be happy until they're joined to their Papist pals in the South. They won't get that in my time so when they realise that they'll dig up the guns and the bombs again. We've always been the front line against the bastards who're tryin' to end the rule of law in this province. The thin blue line stopping a Papist take-over of Ulster. How many funerals for blown-up or assassinated colleagues do we have to attend before we refuse to buy the line that we're like the police on the mainland?" He turned and looked through the plate glass window at his new colleague. "And now we have to grasp the snake to our bosom."

"If you ever quit this job you'll find a new vocation with a dog-collar," Wilson said trying to lighten the mood. He knew that George wasn't alone in thinking that there was too much change on the way. For men like him, born in the nineteen sixties into a Protestant-dominated world, the thought of power sharing and working alongside Catholics in jobs that were traditionally reserved for Protestants was anathema. He had recently attended a management seminar where the problems associated with the change were discussed and he was told to empathise with people like George. But not while I'm in the middle of a murder investigation, he thought. His head was pounding now. "I understand where you're coming from, George. But we've got to move on and we've got to take our responsibilities whatever the politicians get up to."

Whitehouse didn't reply. He just stood there wearing his hang dog look.

Wilson picked up the Patterson file from his desk and handed it to Whitehouse. "Give this to Constable McElvaney on your way out. I want every available man on this case. If we are talking IRA then I want a name and a number. And I want it yesterday. Got it."

Whitehouse leaned forward slowly and took the file. As he stood back his right foot caught the edge of the document stalactite and files cascaded across the floor tumbling into other stalactites which crumbled in their wake. He bent down in a vain effort to stay the domino effect.

"For Christ sake, leave them, " Wilson waved his hand at the outer office.

Wilson surveyed the mass of documents strewn around his floor and rubbed the palm of his left hand across his forehead. The headache which had begun in Jenning's office and was reaching a crescendo. He opened the top drawer of his desk and flipped the top off a tube of strong pain-killers. He popped two tablets into his mouth and swallowed them. It would take at least ten minutes for the drugs to take effect. Then he could think about calling a secretary to help clear up the mess. He sat with his head in his hands looking out at the still silent squadroom. McElvaney sat at her desk staring at the file which

Whitehouse had dropped wordlessly in front of her. Now I know how Christ felt in the Garden of Gethsemane, he thought.

CHAPTER 9

Moira read the last page of the Patterson murder book and closed the file. She tossed the buff coloured folder on top of her tiny steel desk in the squad room, let out a deep sigh and stretched in her chair. A strong vodka and orange and a hot bath was what she needed right now. The squad room was deserted. All her new colleagues had departed. Thankfully they hadn't bothered to proffer any invitations for a drink. She couldn't have handled that. She'd known that working with six men was going to be difficult. The smell of testosterone was palpable in the room reminiscent no doubt of the locker-room of the Los Angeles Rams. However, her options were limited. It was apparent that she was never going to become one of the boys. That just wasn't going to happen. They were wearers of the sash to a man. Their Thursday nights would be spent in the company of like-minded individuals trading peculiar hand shakes with one trouser leg rolled up. She smiled at the mental picture of the exposed hairy legs. Was she totally mad? What the hell was a Catholic woman doing in the middle of colleagues who were either Masons or members of the Orange Lodge or maybe even both? The only thing they had in common was that they were coppers. Maybe that wouldn't be enough. She stretched her arms upwards and brought her hands together it mock supplication. Who would be a newby in an all male Protestant squad? That was the inevitable process of integration but it might last a bit longer in this case. She allowed her arms to drop as she sank into her chair. For the moment and for the foreseeable future she would have to be 'hail fellow well met'. That would mean laughing at any asinine jokes that would really be intended to put her down either as a woman or a catholic. Eventually she might be admitted to the after-work drink ritual. But that would depend on whether her new colleagues would appreciate being seen with her in their usual watering holes. She came from a town with two Chinese restaurants, one of which was the catholic Chinese while the other was the protestant Chinese. After all this was Ulster. What the hell am I doing here? she thought. More importantly what the hell am I trying to prove? There were women detectives all over the United Kingdom. Some had been in the job for eons more than her. Also some of those women were also Catholics. So there was nothing special about her. Why then did she feel like she was a test case? She looked towards the end of the room where Wilson sat pouring over files. His desk lamp illuminated his face. He definitely doesn't want me here, she thought. But he has to play along with the game. They had leaned on him to take her. Everybody would be waiting for her to screw up and when she did they would dump on her like a ton of bricks. And I asked for all this, she thought. She felt a sudden dart of pain in her stomach and wasn't sure whether it was hunger or fear. Don't be such a wet, she thought. You knew what you were getting into. Nobody said it was going to be a rose garden and anyway what do you care. Two years at the most and then it will be back to Strabane and a bit of family support. Her eyes began to fill as she thought of her parents. They were so damn proud of her. She had worked hard to get into University. After the African adventure she managed to land a good job with the Ministry of Social Welfare. Her parents thought that she had hit the jackpot with her marriage to an up-an-coming accountant. Then it all went down the toilet starting with the day her husband had decided to show her his true colours by giving her a good thump. She'd given him the mightiest kick in the balls she could muster and then packed her clothes. That was the end of the marriage and the job at the Ministry. Her parents tried to convince her to go back but she'd hit a watershed. No son-of-a-bitch was ever going to lay a hand on her again. They had stood by her when she had joined the Police Force. And her mother had shed buckets of tears when she had been posted to Belfast but at least she had made it to detective constable. She had seen tears form in her father's eyes also but he wouldn't allow himself to show weakness in front of her. He was too old-school for that. A tear crept out of her eye and she brushed it away. Maybe she was a bit old-school herself. Christ she had to get out of this mood or she would be on the next train home. She looked down at the file on her desk. The details were skimpy. She thought that perhaps Sergeant Whitehouse was right. On the surface it looked like James Patterson had joined the long list of sectarian murders. There were no witnesses to the event and there appeared to be no clues as to who might have been responsible. The murder appeared to be a classic act of mindless violence. A death based on no other motive than religion.

She glanced up at Wilson's office and remembered how chuffed she had been when she'd heard that he was going to be working for the most famous detective in the PSNI. She was pleasantly surprised when she realised that the legend was actually flesh and blood just like everybody else. She assumed that it was the same with all heroes. From a distance they appeared to be supermen but up close they were pretty ordinary. It wasn't Wilson's fault that the recruits had pictured him as some kind of Irish Dirty Harry. What they would have got in reality was a soft-spoken gentle giant who wore a stained sports coat and a shirt that looked like it hadn't seen an iron in months. She picked up the file and walked towards Wilson's office.

"Excuse me sir," she remained at the door to the office.

Wilson looked up slowly from the papers he was working on. "Constable McElvaney, what can I do for you?" he said in a bored tone. It was going to be difficult not to think of the young woman in front of him as the 'father of all things for to bother him'.

She held up the résumé of the Patterson file. "I've been reading this file, sir, and I can't help thinking that there must be some way we can get the bastards who're doing these killings. There must be some way of putting the evidence together so that we can put them away." She didn't usually use strong language but she realised that within the context of her current situation a concession to the vocabulary of her colleagues would be a necessity.

Wilson stared at the young woman wedged between the door-jams of his office. My God, he thought, what wouldn't I give to return to the state of innocence in which crimes of murder could be solved by diligent policework. The sifting of facts and the testing of hypotheses was the stuff of classic detection and had no relevance to solving crimes in the province of Ulster. This was the land of the informer and the super-grass. It was the land of the confession beaten out of the miscreant during his six days of incarceration in Castlereagh. What price police work in a province where a serial killer can give an interview to a mainline British newspaper concerning his crimes and still walk free? Maybe the idea of the Truth and Reconciliation Commission wasn't such a bad one after all. It was high time that the Province gave up its psychopathic killers to justice. The families of the dead and injured deserved no less. It was time to dig out the King Rats and the Mad Dogs and to be rid of them forever. He looked into McElvaney's fresh freckled face and wondered whether he should begin

76

the process which would result in destroying the innocence and replacing it with hard-bitten cynicism. There was a major job of mentoring to be done here and he realised that if Constable McElvaney were a man he would have jumped right into the role. Mentoring a woman, especially for someone with his chequered sexual past, might raise more problems than it was worth. The common perception was that he had screwed most of his female colleagues. That wasn't quite true but he had never taken advantage of his rank while pursuing his colleagues. They had all come willingly.

"When you were on the beat did you ever help out in a murder enquiry that was sectarian?" he asked.

"Once or twice," she replied.

She was leaning against the door-jam now in a pose which in other circumstances Wilson might have considered provocative. For God's sake, he gave himself a mental slap in the face. You're old enough to be her father. "How did it go?" he said putting the cap on his pen. "Did they collar anyone for the crime?"

"Everybody in town more or less knew who was responsible but there was no evidence and his alibi was rock solid. He was lifted and interrogated but nothing came of it."

"Welcome to the real world," Wilson said looking directly into those hazel eyes. It was day one and he was going to have to get his head around the fact that he was going to spend a lot of time around a very attractive young woman that he could not possibly touch. It would be a difficult enough task for an ageing Lothario. "A group of suspects with cast iron alibis is an Ulster phenomenon."

"How can we win in a situation like that?" she asked.

"Moira," he was about to add darlin' but stopped himself just in time. He covered the hiatus with a smile. "Today, I'd like to begin your initiation as a real murder squad officer by telling you a few home truths."

Wilson beckoned her into the room.

"That file in your hand," Wilson began, "constitutes all we know about that particular crime. You know that we call it the murder book." The look on her face said 'don't treat me like a child'. "In other words there's no further evidence, no new witnesses, in short, nothing else. Most of the murders we do solve are the results of either confessions by the perpetrators or information provided by informants. Confessions are always dodgy and since the `supergrass' period there's been a distinct lack of individuals willing to put their entire kith and kin at risk by informing on their mates. So we're left with the files. You've been told that this job was paperwork, paperwork and even more paperwork. There is no super detecting work. We will not sift clues and develop startling conclusions. That's Agatha Christie and Jessica Fletcher. You've read the file. What do you think of the Patterson case? Is it a sectarian murder?"

"I know next to nothing," she sat gingerly on a pile of folders. "But if we're going to play the Socratic game that we did in tutorials in college so be it. There's always a motive. That motive might be sectarian which might make the victim random or there might be a motive which concerns this victim alone. Since we cannot test the hypothesis concerning the sectarian motive because of the random nature of the victim, then we should begin by testing the hypothesis that the victim was intended and that there is a motive. If we find nothing in that direction then we would be justified in accepting that the killing was sectarian."

Not just a pretty face, Wilson thought. "Your approach is right of course and I'd agree if this murder had taken place on the mainland. A large proportion of murders are domestics and another major category is targets of opportunity, criminals killing each other or murders committed in the course of another crime. The killer and the victim are generally known to each other. Police work consists of rooting around in the rubbish of human relationships until a motive for X to murder Y is found. It might be money or sex or both or any combination of factors but once you've found it you're half way to solving the crime. Let's get back to the case in point. Patterson had no family, no friends, no pets even. He was a loner who apparently didn't bother a soul. We've only just scratched the surface of his life but for the moment that appears to be it. So what are we left with. George's theory - an act of mindless violence . The wrong man in the wrong place at the wrong time. It could just as easily have been any other citizen. We've had too many examples of that kind of crime to discount the possibility. That means no motive other than religion. We could waste a lot of time following your approach. In the meantime the pressure cooker begins to boil. We don't locate your motive and the boys who still have a gun buried somewhere in the back-garden decide that the scores have to be evened. Then we're not looking at one murder but two and possible three or four before we can put a stop to the mayhem. This is not Police College and this is not the Big Island. So we start by showing the men with the guns and the public that we're looking at the bad boys for this one. If in the course of our enquiries we stumble across drugs or women or men for that matter then we go in that direction. But first we try to contain a reaction. Not classic police response but par for the course. This way nobody gets to drag us back into the maelstrom."

"You make it sound so damn futile," there was a note of tiredness in her voice.

"Just remember that you're talking to an old cynic" He had no wish to cut off the young woman's enthusiasm completely. "Sometimes we do some police work and we nab a real bad one. But generally the real bastards deal with each other. I suppose you've heard about the `Shankill Butchers' case."

"We discussed it during training," she said.

"It wasn't exactly our finest hour in this station. Eighteen people murdered on our patch. Most of them mutilated with hatchets and knives. The early victims were Catholics. Then it was anyone who got in their way. We did all the police work, forensiced the evidence until we were blue in the face but in the end of the day we couldn't break the suspects' alibis. We knew that Lenny Murphy and his pals were the culprits but we just couldn't nail the bastards. Thousands of hours of careful police work and the murderers were still on the streets. Just when we were despairing of ever gettin' the swine, the IRA took Lenny out and the rest of the gang folded. We jailed them but they discovered God and now they're rambling the streets just like you and me. They hacked people to death and they're back in society. It's just another example of justice Ulster style. Depend on one set of psychopaths to take out another and let the justice system deal with the camp followers. We don't have to agree with it but when you've been here as long as me, you'll settle for what you can get."

She smiled "What's that line from Gilbert and Sullivan – 'a policeman's lot is not a happy one."

"Ain't that the truth," Wilson smiled back. It was quite a while since he'd smiled with one of his colleagues. "Receive any warmth from your new colleagues?"

She rubbed her hands together theatrically. "A cold wind has been blowing all day. I appear to have upset the equilibrium of the squad room," she lifted herself gently off the folders making sure not to tip them over.

"Don't worry. They'll come round," he lied knowing full well that it would be a cold day in hell before George Whitehouse would accept her. "Nobody said it was going to be easy." He leaned forward. "You can always demand a transfer."

She threw her eyes up to heaven. "Every one of our conversations contains an exhortation from you for me to quit and go back to where I come from. I could develop a complex, sir. I could begin to feel unwanted. If I weren't so thick skinned." Christ, I'm flirting with this guy, she thought to herself. She could feel a blush rising in her face at the thought.

Wilson saw her cheeks redden. I've gone too far, he thought. And it wasn't fair. She was having a difficult time with the other officers. It was time that he gave her a break

"What about a drink after work?" he asked before he'd thought about the ramifications.

"Thank you, boss," she said formally. "I think I'd like that."

"OK," Wilson felt that he had been hooked on his own line. He was suddenly embarrassed and shifted awkwardly in his seat. "Outside the station at eight o'clock. In the meantime why don't you run along and learn how to play with our computers. Take along the Patterson file and see what you can come up with."

"By the way," she said looking back into the squad room. "I don't like mentioning it but there's a funny smell in the squad room underneath the normal male smells of testosterone and farts."

81

Wilson smiled. "Before it became a police station the building was a brewery and they never quite got rid of the smell of stale beer. Don't worry you'll get used to it."

CHAPTER 10

Case was getting slightly pissed off. He stood sheltering from the rain in a doorway across the road from Charlton's Garage in the Newtonards Road on the Southern shore of the Lagan River. The heavy rain which had threatened all day had finally started to fall. Away to his right a neon light tried in vain to pierce through the enfolding mist while overhead the rain fell from an impenetrably dark sky. Water vapour sprayed into his face but still his eyes remained fixed on the glass booth in which two men sat talking and smoking. A combination of rainwater and condensation had made the glass of the booth almost opaque and Case was forced to strain his eyes in order to concentrate on the object of his attention. Theoretically this should have been the easiest of kills. The man he was straining to see was a well built young man of about twenty-eight and according to Case's own timetable the guy should already be explaining himself to Saint Peter. He smiled at the thought of Saint Peter drumming his fingers impatiently over the non-arrival. The plan had been screwed when he had arrived at the garage and found his intended victim was deep in conversation with a visitor. The hitch was unforeseeable but would only serve to delay the inevitable. The filthy weather had reduced business at the filling station to a trickle and he had watched the attendant leave the booth on only two occasions to dispense petrol. He glanced at his watch: it was almost eight o'clock. He stuck his head out from his shelter and looked in both directions. The normally busy street was dark and virtually deserted. A few stragglers, bundled up against the rain and cold, rushed unheedingly along the street anxious to reach the comfort of their homes. Case was completely impervious to both the cold and the damp which easily penetrated the narrow opening in which he had chosen to wait. He had been trained to ignore the elements and concentrate all his attention on one particular task. Soon he would have to make his move, visitor or no visitor.

He pulled a small passport photograph from his right hand pocket and examined the face yet again. There could be no mistakes. Everything had to be done correctly and on time. One mistake could screw up the whole operation. He shuffled his feet in impatience. Get out of there you stupid fucker, he addressed his thoughts to the visitor to the booth as if trying to will the man to leave. His hand slid into his inside pocket and closed around the handle of the Browning. He couldn't wait any longer. Both of them would have to go. He pulled his balaclava further down over his eyes and left his doorway shelter. The deserted street was a near perfect killing ground. The dim light from the booth illuminated the silhouettes of the two men.

He smiled to himself as he slipped quietly across the road. The majority of Belfast's citizens were cursing the weather while for him it was a Godsend. As he crossed the thirty yards which separated him from the petrol attendant's booth, his view of the two men became clearer. His target was wearing a blue overall and was sitting with his feet perched on top of a small cluttered desk. The second man sat facing the door, his chair wedged against one of the angles of the booth. As he approached, he heard the two men burst out laughing. It had to be some bloody good joke. It wasn't a bad thing to die with a smile on your lips. He continued at the same pace satisfied that neither man appeared interested in him. He approached the booth and pulled the glass door open. By the time the men's eyes raised to face the open door, the Browning was already in his hand. The smiles froze on the men's faces then faded to fear. Case saw a level of understanding strike them as he raised the gun. They knew they were about to die. The noise from the first shot ripped through the confined space of the booth. The bullet passed through the attendant's head before shattering the glass panel directly behind him. Case swung the gun in a smooth movement and fired just as the second man began to rise from his seat. The bullet caught him in the throat and he was flung back against the steel stanchion which held the glass panes together. He gurgled like a baby through the torrent of bright red arterial blood which was already issuing from the gaping hole in his neck. Case didn't have to examine either man to know that they were both dead. He moved quickly to the attendant's body and fired two more shots at close range one to the head and one to the heart. He put the Browning back into his coat pocket and turned immediately away from the petrol station. He walked briskly until he came to a corner and after turning it dropped his pace slightly. Footsteps sounded somewhere behind him. He didn't look behind but simply ignored the sounds and continued walking away from the murder scene. On these streets he was just another evening straggler caught in the rain and impatient for the warmth of his home.

CHAPTER 11

Wilson stood at the front door of the police station. Most of the fortification which had marked the station in the 1980's and 1990's had been removed. The few bits of concrete which had been left were now the subject for the cameras of foreign tourists on the "troubles' tour. Tennent Street Station now presented a more benign face to the public. The rectangular building had begun its life as a brewery and despite its conversion to a police station many years before, still had a faint smell of beer in the air surrounding it. Wilson wasn't sure whether he preferred the new approach or the old Fort Apache-like fortifications. The concrete remnants of the protective barrier only remained because the overhaul budget had run out. Unlike the pieces of the Berlin Wall there was no value on the concrete which had protected the PSNI from the people they were employed to protect. He sniffed the air. No beer smell this evening. Full scale rain was up there somewhere and the light stuff that blew through the open door and ran along his cheek like fine oil was simply the precursor of more substantial rain to come. Just at that moment the rain started in earnest. For the past ten years he'd thought of himself like a medieval lord looking out from his moated castle, he'd had the impression of being besieged by some outside foe, someone unknown, but dangerous. Separated from the danger by the dark masses of concrete and mounds of sandbags looking for all the world like a row of basking whales on a dark November evening. Future generations would look at photographs of the barricaded police stations and wonder whether their forefathers had been mad.

He stuck his arm out through the open door of the station and turned his palm upwards. His skin was covered instantly in a thin film of water. Belfast wasn't immune to pollution. He withdrew his hand and rubbed it on the side of his grubby anorak. If he'd opted for an evening at home in Malwood Park, he would toss a few logs on the fire, open a bottle of Black Bush, microwave a lasagne and watch Inspector Morse solve a nice clean crime in nice clean sunny Oxford. But for some silly reason he had foregone that pleasure out of some feeling of empathy with his new outcast colleague. The more he thought about the similarity of their situations the more it bothered him. He shuffled from one foot to the other. Nobody in the station ever invited him for a drink. He was not 'one of the boys' and he hadn't invited a woman out since the death of his wife. He wondered what else he and Moira might have in common. The evening ahead filled him with trepidation. One drink and he would be off home to Inspector Morse and the lasagne.

He felt rather than saw the presence of someone behind him.

"Ready," Moira stood directly behind him stuffing a handful of computer printouts into a well-worn black attaché case. A wide grin covered her face and her earlier gloom appeared to have disappeared.

Wilson looked furtively around the hall. The Duty Sergeant stared in their direction with a leer on his face. Screw you, Wilson thought. The news would be around the station before they had their first order in. The inferences people would make would not be very complementary for Moira.

"Let's get on," Wilson smiled warmly at the young constable. "I've a thirst that'd do justice to a camel."

As he walked through the door, Wilson flicked up the hood of his anorak. "Where's your car?" he asked

"I wouldn't dignify my mode of transport by calling it a car," she nodded at a battered and rusted white Lada looking abandoned in the corner of the car-park. "My Polish made chariot - without horses of course."

He looked in the direction she indicated. "We better go in mine," he said. "The weather's too bad for push starts."

"No Lada jokes, please. I've heard them all," she said following Wilson at a run across the parking lot.

Wilson settled himself in the driver's seat of his Toyota Corolla and flipped open the passenger door. He put the key in the ignition but didn't turn it.

"I don't want you to take this in the wrong way," Wilson said staring out through the water streaming down the windscreen. "But I think that we shouldn't go local."

Her lips curled into a knowing smile.

"Most of the lads from the Station drink locally and I don't want a sea of faces staring at me every time I lift my pint. This is only day one. Let's give them a bit of time to get used to you."

"You're the expert around here," she said maintaining the smile. "If we go local tongues will wag. If the look on the Station Sergeant's face is anything to go by they may already have started. To be honest I wouldn't feel comfortable in a cop bar right now so let's go somewhere quiet."

"I think that you have a future in this business, Constable," Wilson smiled and flicked the ignition switch and the Toyota's engine sprang into life. "There's a couple of yuppie pubs on the Malone Road where money is more important than religion. If you can deal with the sound of mobile phones ringing every second or so we could head up there."

Wilson manoeuvred the car carefully through the crowded carpark towards a barrier between the remains of what had been two mounds of fortifications. Like a mining district it was difficult to put back the police stations in Ulster to their original state. There would always be a scar of what had been. Water ran down the shiny black raincoat of the constable on duty at the barrier and there was a suggestion of reluctance in the man's salute as he raised the barrier to permit the Toyota to enter the outside world of Belfast. The city they entered was grey and dark. The clouds were so low and heavy that they appeared to be right on top of them. It was not the kind of weather which lifted the spirits. He piloted the car down the Shankill Road and on towards the Westlink and then southwards to the Malone Road. He tried to remember what Belfast had looked like before the bombings and the 'peace wall' dividing the communities had turned the city into an obstacle course for motor transport. Normality had gradually returned to the city but there was still an edge to people's thinking. The fat lady hadn't exactly finished singing. Peace had brought prosperity. And prosperity had lured the speculators who had started to re-develop the city and provide jobs. The whole thing had even snowballed like the economists predicted and a minor economic miracle had ensued. House prices escalated and most of the population were basking in a secure future. It was even possible that Protestants and Catholics would begin to see each other as fellow human beings. But there were still buggers out there who could screw the whole thing up. Some idiots didn't want peace and prosperity. There were still religious bigots keen on fighting the religious wars of the Middle Ages. Wilson prayed silently that whoever had killed Patterson wasn't one of those religious bigots. The peace and prosperity were as weak and fragile as a new-born baby. A series of sectarian murders could be the torch-paper that would set off the whole cycle of violence again.

"It's amazing but you remind me so much of the first RUC man I ever saw back in County Tyrone," Moira's voice cut across his thoughts.

"Well it wasn't me."

"I know that," she laughed, "It's just that he had exactly the same build as you. A great big bloke. Tall and strong like a big black mountain. His head was like a giant white globe held in place with a neck like a tree-trunk. Dressed in the long black coat and with a big pistol strapped to his hip he looked like some kind of ogre to us kids."

"All us Protestant RUC men look alike. Haven't you heard that? We're all big burly blokes. Just look at George." A wide smile creased his face.

"In a way you are, you know. It always amazed me that the RUC constables always seemed to be bigger than the rest of the population. Like the Protestants were breeding some sort of supermen just to look after them. I remember seeing the constable towering over my father who was no small man himself. But he cowered before him. The whole scene made the constable grow bigger while my father seemed to grow smaller."

They approached the lower Shankill Road. Wilson waited in a line of traffic before turning onto the Westlink and heading south. Because of the filthy weather, the road was relatively clear of traffic. The office workers had cleared off early.

"At least you seem to have respected your first constable," Wilson moved the car up through the gears.

"I suppose you're correct up to a point."

"Why only up to a point?" Wilson asked.

"Because whatever respect I might have had for him died the day I saw a photograph of him in our local paper. He was standing in about eighteen inches of water in a stream with a big stick in his hand and appeared to be about to unleash the most almighty blow on a poor girl who was on her knees in the water. All that force and strength was just being used to beat up on a poor defenceless girl. It's pretty hard to respect someone who'd do a thing like that. We're only public servants whether we work in the Ministry of Social Welfare or for the PSNI. If we can show that we're honest and fair with all sections of the community then we'll have done a good job."

Wilson knew that there were too many people in Ulster who had had Moira's experience. There were times that he could imagine Whitehouse wielding that baton to the shouts of encouragement from his Orange brothers. But it was worth remembering that everyone is a product of his or her upbringing. If George was a bigot then someone had fed him that particular line of bullshit.

"Good luck to you," Wilson said. "You may have three A-levels and a university degree but you still have a lot to learn about human nature. That poor stupid copper was only doing what he and a large proportion of the population thought was right. People don't like change. In fact they hate change and they'll resist it with every fibre of their being. That's a fact of life. And a lot of them are willing to fight and die to preserve the status quo. Their actions sometimes reduce them as human beings."

They drove on in silence until they left the city and began to enter the more obviously prosperous suburbs of the Malone area. He turned onto Balmoral Avenue.

"Do you like computers?" Moira asked breaking the silence.

"I'm afraid I missed the computer boat," Wilson smiled. "Computers, videos, even microwaves. All that kind of stuff is a mystery to me."

"I'm crazy about them," she said as Wilson pulled into the courtyard of a pub called the `Windsor Arms'. "I did a course while I was stationed in Strabane. I really got into it."

The threat which had been implicit in the dark clouds had been real and the light rain had been replaced by the heavier variety of the previous evening. The two police officers sat staring out through the rain stained car window. Wilson switched off the car and the windscreen wipers stopped in mid sweep.

"Don't ask me why but I guessed that new technology would be your game alright." Wilson smiled at her enthusiasm. The coldness her recollections had engendered had evaporated. "You people with the big brains are always looking for ways to exercise them. Let's get ourselves that well deserved drink."

They sprinted through the heavy downpour and arrived almost together at the door of the pub. At the last moment, she slackened her pace slightly to allow her superior to pass through first. Their bodies touched as they crowded into the doorway and Wilson quickly moved ahead. They stood in the hallway of the pub and shook themselves like a couple of wet dogs.

"If I remember well, this place has a real log fire," Wilson said pushing open the lounge doors. "Ah! There we are." He led the way to where a half dozen logs burned brightly in an open grate, pulled out a chair and placed it directly in front of the fire. "What would you like?" he asked.

"Double vodka and orange, please," she set her briefcase on the floor, took a chair and put it beside Wilson's and removed her coat. "It's been that kind of day."

Wilson went to the bar and returned with a pint glass of Guinness and a tall glass containing an orange liquid which he laid on the table before her.

He was suddenly struck by the fact that this was the first time since his wife died that he had taken a woman for a drink. What the hell was he thinking? This wasn't a date. This was his new officer. He was being kind and considerate to someone who happened to be a woman. It was just a bonus that she was young and attractive. "Good luck," Wilson said and without waiting for her response he took a long swallow of the black liquid. "By God, I needed that." He laid the glass on the table and flopped into his chair immediately feeling the warmth of the alcohol and the fire coalesce into a general feeling of wellbeing.

She sipped her drink and laid her glass beside Wilson's. "It's great that we all have computers now." she said after settling herself in her chair.

"From what I hear they're a waste of bloody time," Wilson slipped off his anorak and laid it on the back of a chair. "I know they perform all sorts of miracles but I couldn't tell you the number of times I've walked past someone looking up the newspapers or booking their holidays when they should have been working. A couple of years ago some boffin type gave me a training course on them. He lost me when he started to talk about something called binary numbers. That's was when I decided to leave the computers to educated young people like yourself"

"I spent the best part of the day on one of the terminals" she pulled a sheaf of computer printouts from his briefcase. "I tried to do some correlations on the Patterson case."

"And what brilliant insights did the magic machine give you?" Wilson took another swallow from the Guinness glass and looked at the mass of paper she was spreading on the table.

"The computer doesn't give you insights," Moira said picking out one of the sheets. "It only saves and sifts information. The main computer links to the Criminal Records Bureau database in London. It has a store of information on every murder in the United Kingdom. You know the kind of thing that you find in the case file: name, address, religion, social status. Then we get some more pertinent details like the results of the pathology like the location and extent of the wounds and the type of weapon used."

"Etcetera, etcetera," Wilson said cutting into what he thought might be a never ending list. The lads from the squad should be here, he thought. She might be a Catholic but she was exactly the same as every young enthusiastic Protestant copper Wilson had met. He'd just put in ten hours at the office and he had opted to be bored out of his tree with this young computer nerd.

"Yes," she said some of the enthusiasm draining from her face. "Anyway," she launched forward again. "To get to the point." She noticed Wilson gazing into outer space. "I ran this guy Patterson through the database. The modus operandi was unique. Thousands of people have lost their lives in Northern Ireland but most of them have been either caught in explosions or wasted in a hail of bullets. Those who have been executed were in general lifted first, interrogated somewhere, shot in the back of the head and then dumped where they could be found. Patterson looks more like a gangland killing than a sectarian murder."

"So far you're teaching your grandmother to suck eggs," Wilson said sipping his Guinness.

"I don't think that Patterson was a random victim," she watched Wilson's face as she took another sip from her glass. Wilson's brow was furrowed.

"I knew that the minute I saw the body," Wilson said. "I didn't need to spend endless hours staring at a bloody blue blinking screen. It was too damn professional. Too damn cold. Too emotionless. Too gangland. Except that Patterson had no previous. As far as we're concerned he's snow white." His mind flitted to a mental picture of Patterson's bed-sit. Who would want to remove such an insignificant human being? "Did the magic machine give you any clue as to the motive? In the end it's all down to motive. If we can find out why someone wanted to kill a nonentity like Patterson then we'll be half way to a solution. Without a motive Patterson's file will join all those back at the station that have become as cold as a block of ice. If there's no motive or if the killer simply picked Patterson at random then we're up the creek without a paddle. That's what's such a pain in the arse working in this Province. Once they get a lust for blood they don't care who they kill. But rest assured that there's a motive in this case. Patterson wasn't just murdered, he was assassinated. That's the difference. Someone wanted him in particular to die. Somewhere in his nondescript pathetic life there is a nugget which will tell us why someone wanted him dead. Count on it. If we find that nugget then we'll be on our way. "

"So far I've found nothing that could be called a motive," she said. "But let's just suppose that the IRA or some crazy splinter group are responsible. Why should they claim this kind of murder at this point in time? As far as they're concerned sectarian killing is a thing of the past. They know that killing an ordinary unconnected Prod will raise the hackles of the UVF or the UFF. Okay things are always tense but everybody wants peace. If Patterson was killed because he was a Protestant then whoever's behind the killing looks like he wants to re-start hostilities. I just can't believe the idea that he was targeted by a terrorist splinter group anxious to get the war going again."

Wilson drained his glass. He'd almost forgotten what it was like to have such boundless enthusiasm. If she lasted a couple of years on the Murder Squad a lot of that youthful exuberance would be well and truly dissipated. But she was right about one thing. Whatever the pols might say Northern Ireland was still a tinderbox. Yes the big boys had all moved on. They'd signed up to the Good Friday Agreement and appeared on television saying they were sorry for what they did but beneath them the rats were still around. Only now that their political justification had disappeared they had simply become gangsters. Just like their counterparts in London or Birmingham or Glasgow they had established their turf and they had entered the world of free criminal enterprise as though to the manor born. They had embraced drugs, prostitution and protection. They were making money and if the social system that protected them was attacked by some idiot killing for religious reasons they would be forced to retaliate with inevitable knock on consequences. It didn't bear thinking about.

"Some of the many people I've run across in this job don't always think with what's between their ears," he said laying down his empty glass on the table. He laughed. "Even those lucky enough to have had something operational between their ears."

"Another one," she said quickly finishing off her own drink.

"Trying to butter up the boss," Wilson barely had the words out of his mouth when his mobile phone began to play the Ode to Joy. "Hold on a minute," he said as she started to rise. He took the mobile from his pocket and listened without speaking. "There won't be time for another one to-night. Let's go," he said closing his phone and pulling his anorak from the back of the chair. "Some bastard's just topped two men at a filling station across the river on the Newtonards Road."

CHAPTER 12

Case stood in the telephone box on Donegal Square in the heart of Belfast and slowly composed a number in London. It was time to report in. Case's body was still buzzing from the excitement of the hit. Everything was going like clockwork. Just doin' my fuckin' thing, he thought to himself as he composed the numbers. Everybody's got to be good at something and he was good at killing. A man has just got to love his job to be good at it and Case loved his job. The adrenalin rushing around his body was ample proof of the pleasure he got from killing. They'd been right in the Regiment, he had a talent for it. The shrinks who had booted him out of the Army had been right. Joe Case was one sick, fucked up bunny. Maybe he got his violent streak from his dad. That bastard had fucked off as soon as young Case had been born and had never been seen again. His mother had looked at his scrunched up red face in the hospital and decided that she didn't want the ugly bundle. So she had dumped him into care. His old gran had retrieved him and spent the last years of her life looking after him. When she died his mother reappeared looking for her inheritance which happened to include him. That's when the fights at school began. He was little but he could give as good or better than he got. Nobody screwed with Joe Case. His mother encouraged his talent for violence. And by God she'd used it. He was twelve years of age when she'd shown him how to roll the poor suckers she brought home to screw. Sometimes he went over the top on the violence bit but nobody seemed to care. The old scumbags he rolled never went to the police. They didn't want their better halves to know that they were screwing an old slag. He made ten times as much from mugging as his old woman could make on the game. Then the old bitch had sold him on to the pimps, pushers, villains and loan-sharks who ran the East End. And he'd loved every minute of it. He wasn't the biggest but when things got violent Joe Case was the bloke they sent for. They introduced him to shooters and he had taken to guns like a duck to water. He'd stand for hours in an empty warehouse in the Docklands and blast the shit out of tin cans. But that's where it ended. Nobody used shooters back then. They just waved them around to scare people. That was when he decided that he wanted to be in a business where people used shooters all the time. The Army were happy to sign on a fit young lad with no hint of a police record. It hadn't been hard for him to become the star in basic training. He was fit, tough and he had this natural talent with weapons. There was no type of gun he couldn't master in double quick time. His complete disregard for his own safety and incredible endurance put him at the top of his class for physical training. The books were a different matter. It wasn't that he was dumb, he just didn't take to it. Nothing from the printed page seemed to stick in his head. At the end of basic training, one of his instructors suggested that he try out for the SAS. Why not, he thought, the more action the better. During his basic training with the Regiment, he'd met and married Norma. That's when the trouble started. They say it's everyman's dream to marry his mother but he'd actually done it. That was the nightmare. Who would have thought that the skinny little bitch was a bleedin' nympho? Every man in his training squad had been in her pants. They laughed their arses off the day he married her and he didn't even know why. Two months after they were married he came home and found her in bed with some big black soldier. He'd beat the bastard unconscious and then started on Norma. His officers could have overlooked the black man but nobody was amused by the way he'd left his wife. So, they'd posted him to wherever the action was, Northern Ireland, then Iraq and Helmand before he did a second tour in Ulster. The army was the happiest time of his life. Most of the regular soldiers used to piss themselves when their units were transferred to a hot spot but not him. What was the point of being trained up to the hilt if you never got the chance to use the things you learned. He loved war the only problem for him was that there wasn't enough of his kind of war. Fuck the rules of engagement. If some raghead wanted to get it on then Joe was ready to oblige. He thrilled every time he thought of the action. Being dropped in by chopper, doing the business and then being ferried out before the opposition arrived. It was heaven. Just like appearing in a Rambo film every day of the week. And nobody could touch him. During his time in Northern Ireland, he discovered his second talent; he could mimic any accent. He could speak in a Belfast brogue that would convince even a Shorts and Harland ship-worker or he could drink with the locals in a border pub without raising the slightest suspicion. His superiors quickly realised his usefulness and started using him on undercover work. He specialised in frequenting well known IRA drinking dens and keeping his eyes and ears open. But it was flat beer when compared with blowing the shit out of a couple of Provos. He needed action. No buzz made Joe a very angry boy. The maggot in his brain needed to be satisfied. One night he picked up a girl in a drinking club on the Shankill Road. She was just a slag just like his mother and his wife so he beat her senseless. The brass weren't too pleased with that one and he spent two months in the stockade. But the maggot kept chewing away. Two weeks after the Army put him on the streets again, he beat another bitch senseless. This time the brass couldn't take it and handed him over to the shrinks.

He laughed when he thought about his sessions with the shrinks. They pissed themselves when they unlocked what was in his head. Then they couldn't get him out of the Army quick enough. Best thing that ever happened. There was plenty of freelance work in London for blokes with balls who could use shooters. A man with a talent like his was never going to starve.

The phone at the other end rang twice.

"Yes," the voice on the other end of the line was clipped and cold.

Case listened without speaking. He wondered what the man behind the voice looked like. That was one of the snags of being a professional. You never got to see the face of the man you worked for. You could never tell whether the bastard was chuffed with what you'd done or not.

"Number two has been taken care of," Case said unable to keep a tone of self-satisfaction out of his voice.

"Congratulations, Mr. Case," the voice said without emotion. "Keep me informed."

The phone went dead before Case could say 'Yes sir." He would have liked to describe the mayhem he was leaving behind him but it was his experience that the blokes who gave the orders seldom wanted to know about the dirty stuff. Death for them was like watching television. They knew that the 'dead' guy got up and walked away when the camera was switched off. The bosses never equated what they wanted done with blood and shit all over the place.

He left the phone booth and began walking slowly back towards his small flat. The assassin of a few hours ago had become an ordinary Belfast working man. Only two things could tie him to the murder in Charlton's Garage: the Browning sitting snugly in his inside pocket and the dossier on Stanley Peacock, former petrol pump attendant. He

101

ducked into an alleyway and took the two A4 pages which described what had been Peacock's life out from his inside pocket. Might as well get rid of them here, he thought. He produced a Zippo lighter from his jacket pocket, flicked the flame into life and then touched the naked flame to the white typing paper. The two pages caught fire and burned away in a few seconds. Bye, bye, Mr. Peacock, he thought as he dropped the charred remains on the wet ground. There was only the Browning but nobody in Belfast was going to question a man who could produce a bona fide Special Branch ID card. So, no loose ends.

"Sweet Jesus," Moira surveyed the scene of devastation inside the tiny attendant's cubicle at Charlton's Garage. The concrete floor was covered with a dark slick of deep red blood and the glass walls of the booth were streaked with blood. A single naked hundred watt bulb cast an eerie light on the dead bodies as it swung gently from the ceiling impelled by the rain-soaked wind which entered through the open door. A pool of vomit lay directly outside the door.

"Stand back," Wilson said pulling on Moira's arm. "It's a crime scene."

Two uniforms had already reached the scene and were standing well back from the booth.

"I know, boss," she said choking back the bile that rose instantly in her mouth. The last thing she wanted to do right now was to get sick. That would undermine her completely with her new colleagues.

"Someone has barfed," Wilson said glancing at the vomit. "I doubt it was the killer. Probably some poor bastard who happened on the scene," he glanced over his shoulder at the uniformed policemen stationed at the edge of the garage. "Or maybe one of the uniforms. Anyway SOCO will have to bag it but I doubt the analysis will do us any good."

Wilson was careful to stay outside the door of the booth and looked inside. Two men lay dead. One wore the uniform of a petrol pump attendant and had been shot several times in the head. The man's head lay in a pool of thick red blood was split open like a cracked coconut. The second man in the small cubicle lay propped against the stanchion. He was dressed in windcheater and cheap jeans and his head hung to the side of his neck giving his body the appearance of a discarded Pierrot doll. The killer had blown a hole in his throat which had almost severed his head and the front of his windcheater was drenched in bright red blood. There was no point in checking their pulses. Both had been killed with a single shot and the pump attendant had been shot in the head for good measure. Wilson's stomach turned and it wasn't because of the sight. He'd already seen enough corpses to ensure that his sensibilities had not been assailed at the sight of two more. He was beginning to get a very nasty feeling. Three deaths in two days. Very professional hits. Wilson's stomach heaved again. He'd bet a month's pay that this was the same guy that did Patterson. He took another look around the booth and noticed four shell casings. The killer hadn't bothered to clean up. He obviously wasn't worried that the police would find the shell casings. He'd done his job and moved on. What the fuck was the killer up to? This shit was liable to start a small war.

The air outside the glass booth stank of petrol fumes but Wilson preferred it to the coppery stench of fresh blood in the booth. A police car and van pulled up on the station forecourt some distance from the booth. George Whitehouse alighted from the car and some of the forensics team disgorged from the van.

"Busy week, boss," Whitehouse said a bag containing a plastic overall to Wilson, "I see you've taken to travelling with your new 'friend'," he nodded in Moira's direction before starting to don his own plastic overall.

The emphasis on the word 'friend' was clear. Everybody and his neighbour would now know that he and Moira had left the station together and had arrived at the crime scene together. Somebody might even have seen them having a drink together and already the station rumour mill would be putting two and two together and getting five.

"Now, now, George," Wilson said pulling himself up to his full height. "Jealousy will get you nowhere," he poked Whitehouse in the chest with his finger. "I'm old enough to be her father and I feel it. Furthermore if I catch any idiot spreading rumours about me and Constable McElvaney I'll see to it that they're pounding a beat in South Armagh next week. Spread the good word, George. I want everybody to know who they're playing with."

"Okay, boss, okay" there was a look of apprehension on Whitehouse's otherwise bland face. "Just making an observation."

Yeah, sure, Wilson thought turning towards the shattered booth. The forensic team were already setting up crime scene tape and arc lights. "I've got enough problems without adding you and your mates to the list. We've got two stiffs inside," he nodded at the booth. "One of them has got two bullets in the head and one in the heart. The other boy was shot only once. Conclusion, somebody wanted the boy in the pump attendant's uniform stone dead and wasn't taking any chances. The lad who was shot in the throat probably didn't die straight away but the killer didn't bother to give him a coup de grace. He got who he came for.

The hit was very professional. We've picked up four shells. In my opinion the second poor bastard happened, as you would say George, to be in the wrong place at the wrong time. I want you to supervise the forensics examination. I don't want SOCO to miss anything" He pointed out the shell casings on the floor of the booth. "Get those to ballistics and put a rush on it. We'll have to wait for the report but I'd bet a pound to a penny the two blokes inside were killed with the same gun that killed Patterson."

A series of arc lights suddenly lit up Charlton's petrol station like a Christmas Tree. Wilson looked beyond the glare of the lights to the dark deserted street. Police Landrovers had been drawn across each end of the road and the area around the petrol station had now been sealed off with streamers of plastic crime scene tape. Uniformed RUC men with Heckler and Koch automatic rifles stood stationed along the street.

"My gut is kicking up on this one," Wilson said as he and Whitehouse walked away from the garage. "Three men dead in two days scares the living hell out of me. If we don't break this case soon then there's going to be retaliation and that means more dead bodies, and lots of them. This guy is on a killing spree and we have no idea where or when it's going to end."

"Somebody wants to start trouble," Whitehouse said defensively. "In the past we know who that usually was."

Wilson ignored the remark. "I'm becoming more convinced that we have a new player in the game. And a very dangerous player he is too. Some things don't quite gel." They crossed the road from the booth. "Why these guys? Why Patterson and why this poor asshole. If it's the same killer and I'm sure it is, what has he got against the men he kills. Patterson didn't have either a friend or an enemy. And then he's too damn professional. Most of the so-called gunmen in this town wouldn't have been able to hit that booth with a burst of automatic fire. If they had managed to hit it, they'd probably have succeeded in breaking every pane of glass and leaving the two occupants completely untouched. But not our boy, he marches in cool as you like, fires two shots and scores two hits. Then he stands over the attendant's body and delivers a coup-de-grace." He looked along the darkened doorways which lined the street. "I bet, Sergeant, that if your boys look really hard, you're going to find some trace of our friend in one of those doorways." He was beginning to get a feel for his new adversary. The killer was cool and calculating. "He waited, sheltered in one of those dark hollows, until he couldn't wait any longer. The second man must have bothered him. I get the distinct feeling that our man likes to leave things all neat and clean. Let's get the photograph boys and the forensics people in here." Wilson stood up and turned towards the door.

Moira appeared at Wilson's shoulder. "The garage owner's just arrived, sir. The pump attendant was one Stanley Peacock. He's got an address in Sydney Street. No ID. on the second man yet. Peacock was on the late shift. Due to finish at eleven."

"Any next of kin?" Wilson asked.

"Wife or at least partner," she replied. "So the owner thinks. He isn't big on human relations. They operate the basic employment contract - the staff worked and he paid them. End of story."

Whitehouse studiously ignored his new colleague. "Sydney Street. It looks like two more Prods bite the dust."

Wilson nodded in agreement. "It's a safe bet."

"If this new player of yours is a rogue, he's got balls of steel. Once in here he wouldn't stand a dog's chance of gettin' out," Whitehouse said

"But he did," Wilson started back towards the petrol station. He was dealing with a ghost or someone very familiar with the area. Maybe not someone from the area but at least someone who had spent some time casing the petrol station and its environs. Nobody would have noticed him as he checked out his victim and established his escape route.

"George, check if anyone at the petrol station saw a stranger lurking around the area over the past few days," Wilson said. He doubted it would lead to anything but you never knew. Thirty years of 'troubles' had led the citizens of Belfast to ignore people they did not recognise. It was just another puzzle to add to those already occupying his thoughts.

Moira and Whitehouse fell into step behind their chief. Each avoided looking at the other.

"I hope you weren't planning on an early night," Wilson said glancing around the assembled ranks of PSNI men. He could feel the resentment coming off them with the steam from their breath. It was cold and wet and combing the area for evidence was going to be a shitty job. "I want this street fine combed," he addressed the grumbling policemen. "Everything is to be bagged and handed to SOCO." He turned to face Whitehouse. "Every house is to be canvassed and I want the results of the canvas written up and on my desk to-morrow morning." He turned to Whitehouse and Moira. "Time to give the bad news to the next of kin. This is one of those occasions when it's useful to have a woman constable on the team. Eh, George?"

Whitehouse ignored the remark.

"And since Constable McElvaney is new to this business, I think I'll go accompany her." He turned to Moira. "Let's go tell Peacock's nearest and dearest that they've been bereaved before some 'presstitute' from the 'Sun' beats us to it."

CHAPTER 13

Wilson piloted the Toyota through the deserted streets of West Belfast lost in thought. Two professional killings on his patch in such a short space of time was certain to bring all kinds of shit down on his head. The brass in Castlereagh would be watching events with more than their usual interest. He had never been near the top on their list of high fliers but he was well aware that he topped their list of people they could easily do without. More than once a Lodge brother had stood in the wings waiting for him to fall on his face. The drop had been avoided only with large helping of good fortune. Maybe his luck was about to run out. These killings could be the loose canon that was finally going to blow him out of the water. The stakes were too damn high. The Province was living on a knife-edge between peace and a full scale return to violence. Nobody in their right mind wanted a return to the bombing and killing but history had already proved that there were a lot of people in Ulster who could be described as having mental aberrations. The politicians would be running around like chickens with their heads chopped off trying to keep the lid on the rapidly boiling kettle. There was a more than even chance that some crazy was already planning a retaliation for Patterson. Peacock's death would only add to the pressure. If the situation boiled over, heads would roll and the first sacrifice would be the senior investigating officer.

Moira peered through the side window searching for house numbers as Wilson turned into Sydney Street. "It's on the left hand side about ten houses down," she said well aware that she had spoken the first words since the two had entered the car.

"Let's get this over with," Wilson said switching off the car and stepping onto the pavement in front of a decrepit row of red brick houses.

Being the bearer of sad tidings was Wilson's private version of the hell. He had listened far too often to the anguished screams and the howls of pain. He knocked on the door wishing the distasteful task could have been delegated to somebody else.

"Yes."

The woman who opened the door was so pale and haggard that Wilson assumed that he had been beaten to the punch. He noticed that the area under her left eye was dark and puffy. He fished around in his pocket for his warrant card and flicked it open.

"I'm Detective Chief Inspector Wilson and this is Constable McElvaney."

The woman made no attempt to speak.

"You're Mrs. Peacock?" he asked.

She laughed bringing a vestige of animation to her pale visage. "You could say that."

Wilson raised his eyebrows.

"I'm Jean Black, Chief Inspector," she said. "There's no Mrs. Peacock. But I suppose I'm the closest thing to it."

A baby screamed inside the house but Jean Black ignored the shrill sound.

"May we come inside?" Wilson asked.

A look of apprehension passed over Black's face. "What the hell's goin' on? What do you want with me?"

Wilson forced himself past the woman at the door and entered the narrow hallway of the house. Moira McElvaney followed him. "We're sorry for disturbing you but I'm afraid that Mr. Peacock was involved in a shooting accident earlier this evening."

The look of fear disappeared from her face. "Nothing trivial I hope," she said her mouth curling in a sneer. Wilson was slightly thrown by her demeanour. He felt like an actor who was being fed the wrong lines in a scene he had often played before. Where was the terror and fright at the thought of a loved one being injured or possibly killed?

"I'm afraid Mr. Peacock is dead," Wilson said trying to get the right amount of solemnity into his deep voice. "He was shot at his place of work earlier this evening."

"Who did it?" she asked matter-of-factly.

This was going all wrong for Wilson. He'd expected her to collapse at the news but she stood directly beneath him in the narrow hallway her pale tearless face turned up towards his.

"So far we're in the dark on that," he answered.

A smile creased Jean Black's thin lips. "Well if you do manage to find him. Tell him thanks from Jean Black will ye." She noticed the look on the two copper's faces and began to laugh out loud. "I've spent the last six months tryin' to get that bastard barred from this house," she said. "But the little fart down at the court wouldn't give me an order because we weren't married. Common law doesn't count. The man with the gun has given me what the beak wouldn't. Thanks mister." She tipped her forelock in salute.

"Was Mr. Peacock involved with any paramilitary organisation?" Wilson asked.

Jean Black laughed again. "Are you kiddin'. That bastard was only good for beatin' on women." She leaned forward towards Moira displaying the eye Wilson had noticed earlier. "This is what you can expect from your man, dearie. And that was only a taste. I've been in the Royal Infirmary twice. I had my jaw wired for three months. Stan wouldn't hit anything that might hit back. He was a fuckin' coward. A yellow-livered bastard to his boot-straps." A tear slid out of her eye and rolled down her cheek.

"Do you have any family that might be *'involved'*?" Wilson asked.

She hesitated for a moment. "Involved in what?" she said more firmly than was necessary.

"Drugs, maybe something on the other side of the law."

"You people are a fuckin' joke," Jean Black spat at them. "The poor man is probably lyin' in the morgue and you're tryin' to blacken his name. Well fuck you."

Wilson saw McElvaney take a note.

"Do any of your family feel strongly enough about Mr. Peacock to want to do something about him?" Wilson asked.

"You could fill a football ground with people that Stan had pissed off."

"About your family," Wilson said quickly. "I assume we could add them to the list."

"You can leave my fuckin' family out of it," Jean Black folded her arms across her thin chest. "If Stan was thick enough to get himself killed that's his business. I won't have my relations bothered over that lousy bastard." The baby's screaming had reached a crescendo. "What happens now?" she asked suddenly busy to get on with her life.

"His body will be taken for a post-mortem examination," Wilson said trying to be delicate out of habit. "His boss identified him so at least you've been spared that. It wasn't a pretty sight. Because he died violently there'll have to be an autopsy. After they release the body you'll be able to arrange the funeral."

"You can keep him as far as I'm concerned," she said. "Why the hell should I bury him?"

"No reason," Wilson said turning towards the door. Moira already had it open. "One of my officers will be along to-morrow morning to take a detailed statement. In the meantime if you could make a list of those who might possibly have wanted to do your husb... partner harm. And the press will probably bother you to-morrow," he said by way of a parting remark.

"Do they pay for interviews, photos and the like?" she asked.

Wilson turned to face her and saw her previously dull eyes sparking at the thought of financial gain.

"I suppose so," he said and turned towards the car.

"So much for the grieving Common Law widow," Wilson said as he and Moira settled themselves into the seats of the Toyota.

"Another of those partnerships forged in heaven," Moira said. She didn't notice Wilson looking away. "You think she could be involved?"

Wilson's brow furrowed. He was wondering whether every relationship in the world between men and women was fucked up. His certainly had been and from what he had gleaned from McElvaney so was hers. Who were they to throw stones at Jean Black?

"I think she would like to have been involved." The ranks of murderers were littered with unhappy spouses who had topped their 'better haves'. He'd seen it plenty of times himself and visited many a hospital ward to visit a victim where the murder process did not reach its culmination. He turned the key in the ignition and the car's engine sprang into life. "It never ceases to amaze me that people who hate each other as much as they must have actually can stay together. I'm no expert on children but I'd guess that the squealing baby was probably less than one year old which means that Miss Black was probably intimate with the victim fairly recently."

"Unless the child wasn't his," Moira said.

"Point taken," he said smiling. That was a woman thinking like a man for a change. "But if I had to hazard a guess I'd say that Jean Black is not involved. To-night's events have also convinced me that there may be more to these killings than meets the eye. You might just be in for a lesson in real old style police work. What really bothers me is the time question. We've got three dead bodies in the past two days. All three probably killed with the same gun. That usually spells either a sectarian murder spree or a turf war. An outside bet would be a serial killer but they usually start by being messy and then refine their method. The Shankill Butchers were another good example of serial killers refining their technique as they progressed. Since as far as we know none of the victims appears to be 'connected' we can probably rule out the turf war. And much as I hate to admit it it's beginning to look like George was right about the sectarian angle. We've got to stop this lunatic before there's any escalation. The fact that he leaves us no clues bothers me. The crazies aren't usually so professional. This asshole knows how to kill. That means he's done it before. We start with the usual suspects. That'll mean leg work and hours of overtime. We're going to have to beat the bushes to force this guy into the open." He piloted the car away from the curb. "We've done enough for one day and I'm not as young as I used to be. I'll drop you back to the station. Your Lada's probably pinning for you."

Moira sat before the screen in the basement of Tennent Street station. Lines of computer generated text stared back at her. For the previous two hours she had scoured every data source for information on Patterson, and Peacock. She had ignored the second victim at the garage since Wilson was sure that he had been in the wrong place at the wrong time. The 'magic machine' as Wilson had called it had thus far yielded paltry results. Patterson was as clean as the driven snow while Peacock had two arrests for aggravated assault. Jean Black had sworn both warrants. All Moira had for her trouble was a pair of sore, red-rimmed eyes. Neither of the victims appeared to have any connection with the Belfast criminal underworld and she has found no evidence to support a connection with paramilitary activities. Yet there had to be some reason why these specific people had been selected. She sat back and rubbed her aching eyes. The action only served to increase the discomfort. What a sad case she was. Wilson had dropped her at the car park and instead of heading back to her small apartment she'd decided to spend a few hours on the computer. Sad. Twenty-eight years old. Failed marriage. New job with unappreciative colleagues. What she needed was a couple of belts of Stoly and a curl-up in front of a rom-com. And maybe a good cry. What the hell was she doing in this bloody police station in the middle of Protestant West Belfast? What was she trying to prove? Was she totally bloody insane? She looked at the lines of text on the screen. Perhaps the random theory was correct. If so, she was currently embarked on the biggest waste of time of her career. It was time to think outside the box. There may be nothing in the Criminal Records Bureau but there had to be some link somewhere. Officially she had no access to either the Home Office computer or the Department of Social Welfare. But when you've already hacked in once the second time is easier. She pushed a series of keys and a new menu appeared on the screen. In the centre of the screen was a panel which asked for her password. She pulled a

Moleskine notebook out of her bag and leafed through some pages. After a few minutes she found what she was looking for and typed the password. Miracle of miracles it still worked. She now had access to UK Government databases. It was inconceivable that no reference existed to either of these men on some government database or other. She moved the cursor down the line of available data until he reached the words 'social welfare'. She pressed the 'enter' key and screen went blank. After a few seconds, the prompt 'name' appeared on the screen. She typed 'Peacock' for the umpteenth time. The screen cleared and the prompt 'first name' appeared. She typed 'Stanley' and leaned back in her swivel chair. The screen went blank and after half a minute the word 'wait' appeared in amber letters. Why not. It was too late for Stoly and a Rom-Com that would turn her into a teary mess. She'd already spent half the night messing around with the damn thing. A few more minutes wouldn't matter.

She leaned back and closed her eyes. There was another life. At the week-end she'd put her glad rags on and hit the night spots. Maybe she'd meet someone who had even a trace of a brain. Most of the men she met were only interested in a quick lay. She'd had more than her fair share of those and that part of her life was over. Christ but I need a friend. She thought of Wilson. She'd been told he was attractive and that his personality drew women like bees to honey. And she had to concur. He was old enough to be her father but he had a certain something. Maybe if he had been just a bit younger. At least he'd had the good grace not to proposition her on her first day. But she had the feeling that he found her attractive. Get those damn ideas out of your head girl, she thought.

She opened her eyes and looked at the screen. The life and times of Stanley Peacock, she murmured softly as she bent forward to examine the information on the screen. She read quickly moving down through the standard Social Welfare template. Name, address, age, details of the dead man's schooling and early life were scrolled down the screen for his benefit. When she came to the end of the text, she continued to push the 'page down' button. There had to be something else. She wanted so badly for the computer to give her the motive for Peacock's murder that she almost kicked the machine in frustration. There was nothing of any use in the file. What use was the name of his schools, mother's and father's first names? She scanned the text again. It's in there somewhere, she thought looking at the orange letters. She just wasn't smart enough to see it.

"Sad bloody cow!" She bashed a series of keys and the printer beside the computer terminal began to whirr. When the noise stopped she pulled the typewritten pages from the tray and put them into a blue coloured folder. She slammed back the swivel chair and switched off the computer terminal. What an unmitigated waste of time, she thought as she started towards the Squad Room.

CHAPTER 14

Case entered the hallway of his lodgings in Leopold Street and dumped his rain-soaked donkey-jacket on a free hook on the hall-stand.

"Filthy night, Mr. Case," Betty Maguire's head peeped around the door of the downstairs parlour.

"Filthy night, indeed, Misses M," he replied employing the Scouse accent he used with the landlady. He was well versed in laying a trail of confusion. Different accents, different identities, lies built on lies, built on lies. When he left Belfast it would take a genius to hang the different people he had created onto one man. And nobody would be looking for Joseph Case.

"Would you not come into the parlour and warm yourself in front of the fire, Mr. Case," the landlady's Belfast accent was so thick you could cut it with a knife. "I'll make us a lovely cup of tea and we could watch television together."

"No thanks, Mrs. M," Case smiled his most engaging smile, "I've had a hard day and I just want to crawl into bed with a book."

"Lucky book," Mrs. Maguire said and gave him her version of a demure smile.

"Night, Mrs. M," Case ascended the staircase towards his room on the second floor.

That silly old bitch could become a problem, he thought as he closed and locked the door behind him. What I don't need at this point in time is a widow in heat looking for a bit of sex.

"Lucky book," he said mimicking Mrs. Maguire's accent perfectly.

It just needed one word of encouragement and the silly bitch would have her pants down before you could say

'Jack Robinson'. In a way he was tempted. Betty Maguire wasn't a bad looker and although she was nearing the top of the hill she wasn't over it yet. Why shouldn't he have all the creature comforts while he was in this shithole. But a relationship with somebody as desperate as his landlady could lead to problems. And his boss in London had been very insistent that there should be no problems. So he would just have to go on playing the perfect lodger. He would continue to go to his non-existent job at exactly the same time every morning and he would be perfectly polite to all and sundry. Two weeks after he left nobody would be able to remember anything about him except that he had always been cheerful and helpful. They wouldn't remember whether he was tall or small, fat or thin, nothing. As long as he could resist Betty's amorous advances, nothing of him would be left behind.

Case took the Browning out of his pocket and slipped it into the drawer of the battered locker which stood beside his bed. He needed, no he deserved, a drink. So far so good. He pulled out the bottle of Black Bush from beneath the bed and poured himself a large measure. The golden liquid burned down his throat and warmed the pit of his stomach. He sat down in the decrepit stuffed armchair which along with his bed dominated the room of the old Victorian house. The control for the television lay beside his hand and he flicked the button that would bring the ancient set into life. The screen flickered and an image of a game show host came slowly into focus. Case lowered the volume until the host's voice was simply a purr. He didn't need to listen to crap. What he wanted was to savour the success of this evening. His mind ran back over the hit and he could feel a mild adrenaline rush as he relived the scene in the petrol station. It had been bloody perfect. There would be no trace of him having been there and the second bloke's death would confuse the local coppers. The only thing that was missing was someone to share his triumph with. Back in his army days there were always mates in the mess to boast to. Deep inside there was a need to belly up to the bar and fill someone's ear with the story of how MI5 had picked him to get rid of some Belfast shit and what a great job he was doing of it. But that wasn't the way it worked in his new life. He'd have to get used to keeping his scores to himself. He emptied his glass and poured another large measure of whiskey. He made an imaginary gun with the thumb and forefinger of his right hand. Pow, pow. Two shots fired from the doorway and two direct hits. It was real 'Dirty Harry' stuff. Make my fucking day and nothing personal. He'd come a long way from the skinny-arsed kid that had rolled the punters.

He poured himself a third measure of whiskey. Just another week and he could join the rest of the boys on the Costa. A winter of sun, sea and sangria with maybe a bit of sex thrown in. He made the imaginary gun again with the thumb and forefinger of his right hand. Pow, pow.

CHAPTER 15

The police car dropped Whitehouse at the corner of the Shankill Road and Snugville Street. He glanced at his watch as soon as the car pulled away from the footpath. He had five minutes before the appointed time of his meeting with Richie Simpson in the 'Linfield Arms'. To hell with Wilson, the bloody slave-driver, he thought to himself, as he bundled his coat around him and started off in the direction of the pub. He'd spent two sodding hours picking up bits of crap from around the murder scene. And what did they have to show for it. Sweet bugger all. A selection of trash that could have been picked up on any street in Belfast but not one single shred of what the 'Great Detective' would call evidence. He scowled. He'd love to dump all the shit we've collected onto Wilson's desk and see the expression on his face. Whitehouse hustled along the darkened streets. He had been born and raised in this warren of tightly packed houses. He knew everybody who lived here and everybody knew him. That was an edge that Wilson would never have. Most of the hard men of the area had been at school with him and he had used that connection to break a few cases but he wasn't that stupid that he didn't know he was being fed what they wanted him to know. George Whitehouse had spent his life walking a very fine line between doing his job and maintaining his position within his community.

He quickened his pace when he saw the entrance of the 'Linfield Arms' directly ahead.

Richie Simpson looked up from his drink as the front door of the pub opened and Whitehouse came in. About bloody time, Simpson thought. He had been wondering whether to abandon his vigil but the stakes were too high. The PSNI Detective Sergeant looked more harassed than usual. Simpson watched Whitehouse search the crowded bar until their eyes locked.

Whitehouse pushed his way through the crowd at the bar towards the back of the pub where Simpson was sitting at a table.

"You took your time," Simpson pointed to the wooden chair opposite him.

Whitehouse removed his sodden overcoat and threw it over the back of an empty chair. Simpson watched as Whitehouse's short body slumped into the chair across from him.

"You look bolloxed. You need to get one down you." Simpson raised his hand and the barman arrived instantly. "What'll ye have?

You're not looking so great yourself, Whitehouse thought. Simpson's face hadn't been made to conceal his thoughts. The heavy crows-feet around his eyes mirrored the deep frown lines etched into his forehead. His dark greasy hair was tied back in a ponytail. It didn't take a genius to see that Simpson was a man with something on his mind.

"Bushmills," Whitehouse said settling himself in the chair. "Make it a double," he added before the barman could disappear. "I've spent half the night arsein' around in the dark tryin' to find *'evidence'*."

"I thought that's what you coppers live for," Simpson smiled and took a drink from the pint of Guinness in front of him.

"Very sodding funny," Whitehouse said feeling the bottoms of his trousers sticking to his legs. He let a smile slip from his lips after the remark. He didn't want to get Simpson's back up. He was a direct connection with the Protestant politicos and a harsh word dropped in the wrong ear could put an end to Whitehouse's career such as it was. Being a Lodge brother wouldn't save him if he didn't prove to be a loyal brother.

"What's on your mind?" Whitehouse asked. "You didn't ask me here to pass the time of day." The two men had known each other since their schooldays. While Whitehouse had joined the Royal Ulster Constabulary, Simpson had clawed his way up the Loyalist political ladder from street bullyboy to semi-respectable political hatchet man. Nowadays Simpson and violence had parted company. That didn't mean that he couldn't have an assassination carried out or a good beating delivered. It had been easier to arrange for the headbangers with the skinhead haircuts and tattoos from their arses to their necks to carry out the dirty work. Simpson had paid his dues via a couple of years behind bars for attempted murder. If the bastards in Whitehall decided to ditch the province, he could see Simpson and his pals governing an independent Ulster. And why shouldn't he, others had marched the same demagogic road to power as him. He glanced around the pub and noticed Simpson's 'minder' leaning against the bar about fifteen feet away. Even in a staunchly Protestant area, Simpson's life was so important that he had to be protected at all times.

"Right you are. Bein' a policeman hasn't interfered with your powers of perception," Simpson said.

The barman arrived and put a small jug of water and Whitehouse's whiskey on the table.

"And just because you've graduated to wearing a suit you've no reason to look down on people who you've used in the past," Whitehouse ignored the water and immediately lifted the whiskey. "Death to the begrudgers," he said looking into Simpson's brown liquid eyes. He took a mouthful of the golden liquid and felt the heat passing from his throat to his stomach. "Let's have it? I still have a home to go to."

"I heard what happened to-night over by the Newtonards Road," Simpson began his voice barely above a whisper. "Some very important people are gettin' their knickers in a knot about three Prods being killed. You know the way things stand in West Belfast, the Prods look to the local leaders to make sure that they sleep quietly in their beds at night. It's all about protection. As soon as a few Prods bite the dust out come the hard men with their guns and the next thing you know you're walking down to the local boozer tryin' to avoid the dead bodies they leave scattered about. End result a return to lots of funerals, a return to the bad old days when nobody could make money. Returning to that shit is in nobody's interest but unfortunately some of the younger headbangers might not know that. Can you see where I'm goin'?"

Whitehouse nodded. His eyes were hooded from fatigue.

"We need to know what you know," Simpson said. "That's why you're here. Our relation is mutually beneficial, George. You help us to help you."

Whitehouse leaned forward conspiratorially. "It looks like the same bloke pulled the trigger on all three."

It was Simpson's turn to nod his head.

"I've never seen anything like it. The bastard does them dead cool then stands over them and makes sure with one dead centre in the skull. You should see the mess he leaves behind. It looks like the same gun was used in the three killings this week. A nine millimetre. I'll know more when ballistics get through with testing the new shells. As far as we can tell he works alone. But up to now nobody has come up with anything. For all we know he might be part of a team. So far we've got nothing."

Simpson sat quietly digesting the information while Whitehouse utilised the pause to take another gulp of whiskey. "Have your people got an idea of the reason why?" he asked.

"Not a fucking clue. Three dead and no apparent reason. Either there's a psycho on the streets or those boys were into something that we don't know about."

"We've checked the first one out. Nobody's heard of him. Patterson drank in the 'King's Head' but he wasn't part of the scene there. The boys reckon he got his kicks by rubbin' shoulders with them. He was a bloody joke, man."

"That's not the only way he got his kicks," Whitehouse took a gulp of whiskey and launched into a description of the search of Patterson's flat.

Simpson took in the information without blinking. "Maybe it's a queer thing."

"The kills are too clean and clinical for queers," Whitehouse remembered Wilson's deduction. "Queer killings are crimes of passion. Mostly carve ups. Wilson thinks ...." Whitehouse stopped himself.

"Let's have it. That bollocks might have caused us more trouble than he's worth but at least I know there's something more than butterflies runnin' around in his head."

"Wilson might have his head up his arse. He thinks that there's a totally new player out there. A professional killing selected victims."

"Why only Prods?"

"How the hell do I know." Whitehouse finished his glass of whiskey. "Why don't you ask the great soddin' detective himself?"

Simpson could feel the frown lines on his forehead deepening. As soon as the night's news was out there was going to be hell to pay. The denizens of the Shankill would be baying for blood in a big way. "Okay, I want to know everything that happens on these ones. Right."

A wicked grin came over Whitehouse's face. "I've one other titbit of information that might tickle you," He glanced at the empty glass of whiskey but Simpson ignored the manoeuvre. "There's a Taig working in the squad. A young woman PC called McElvaney. Before we know it the PSNI will be overrun with Catholics. It's the tip of a giant fuckin' iceberg."

Simpson shook his head. "Grow up, George. Take my advice and learn to live with it. If the Brits have their way, you'll be pile suckin' McElvaney long before you reach retirement age. Get your mind off the Taig and get concentrated on my business. I want to know what's happenin' before it happens if you know what I mean. Thanks for the information, now piss off home."

Whitehouse picked up his wet overcoat and reluctantly put it on. He moved off towards the door of the pub without looking back.

Simpson watched Whitehouse's departure. As soon the PSNI detective had closed the pub door behind him, he stood up and walked over to the bar. The barman instantly moved to his side. "Where's the private telephone?" he said curtly. He had a mobile in his pocket but after Prince Charles had announced to the world via his mobile that he fancied being a tampon, he and the boys had decided that land lines were the only way to go.

The barman led the way to the rear of the pub and inserted a key in a door marked 'PRIVATE-Staff Only'.

"Wait a minute I'll switch the line over from the bar." The barman withdrew and left Simpson standing in the doorway.

The smell of stale beer was worse in the office than in the bar. Simpson entered the cramped room, picked up the phone dialled a local number. "It's Richie, is he in?" he said when the phone was answered.

"Please hold on," the female voice on the other end sounded warm and friendly.

He stood holding the phone for twenty seconds. "Yes," the high pitched Northern Irish accent which the public knew so well came over the line.

"I just had a little chat with Whitehouse," Simpson said. "You were right on the button. They're as much in the dark as we are. I've been in touch with the other side but they swear blind that they have nothing to do with it. They're as bloody worried as we are. Something smells to high heaven and you know what that means. Somebody's out there makin' mischief for both us and the Fenians."

"What do you recommend?"

"The first thing is to avoid a bloodbath. We'll have to keep the 'hard men' in line."

"How?"

"I don't bloody know but I'll come up with something. In the meantime we'll have to find out who's behind the killings. If it's some rogue from the other side they've agreed that they'll clean it up."

"That's big of them," the voice said sharply. "What if it's a rogue Prod? It's happened before."

"We'll stop it," Simpson said emphatically.

"I hope that you're as good as your word. I'll make sure that the police concentrate their minds on finding the culprit. Meanwhile, I'll leave the day to day business in your capable hands." The phone went dead.

Simpson replaced the handset on the cradle and sat down in a dilapidated office chair. What in God's name was going on? he asked himself. The only positive thing was that Wilson was in charge of the case. He thought about his conversation with Whitehouse. The idiot's mind was back in the dark ages. But he could be very bloody useful. It takes all sorts to make a cause, he thought and he started to laugh.

CHAPTER 16

Wilson finished reading and then closed the file which Moira had left on his desk. Nothing. Peacock was just a twenty six year old nobody. So much for the common points with Patterson. Neither man seemed to warrant the trouble it had taken to murder them. And yet someone had gone to considerable lengths to ensure that they died.

"That's all?" he asked.

"That's everything that the government knows about Peacock. Where do we go from here?" she asked.

Wilson looked up into her red-rimmed eyes. One day on the squad and she was already beginning to look washed out. But even washed out she would still turn heads. Welcome to the PSNI. It wouldn't take long before she was wishing that she was working sixteen-hour days for an investment bank. At least there she would be paid for being shat on.

"First off if we don't find a link between Patterson and Peacock then we're in real trouble because that will mean that our killer is selecting his victims at random. That will make him very hard to find. So we need the link. In the meantime we start by following classical police procedure. We're coppers and that means that we start shaking trees and seeing what falls out." He pushed back his chair as far as it would go and leaned back. "Since I saw the shambles at the petrol station last night, my stomach's been as tight as a ducks arse. We're not dealing with the usual sort of trigger happy Provo or UVF man. From the minute I saw Patterson's body I've had the feeling that we're dealing with a professional killer. This man knows his business as well as I know police work. I'd guess that he's had some training. Probably army or at least high-quality paramilitary. That means we can limit the suspects to any one of a couple of thousand men."

"How can you deduce that?"

Wilson raised his eyebrows.

"Seriously," she said. "I want to learn."

"There are two general categories of murderer in the province. The first is your common or garden psychopath. Ulster is fertile soil for this boy. Take Lennie Murphy. He and his merry men liked to lift their intended victims out on the street. The poor unfortunate bastards were taken back to a drinking club for a bit of fun and frolics before being taken to some waste land and hacked to pieces."

She screwed up her face in mock pain.

"Exactly," Wilson said. "There have to be a few marbles loose up there," Wilson tapped the side of his head, "before you can get into that kind of business. It's always bothered me that it took us so bloody long to get a fix on those bastards. The butchers were just a gang of psychopaths who got their rocks off by hacking up people. Any people. After a while Lennie and the boys didn't bother to ask your religion. But they weren't alone. Anywhere else in the world serial killers like Lenny Murphy, the King Rats and the Mad Dogs would be classified alongside people like Fred West, Ted Bundy and Jeffrey Dahmer. But Northern Ireland is a special case. Justice British style ends at Stranrar. This place used to be awash with mass murderers who are downright psychopaths. We just give them stupid tabloid names like 'King Rat' and 'Mad Dog' but they were real live people who got off on killing people. The fact that they were so-called political didn't make our life any easier."

"But why doesn't the justice system just treat them as serial killers?" she asked. "What's so bloody political about killing a vagrant?"

Wilson let the question hang on the air. He had devoted his life to bringing killers to justice and he had no answer to the Constable's question.

"Okay what's the second kind of murderer?" she asked when she saw that Wilson wasn't going to answer her original question.

Wilson broke out of his reverie. "The second type of murderer is the hapless volunteer. He's so hyped up on twisted political claptrap that he blindly follows orders. Someone decides that a particular person has to die and the murderer simply fulfils the contract. This bloke is the complete amateur. He comes in blastin' with whatever weapon the godfathers stuck into his hands and he takes out everybody in the vicinity of the target. The UVF did it with automatic weapons. The AK-47 was the ideal invention for this guy. The object is to hit as many poor buggers as possible with a hail of bullet and then scarper. The IRA favoured your bomb. Both are indiscriminate and there's no specific target. It was the local equivalent of the suicide bomber. We're talking fear and carnage. Have you ever seen the results of a bomb or a wild shooting?"

She shook her head.

"Not a pretty sight. I sometimes think the dead are the lucky ones. Most of the detectives in this office have been to counselling. Murder is one thing but to accompany it by tearing the bodies to pieces adds a level of sickness that's hard to square with human beings. Am I boring you?"

"No," she said. She'd heard most of this before at the college but not from someone who had been at the coalface. "Go on."

"Sometimes the two general types cross the line. They begin by killing to order and then become psychopaths. Other times the psychopaths can disguise their blood lust and kill only when ordered. That's what makes Patterson and Peacock different. In each case the killer got the man he wanted to get. He's not indiscriminate and he's not sick. Also he's left us nothing to work with and no clue as to where he'll strike next."

"Maybe he won't strike again," she said.

"Chance would be a fine thing." The phone on Wilson's desk rang and he picked up the receiver. "Yes. Right away," he replaced the handset slowly. "Two calls from the DCC's office in one week. It's a royal pain in the arse being so popular."

She watched the big man squeeze his way out from behind the desk. Bead's of sweat stood out on the Chief Inspector's brow. There was a faint odour of stale whiskey in the air as Wilson moved towards her. Was this what twenty years of police work can do to you?

"I'm getting fed up to the teeth of these confession sessions with the DCC," Wilson said as she retreated into the main Squad Room to permit her chief's exit from the cramped office. "When I was a kid in Sunday school they taught me that Protestants were against confession. But I think they're only against it when there's a priest involved. Why don't you go through those files again." He picked up a small file from his desk and handed it to her. "Here's the report on last night's canvas of the houses close to the garage. There's nothing of interest but go through it before passing it on to Eric. Find me something, anything that'll link the victims and help me get my hand on the bastard who's doing them."

"He's waiting for you," the Secretary looked up from her desk as Wilson entered.

Once more into the valley of death, he thought as he strode towards the open door.

Jennings' face was so long that he looked like his favourite dog had just died.

"Sit down," he said curtly. "Let me get right to the point. I've had the Chief Constable on to me this morning. He's wondering what in the hell you're doing about this damn outbreak of sectarian killings," Jennings picked up a metal paper clip and began to straighten it. "It appears that some political personages have been making representations to him concerning the disquiet in the Protestant neighbourhoods. The Chief Constable is very concerned that your inactivity could lead to retaliatory action by Loyalists. In other words he wants bloody action and he wants it fast. Where do we stand?"

"I've got all my available men working on this one," Wilson eased himself into the chair in front of Jennings' desk. He stared over his superior's shoulder at the montage of photographs which lined the wall. The central subject was always Jennings. He could be seen smiling and shaking hands with several of the principle Protestant politicians. Taking pride of place in the centre of the collection was a picture of the Superintendent shaking hands with the former Prime Minister of Great Britain while a prominent Evangelical Protestant politician looked on. Mixing with the great and the good was Jennings' stock in trade. He would soon have to make room on the wall for photos of himself in cahoots with Nationalist politicians. Wilson was sure that his smile would be as wide for both sides of the political divide.

"We think that the same gun was used in the three killings," Wilson continued. "But that hasn't been confirmed. Two of the men, Patterson and Peacock, were the intended victims. We think that the third man was in the wrong place at the wrong time. There's no real evidence other than the ejected shells. The gun doesn't feature in any previous shootings in the province and we haven't come up with a witness for either of the killings. We've established a hot line but so far that hasn't produced a lead. As you might have already concluded, an arrest is not considered imminent."

"So the killings are random and might possibly be sectarian," the DCC looked at the file on his desk.

"They could be," Wilson leaned back in the chair. "But I don't buy it."

"What exactly are you trying to tell me?" the DCC has dispensed with the paper clip and had graduated to turning the silver buttons on his tunic absentmindedly.

"Whoever did these killings was very careful about the selection of the target and he made damn sure that the target wasn't going to make a miraculous recovery." Wilson was suddenly aware that Jennings was hanging on his every word. What the hell is going down here, he thought as he watched the anxious face of his superior. He'd handled dozens of murders in his tenure at Tennent Street but Jennings had never taken a blind bit of notice. The Chief Constable had dropped a ferret down Jennings' trousers and that meant the Chief Constable himself was being squeezed, big time. "If you want my opinion I don't think that there is any paramilitary involvement. Nobody is stupid enough to get involved in carrying out assassinations like Patterson's and Peacock's. Also," Wilson added quickly before the DCC could intervene. "Neither of the two men had any relation with any of the paramilitaries or the criminal fraternity. So we're looking at two random murders carried out by a professional killer. It doesn't gel."

"I don't see where this is leading us," Jennings' left eye twitched as he stared at Wilson.

"I think we've got a new kid on the block. I have no idea what he's up to but he's been in this business before. I

134

also have no idea whether he belongs to a grouping or whether he's a lone wolf. All I know is that he picks the target, he makes sure of the kill and he leaves nothing for us to work with. We've given the 'usual suspects' a quick once over but there's no obvious candidate."

"An interesting theory but complete conjecture," Jennings was coming alive again. "Now I don't like telling you how to conduct your investigation but it is imperative that we solve these murders. I don't have to remind you that we are sitting on a powder keg and if somebody has been stupid enough to be playing with matches we could be looking at another twenty-five years of conflict. I want you to get in touch with Frank Cahill. Set up a meeting with him. Find out what he knows about the killings. Somehow we have to convince him that it's as much in his interest as it is ours for him to put a stop to this damn foolishness."

Wilson winced at the mention of Cahill's name and a bolt of pain shot through the back of his head. 'Two-gun' Frank Cahill had been, and possibly still was, the chief IRA 'godfather' in Belfast. Although nominally a brigade commander in the IRA, Cahill used his position to set up a criminal operation which would have done credit to the Mafia. Cahill controlled extortion rackets, building scams, booze, robberies and prostitution over a large area of West Belfast. No kind of economic activity was possible in Cahill's area unless tribute was paid to the 'godfather'. The man was scum.

"It won't help," Wilson said staring into his superior's eyes.

"That remains to be seen," Jennings replied coldly. "I want you to get them to stop before the other side starts and we have an all out war on our hands. Frank Cahill can help us to stop that war and you're the one who is going to ask him for that help."

" Take my word for it Cahill's not involved. There's no profit in killing civilians."

"In words of one syllable, see him right away and get this bloody thing stopped," Jennings began to shuffle the papers on his desk. "You've led a rather charmed life in the Force. I'm sure that it's no surprise to you that there are some people here at Headquarters who've been waiting quite a long time to see you land on your arse." Jennings lifted his eyes from the papers and looked at Wilson. "Of course, I've never numbered myself among them. However, if things go wrong on the Patterson and Peacock cases you could very well find yourself pounding a beat in Pomoroy."

Wilson felt the twitch at the corner of his mouth and wondered whether it had been visible to Jennings. He knew that his rejection of earlier approaches to become 'one of the boys' would stifle his chances of promotion but he never thought that the 'Lodge brothers' would actually go gunning for him. Jennings' message had been received loud and clear. And despite his assertions to the contrary, the DCC would be the first to ram the knife into his back.

"By the way," Jennings said. "How's McElvaney working out?"

"She's bright," Wilson stood to leave. But not bright enough to pass on a poisoned chalice, he thought.

"Is she working on the Patterson and Peacock business with you?"

"Yes," Wilson stood in front of the desk.

"You'll keep an eye on her of course." Jennings smiled. There was no doubting the double meaning in the statement.

Wilson began to open his mouth but closed it again. Jennings would only draw pleasure from any reply that he might make. His eyes fell on the photograph with the beaming smiles of the DCC and his political friends. The pressure was only beginning. If he didn't find the bastard behind the killings Jennings would use whatever clout he had to put an end to whatever career he had. The ante was being upped and Wilson could see that he was being prepared as a sacrificial lamb. So be it, he thought as he turned and without saying a word marched towards the door of Jennings' office.

Wilson finished reading the last file which had been prepared by his lads on the Patterson and Peacock killings. The ballistics report had confirmed his suspicion that the same gun had been used in both killings. The pathology reports added nothing new. The regulars at the King's Head had been questioned but nobody had any knowledge of Patterson. So what was new. A second canvas of the residents of the Newtonards Road had produced one nugget. A resident who had been on night shift remembered seeing a man wearing a donkey jacket sheltering in a doorway across from the garage. It had been dark and raining so the witness had hurried on. The man might have been tall or short, thin or fat, black or white. He'd read Jean Black's statement on Peacock and concluded that she would have been the prime suspect in his death under normal circumstances. A check on her family had thrown up two brothers who had served sentences in the Maze. Both had been questioned and had produced cast iron alibis for the time that Peacock had been gunned down. So what was new. The work of six detectives and any number of uniforms had produced absolutely nothing to go on. He closed the final report and thought about his meeting with Jennings. It stuck in his craw to have to meet with a former IRA boss in the hope of getting a lead. He rubbed his eyes and tilted his chair back. He would have been a total fool if he hadn't realised the exposed situation the three killings had put him in. The situation on the streets, where the tension had increased appreciably, would increase the pressure on the Chief Constable for a quick result. That pressure would manifest itself eventually in a move to get him off the case and to hand it to a more politically in-tune officer. That eventuality might even suit most of the men sitting in his Squad Room. He stood up then stretched before moving his head from side to side to release the tension. He walked into the Squad Room and stood beside Whitehouse's desk.

"What's the word on the streets on the Patterson and Peacock business?" he asked.

Whitehouse thought about his meeting with Simpson in the 'Linfield Arms'. "Exactly what you'd expect," he answered definitively. "I hear that some people are gettin' pretty pissed of. They want to know what the hell is going on."

"Anybody in particular?"

"You know as well as me, boss" Whitehouse said slowly. "As far as ninety per cent of the population are concerned this kind of thing is finished. They can accept the drug gangs killing each other but not John Citizen being plugged for no reason at all. The press have put the word out that neither Patterson or Peacock had any involvement with the criminal underworld in Belfast. So what are people to think? Add to that the fact that all the dead are Protestant and some of the old fears start coming back. Word on the street has it that some of the former Loyalist paramilitary leadership are not too happy with Prods bein' blown away in their own back garden. A few hotheads are callin' for retaliation. You know the way it is with them boys. Nobody can say how long they'll be kept in check. It might be that things could blow up at any minute. Everybody's on edge. It could get hectic."

"Great minds obviously think alike," Wilson slapped his sergeant on the back. "I just had the same message from the DCC. He suggested that I go and talk with Frank Cahill."

Whitehouse frowned. "Not that old bugger," he said between clenched teeth. "We should have put him away years ago. He's not political any more so he should be fair game but he always seems to be one step ahead of us. "

Wilson watched McElvaney glance up from the file she was studying.

"I'm sure you'd find lots of people who'd agree with you. However, the law requires proof before we can put someone away. Whether we like it or not some stupid bureaucrat thinks that Frank Cahill has developed a certain political status which puts him in the 'difficult to apprehend' category."

"To hell with the sodding bureaucrats," Whitehouse's face was flushed. "Frank Cahill is nothing but a bloody criminal. When the chips are down I'd put him in the same category as the Krays."

"Then maybe the DCC's suggestion wasn't so far of the mark after all. Maybe a word in his ear might get things moving in some direction. To be honest it might do more good than sitting around here on our collective arses."

"You really think that Cahill is involved somewhere in this business, do you?" Whitehouse turned his head to face his superior.

"As a matter of fact, George, just like you, I don't," Wilson replied taking a black leather address book from his pocket and skimming through the pages.

Whitehouse watched as Wilson leafed through the book. "Pull the bastard in," he said. "Lock him up in

Castlereagh. Sweat him and maybe he'll give you your killer."

"That's not on and you know it," Wilson had located his page and held the book open with the palm of his right hand. "Suppose for the sake of argument that I'm right and Cahill isn't involved. He's going to be bloody curious about the killings looking like IRA executions. And don't think for one second that the thought of 'tit for tat' killings wouldn't have crossed his mind. He can only maintain his position in the Catholic enclaves as long as he's seen as the great protector. If there is a backlash and if the Catholic community blame him for it, that's Frank Cahill up the Swannee. He'll want to know who's responsible for the killings as much as we do. Maybe we can flush the bastard out between us. That is unless you have some better idea?"

Whitehouse stared ahead blankly.

"I didn't think so," Wilson said picking up the phone from Whitehouse's desk.

"Jesus, I've seen it all now," Whitehouse said. The red colour had moved from his cheeks to his entire face. "A DCI in the PSNI ringin' up to make an appointment with a murderer."

"Careful, George, I don't want you in the Royal Infirmary with a stroke," Wilson said composing Cahill's number. "It's bad manners to drop in unannounced."

"I wouldn't talk to that bastard to save my life," Whitehouse said setting his jaw.

"You won't have to," Wilson finished dialling. "I'm taking McElvaney with me on this one."

"What!"

Moira had her head buried in a file.

Whitehouse was about to continue when Wilson held up his hand.

140

"This is Detective Chief Inspector Wilson from Tennent Street," he said into the phone, "I'd like to meet Mr. Cahill as soon as possible." he cupped the mouthpiece with his hand. "Moira, finish up there. We're going on a little excursion."

Whitehouse ground his teeth and stared ahead.

Wilson pretended not to notice. Whitehouse was a good copper but he was mired in the past. Someday he would recognise that it was time to move on.

"Yes," he returned his attention to the phone, "I know it. We'll be there in twenty minutes."

CHAPTER 17

When you had lived in Belfast for more than twenty years you developed an antennae which could calculate the level of tension in the city in an instant. As soon as Wilson left the station his antennae told him that the level of tension on the streets had reached seven on his scale of one to ten which put it very definitely in the red zone. He had seen it higher but this was definitely the highest it had been since the end of hostilities. The air of tension even permeated to the unmarked police car that carried Wilson and Moira away from Tennent Street and onto the Shankill Road. The most notorious street in Belfast's turbulent history was deserted except for a few housewives doing their early morning shopping. The car passed the filthy facade of the 'Balmoral Bar' which had gained notoriety during the 1970's as the home base of the 'Balmoral Bar Gang', a rogue group of the Ulster Volunteer Force which terrorised the Catholic population of West Belfast through murder and torture. The building looked shabby and run down. All peeling paint and black soot stains. It was impossible for the onlooker to divine the atrocities which had been conceived and perpetrated behind the crumbling facade. The Shankill had not yet benefited from the peace dividend and still wore a shabby and run down look. The police Vauxhall moved through the centre of the Protestant ghetto and turned right onto Northumberland Street before heading towards the Falls Road and passing the concrete barrier that divided the city's two communities. Walls had fallen in Berlin while walls had been constructed in Belfast

Wilson sat silently in the back of the car. A loud gurgle emanated from his stomach. The portents were not good. He popped two antacid tablets into his mouth hoping that they would calm the impending storm in his stomach. The driver turned onto the Falls Road. Moira scanned the streets through the side window like a newly arrived American tourist.

To their left the towers of the Divis Flats dominated the gloomy skyline. They passed a burned-out building on which a large mural depicting a hooded figure raising a Kalashnikov above its head had been painted. Above the mural was the legend 'Provisional IRA', while the words 'You are entering free Belfast' were painted in bold white letters at the figure's side. He wondered whether such a thing as 'free Belfast' had ever existed. Since the Battle of the Boyne, Belfast had been synonymous with religious hostility, slums and economic exploitation. Desperation and deprivation were the bedfellows of Belfast's citizens. The back streets of Belfast were the equal of the worst slums of Glasgow or Liverpool. In the twentieth century, the city had distinguished itself for its pogroms and its current notoriety resided in its position as the former murder capital of Great Britain. So much for freedom. A few yards down the street a second giant mural depicted the virgin and child. The local population saw nothing incongruous in the appearance of the two contrasting murals on the same short stretch of road.

Wilson rolled down his window and sucked in a deep breath of dank polluted air. His joints felt stiff and he had the beginnings of a pain at the base of the small of his back. They were travelling into the heartland of republican Belfast. This was the area where the PSNI once feared to tread. Here the uniformed policeman had been considered a

143

legitimate military target. Passing through the lower Falls towards Andersonstown, a police patrol vehicle might have expected to be fired upon or to be blown up, so they just didn't bother to go there. How could their fellow citizens on mainland Britain understand such a situation? This was the stuff of television drama. During the 'Troubles' Belfast had resembled a post apocalyptic world where justice did not exist. A comfortable world of Western plenty turned upside down by the fear of the bullet and the bomb. The reign of anarchy replacing the rule of law. In its time Belfast had been compared to Beirut but it and the capital of Lebanon had moved on. He looked out the side window as the car passed Miltown Cemetery. The graveyard which contained the bodies of many victims of the `Troubles' was eerily enveloped in a shroud of grey misty light. Along the wall of the cemetery the local graffiti artist had composed an Ulster equation 'STOP COLLUSION NOW- RUC/Brits +UDA/UVF = MURDER'.

"We're almost there, Sir," there was a slight catch in the driver's voice and he passed his tongue across his parched lips after he spoke.

"Go straight to the Republican Club on Coolnasilla Avenue," Wilson said. "They're expecting us so there shouldn't be any problems."

Wilson looked at the faces of the passers-by. They looked just like their Protestant counterparts on the other side of the concrete and barbed wire wall which still divided their city. Their strides were heavy with the burden of the murder and hate which they had borne for thirty years. These people deserved hope.

"Who exactly is Frank Cahill?" Moira asked breaking the silence in the car.

Wilson smiled. If you lived in Belfast you assumed that only visitors from another planet didn't know who Frank Cahill was.

"Frank Cahill is the model of what they call a 'godfather'," Wilson said. "Officially he's a member of the Command Staff of the Provisional IRA but unofficially he runs one of the largest criminal organisations in the city. He's the man behind illegal drinking clubs, protection rackets, prostitution, drugs and illegal taxis. You name it and Frank Cahill's got a greasy paw in it somewhere. He's spent most of his life in one prison or other but always for 'the cause'. He was released under the Good Friday Agreement. Frank Cahill has paid his Republican dues and now he's collecting the rewards."

Moira looked across at her superior. "I hate to find myself in the company of DS Whitehouse but if he's nothing but a common criminal, why don't we lift him for straight-forward criminality?"

"Two reasons," Wilson said looking out at the dismal rows of red-bricked terraced houses plastered with graffiti depicting balaclava wearing freedom fighters holding Kalashnikovs above their heads. "Firstly, Cahill is so bloody careful you wouldn't believe it. There's probably not one single piece of paper in his whole operation. Nobody in their right mind would testify against him because not only would they be signing their own death warrant but they'd also be putting every member of their family on the firing line. Secondly, if we did have the goods on him, which we don't, the political fall-out would probably mean that a warrant wouldn't be issued. In any case if we did issue a warrant he'd probably skip to the South." He nodded at the terraced streets. "This is his area. Everybody here knows Frank Cahill and a lot of people here would still protect him with their lives. Our local mafia chiefs have learned a lot from their Sicilian cousins."

The car turned into a deserted street. Rubble and uncollected trash lay strewn around the ground.

"It's the blockhouse looking place at the far end," Wilson pointed over the driver's shoulder.

The edifice which Wilson had indicated stood alone at the end of the street. It was a low red-bricked building distinguished by a series of small barred windows running along the side. The red brick facade facing the street had a large steel door in the centre. On either side of the door was a life sized painting of a hooded Provisional IRA man standing beneath the tricolour of the Irish Republic.

As the car drew to a halt in front of the building, the steel door opened and two men emerged. Both were short and thickset. They were dressed identically in jeans and leather jackets.

"You're Wilson?" the young man who opened the door on his side of the car smiled showing a row of brown stained teeth.

Wilson nodded.

"He's waitin' inside for you."

As Wilson emerged from the car he looked down at the hand of the man who had opened the car door. A tattoo of a machine gun with the letters IRA in green white and gold had been crudely sketched on the back of the man's hand.

"The driver can wait here," Wilson said as he stepped onto the footpath. Moira had exited from the other side of the car.

"That's an improvement of the usual Protestant tart," the IRA man said letting his eyes roam over Moira's body.

"It's nice to be appreciated," Moira said. "But why do I feel I need a shower?"

"Enough of the repartee," Wilson said. He could smell whiskey and stale tobacco on the IRA man's breath.

"I wouldn't touch you, skank, if you were the last woman on earth," he indicated the second IRA man. "My comrade will hang around outside to make sure that your driver doesn't get into any trouble. Someone might take it into their head to run away with your nice unmarked police car." He nodded in the direction of the driver. "Can we assume that neither of you is carrying. I'd really like to search your friend," he smiled exposing the full range of his stained teeth.

Wilson laughed. "Dream on. Neither the Constable nor myself are carrying a weapon and you'll just have to take our word for it. Touch one of us and you'll live to regret it. Go inside and tell Frank I'm having none of this bullshit."

The bouncer reflected for a moment and then stood back. "Inside," He pulled the door open and ushered Wilson and Moira into the building.

Wilson stepped into the club and was immediately enveloped in darkness. He stopped just inside the door to give his eyes time to become accustomed to the low level of lighting. Gradually the dark shapes began to take form and the two policemen found themselves in a small hallway. The outer and inner steel doors were shut and bolted behind them. The doorman walked to an electronic box situated on the wall directly across from the entrance door.

He typed in a series of numbers and a door in the dark wall slid open.

"We don't want any uninvited guests," the man in the leather jacket pushed the door fully open. "After you."

The two detectives walked into a large room which constituted the drinking area of the Club. Wilson's eyes were gradually becoming accustomed to the dim lighting. The left hand side of the large room was dominated by a long bar at which three men sat. All three turned as Wilson and Moira entered. Their scowling countenances displayed their antipathy to the new arrivals.

"Come on," the man in the leather jacket bustled the two policemen forward.

Wilson started walking towards the rear of the room passing the tables and chairs which littered the open area. As he reached the end of the bar, he saw two men seated in a booth located directly behind the bar area. Frank Cahill and one of his lieutenants sat at a small table on which a lamp with a grimy shade stood. Wilson walked directly to the booth and sat on the side opposite the two men. Moira pushed in beside him. She didn't like the look of the men seated at the bar but she wasn't about to show it. Her heart was pounding but as long as she was close to Wilson she felt she could keep her courage up.

"I hope that they're all as pretty back in Tennent Street, Ian," Cahill's voice wheezed as he forced out the words.

"They surely are, Frank," Wilson said settling himself into the booth. It had been nearly two years since he'd last set eyes on Cahill. Time had not been kind to the 'godfather'. Even in the darkened room he could see the pallid skin and the sunken eyes. Cahill's hair or what was left of it had turned snow white and stood out in tufts from his cadaverous face. His jacket might once have fitted his frame but now looked a couple of sizes too big. Wilson could smell something on the fetid air and he imagined that it might be death.

"This is Constable Moira McElvaney," Wilson laid his hand on the arm of the young woman sitting beside him and he felt her tremble at the touch. The poor lassie is probably scared out of her wits. "Frank is one of the old school, Moira. He's too smart to harm a police officer. Isn't that so, Frank?"

Cahill smiled. "Well not such a pretty one anyway."

"Moira's a strange name for a Protestant," the young man beside Cahill spoke.

"Maybe I'm not a Protestant," Moira heard her own voice and was astonished at how steady it appeared. Wilson put his hand on her arm and squeezed. She took it as a sign of approbation and smiled.

"I won't bother introducin' my young associate," Cahill's hissing voice broke the silence. "For obvious reasons," he continued, his thin wizened face breaking into a smile. "Let's just say that he helps me with my business affairs."

The young man at Cahill's side was in his thirties which meant that he had been brought up in the "Troubles' but he had a more polished look than the thugs at the bar. His hair had been professionally cut and his features had not been ravaged by drink. He gave the impression of a personable young man wearing a well tailored pin striped suit and if he hadn't been sitting beside Cahill, Wilson would have taken him for an accountant or a lawyer.

"So Chief Inspector," the young man said. "It's rather strange to be getting a visit from you these days. We live in a period of peace and economic prosperity so our interactions with the police are limited. As you can see by the surroundings Mr. Cahill runs a successful bar business. So what can we do for you?"

Cahill looked sharply at his colleague. "Relax, the Chief Inspector will get to the point in his own time" he turned to Wilson. "The young people are always in a hurry. It's been quite a while since you and I drank together." Cahill made a slight motion with his right hand towards the bar. One of the three men Wilson had seen when he entered picked up a bottle from the bar and brought it and four glasses to the booth.

"This is how business between men should be transacted," the old man hissed and slid a glass into position before each of them. He screwed the top off a bottle of Jameson and held it out towards Wilson. The Chief Inspector nodded and Cahill poured a large measure into the glass. Cahill moved the bottle towards Moira. She placed her right hand over the glass.

"No thanks," she said looking directly into the old man's eyes.

"You know what they say, Moira," Cahill's companion said, "You lie down with dogs you get up with fleas."

"Enough," there was menace in the hiss from Cahill's mouth. He poured himself a large measure of whiskey and screwed the cap back on the bottle. "Fuck the begrudgers."

He lifted the glass to his lips and drank deeply without looking at Wilson. "The doctors tell me that this stuff is slowly killing me;" he let out a wheezing laugh. "They're starting to tell me that everything I do is slowly killing me. If they're right about how long I've got, I'm afraid that you and I have concluded our business together. You won't ever have the chance to put me away again."

Wilson sipped his drink. "That would be a great pity. It would make many a copper's day to see you banged up again."

Cahill smiled. "You're too damn honest to be a policeman." He took another sip of his whiskey. "I know that you probably won't believe me but I've always respected you. It's a hard enough job to find an honest copper these days."

Wilson could recognise the incipient rattle of death in Cahill's voice and realised that he wouldn't be long for this world. Justice was about to be thwarted by nature.

"Now to business. To what do we owe this particular visit?" Cahill put his glass on the table and dissolved into a fit of coughing. The man at his side patted the old man's back gently. Cahill's coughing subsided and he wiped his mouth with a handkerchief which his lieutenant proffered. "It must be something mighty important for the RUC, sorry the PSNI, to call on us personally" Cahill's voice was no more than a whisper.

"We've had three Protestants murdered in 'C' Division over the last few days," Wilson began. "Three Protestants shot with the same gun in two separate incidents. All killed deep inside Protestant territory." Wilson gave the exact locations of the murders. "The three hits were professional, very professional. Everyone is afraid that trouble is just around the corner again. It follows that a lot of people might think that you or some of your friends are responsible." He paused and looked directly at the two men opposite. Neither spoke. "You know as well as I do how these things work. The hotheads are already rattling the sabre. Unless it stops more bodies are liable to end up in the morgue. That worries me. Also there's the question of putting the bastard who did this where he belongs – behind bars."

"Look me in the eyes," Cahill said and locked his stare on Wilson. "It's over. We've all decided to move on. Some of us have even decided that the whole thing was one big bloody mistake." He let his eyes fall to the table and he gripped his whiskey glass. "We've known each other a long time. I hope that you don't take me for a bloody fool because that's what I'd be if I allowed any of my people to get out of line. We don't kill people any more, especially Prods. Full stop. I don't suppose you'd be here if the victims were connected with any paramilitary group."

"As far as we're concerned they're as white as the driven snow," Wilson replied.

"That means nothin'," Cahill said.

"So you come to us first," Cahill's lieutenant said. "A case of rounding up the usual suspects."

"Since the murdered men were Protestants, we got the bright idea of starting our enquiries with you," Wilson stared at the young man beside Cahill. His eyes were now fully accustomed to the light and he looked beyond the suit and the grooming. He concentrated on the eyes because that's where you could see the damage of years of conflict. The young man's eyes were dark and lifeless. Wilson considered himself a fair judge of character but he could read nothing from those eyes. They were as cold as the eyes of a dead man. As long as men like this existed then the province would never be safe. Born in conflict and raised on a diet of sectarian violence. As a young child, he'd probably begun by throwing stones at British Army patrols before graduating to Molotov cocktails. They would have blooded him early and then put him at the feet of the master to learn his trade. And there was no better tutor in terrorism than Frank Cahill. He wanted desperately to believe that Cahill was right and that the conflict really was over. But he was afraid that there was more than one man with the dead eyes of the true fanatic out there on both sides of the divide. As long as that was true the conflict would never really end. Peace and reconciliation was the new cry. It was said that there would be no real peace until both sides were reconciled. The peace was holding but the reconciliation would be the most painful part of the process. Men would have to bear their souls and admit to acts which would horrify their neighbours and possibly the world. He wondered whether Cahill's young lieutenant was ready to bear his soul. He doubted it.

"There's no offence intended," Wilson continued. "We had to start somewhere and here is as good as anywhere else."

"That's a load of shite?" Cahill's speech was almost inaudible. "We're playing by the rules these days. The guns have been put away except for a couple of gobshites and we're takin' care of them ourselves. The killing is over. We're all going to live happily ever after."

Wilson raised his eyebrows. "Put yourself in my shoes, Frank" he stared at the old man. "The three stiffs were Prods. They were done professionally. Your people could have done it whether you authorised it or not."

"That's bullshit and you know it," Cahill's lieutenant interjected angrily. "Our discipline is tight. None of the people associated with Mr. Cahill are going to jeopardise the peace. Unlike others we haven't become politicians. We're businessmen. And we're not about to screw up our business interests."

Cahill shot a glance at his young colleague.

"What we're saying is that we weren't involved," Cahill paused and wheezed in a long breath. "If a flea farts in Republican Belfast then I know about it. There may be some stupid fuckers about but I don't know anyone crazy enough to assassinate a target so deep in the Prod's territory. If the Prods didn't get him then I would."

"What about a rogue? Somebody acting alone," Wilson asked.

"Not a chance. Like my young associate said, our discipline is tight. The politicians have convinced us that demographics are on our side. Some day there'll be a united Ireland although I don't think that I'll be around to see it." The end of Cahill's sentence dissolved into a fit of coughing.

"What kind of gun was used?" the young man beside Cahill asked.

"A 9 millimetre," Wilson said.

"Brilliant, a nine millimetre," the young man said through the noise of Cahill's coughing. "The province was full of nine millimetres. Is it new on the streets?"

"As far as we can tell. The ballistics tests don't match anything we've come across before." This fact had been bothering Wilson. The majority of shootings in Belfast took place with guns that had already been used in many such incidents. Gunmen rarely held their own weapons but picked up the requisite hardware from an organisation 'quartermaster' just prior to a murder. As soon as the killing was done, the first task was to return the gun to the 'quartermaster'. The appearance of a 'clean' gun was an event. He had no doubt that Cahill had squirreled away more than a few guns during the de-commissioning exercise but he would maintain a strict control over them.

Wilson looked away from Cahill to the bar. The three men who had watched the entrance of the police officers had adjusted their stools and were seated directly facing the booth in which Cahill sat.

"Our first priority is to get the murders stopped," Wilson began when Cahill's coughing had subsided. "If he's one of yours, call him off before this thing escalates. Give me a name and I'll do the rest. We need this asshole off the streets."

"I think that you need to get your ears tested," Cahill's lieutenant leaned forward towards the two police officers. "You've been told that our people had nothing to do with the killing of working class Protestant civilians. We fought a war against the British Army and the oppressive sectarian security forces. That war is over but some of the shit is still clinging to this Province. You people think you can con us just because you recruit a few Catholics and stick blue uniforms on them. You and your friends have killed over three hundred and fifty civilians since this 'trouble' started. And how many of you have been jailed for it? Not one man jack of you. You give your evidence from behind screens while some judge whitewashes you. If it's murderers you're lookin' for, you won't have to look very far. And you," he turned to face Moira. "You're the face on the new PSNI. A good-looking catholic woman that the

Chief Constable can point to when the people from the Mainland ask about religious integration. You'll go far. And if they dump you out for any reason I'm sure we can find a place in our organisation for you." He smiled broadly when he'd finished speaking.

Moira ignored the smile and looked straight ahead.

Wilson stared at Cahill who seemed to have retreated into himself. "What do you say, Frank?"

"He may not be far wrong," Cahill said to Wilson his weak voice was in direct contrast to his colleague's shouting. "It wouldn't be the first time the Prods topped one of their own kind. They're more famous than us for their feuds. Sometimes it's not a question of religion but just plain old bloodlust."

"You're not listening," Wilson said. "This isn't a replay of the past. I don't think that this guy is a psycho. The man who did these killings was a pro. I think that maybe he does this for a living but I can't for the life of me think of why the victims warranted this level of attention."

Cahill opened his mouth to speak but Wilson held up his hand.

"Don't ask me for details just take my word for it," Wilson said. "I've seen more murder victims in my life than most coppers and I can recognise the difference between the work of a pro and a 'cut-up' job. I'll take your word for it that nobody from your side was involved." He stood and motioned to Moira to do the same. "We're leaving."

Wilson saw the three men at the bar stand up and push their stools aside.

"Don't think that I'm so naive that I don't understand what's going on here," Cahill stood with some difficulty and faced Wilson. "I may be on my last legs but I don't want to see this Province returned to a permanent state of war. There are still a few stupid buggers in the movement who can see a day when the Brits will pile into the long boats and sail off the island. But it probably isn't going to happen that way. The way forward is through the ballot box. You wouldn't be here if you didn't think that something smelled almighty queer. I get the same pong. Somebody's messin' around in our back yard. Maybe he's tryin' to create grief between us and the Prods. That's for you to figure out. And I'm glad that it's not up to me to solve. Maybe we'll see each other again but I don't think so. And if we do it'll have to be on the other side."

"We'll keep it in mind," Wilson said.

"I'm bunched, Mister Wilson" Cahill said standing with difficulty. "A couple of weeks the doctors tell me. I know that you think I'm scum but that's not the way it started out. I really believed in what we stood for. It was all fucked up and too many people died because of it. I was just a pawn in the game. I want you to believe that. I always respected you."

"I heard you on the television, Frank," Wilson said. "But saying sorry won't bring back the dead or re-grow lost limbs. No cause was worth the collateral damage."

Cahill stuck his hand out to Wilson.

Wilson took the old man's hand and shook it without speaking. Cahill looked frail and bent as the two police officers towered over him. He held out his hand to Moira and the young constable waited for Wilson's nod before taking it.

"Be careful around this fellah, Moira," Cahill said as she released his hand. "He's got a reputation for getting people into trouble. Even with his own people. Now, be off the two of you." Cahill slumped into his place in the corner of the booth.

"A pleasure doing business with you, Chief Inspector," Cahill's lieutenant motioned towards the door. As he passed the men at the bar, he signalled for them to retake their seats. He opened the inner door and led the two police officers into the hallway. As they left the drinking area of the club and the steel door clanged shut, Wilson thought that on a humanitarian level he should feel some sorrow for the sick old man they had left behind. But whatever sorrow he might have felt was submerged by the grossness of the crimes which the man had committed during his lifetime. Like many others who had been involved in the 'Troubles', Frank Cahill had repented publicly but he had sent many innocent men and women to meet their maker. Cahill's lieutenant opened the front door and a flood of grey light entered the hallway.

"I hope we can avoid you visiting us again," he said holding the door fully open.

"So do I," Wilson said looking directly into his face. "But I have a feeling both of our hopes will be dashed. See you around."

Moira walked to the car and held the door open for her superior. Wilson noticed that while they had been inside the building the driver had turned the car around so that it was facing back the way they had come.

"On the other hand, Moira," the lieutenant said from the doorway. "You're always welcome to visit."

Moira stiffened and released her hold on the door-handle of the car.

"Looks like you made a conquest," Wilson called from the backseat. "Get into the car before they kidnap you."

Moira stood glaring indignantly at Cahill's assistant for several seconds before she turned and sat into the back seat alongside Wilson. She slammed the door shut behind her.

As soon as the door closed, the driver slipped the car into gear and they moved off in the direction from which they had come. The driver's relief at moving off was noticeable to Wilson in the backseat.

Moira let out a long breath. "I could kill that bloody sod," she said. "He's so smug and superior. They're the one's who are in control now. We created a power vacuum and those people have just jumped into it. I've had the same reaction from some of my parent's neighbours. How do they expect to get a fair crack of the whip if they don't appreciate Catholics who join the police force." Her hands were shaking and she felt a shiver run along her spine. "They make me so bloody mad."

"It's not so funny when you get it from both sides," he said. He noticed that she was shivering and his first inclination was to put his arm around her. In a fatherly-way he told himself. But she was a twenty-something very attractive woman and he was her direct superior. He saw the eyes of the driver in the rear mirror. Think about your pension, he told himself. "Don't worry about it. It's always tough when you cut trail. Just think the next Catholic detective at Tennent Street will have a much easier ride."

She felt the shivering subside. She was bigger than a few stupid remarks from a petty criminal. She'd hung tough when it was necessary and Wilson was right – it could only get easier. She sucked in a few deep breaths as they rode along in silence.

"What did you think of Frank Cahill?" he asked when he felt she had regained her composure.

"He reminded me of my father," she said. "A grey-haired old man with a twinkle in his eye and a liking for a drop of the hard stuff."

"It just shows that appearances can be deceptive. Frank is as tough a customer as you'd hope to meet. As is your father I suppose."

"So we learned nothing."

"I wouldn't say that," Wilson sat back. "I have a sneaking feeling that Cahill is telling the truth. They don't know anything and a blind man could see that they're as worried as we are." He sat in silence for a few moments. "I don't like this one at all."

"Then you definitely don't agree with DS Whitehouse," she said.

"Somebody is using their modus operandi as a blind. That somebody wants us to think that the IRA is behind the killings. Maybe the plan is to get the paramilitaries back into business and at each others throats. Maybe the Chinese are not happy with the restaurant trade and want to move in on the crime business. Maybe it's the Russians or the Albanians. Or maybe it's the bloody Martians. I don't know. The peace is still a fragile thing perhaps somebody doesn't want peace. The question is who the hell is that somebody."

"So we exclude Cahill and his associates?" Moira asked.

"At this point in time we exclude nobody. We've managed to pass the ball to Cahill for a while. He doesn't want rogue operators queering his pitch and causing trouble between him and his new Loyalist friends. I reckon that it won't take him long to get the word out that if there is a rogue out there he wants to know who it is. Maybe he'll flush the bastard out for us."

Wilson sat back in the car and fished around in his pocket for his packet of antacids. Nothing in Northern Ireland was as simple as it seemed and the Patterson and Peacock murders already looked complicated. It didn't auger well for the future.

Cahill's lieutenant watched the police car accelerate down the street. He'd heard of Wilson but then again everybody involved with the criminal fraternity in Belfast had heard of Ian Wilson. For some weird reason Frank had wanted to see him. Frank was old school and his generation were moving on or at least moving out. He was willing to humour the old man during his last days but his successor was already flexing his hands around the reins of power. They had made the transition from terrorism to business. There was no longer a need to collect money for bullets and bombs so it could be used in developing the business opportunities that arose from the strategic advantages they had developed during the troubles. Most of their footsoldiers were adept at running clubs, organising protection and robbing banks.

There were also those who had already killed and who could kill again but it was best to keep those individuals in check. The Prods were in the same business on their side of the line and that didn't bother him. The two opposing paramilitary groups who had fought each other during the 'Troubles' had learned that coexistence was preferable to annihilation. It was always dumb that the Protestant and Catholic have-nots had gone for each other's throats while the fat cats had kept a respectable distance from the fray. He watched as Wilson's car disappeared into the distance. He had the idea that Wilson was not the kind of copper his new organisation would be able to deal with. He re-entered the club and made his way to the booth were Cahill sat. The old man's face was so grey that he already looked dead.

"First Richie Simpson, now Wilson," Cahill's lieutenant said sliding into the seat directly across from his mentor. "This thing could get out of hand. What do you think, Frank?"

"That was about trouble, Sean me boy," Cahill coughed into the white handkerchief and Sean noticed small flecks of red appearing through the white linen. Cahill glanced up and saw the look on the young man's face. "Yes, Sean, I know what you're thinkin' and you're right. It won't be long now. You'll soon be in charge but you won't last long if you don't stop shoving that shit up your nose."

"For God's sake, Frank, you'll live to be a hundred," Sean doubted seriously whether Cahill would see out the month. "And the shit I shove up my nose is as recreational as the Jameson you drop down your gullet. So why are we in trouble?"

"We're not in trouble, yet," Cahill drew in a deep breath. "Wilson is something of a strange cat for a Peeler.

162

We have it on good authority that he isn't one of the boys. Not a Lodge man. The PSNI is a bad place not to be a Lodge man. No promotions. Lots of grief." He paused to draw in another large breath and used the hiatus to refill the glass that still stood before him from the bottle of Jameson.

"So?" Cahill's young lieutenant was not well known for his patience.

Cahill sipped the whiskey and felt the golden liquid sting his throat as he swallowed it. "So when Wilson decides he has to visit our neck of the woods to deliver a message, I'm inclined to listen."

"What message?"

Cahill looked into the young man's eyes. What the hell are things coming to? The man who would take over from him was a fuckin' drug addict. Off to the fuckin' toilet at every hands turn to light up whatever bit of brain he had left by snorting cocaine. Death would be a release not only from the pain but from the shit he was leaving behind. The struggle used to mean something but now you were either a politician or a criminal and Frank Cahill had never been much of a politician.

"Get your fuckin' brain in gear. The message is that there's some bollocks running around the Protestant area gunning people down," he paused and coughed "And that our friends on the other side aren't goin' to be allowed to stand around watchin' it happen. So sooner or later, maybe to-day or to-morrow, they're goin' to have to show their balls by comin' over here and wastin' a few of our people."

"Nobody's that stupid," Sean said. "We've all learned that killing each other is bad for business. The fact that

Richie came here to discuss the situation with us shows that we're all on the same page."

"You stupid young git. Don't you think that there's some idiot in the Shankill with shit for brains but a nine millimetre buried in his back garden who's just itchin' to add to his tally. Richie and his lads might be able to put two and two together but they're not in control of all the psychos and neither are we. We have a legacy here in this Province. There's more than one man who has already killed walkin' the streets of Belfast. You know the psychology as well as I do. Once you've tasted the power of the gun you want to feel it again. You and your generation are goin' to have to live with the legacy we've left you until all the psychos are dead. If we don't put a stop to this then we're all up shit creek again."

"What do you have in mind?" Sean asked.

Cahill looked at the three men seated at the bar. "We start by gettin' those lazy bastards off their arses and out on the streets." For the first time that morning Cahill's voice had something of its former strength. "It wouldn't be the first time some fool went over the top. If there's someone operating outside the organisation, I want him. Do I make myself clear, Sean."

"Aye," Sean was surprised by Cahill's transformation. "What do we do?"

"Contact all our people on the street. Grill the bastards. If they know anything about the murders I want to hear it. And check the guns we put away. I want the name of every bollocks who's in the know and who might have got his hands on a nine-millimetre. Get every available man on the streets now. They're to pump the locals. I want every ounce of gossip."

"That's a tall order," Sean stared at the rejuvenated Cahill.

"Just do it, Sean." Cahill watched as his heir apparent left the booth and strode towards the bar rousing the men from their lethargy. By the end of the day every former IRA man in the city would have a bug up his arse about the murders in West Belfast. Something or someone would crawl out of the woodwork. If there was a rogue operating on the other side of the Shankill Road, Frank Cahill wanted to meet him. He picked up the glass of Jameson and drained it. The whiskey was beginning to drown the pain which was his constant companion. He thought about what Wilson had said. Neither side wanted to be drawn in a renewal of the conflict.

The godfather' refilled his glass from the whiskey bottle. "Ian Wilson," he said raising his glass in a toast. "The only honest Peeler I've ever met," he added and finished off the contents of the glass in a single swallow.

CHAPTER 18

Case made sure that the door was locked before he prised up the loose floorboard and took out the small metal suitcase containing the tools of his trade. He laid the box on his bed and carefully composed the combination on the two locks. After double checking the combinations, he flicked the twin catches open. Moving his hands slowly, he carefully raised the lid of the metal suitcase. Opening the damn thing was always a tricky business. A small charge had been inserted in the combination mechanism so that if anyone tried to open the suitcase without knowing the combination both they and it would disappear in a puff of smoke and a blast of hot air. While he was completely at home with weapons, he always felt a tinge of fear running down his spine when explosives were involved. Guns could be trusted. Explosives were temperamental. The lid gradually moved back and revealed the contents: the Browning automatic used in the three murders, spare ammunition clips, and a small container of Semtex, the Czechoslovak manufactured explosive which had been favoured by the IRA. The metal suitcase had been fitted with a special felt lining into which depressions had been made to hold each item of contents snugly. He lifted the Browning out of the base and removed an oil can and rag from their positions. He began to clean the gun methodically, just as his sergeant had taught him. The feeling of power and pleasure he got from holding the gun spread slowly through him. It was a pity that it was going to be one whole day before he could use it again. A simple phone call earlier that morning confirmed that the next victim would not return to Belfast until to-morrow morning. It didn't matter, he thought as he cleaned the barrel of the gun, he was well within schedule and the local coppers would be running around like chickens with their heads up their asses. He sat back and considered the chaos he must be causing the poor bastards in Tennent Street. They'd have enough on their plate without trying to solve the little problem he was setting them.

Case laid the Browning on the bed and walked to the sideboard. He picked up the remains of last night's bottle of Bushmills and a glass and then put them down again. He poured a double measure and dropped it back in one gulp. He resumed his cleaning of the Browning until he was satisfied that the gun was in mint condition. He replaced the gun in the metal suitcase, slipped the catches, turned the combination locks and returned the case to its hiding place beneath the floorboards. To-day would be a day of rest. He'd ramble into the centre of town and take in a flick. Why not? He thought about the policemen trying to solve the murders he'd committed. Poor bastards. No rest for the wicked, he said softly under his breath. He donned his coat and let himself out of his bedsit.

It was almost lunch time when Wilson and Moira arrived back at Tennent Street Police Station. Wilson ignored the greeting of the Duty Sergeant and made his way directly to the office which housed the Murder Squad. The only occupants of the room were Eric Taylor and Harry Graham.

"Where's George?" Wilson asked from the doorway of his office.

"Don't know," Taylor replied without looking up from his paperwork. "He was here a minute ago."

"What the hell do you mean you don't know," Wilson's voice was raised well above its usual level. If he was going to be put under pressure then he was going to observe his managerial prerogative by passing it on. "This *is* a police station, isn't it? People do work here, don't they?"

Taylor and Graham looked up slowly from their desks. They had both been with Wilson long enough to recognise his mood. There was great pain waiting around the corner for someone.

"George stepped out a few minutes ago, Boss," Taylor said quietly. "He didn't exactly say where he was going."

"Did he exactly say anything?" Wilson asked.

"No," Taylor wished there was some other answer he could have given.

"Well go and find the bugger for me. And don't come back without him." Wilson pealed off his anorak and tossed it at the coat-rack in the corner of his office. "You," he turned to face Moira, "you write up a detailed note of our meeting with Cahill and don't forget to put in a description of that young lieutenant of his."

Taylor stood up and started for the duty desk while Moira took off her coat and took her seat behind her desk.

Wilson sat behind his desk and ran his hand through his hair. He was beginning to wonder whether he had been too hasty in buying Cahill's 'not us boss' story. The lack of a connection between Patterson and Peacock was the factor that bothered him most. If the killer was selecting his victims at random, it could take months or forever to uncover the bastard. And all the time Jennings was waiting in the wings ready to pounce on him if he failed to stop the murders. Outside in the pubs the Protestant avengers would be stoking their anger with Guinness. Unless they were restrained some poor Catholic randomers were going to pay for the three killings with their lives. It was a heavy burden for him to bear that it was up to him to stop such a scenario.

"This job shits," Wilson said quietly under his breath. He rummaged around his desk rearranging papers into new bundles as he went. "Now where the hell did I put those computer printouts?" The piles of paper refused to yield the computer sheets that he sought.

"You were looking for me," Whitehouse said from the doorway.

"Glad you decided to join us," Wilson looked up from his cluttered desk. "Where the hell were you?

"Here and there," Whitehouse said.

"Out and about," Wilson said sarcastically.

"I suppose that Mr. Frank 'Arsehole' Cahill gave you nothing," Whitehouse said.

Wilson didn't reply.

"I told you not to bother with that bastard," Whitehouse sneered. "You should have listened to me. Haul the bollocks in and give me and the boys a couple of days with him. The bastard's in it up to his scrawny neck."

"Ever hear of innocent until beaten guilty," Wilson said. "You better haul him in soon if you want to give him the rubber hose treatment. He's on the way out. In fact one blow of a rubber truncheon would probably be enough to send him to his Maker."

"You're jokin'?" a wide smile creased Whitehouse's face. "That's the best news I've heard all year. God must be a Protestant."

Whitehouse's lack of humanity didn't surprise his chief. "The poor bastard's dying," Wilson said. "From the look of him he could be gone soon."

"It can't be too soon for me," Whitehouse spat out of the corner of his mouth. "Good riddance to bad rubbish."

"I wouldn't celebrate just yet if I were you. Sometimes the devil you know is better than the devil you don't know." Wilson thought of the cold eyes of the young man who had been at Cahill's side in the club.

"I'll settle for spittin' on the old bastard's grave."

One more or one less, Wilson thought, wouldn't make too much difference. The PSNI had been responsible for taking lots of murderers off the streets but that had never seemed to slow down the level of violence. He had always believed that they should have been attacking the cause and not the effect. Thank God the politicians had woken up to that fact eventually.

"I might be losing my marbles but I'm inclined to believe Cahill this time," Wilson said. "I don't think he's involved."

"You're sodding mad," Whitehouse said, his colour rising. "If it quacks like a duck and it looks like a duck then it's a fucking duck. It's the way they operate. They bloody did it. Now they're tryin' to crawl their way out. Rotten sodding bastards."

"Don't ask me why," Wilson said raising his hand to stifle Whitehouse's tirade. "But I don't believe he'd try something like this right now. There's something else that worries me. Both the Chief Constable and the DCC are watching this investigation like hawks. The politicians are beginning to pass water in case the three deaths start the whole cycle of violence off again. That means pressure all the way along the line. If it was drugs or a turf war they wouldn't give a curse. But the problem with these murders is that it looks sectarian and that's what keeps the big boys awake at night. Has anyone from the Press been on?"

"Not so far."

"We should be thankful for small mercies," Wilson said knowing that it was only a matter of time before some smart jurno would get on the bandwagon to stoke up whatever flames were out there. Playing on fear and prejudice was always a winner. "It's bad enough trying to catch these bastards without having the brass breathing down our neck. Hopefully the Press will stay out of it for a few days yet. Until we turn up whoever's behind the killings I want maximum presence of police on the streets."

"Wise up, Boss," Whitehouse said. "Do you really believe that the Super is goin' to saturate the streets for a couple of dead Prods. Think of the cost of the overtime. If this professional bloke of yours knows the game, he'll close down for a few days and we'll be back where we started. The 'randoms' are the worst to second guess."

"It's not random," Wilson said with more conviction that he felt. The only way the killer could be caught would be by finding the pattern. "This guy is screwing around with us. Three dead bodies and no clues. If he was into the numbers game he'd hit a pub or a betting shop just like the rest of the crazies. No, it's not random. He's got the names and he's got a schedule and if we don't get a break soon he'll be finished and we'll be none the wiser."

"Maybe we're missing something," Whitehouse said. "It could still be something personal. Drugs, women. Nothing to do with politics or religion."

Wilson turned and looked at the whiteboard in the squad room. On it were pinned the photos from the two crime scenes. Beside each set of photos was a brief description of the victims. "This bastard has me stumped. There's something that connects our victims. It could be anything. Maybe they look like his old man. Maybe it's the colour of their eyes. Maybe they both screwed his wife." He slammed his hand on the desk and the paper piles jumped. "It's not drugs, it's not a turf war and it's probably not religious or political. We could just have an old-fashioned serial killer on our hands. If he was killing women, that might be a valid hypothesis. We've got to find what connects the victims."

"That could be a tall order, Boss," Whitehouse said. "These are nobodies. We've interviewed Peacock's friends. It's work, boozer and home for a burnt offering from the Misses and maybe a bit of a punch up if he's in the mood. Patterson didn't have a life, just an existence. The wanker didn't even have a pet."

"For the sake of argument let's assume that Cahill's telling the truth," Wilson held up his hand again to stifle Whitehouse's incipient protest. "You yourself said that it would take balls of steel for a Catholic to march so deep into Loyalist territory to carry out assassinations. So let's start by eliminating some possibilities. What about a new Loyalist feud?"

"No sodding way," Whitehouse said. "Since the last UVF/UDA action there hasn't been a peep in that direction." His round face hardened. He hated to think of his own people shooting each other. But they had and he was in no doubt that if another turf war erupted then they would do it again. He thought back to his meeting with Richie Simpson. If there had been a Loyalist feud, Simpson wouldn't have come near him but he couldn't tell Wilson that.

"You're pretty damn sure about that," Wilson stared at his colleague. After ten years together he could read his Sergeant like a book. George was holding something back and this wasn't the time to be playing secrets. "Is there some nugget of information you'd like to share with me?"

Whitehouse delayed replying a little longer than was necessary. "What are you gettin' at?" he said defensively. For the past few months Wilson had a habit of making insinuating remarks about Whitehouse's Loyalist connections.

"Don't get your knickers in a knot," Wilson was amused by Whitehouse's unease. "It's just that you're a Shankill lad yourself. You went to school with most of the Loyalist leaders. You drink in the same pubs as them. You attend the same Lodge as them. It's only natural that they might let something slip to you every now or then." Wilson saw a fine bead of sweat burst from Whitehouse's hairline. "I'd never think of suggesting that you might be in collusion with them."

"You'd better fucking not," Whitehouse's colour heightened further.

Wilson watched Whitehouse's discomfort with pleasure. It was another little demonstration, if more was needed, that his loyal Sergeant was not to be totally trusted "Maybe it's time we made some use of these Loyalist contacts of yours. You could ask around and find out whether there's a 'new 'player' on the Protestant side."

"That's if anyone will talk to me," Whitehouse said.

"Don't underestimate your powers of persuasion," Wilson said smiling. "It never ceases to amaze me that we're so much better informed on the activities and personnel of the Republican side than we are on the Loyalist side."

Whitehouse said nothing and continued to lean against the door-jam. He stared at the bulky figure sitting behind the desk. Why was it that he had to work with the only officer on the Force who didn't regard the Fenians as the enemy? If the rumours in the station were to be believed Wilson wouldn't be sitting behind that desk for long. The boys at the top wanted people they could trust implicitly. There was no doubt that Wilson was probably the best detective on the Force but he was a loose canon himself. You never knew what he was going to do and that didn't sit well with the top brass.

"Get on with it George," Wilson looked at the papers on his desk. "We won't catch our man by spending our days holding the wall up. Let's find out whether your contacts can solve our little problem."

Whitehouse turned quickly from the door.

Wilson bundled up the scattered documents on his desk and formed a neat pile. Maybe, he thought, if he were to throw the handful of A4 pages into the air, the one with the piece of information which would lead to the professional with the nine millimetre would land on the top of the pile. That police work should be so easy. He looked through the glass partition into the squad room where four detectives from his staff of six were working. He continued to stare at the group until Harry Graham raised his head and met his superior's eyes. He beckoned Graham by crooking the index finger of his right hand. The detective stood up wearily from his desk an approached Wilson's tiny office.

"Let's go through the statements you collected from Peacock's neighbours, Harry," Wilson said when Graham presented himself in the doorway.

There had to be a clue somewhere. No matter how clever the murderer had been he had to make one small slip. But it would certainly be buried in a mountain of crap and would require hours of sifting and examining to turn it up. But that was what the British taxpayer paid him to do. He and his men would continue to wade through the crap until they located that nugget of information. No matter how long it took.

CHAPTER 19

Simpson looked around the faces of the four men who sat in the back room of the `Balmoral Bar'. He coughed and felt bile in his mouth as his nose and stomach reacted to the smells of stale beer from the bar and the ammonia from the open door of the toilet that competed with each other before combining to create a mixture with the potency of mustard gas. He decided to make the meeting as short as possible. The men sitting around the table in the back room of the bar had at one time constituted the entire Belfast High Command of the Ulster Volunteer Force, the most hard-line and vicious of the Protestant paramilitary groups. Each man sitting at the table had murdered in the name of Ulster. In Mafia parlance, each of the former UVF chiefs was a `made man'. Some many times over. All four had served terms of imprisonment in the infamous `Long Kesh' prison outside Belfast. But now all four were free men unstained by their 'criminal' pasts. He felt uncomfortable in the company of these dinosaurs. But even dinosaurs were useful to the political movement. The connection between the Protestant political parties and the paramilitaries went back to the establishment by Edward Carson of the original Ulster Volunteer Force which was intended to safeguard Ulster from invasion from the Catholic South. The best known UVF was created with political connivance in the 1960's but the membership lacked the discipline of Carson's original force and the UVF had become synonymous with brutal sectarian murders. Many of the Protestant politicians regarded the UVF as an evil, but a necessary evil. The organisation was often the instrument which had been used to terrorise the Catholic population. However, like their IRA `brothers', the former UVF chiefs had slowly gravitated

176

towards the status of 'godfathers' and each man made his living exclusively from the proceeds of his criminal empire. As the organisation metamorphosed from a sectarian strike force to a criminal conspiracy, so the hold of the politicians over the organisation had diminished.

The two major chieftains sat on either side of Simpson. Sammy Rice, whose fiefdom covered East Belfast sat to his right while to his left sat Jimmy McGreery, the 'godfather' in Central Belfast. The other two participants, Norman White from North Belfast and Ross Younger from South Belfast sat facing the other three men.

"This better be good," McGreery adjusted his fat body on the small wooden chair and glared into Simpson's face. McGreery, overlord of Sandy Row, was in a hurry to get away from the meeting. He was as busy as any other executive in Northern Ireland and his business empire needed his constant attention.

"I'm just a messenger boy," Simpson started defensively. He glanced over his shoulder before remembering that his 'minder' had been left outside along with the other bodyguards. He was in no doubt that if these men decided to kill him, he would end up very dead indeed.

"Some messenger boy," Rice was the veteran of the group and the unchallenged leader. As a young man, he had proved himself to be a vicious, resourceful killer and had climbed to the top of his organisation by demonstrating the inability of the previous leadership to control him. He led the largest and most violent gang which was centred on the Protestant heartland of the Shankill Road. The fact that the meeting was taking place on his turf was not insignificant. Of all the men in the room, Rice was the most dangerous. "Get on with it Richie, we've other fish to fry."

"Yeah, what's your fuckin' problem?" McGreery looked pointedly at his watch.

"You all know that there've been three Prods killed during the past few days," Simpson concentrated on a point on the table between his outspread hands.

The four faces surrounding him hardened.

"If you decide to stop tryin' to be a second rate politician, you could try your hand at bein' a comedian," Rice said. "Of course we know three Prods have been murdered. If three Taigs had been killed we'd be tryin' to find the bloke who did it to congratulate him. As it is we're tryin' to get our hands on the bastard who did them three boys in. If we do get him, we'll switch his light off."

Simpson looked directly into Rice's face. He'd known the former UVF chieftain since he was a pale-faced Belfast hood with a single gold chain around his neck. Rice had graduated to having an all year round tan, a pompadour hairstyle that would have been over the top even for Elvis and enough gold jewellery to set off an airport metal detector at twenty feet. He'd heard that Rice had recently become the owner of a half a million pound villa in the Canaries. Not bad for a boy from the back streets of Belfast.

"My boss is gettin' a little worried that you boys are goin' to overreact and start toppin' a load of Taigs," Simpson let his gaze pass along each man's face in turn. He didn't much like what he saw. These men were not the type who would sit idly by.

"You can bet your fuckin' arse that we're goin' to over-react," Rice said. "The Taigs know the story. They kill some of ours and we fuckin-well kill more of them."

"That's the gist of it," McGreery said smiling.

"Bad move," Simpson said. "What happens if you go ape-shit? The peace goes up in smoke. The other side plant a bomb and kill a load of Prods. The Brits get even more pissed off with us than they are right now and shovel us down the tubes even quicker. The Assembly gets suspended again. You guys are livin' in cloud cuckoo land. The Brits want out and an all-out killin' war after a solution looks on the cards is goin' to send them running for the door. Think about it."

A sly smile spread across Rice's baby face. When he smiled, he was a most unlikely looking killer. "You people make me want to puke," he said. "You sit in your safe fuckin' house and draw your state salaries as so-called politicians. But who do the people on the street blame if the Taigs shoot them up." He swung his arm around the assembled chiefs. "Us. They won't hassle you in the streets. But they'll give the shit to me, and Jimmy, and Norm, and Ross. We don't draw the salaries but we get the fuckin' blame. It's fuckin' typical. You call the general strike. We enforce it. And what do we get out of it? Sweet fuck all, that's what. You and your fuckin' buddies think that you're goin' to carve up this province between you. But I've got news for you. We've still got the guns and the explosives and it just might be that we won't like your form of government any more than we liked Westminster's. So when the dust settles, we won't ask for something, we'll just take it."

"Okay, Sammy," McGreery said holding up two fat hands, "Richie gets the gist of it. Don't you, Richie?"

Simpson nodded in assent. Handing Ulster to these boys would be the equivalent of giving Italy to the Mafia.

"We know only too fucking well," McGreery continued glancing around the faces of the other chiefs. "About the three Protestants that have been topped in the past few days. And as sure as shit at this very minute on the Shankill, Prods are workin' themselves up to take a couple of Taigs out. From what we heard, the boys who were shot were civilians. That means we can hold off for a bit but not too long, mind."

The door opened and the barman entered carrying a tray of drinks. The five men seated at the table remained silent until the drinks had been served and the barman had left.

"I'm here to ask you to make sure that the killings don't escalate," Simpson picked up his glass of whiskey and sipped the contents.

The four men looked at each other.

"What's in it for us?" Rice asked.

"The same as what's in it for the rest of us," Simpson replied. "The Brits let us hold on here longer than if we force them to abandon us."

"I mean in the fuckin' short-term," a malevolent smile creased Rice's boyish features.

Oh Jesus, Simpson thought as he looked into Rice's face. This was a perfect example of the Ulster political process. Sitting in filthy backrooms of bars with four common criminals who would make even the Medelin

180

cartel look saintly. The men surrounding him were totally without honour. They had all proved themselves to be sociopaths. They cared nothing for the people of their area only what they could get out of them. Just a short time ago they had feuded with each other over turf. Now each one wielded power within his own fiefdom carved out after the dead bodies had been dragged off to the morgue. The `foot-soldiers' did their chief's bidding because failing to do so laid them open to a code of punishment which could have been lifted directly from the Mafia code of *Omerta*. This was the legacy of the 'Troubles'. Men who had killed and killed badly without compunction. Men who were to all intents and purposes uncontrollable.

Simpson took a mouthful of his whiskey. He had only one card to play and now was the time to play it. "Maybe we can put some business your way," he began looking around the faces at the table, "I didn't come here with anything concrete in mind. Maybe you can think about what you might be interested in."

"Maybe we can," Rice said without consulting the other men. "I wouldn't advise you to renege on this one Richie."

"We know better than that," Simpson could feel the bile rising in his throat. He was well aware that if Rice wanted him dead then it would be done without the batting of an eyelid.

"Right," Rice said. "That it? We'll hold off and give the Peelers a shot at clearing this one up"

The four men around the table laughed in unison. "Fat fuckin' chance," McGreery said. "Most of the Peelers in Tennent Street would need a map to find their own arseholes."

Simpson shook his head and rose from the table.

"Don't you forget our bargain, Richie boy," Rice laughed and nodded towards the door. "You've got forty-eight hours."

Simpson accepted his dismissal and left the room.

"Fuckin' crawlin' bastard," Rice said when the door had closed behind Simpson. "Get the word on the streets. No retaliation until we give the order. Anyone who breaks ranks will be lookin' for a new pair of knees. Any word on who topped the Prods?"

"It happened on my territory," Ivan McIlroy, Rice's lieutenant, stood behind his chief's chair. "I've been bangin' heads together but nobody is sayin' a word. The Other Side swear that they have nothin' to do with it."

"You can't trust those fuckin' bastards," White said angrily.

"One thing you should have learned in the `Kesh', Norman," Rice said harshly. "Is that we can trust them a damn sight more than we can trust fuckers like Simpson and the politicians he works for. The Provies and us are the same people. We're both in business now. At least in Ulster the poor will get to inherit something. They say they're not involved I believe the buggers." He turned to McIlroy. "Get the boys onto the streets. Somebody or other saw or heard something, then I want to know it." He ran his fingers over the stubble on his chin. "If the Fenians didn't kill the Prods and we didn't do it then who the fuck did? More to the point why were three nobodies topped? Find the answers, boys. Find the answers."

McGreery moved with a speed which belied his bulk and was through the door of the backroom almost before

Rice had finished. White and Younger turned to bid Rice good-bye but he was already lost in thought.

Rice's intuition was telling him that somewhere in this mess there lay an advantage and he was straining all his senses trying to listen to his inner voice. He didn't see White and Younger leave the room nor did he hear the door close behind them. Even though he held the guns, the politicians held the power. Fuck power he wanted cash and lots of it. When you're forced you have to turn your hand to what you know. And he knew how to wreak pain on people to get what he wanted. This business might allow him to squeeze the balls of some of the bastards that looked down on him. That was the content of the message running around inside his head.

CHAPTER 20

Wilson hadn't noticed the light outside the office change from winter gloom to dark of night. The review of the statements Graham had taken from Peacock's neighbours provided him with a picture of a seriously troubled young man. Nobody seemed to mourn his passing but at the same time nobody had any idea who might have pulled the trigger on him. It was evident that Peacock was an alcoholic and a wife-beater. He was also unsociable and withdrawn. There was no evidence that he had been involved in either politics or criminal activity. He had few friends if any and the results of the post mortem had shown that he had been cutting himself over a long period of time with either a scalpel or a razor blade. His arms and legs were covered in scars. The question still remained as to why someone would have wanted both him and Patterson dead. The investigation was as stalled as it had been before the review of the statements. Graham had left his office just after four o'clock and Wilson had spent the past three hours immersed in the paperwork associated with the running of a small police squad. He was faintly aware of desk-lamps being progressively switched off in the main squad room. When he finally raised his head from a pile of staff reports at ten minutes past seven in the evening. He saw that only Moira's desk-lamp remained lit although there was no sign of the young red-haired constable. The squad room looked dark and gloomy with the light from the single desk-lamp casting an eerie glow around the walls of filing cabinets and the mountains of loose files which surrounded the steel desks. The light barely illuminated the array of black and white crime scene photographs which had been pinned to the whiteboard.

This was surely a job for an optimist, he thought as he looked back on a day which had yielded not one centimetre of progress on any of the three active murder cases currently being handled by his group. It was night again with the attendant problem that the killer of Patterson and Peacock could be preparing to strike again. If there was a schedule or a pattern to the killings, he was no nearer finding it than he had been the previous evening.

He rubbed his tired eyes and tried to concentrate on the typewritten documents before him. Lines of black lettering coalesced and separated as he blinked to clear his vision. He needed to rest. God, how he needed to rest. At this point every evening he longed for a home and family to help him deal with the frustrations of his daily life. He leaned back and closed his eyes. Where in God's name had it all gone wrong? Over the past year he'd had plenty of time to replay the events of his life searching for the one moment which had soured his relationship with his wife. There was a time when he and Susan could have made it work. They could have been happy. Produced their two point four children and lived like other people. Somehow his commitment to the Force had always managed to get in the way of their happiness. That was bullshit. The Force was only one small part of it. It had mostly been down to him personally. Maybe the defining moment had been the night when the piece of shrapnel tore his thigh away and ended his brilliant rugby career? Or perhaps it was the night he had decided to cheat on his wife for the first but not the last time? Or maybe it was his father's obsession with both the Force and rugby which had defined him and his place in the world. When he was playing rugby the women had flocked around him and he had gotten used to having sex with whoever he pleased. Sex and work became his drugs. If he lived in the US he would have declared himself a sex addict and attended a clinic. But this was Ireland. Sex addicts just had to get on with their lives. Why was it that he couldn't shake the thought that he personally was responsible for Susan's death? All the articles he'd read supported this hypothesis. Sure, hereditary could produce cancers. But so could stress. And he had brought more stress into that poor woman's life than any person deserved to endure. After her death he was left with the guilt and the house in Malwood Park. Both he and the dwelling his wife had desired were cold and lonely, devoid of comfort. It was too late to think of what he might have done to avoid what had happened between them. It was time to tread steadfastly on. Work to house and house to work.

"Boss."

Wilson started at the sound. He shot forward and banged his knee against his desk. Moira McElvaney stood in the doorway, a smile lighting up her attractive face.

"Oh shit," Wilson bent forward and began to rub his injured knee.

"I was just wondering whether you'd dropped off," she said trying to suppress a smile.

"Fat bloody chance with idiots like you around," Wilson pushed his chair back from the desk. "I was just getting ready to leave," he eased his bulk out of his battered armchair. He had suddenly stopped feeling sorry for himself. This nice young woman was possibly the only person in Belfast who was lonelier than him and yet there she was smiling away. "What would you say to finishing that drink we were having last night?" Loneliness will be the death of me, he thought as he issued the invitation.

"Great," Moira said enthusiastically. "Maybe we'll get bleeped again."

"You blood-thirsty young cub," Wilson squeezed around his desk. He sometimes thought there had been more than a little malice in Jennings assigning him the cubby hole in the corner of the squad room as his office. Nobody in his right mind would put a man of his size into such a confined space. "Maybe tonight all the murdering bastards will stay at home and we'll be allowed a peaceful evening," he pulled on his anorak.

"Let me get rid of these," she held up a handful of files. "My eyes are bugged out from looking at those damn screens. There's so much bloody information on the mainframe. It'll take me years to sift it." She went to his desk and laid the files carefully in the centre.

Oh Christ, Wilson thought picturing the dark cloud laden sky and streaming rain outside. Ireland would be a marvellous place if it wasn't for the weather.

"Let's forget the pub and have a drink at my place," Wilson said. He didn't need the impersonal jollity of a bar right now.

"Are you sure?" her eyebrows raised. She was mildly surprised at her chief's suggestion. She had heard of Wilson's reputation with women and she didn't need this kind of complication. "Two nights in a row and already I'm invited home. Tongues will certainly start to wag if that gets out. Wouldn't we be better off in some pub or other."

Her earlier enthusiasm had faded and he could see the concern in her eyes. "Damn it all, I'm old enough to be your father."

"I've had guys older than you come on to me," she said. She was beginning to feel that she had over-reacted and she wanted to defuse the situation. "I'm aware that you have a reputation so I'm assuming that we're really only talking about a drink."

"OK then, I'm your superior officer." He wanted to smile but he kept it inside. The evil that men do follows them, he thought. The poor wee lassie was scared that he was going to proposition her. Twenty years ago, no ten years ago there would have been a bloody good chance.

"I suppose I'll just have to trust you." The smile was back on her face.

"Do you know Malwood Park?" Wilson asked. His mouth suddenly felt very dry and he had the strong need for a large whiskey.

She shook her head.

"OK. You follow me in the heap of shit you call a car and I'll do my best not to lose you."

A gust of wind blew a sheet of rain over the two detectives as they left the station. They sprinted for their respective cars through the driving rain.

"Jesus!" Wilson said as he slid into the front seat of his Toyota. He brushed his hand through his damp hair and a stream of water ran down his neck. Across the car park he saw a slow moving windscreen wiper blade alternately hide and display McElvaney's smiling young face. Oh to be back there again, he thought looking at the happy expression on the young constable's face. Such innocence. Was he ever that innocent? Perhaps once, a very long time ago. He searched for that innocent Ian Wilson in his memory but couldn't find him. He put the key in the ignition and started the car.

The Lada followed closely behind Wilson's Toyota as the two cars left the police car park. Wilson looked at the gloomy scene of darkened streets and equally darkened terrace houses through the swishing wiper blades as he turned left onto the Shankill Road and away towards the security of his stockbroker belt abode. The Shankill was deserted. Lights burned brightly from dilapidated public houses. The 'troubles' had caused a re-evaluation of building improvements. What was the point of refurbishing a faded paint-peeled facade of a pub if the place could disappear off the face of the earth at any time? Since the end of the 'troubles' that had all changed. The carpetbaggers had arrived and the price of property had sky-rocketed. Old fashioned pubs had been replaced by entertainment palaces. Except in the old working class areas where the drab exteriors were maintained to reflect the drab lives of the customers. He drove slowly glancing occasionally into the rear view mirror to ensure that McElvaney's Lada was behind him. To his right a man burst through the front door of a pub caused him to pull sharply to his left. The man staggered a few steps then braced himself against the wall of the pub before launching a stream of vomit in the direction of the gutter. Good old Belfast, he thought, nothing ever changes. He piloted the Toyota onto the Westlink and south towards the M1 motorway. As the city centre fell away behind him, he unconsciously pushed his foot on the accelerator and hoped that McElvaney's Lada could keep pace.

Wilson pushed open the glass-panelled front door and ushered Moira into the hall.

"Wow," she said looking appreciatively around the large expanse. "This is some place," she ran her fingers along the walnut case of an antique grandfather clock which stood at the foot of the staircase which led to the upper story of the house. "I bet this clock cost a few bob." She looked around but Wilson was no longer in the hallway. She deposited her coat on a brass hook which protruded from an old wooden hall-stand.

"In here," Wilson called from the living-room.

She entered the living-room and saw Wilson standing before a small mahogany drinks cabinet already sipping from a glass of amber liquid.

"Sorry I started without you," he held up a bottle for her approval. "Jameson all right?"

"I'm not really a whiskey person," she said lowering herself into a leather club chair. "Any chance of a vodka and diet Seven Up?"

He frowned and then searched among the bottles on the bar. "Smirnof alright."

She nodded.

"No Diet Seven Up. Tonic?"

"Please."

Wilson poured her a liberal shot of vodka and topped it up with a bubbling bottle of tonic. He then gave himself a quick refill. He handed the tall glass to Moira and immediately raised his own.

"Cheers," she said.

"Down with the criminal classes," Wilson said taking a slug from what was a very large whiskey and soda. He smiled at the way she looked about the room.

"It's a hell of a house, eh," Wilson said savouring the taste of the whiskey and soda. "You too can have a house like this. That is if your husband is acquisitive enough and if you wish to spend most of your life up to your ears in hock."

"I resemble that remark already," she sipped her drink. "I don't think I'll ever have a house as imposing as this."

"Imposing, is it?" Wilson smiled. "Now that's the benefit of a good education for you. There probably isn't another constable in Tennent Street who can pronounce the word 'imposing' never mind using it in it's proper context." Wilson downed the contents of his glass and poured himself a refill. He raised the vodka bottle in his guest's direction but Moira shook her head. "Susan, that's my late wife, made sure that we scrimped and saved until we could afford this place. She called it her dream house. Then she scoured the auction rooms so that we could furnish it. Most of this stuff was bought for a pittance."

"I'd say it's worth a fortune now," she said. She remembered that someone had told her that Wilson was a widower but in her nervousness she had forgotten.

"So they tell me," Wilson walked to the window and looked across the rain-soaked neglected lawn. An awkward silence flooded the room.

"Are they real?" she asked after a minute of total silence.

Wilson turned and saw that she had left her seat and was standing before a display case containing a collage of four international rugby jerseys and tasselled caps.

"They are indeed," Wilson was beginning to feel the mellowing effects of the alcohol. "You can buy them in the shops now but when I collected them they came off the backs of men I played against."

"You actually represented Ireland," there was awe in her voice. She stood staring at the glass-windowed case.

"So it appears," Wilson moved to the drinks cabinet and poured himself another drink. "But long before your time. I was a flank forward to be reckoned with in those days. Tackled like a train and ran like a gazelle. Then I took part of a Provo bomb in the leg and I wasn't so fast about the field after that."

"There's a Lions jersey in there," she said. "You actually played for the Lion's"

Wilson seldom thought of those halcyon days now. If it wasn't for the constant reminder of the display case he would have thought it simply a dream. Susan had erected the case as a reminder. Not only to him but to all those fortunate enough to be invited into their living-room. While he had been at his peak, Susan had harboured delusions of him as a future Chief Constable. Malwood Park was part of that dream. The poor deluded woman, he thought. If the Provo bomb hadn't stopped him, he might have continued for another couple of seasons but he already knew that rugby wasn't going to be his fortune. He'd been born twenty years too soon for that. There had been as little chance of 'Ian Wilson plc' in those days as there had been of him ever achieving his wife's ambition for him. As soon as his sporting prowess had disappeared, his honesty permitted the jackals of RUC Headquarters to descend on him. That was why he occupied a cubby hole in Tennent Street instead of a sumptuous office at Castlereagh.

"Let's blame the Provos," Wilson said lifting his glass in a toast.

"I never heard about your sporting accomplishments," she said turning away from the case for the first time. "My dad is a big fan. I bet he's heard of you."

"Former sporting accomplishments," Wilson said. "It's all ancient history now. A glass case full of ageing jerseys and tattered caps." He looked at his almost finished glass. "I'm drinkin' too much." His words contained the scent of a slur. "But I suppose it comes with the job. We're two bright sparks, aren't we? Not a real friend in the world between us." The thickness was now evident on his tongue. "Not one single real friend. They hate you because you're a woman and a Catholic and they hate me because I'm not one of them. Some life. Eh!"

Moira shuffled uneasily. She could see the redness in his cheeks and noticed that his eyes were watering. He had already drunk three large free-poured whiskeys and he obviously hadn't eaten all day. That was probably enough to put an elephant to sleep. It was time to beat a retreat. She certainly didn't want this to get embarrassing.

"You should have stayed in that job in the Civil Service," Wilson continued. "Take my advice and go back to your family. Forget all this business about contributing. You're a nice intelligent lass with a future. Forget the PSNI. There's only pain in this job." He finished the contents of his glass and poured himself another.

"I think I should be off," she said laying her glass down on a stained mahogany coffee table. She hadn't expected that she would be drawn so closely into Wilson's private world. She'd heard that many officers suffered from burn-out and suspected she was witnessing at least part of Wilson's trauma. Too many dead bodies followed by too many fruitless investigations created cynical husks of men who had once really cared.

"Good-night, Moira," Wilson said sitting on the sofa with a thump. "I'll be alright here. You see yourself out." He watched the young woman's back disappearing into the hallway. "Christ, I'll have to eat something or this bloody stuff will rot my guts." He tried to rise from the chair but then thought the better of it. He'd phone the Chinese take-away later. He sipped on the whiskey and sat back. He never felt his eyes closing.

CHAPTER 21

The little alarm bell had been ringing inside Joe Case's head for several minutes but he chose to ignore it. His day had been the model of inactivity. After lunch in a city centre pub, he had spent the afternoon at the movies. Now, completely relaxed, he was seated at a corner table in the `Black Bear' in Agnes Street. Case raised his pint glass to his lips and glanced around the room looking for the source of his internal disquiet. There were about fifteen other people in the pub scattered in groups around the bar. His eyes flitted over the groups assessing them before dismissing them as potential threats. He stopped as his gaze fell on a group of four men standing drinking at the bar. The level of his alarm bell began to increase. There was something about the four men that wasn't quite right. He put down his pint glass and resumed his reading of the evening paper in such a way as to keep the group at the bar under observation. It was always a bit dangerous hanging around known Provo or UVF haunts. The highest thrill for SAS men serving in Northern Ireland was to pass themselves off perfectly in Republican or Loyalist strongholds. To do that you needed the right accent and a repertoire of the right songs. He loved feeling the adrenaline flowing in torrents as he had sat there right in the midst of the enemy belting out either 'Kevin Barry' or 'The Sash'. The high was incredible but so were the risks. Anyone found to be playing that game was liable to end up wrapped in barbed wire and face down in a field in South Armagh. The internal alarm bell was proving reliable yet again. The four men at the bar were talking animatedly and he could see occasional glance being shot in his direction. Instinctively, he rubbed the inside of his right foot against the inside calf of his left leg feeling the comfort of the sheath containing his combat knife. Four to one was pretty steep odds and considering that this was Belfast it was odds on that if the boys at the bar were 'connected' and that some kind of weapon would not be too far away.

Case slunk back in his seat as two of the men at the bar detached themselves from the group and made their way towards his table.

"My friend here says that you're a fucking Taig," the man who spoke was in his thirties and of medium height. A large paunch drooped over the belt of his trousers and his forearms were covered with the obligatory tattoos.

Case looked up slowly from his newspaper. His glance passed from the speaker to the `friend': a lanky youth of about nineteen with long mousy brown hair. "Your friend has his head up his fuckin' arse," his Belfast accent was faultless.

"You're not from round here, are ye?" the heavy set man spoke again.

"Mind your own fuckin' business," Case resumed his reading of the newspaper.

The young man leaned over the table and laid a bony hand on the newspaper. "My two mates at the bar," he flicked his head in the direction of the other two men. "They think you're a Taig too."

"Then you've all got your heads up your arses," Case pushed the young man's hand off the newspaper. He smiled as he felt his heart rate dropping and his emotions becoming cold. He had been astonished when he had seen some of his comrade's reactions to battle. Their hearts pounded and their palms began to sweat. He was the complete opposite. He was now completely ready for action. He would deal with whatever was coming whatever the consequences to himself.

The heavy set man looked around the pub. "There's a yard at the back of the bar. We'll talk there. If you're not a Taig, then you've nothing to worry about."

Case sat looking into the two men's faces. This was trouble with a capital T. He was in no doubt that he'd had the misfortune to run into a group of the local crazies. At best he was going to pick up a beating and at worse the bastards might actually go the full distance and kill him. Since he had urgent business to conduct, he couldn't afford either. "OK," he said folding the newspaper neatly. "Should I finish my pint before we leave?"

The two men looked at each other and the younger one smiled.

"I think maybe you should finish the drink," the older man said suppressing a grin.

Case picked up his pint glass and swallowed the contents. "Let's get this over with." He was aware of every eye in the pub watching as the two men led him to the bar. He ran his hand along the left side of his face obscuring it from the view of the onlookers. It wouldn't be wise for him to be recognised. If the police were to enquire in the future whether he had been in the pub, none of those watching him so intently would remember. They were all `non-witnesses' to what was happening. The two men at the bar finished their drinks. He saw one of them nod at the barman and the barman passed a baseball bat across the wooden counter.

Ah shit, Case said to himself. He looked into the face of the man who had received the bat and was slipping it under his coat and resolved to do real damage to the bastard.

The four men led him towards the rear of the pub.

The heavy set man opened a door which led into the yard at the rear and indicated for the group to pass through. "Arty," he said to one of the men who had been at the bar. "Plant yerself here and watch the buggers inside. We don't want some nosy bastard decidin' to take a piss out here."

Sheets of rain poured into the exposed part of the yard. Case and the three men stood under a canopy which covered roughly half the space between the buildings.

"Who the fuck are you then, Taig?" the heavy set man punched Case in the side of the head.

Although the blow stung Case only marginally, he let himself fall to his knees. He felt a stream of rainwater running across the knees of his trousers. He'd been right. This wasn't going to be an interrogation followed by a beating. The beating was going to precede the interrogation.

"You're not so fucking cocky now," the mousy haired youth kicked Case's side and the three men laughed together.

Case moaned and the men continued laughing. The bastards were gettin' off on his pain. He came upright suddenly ramming, as he rose, a bunched fist into the genitals of the man holding the baseball bat. He felt the air exhale from the man's body in one sudden gust before he collapsed onto the soaking wet cobbles. The bat clanged on the stones of the yard skipping away from the four men. The heavy set man stopped laughing just before Case punched him violently in the throat. The man fell to the ground clutching his throat and retching. The mousy haired youth tried to run for a wooden door at the other end of the yard but slipped on the wet cobble-stones and pitched forward across the rain soaked yard.

"You should learn to kick a bit harder, mate. Like this." Case unleashed a kick which shattered the youth's jaw and sent him rushing headlong into oblivion.

It was less than thirty seconds since Case had started moving. The door from the pub into the yard started to open.

"Is everyth..."

Case pulled the door and the man called Arty came flying into the yard tumbling over the prone bodies of his comrades. Before he could regain his wits, Case kicked him in the side of the head and Arty fell senseless onto the ground. The man who had earlier been holding the baseball bat was lying doubled over holding his genitals. Case kicked him hard in the spot where he held his hands and felt satisfaction as the toe of his shoe bit into the soft tissue of the man's groin. The man's scream died in his throat and his eyes widened as he watched Case bend and remove the knife from the sheath on his leg.

"I have a thing about arseholes trying to beat me up," he held the knife up so that the prone man could see it. "You should always try to know who you're screwing with," he put the sole of his right foot on the man's throat. He smiled as he saw the fear in the prone mans eyes and smelled the astringent smell of fresh urine. He pulled the man's right hand towards him and pushed back the cuff of his coat exposing a full white hand.

"Hey your hand's the wrong colour," Case said. He placed the man's hand on a wooden packing case and chopped down vigorously with the razor sharp combat knife severing the thumb at the joint. "Your symbol's the red hand isn't it," he said as he repeated the process with the index finger. "Now you can have one all to your self."

The prone man fainted and his bloodied hand went limp. Case severed the remaining fingers and let the emasculated hand fall across the man's body.

Time to go, Case thought. He moved across the exposed part of the yard and let himself out through the back door. His ribs hurt where the youth had kicked him. "Fucking pussies," he said and moved away quickly.

CHAPTER 22

Sammy Rice was fit to be tied. Nobody but nobody woke up the UVF chief at three o'clock in the morning unless some catastrophe had occurred. Rice sat huddled in his dressing gown in the front parlour of his terraced house in Woodvale Road in West Belfast. A convection heater blew a blast of lukewarm air across his feet and into the cold room.

"This better be bloody good," Rice glowered at the three men standing facing him.

"It is," Ivan McIlroy, Rice's eyes and ears on the streets, stood on the other side of the heater. "This is Bobby Gillespie and Steve Lennon from the `Black Bear' mob. You might remember them." The two men who had approached Case in the `Black Bear' earlier that evening stood at McIlroy's side.

Rice looked at the two men standing beside his principle lieutenant. Both were covered with grime and looked like they'd just about survived fifteen rounds with a sex starved gorilla. The younger of the two had an angry looking black mark down the side of his face. Rice couldn't remember meeting either man but he nodded his head in affirmation.

"You can see from the state of them that the two boys were in a real dust up this evening," McIlroy continued.

"Get to the point Ivan or get the fuck out," Rice huddled closer to the heater. His patience was growing thin.

"Look Sammy, you yourself told me to report anything peculiar and you'll find this very bloody peculiar? OK."

Rice nodded.

"Bobby and Steve were havin' a few jars in the `Black Bear 'this evenin' when they spied a stranger at one of the tables. The boy wasn't one of the locals. Bobby and Steve reckoned he might be a Taig."

"Don't give me that shit," Rice said looking harshly at the two men. "They were out for a bit of fucking violence."

"You're right they were," McIlroy threw an admonishing look at the two men. "The stupid bastards were with a few mates so they decided to ask the stranger outside. You know the score. The guy went along quietly enough. When they got him outside they started asking questions and the bastard went berserk. He beat the shit out of the four of them and get this, he picked on one of them and lopped off all the fingers on his right hand. The guy's in the Royal Infirmary. They're tryin' to sown the fingers back on."

Rice sat upright. "You mean to tell me that some bugger single-handedly beat up four members of the UVF."

"You've got it," McIlroy said.

"Who the fuck was he?" Rice's mind was replaying the conversation the Belfast Command had had with Simpson. Anything out of the ordinary. He'd seen almost everything during his lifetime as a terrorist but this one beat banagher. He looked at the two men who stood in front of him. Whoever had beaten up on these guys was one tough bugger.

"We don't fuckin' know," the young man with the mousy hair spoke with apparent pain. His voice was garbled. "The bastard started on us as soon as we got him into the yard behind the pub."

"Tell me exactly what happened," Rice wrapped himself in the dressing gown. "Leave nothing out."

Gillespie began to describe the events of the earlier part of the evening and the violent happenings in the back yard of the `Black Bear'. "It was all so fast none of us knew what was happenin'," he concluded. "When we came too the bastard was gone and Georgie's fingers were lyin' around the yard. We picked up the fingers and they're bein' sown back on at the Royal. They say that he'll never have the full use of his hand again."

"Lucky it was his hand and not his dick," McIlroy said laughing.

"What did he look like?" Rice asked. The barbarity of Case's actions made no impression on the UVF leader.

Lennon's swollen face frowned as he tried to picture the man who had inflicted the injuries on him. He glanced across at Gillespie. "He was about medium height," he began, "and well built. Aged maybe thirty to thirty-five, dark hair, the face I don't remember so well. Nothing about it stood out. He was wearin' a reefer jacket and he spoke with a Belfast accent." He shook his head. "That's all I can remember."

"That's fucking marvellous," Rice said angrily. "Some arsehole beats the livin' shit out of four of you, lops the fingers off one of you and all you can remember is that he was a pretty ordinary bloke who was wearin' a donkey jacket. Get to hell out of here you pair of gobshites. I'm only sorry he didn't cut your fucking heads off."

Gillespie and Lennon turned and left the room.

"What do you make of it?" Rice's asked as soon as he and McIlroy were alone.

"Damned if I know?" McIlroy asked. "The `Black Bear' mob is one of our toughest unit. Anybody who could take out four of them has got to be somebody to worry about. The bastard must be some kind of superman."

"Who do you think he was?" Rice asked.

"It sounds like SASman to me," McIlroy said using the term applied by both the Protestant and Catholic paramilitaries to the members of the British Special Air Service. "Only somebody of that kind could've gotten out of the `Black Bear' alive."

"Couldn't he be a Provie?" Rice asked.

"No chance. They don't have anybody that good on their books."

"OK," Rice said trying to order his thoughts. "Let's just suppose that this guy was SASman. And then let's suppose that he's the one who offed the three Prods. Then we have to ask ourselves what the fuck is goin' on? Why are they doin' it?"

"Could be they want to get the Provies and ourselves at each others throats. It wouldn't be the first time the Brits've used disinformation tactics," McIlroy said.

Rice sat thinking for a moment. It certainly wasn't beyond the Brits to launch an operation aimed at getting the Provies and the UVF to start slaughtering each other. It had been done before. If that was what was happening then why didn't he know about it. For the past five years he had been secretly working for the Military. Only on the surface of course. They had proved useful allies in his climb to leadership of the UVF. Many an adversary had been lifted off the streets after a tip-off to the Brits. Rice made a mental note to follow that one up with his contact in Military Intelligence. But what if the Brits weren't involved? Could the bloke in the 'Black Bear' be the killer Simpson was looking for? What if the motive wasn't political? What if the killer was a rogue, some twisted bastard murdering for some motive known only to himself? If the bastard was acting from personal motives, why kill only Protestants? Rice knew all the questions but he still had to work out some of the answers. Something was beginning to smell rotten and he wanted badly to be the first man to locate where the smell was coming from. For the present he was one step ahead of everybody else. He was the only one with a description of the guy who might be the killer. Even if that description was half-baked. It wouldn't matter. The UVF had tentacles that stretched into every house on every street in the Protestant ghettos of East and West Belfast. He was going to find the bloke from the 'Black Bear' and he was going to find out why he was topping ordinary Protestants. Then he was going to use that information to squeeze some advantage out of the Brits. Fuck Simpson and his limp-wristed politician friends.

"There's something fucking rotten goin' on here, Ivan," Rice said switching off the heater and standing up. "And I want to be completely on top of it. Right."

McIlroy nodded in affirmation.

"If that bastard is somewhere in Belfast," Rice said. "Then I want to know where he is. Contact the rest of the boys. Give them a run down on what happened tonight and warn them to keep their mouths shut. They're to put the word out on the streets that we're lookin' for a stranger. The description isn't worth crap but give it to them anyway. I don't care what it takes, I want that bastard first." Rice switched off the light in his living room and walked McIlroy into the small hall of his semi-detached house. Gillespie and Lennon stood waiting beside the front door.

"This is top priority. Drop everything else and get on it." Rice slid the large bolt on the steel inner door and let the three men out onto the street. Spits of rain and a cold breeze blew around his feet as he watched the three men disappear into the rain-laden darkness. Arseholes, Rice thought watching Gillespie and Lennon's departing figures. They'd almost got the bastard. As he closed and bolted the front door and the steel inner door, a second thought struck Rice.

The bastard had the four `Black Bear' boys at his mercy, but he didn't kill any of them. Rice wondered why.

CHAPTER 23

Case woke in his small bedsit and turned his head slowly towards the window. A stream of grey light entered through the gap where the two pieces of tattered paisley printed fabric which constituted the curtains met. He pushed down on the bed with his right hand and a bolt of pain shot through his right side where the kick from the dickhead at the 'Black Bear' had landed during the previous evening's fracas. He lifted up the side of his tee-shirt and looked at the black and red streaked weal which covered the bottom section of his ribs. He'd rolled with the kick but the skinny bugger had managed to connect with him. I should have really hurt that little bastard, he thought, taking no pleasure from the memory of the kick which he had delivered to the side of the bastard's prostrate head. He ran his fingers over the weal. The skin hadn't been broken and the bruise would soon fade. He sat up slowly and swung his legs over the side of the bed. No physical jerks this morning. The UVF bastard had made any kind of exercise impossible. He felt another flash of annoyance. The early morning exercises were part of his ritual. He had learned in the SAS that it didn't require brains to kill effectively. The expert killer needed no thought processes to get rid of his victim. Killing for the professionals was instinctive. To keep the instinct honed it was necessary to keep in practice and keep the body in shape. He thought of the fat slob and the weedy youth who had confronted him in the bar the previous evening. The look on their thick Irish faces showed that they were no strangers to violence but there was a world of difference between them and him. They were pack animals. Jackals banding together to hunt and slay the weak and defenseless. He considered himself a sleek killing machine, equally skilled with pistol, combat knife or his bare hands.

He walked to the window and looked down into the terraced street below. A steady stream of light rain washed gently against the glass of the window and blurred the view of the street beneath. Time was running short. Two more clients to service and then he would replace the Belfast gloom with the brilliant sunshine of the `Costa'. Care would have to be his watchword from now on. Under other circumstances he would have preferred to finish off the bastards from the `Black Bear'. But a bundle of dead bodies in the backyard of a pub would lead to a hue and cry even in a city as accustomed to mass violence as Belfast.

Case moved to the battered locker which stood beside his bed. The top of the furniture was scored with deep dark rectangular scorch marks, a testament to the smoking habits of the room's previous occupants. He ran his index finger along one of the many depressions before opening the top drawer and lifting out a fresh white shirt. Nice and clean, he thought holding up the shirt. Just like his business in Belfast. Up until last night that was. There were four sons-of-bitches out there who could recognise him. That was if their brains had been switched on. Nobody would ever connect him with the killing of Patterson and Peacock but there was sure to be four very angry Protestant terrorists roaming the streets today. That complicated matters. All he needed was a couple of crazed bigots hunting for him. He slipped his arms into the cool white cotton, feeling the tingle as the fabric brushed against the weal on his side. He'd have to lie low for a while. To hell with the bastards in London and their schedule. He was going to get out of Belfast alive no matter what schedule they imposed on him.

Case moved to the window and pulled the tattered curtains aside. The rain was still falling in a light silent mist. He looked across at the terraced houses facing him. It could have been a working class area of any big city in England if it wasn't for the spray painted graffiti covering the redbrick walls. The slogans `Fuck the Pope', `Kill the Provos' and `No Surrender' which stared back at him from the walls opposite marked the street as typically Northern Irish. A quarter of a mile away on the other side of the 'Peace Wall' the houses looked the same but the slogans were altered to reflect the different political leanings. He closed the curtains. He didn't give a shit about politics. As far as he was concerned, all the politicians could go screw themselves. The Paddies could slaughter each other until kingdom come. All the conflict in Northern Ireland was good for was to field test the British Army. He prised open the loose floorboard and revealed the hiding place of the steel suitcase. He went through the ritual associated with the opening of the case and removed the file on his next target. He read the three type-written pages for the fiftieth time. It was a no sweat job like the other two. The only trick was that it would have to be done in typical IRA fashion. He looked at the face of the man in the eight by four inch black and white photograph that his principals had provided. He felt nothing for the person behind the photograph. It was simply business. Sometime, somehow this poor bastard had aggravated somebody in authority and he was going to have to pay for it. He slipped the typewritten pages and the photo back into the clear plastic container and replaced it in the side pocket of the case.

He was replacing the floorboard when he heard a soft knock on the door. He hammered the loose board into place with the side of his hand and stood up quickly. "Come in," he said.

The door opened and Betty Maguire stuck her head into the room. "I've a lovely fresh egg for your breakfast, Mr. eh!, Joe."

"Thanks, that's very nice of you to offer, Mrs. M," Case said closing his shirt and moving towards the open door. Maybe to-day wouldn't be such a bad day to lie low, he thought as he slapped Mrs. Maguire's plump departing behind. The hit wasn't until this evening and Mrs. Maguire's backside presented a more enticing prospect than another day at the flicks.

Wilson's eyes were stinging and his throat felt like the bottom of a parrot's cage as he slung his heavy overcoat over the coat-stand in his cluttered office. He hadn't had the courage to look in a mirror but he hoped that he didn't look as bad as he felt. However, he had a sneaking feeling that he did. Then there was the embarrassment. His face reddened when he thought about his performance in front of McElvaney. He was coming apart at the seams. What the hell was he up to? Did he want to get in her pants? If he did he was making a damn poor job of it. Kate McCann's business card stared back at him from a shelf in the kitchen. He picked it up and turned it over in his hand concentrating on the mobile number written in blue ink. He replaced the card on the shelf and turned on the radio. The early morning radio news programme announced the resumption of talks about talks in the Middle East. Nothing changes, he thought. The conflicts just moves around the world. Some gobshite detective in Beirut was probably looking into the death of a Christian killed by a Muslim or vice versa. His Lebanese colleague and he were just a couple of unlucky innocent bystanders. He could not dispel the feeling that the two murders formed only part of a pattern which would eventually involve many others. It rarely stopped at two or three. No detective involved in investigating the sectarian murders of the 1970's could forget how mismanagement compounding ineptitude had allowed gangs of vicious criminals to murder, sometimes in the most horrible fashion, dozens of innocent people. It always bothered him that the RUC had failed miserably to put all the members of the murder gangs away. In the tangled web of terrorism and lies, false accusations and downright perjury that typified the judicial process in Northern Ireland, he had at last begun to accept that the PSNI, or indeed any police force, could only be partially successful against clever terrorists.

The squad room was empty and Wilson settled himself behind his desk to get in a few minutes of uninterrupted work. Every member of the squad would have to pump in all the hours that God would send until they located the man or men responsible for the three murders. Jesus Christ, he thought as he looked at the mound of files lying on his desk. His throat felt so dry that it ached continually while the point just above his right temple pounded with a regular syncopation which would have been the envy of a drummer in a jazz band. He placed the top file in front of him and telephoned his squad's secretary to fetch him up a cup of strong sweet tea. The tea arrived five minutes later and was almost strong enough to keep the spoon upright in the middle of the cup. He drank a mouthful of the liquid which streamed down his throat like a torrent of nectar. Then he opened a file and began to work.

Detective Constable McElvaney looked over the computer printouts for what must have been the twentieth time. She had finally hit on one factor which connected Patterson and Peacock. It had been so simple that she couldn't understand how she hadn't seen it before. But then again maybe it had been too simple and so maybe it meant absolutely nothing. The files from the Department of Social Welfare had shown that Patterson and Peacock had both been orphans. At first sight this fact seemed inconsequential. No policeman in his right mind could believe that there was a serial killer concentrating solely on orphans. But she could not deny that it was the only possible fact which connected the two men other than the fact they lived and worked in the same city. She had spent hours dipping into the Social Welfare computer files. Each of the two men had passed through a series of homes and foster-parents before being released into the community at sixteen. She started to cross reference the two men's lives and came up with only one connection. Both men had been residents of the Dungray Home for Boys between the years 1990 and 1992. She switched her attention to information on the Dungray Home for Boys. The institution was run by a group of Protestant fundamentalists and other than giving the barest of details the Social Welfare file on the Home was useless. She printed out the details from the Social Welfare file and switched to the PSNI and Military Intelligence files. Nothing. Not even the slightest mention of Dungray. She was disappointed because she was sure that she was on to something. She told herself that there was no reason why there should have been police files on the Home. But something was niggling her. Days of examining files had produced only this single tenuous link between the two men and like a dog with a bone she wasn't going to give up this lead easily. She picked up the print-out of the Social Welfare file. A column in the file indicated the names of the individuals who had run the home since its inception. She located the years 1990 to 1992 and ran her finger across the paper until it came to the name Robert Nichol. She interrogated the PSNI files one more time and when prompted by the computer she entered Nichol's name. The amber screen went blank and she sat back while the machine scanned the thousands of files which had been built up by the police and military since the creation of the state of Northern Ireland.

This was the new police work, she thought listening to the whirr of the computer terminal. The 'bobby on the beat' was an anachronism. The old style of police work had its uses in an age where a man in a blue uniform knew most of the people on his beat. These days the information on citizens of a country consisted of patterns of charged particles stored God only knew where. Whereas the old style policeman picked up his information from gossip on the streets, the new police could tap into a myriad of databases that could literally trace the history of an individual from birth to death. Big Brother had arrived. She could feel a tinge of excitement as she waited for the machine to disgorge its information. Something told her that the long hours sitting before the computer screen and pouring over the files was going to pay off. The screen flicked and she leaned forward. She stared at the small box in the centre of the screen. The word 'RESTRICTED' flashed on and off in the centre of the box. The words 'enter access code' flashed in the left hand bottom corner of the screen. She typed in her access code and pressed 'enter'. The machine emitted a beep and the legend 'enter access code' reappeared. She hit the escape key and the screen changed to the data search menu. What the hell was going on? Why should the file on the warden of an orphans home be restricted? She selected the PSNI and Military files and keyed in her access number. When the machine prompted her for her request she typed in Nichol's name for the second time. There had to be some problem with the machine. Her access code should have been sufficient to open up all the files held by the PSNI and Military Intelligence. She waited anxiously as the machine searched for Nichol's file. The screen flicked into life and her heart sank as she saw the same small box dominating the centre of the screen. Angrily she pushed the escape key. What the hell was so special about Robert bloody Nichol that his file had been restricted? Somebody was being very cagey about Mister Nichol. She leaned over the keyboard of the terminal. There was more than one way to skin a cat. It was a certainty that if there was a PSNI or Military Intelligence file on Nichol that there would be a cross reference to him in some other file. She asked the computer to search for the name Robert Nichol in any of the other files. This was going to be a long job. The machine whirred and her eyes glared at the empty screen. Occasionally the word `working' flashed on the screen. The minutes dragged by as in the bowels of the station the computer examined thousands of yards of computer tape. She was about to give up when the screen suddenly filled with text. She blinked her eyes and focused on the fuzzy amber letters. She scanned the text moving quickly from line to line. Finally her eyes lighted on the name `Robert Nichol' buried in a line of text. She returned to the top of the data file and began to read slowly through the words.

CHAPTER 24

It was a bad day in the life of Ian Wilson. As he'd become older, he'd realised that alcohol didn't agree with him but that didn't stop him from over indulging now and again. As he left the weekly management meeting, he headed straight for his office and the biggest mug of coffee obtainable in Tennent Street. The weekly meeting with his colleagues was usually difficult enough to take, but this morning's effort had pushed him to the limit of his self control. Nobody with a pounding head wanted to listen to other people's petty problems and his colleagues were past masters at elevating the trivial to the heights of importance. He could tell from their expressions that they had smelled the booze on him. Poor old sod, they would think to themselves. Used to be a good copper but gone to seed since his wife's death. Then the snickering would start. His throat felt raw and tender. He slid into the narrow space behind his desk, drained his coffee and signalled to Davidson to bring him a refill. He looked at the mass of papers littering his desk and his stomach turned. To-day was not the day to view grizzly photos or read graphic descriptions of torn flesh and ruptured organs. Davidson entered the office and poured the contents of a coffee pot into the empty mug sitting on a beer mat which was placed close to Wilson's right hand.

"It's like that is it, boss?" Davidson said retiring towards the door.

"You playing at being a detective again," Wilson said eyeing the mug of steaming black liquid at his right hand. "It's worse than that."

"Did you take any paracetamol?" Davidson asked.

"Yes," Wilson said curtly.

"And try a few mints. This office smells like a brewery."

Wilson burped. "Thanks for your kind offer of assistance. Your concern has been noted. I'll include the phrase 'full of the milk of human kindness' on your next assessment." He waved the detective constable back towards the squad room.

Somehow, Wilson thought, he would have to slip away for a few hours sleep. Alcohol and lack of sleep were a bad combination for someone in his line of work.

Wilson looked up and saw McElvaney standing at the door with a sheaf of computer paper in her hand. It was the last sight in the world he wanted to see.

"Look, about last night," Wilson began

"Yes," she interrupted quickly. She squeezed into the office and pulled the door behind her. "I wanted to thank you for making my introduction to the squad so easy. I really appreciate your efforts to help me to settle in but I think that we should curtail the socialising until I'm more integrated into the wider group. Two nights in a row might be considered by some people as inappropriate."

"You're quite the diplomat," Wilson took a slug from the mug of coffee and wondered why he bothered with alcohol. "But of course you do have a point. I'm sure that you'll develop a circle of friends of your own age over time."

"Don't get me wrong. I do appreciate what you were doing but I'm alright now."

"I only wish that I had been the one to clarify the situation," Wilson drained the coffee mug. "So what can I do for you?"

"I think that I've got something." The young constable's eyes were shiny with excitement.

216

"OK let's hear it." Wilson motioned to the space directly before his desk.

"I've found a link between Patterson and Peacock," she couldn't keep the excitement out of her voice. "It's tenuous but at least it's something. They were both orphans and residents of a boy's home called Dungray at the same time in the early nineties."

Wilson lifted his head and grimaced as though in great pain.

"I know it's pretty feeble stuff but you asked me to find a link between the two dead men."

Wilson picked up the mug of black coffee before realising that it was empty. "OK," he heard his voice rasping as he replacing the cup on the mat. "Stop playing `McElvaney, Ace of Detectives' for just one second and think about what you just said. This city is so small that you can usually find some link no matter how tenuous between any two of its citizens."

"That's not all," she interrupted her superior. "The man who ran the home at that time was a Robert Nichol." She paused to let the name sink in.

"So," Wilson said.

"Nichol should have some sort of security or social welfare or at least employment file but there's nothing on record about him. Every piece of government information on this man is restricted and none of our codes can access the computer files."

Wilson looked up into McElvaney's face. This was one weird situation. It took some level of authorisation to pull individual files so there was no doubting that Robert Nichol was an important man is some person's eyes.

"That's not all," she said without trying to hide her excitement. "I cross-checked Nichol against all the other

217

PSNI files and this is what I came up with." She tossed the computer print-out onto Wilson's desk.

Wilson looked at the faded typescript on the lined computer sheets and a blinding pain shot through a point directly between his eyes. "Tell me," he said pushing the sheets back towards her.

"This is a computer résumé of a murder case in which Nichol was interviewed," she said. "It was the only reference to Nichol in all the old RUC files. It appears that a young man's dismembered body was found in North Belfast and that there was some reason at the time to believe that Robert Nichol was involved in the murder."

"Right," Wilson said draining the coffee. "Has the original case file been digitised yet?" He was beginning to wake up.

"If it has there's no record of it on the computer."

"What about the original file? Is it still in the archive?"

"I've already looked," she said smugly. "The case file's gone missing."

Wilson sat upright in his chair. "What do you mean `the case file's gone missing'? Files don't just go 'missing'. Somebody must have taken it out."

"So you would think," she replied. "There's a gap where the file should be and the filing clerk doesn't know where the file is to be found. The take-out sheet is also missing so we have no idea who was the last person to view the file. "

"Now that is strange," Wilson said trying to clear his head. Maybe she had hit on something here. He was so desperate for a break that he was willing to clutch at any straw. "Here," he pushed the coffee cup across the desk towards her. "You go and get me another cup of that muck. I need to have both the brain cells that haven't been destroyed by Jameson in action to-day." He reached across the desk for the pages of computer printout and read slowly through the lines of faint print wondering if the PSNI would ever find the money to buy decent printing equipment. Robert Nichol had been one of a series of suspects in a bizarre and macabre murder of a fifteen year old youth whose dismembered body had been found at three different locations in North Belfast. It felt strange to read the details of a murder case which didn't have a sectarian motive. The computer file gave only the basic details but there was no doubt that unlike ninety nine per cent of the province's murders this one had been motivated by something other than politics. Even from the scant information on the sheets, it was clear that the investigating officers were of the opinion that they were dealing with a homosexual crime. The post mortem had revealed that the youth had had anal sex shortly before his death. The case had remained unsolved. He reached the end of the short report. The names of the investigating officers were appended to the bottom of the final page. One of them had been a Detective Constable George Whitehouse.

Moira entered the office just as Wilson finished reading the computer file. She laid the mug of steaming black coffee beside her boss and stood back. "Well, what do you think?"

"Are you absolutely sure about the file in the archives?" Wilson asked. "It hasn't just been mislaid."

"I don't think so," she replied. "The clerk wasn't too co-operative but I could see that he thought it had been lifted."

"Maybe someone took it out for consultation," Wilson sipped the coffee and burned the tip of his tongue.

"That's probably why the take-out sheet is missing."

"What have we got?" Wilson said. "The two men the murderer definitely wanted out of the way have only one connection that we can locate. They were both residents of an orphan's home in the early nineties. The file on a murder which involved the director of the home is missing and his intelligence file can't be accessed. The murder link obviously fizzled out otherwise he'd have been charged."

"There's one other piece of information you should know," she said.

Wilson looked up from his desk.

"I ran a check on the dead youth," she paused for effect. "He was in Dungray at the same time as Patterson and Peacock."

"Now that's a coincidence," Wilson said and pushed his chair back until it came to rest against the partition. Perhaps she had struck something alright but where would it get them. Three dead men had all been residents in a Belfast orphan's home. One had been murdered in gruesome fashion twenty years previously while the other two had been killed by a professional in the past week. Then there was the business of the missing file. He needed to know more. He pulled open his desk drawer and took out the school copybook he had removed from Patterson's bedsit. He flipped open the front pages and stared at the crude drawings. A homosexual murder and drawings of homosexual acts. Was there a connection? Would that connection lead him to the killer of Patterson and Peacock or would it send him on a wild goose chase? He looked through the glass partition which separated him from the squad room and his gaze fell on the burly figure of Detective Sergeant Whitehouse sitting at his desk. Wilson motioned for him to join them in his office. There was going to be no opportunity to slip off home for a sleep today.

Whitehouse was standing at the doorway by the time Wilson put down the coffee cup.

"Any orders, boss," Whitehouse studiously ignored Moira.

"Yes," Wilson said. "Moira here may have found a slim connection between Patterson and Peacock." Wilson noticed that Whitehouse winced at his use of McElvaney's first name. A good Prod didn't address the enemy by their Christian names. "Both of them were residents of an orphans home called Dungray in the early nineties."

"That's some sodding slim connection all right" Whitehouse said keeping his gaze fixed on Wilson.

"Agreed," Wilson said. He noticed the tick in Whitehouse's eye when he had mentioned Dungray. "Do you remember anything about Dungray yourself George?"

"Never heard of the place," Whitehouse replied.

"That's strange," Wilson said. "An ex-resident of that home managed to get himself killed more than twenty years ago." Wilson had forgotten the dead youth's name. He picked up the computer sheets from the desk and scanned the file. "A young kid named Ronald Jamison was found in various bits in rubbish bags around North Belfast."

"So," Whitehouse said.

"So," Wilson repeated. "Maybe its nothing but then again maybe there's some kind of connection. That's what we're going to find out. You worked on the Jamison case."

"I don't rightly remember," Whitehouse said. "Twenty years is a long time. I was a young wet-behind – the-ears detective constable. They might have included me in the investigation but I really can't remember."

"It's in this small memo," Wilson held up the sheets of computer printout. "Moira cross-checked the files for mentions of Robert Nichol and ran across this one." He stopped. Whitehouse had definitely winced when Nichol's name was mentioned. Don't ever be a poker player, Wilson thought. George's face was an open book. Something was badly wrong here. "You wouldn't happen to know where I could find the full file on this case?" Wilson asked.

Whitehouse shuffled his feet. "Nobody tried the archives, I suppose."

"It appears the file hasn't been digitised and there's an empty space in the archives where the file used to be," Wilson said. "Come on, George. You've got a good memory when you want to. You worked on the case. What do you know about Robert Nichol?" Wilson was watching for the involuntary reaction. He got it. Another wince and a bead of sweat exiting from the hairline. There was something to hide and George was in the know. Wilson could smell the work of the Lodge brothers above the stench of booze in the office.

"For God's sake. That was an age ago. In that time we've had fires and floods and God only knows how many changes of personnel. The case files was probably taken out and lost. Every time they renovate this dump half the paper goes missing." Whitehouse shuffled his feet and the sweat was now exiting from his hairline in globules. "I've handled dozens of cases in the meantime. How the hell can you expect me to remember the details of any one particular case?"

"Maybe this'll refresh your memory," Wilson handed Whitehouse the computer output. "Read it."

Whitehouse read slowly through the sheets his lips moving as he verbalised the words. When he had finished he handed the pages back to Wilson.

"Well," Wilson said. "Anything coming back?"

"Bits," Whitehouse said. "As far as I can remember we interviewed most of the people who knew Jamison but we didn't really get anywhere. The kid had been fucked up the ass sometime on the night he died." He looked at Moira expecting to see her wince at his use of crude language but she just stared at him. "We never found out were he'd spent the evening or who he'd been with. We were swamped with murder cases at the time so when it didn't break quickly we were forced to let it go."

"But you did interview Nichol?" Wilson asked.

"Only for background," Whitehouse added quickly. "He wasn't really a suspect. The kid was an orphan. He'd spent time in a home run by a religious group that Nichol was involved with. Big sodding deal. We found that he'd gone on the game as a rent boy selling his ass to anyone with twenty quid in his pocket. The theory at the time was that he had picked up some john, they'd screwed and then something went pear shaped and the john ended up killing him. We trawled the homo scene but nothing turned up. It was before DNA and there was a whole load of other shit going down so we were forced to let it go."

"That's a good boy, George," Wilson smiled. "See how much you can remember when you put your mind to it. And the interview notes?"

"In the case file," Whitehouse said avoiding eye contact with his superior.

Wilson was remembering the scenario he had developed during the visit to Patterson's bed-sit. It bore a remarkable resemblance to Jamison. "Did you check out the orphans' home?"

"Now you're pushing me, boss," Whitehouse said. He wiped his face with his handkerchief. "If only I had them notes to refer to. Like I said it was a hell of a long time ago."

"And the only set of interview notes were in the missing file," Wilson said.

Whitehouse nodded.

"And the orphan's home would be Dungray I suppose."

"I don't remember," Whitehouse said.

"Was there anything more to this guy Nichol than being the warden of an orphan's home?"

"Like what?" Whitehouse said belligerently.

"Like, are you bloody thick," Wilson shouted. His head was pounding. Getting the information out of George was worse than pulling teeth. "Like, was he involved with any grouping? Like, was he political? Like, is there something I should know about this man?"

Whitehouse stood silently for a moment. He looked into Wilson's face and knew that he wasn't getting away without an answer. "At the time," he said forcing the words out. "Nichol was a front man for one of the Protestant organisations, I don't remember the name of it. They weren't exactly paramilitaries."

"They weren't exactly boy scouts either as I remember it," Wilson said.

Moira stood watching her two superiors. She was impressed by Wilson's tenacity.

"Maybe we'll have a little talk with Nichol," Wilson said tilting back in his chair. "Revive some old memories. Maybe he remembers Patterson and Peacock. Maybe he knows why somebody wanted them dead. Then I want to find out why his computer file is restricted and when and how the Jamison file went missing."

"I need to get back to work," Whitehouse said. "Things have been piling up on me over the past week."

"I thought that you might like to join me when I interview Nichol?" Wilson said.

"What the hell do you want to interview that old bastard for?" Whitehouse said. "He's probably dead anyway and I bet that if he is alive he knows bugger-all about either Patterson or Peacock."

"Find out whether Nichol is still in the land of the living," Wilson said to Moira. "And find out where he might be located." He looked towards the doorway and saw that Whitehouse was listening attentively. "I thought you were in a hurry back to your work, George."

CHAPTER 25

Whitehouse looked around the deserted street before he opened the door and stepped into the public phone box. His nose immediately detected the ammoniacal smell of stale urine. The floor of the box was littered with wet pages torn from the telephone book which hung from a chain attached to the side of the cabin. The inside panels of the telephone box were covered with Loyalist graffiti and explicit sexual advice. One crude cartoon depicted a nun fellating a character wearing a tall mitre. He kicked the paper littering the bottom of the cabin into a corner and picked up the phone. He should have made the call from the Station but you never knew who might be listening. All the boys in the squad were true blue except for McElvaney but it was Wilson who posed the main problem. Even after ten years, he still wasn't sure what made the bastard tick. His chief was an obstinate swine who would never bow to intimidation. He could never understand how a man who had been given every opportunity to become one of the boys always managed to misunderstand the invitation. Wilson certainly didn't belong to that group of PSNI officers who saw themselves as being the true protectors of Protestant Ulster. Well that was his tough sodding luck. DCI Ian Wilson wasn't going any further in the Force. Not only that but the day was fast approaching when the powers that be would have to do something about him. He composed the number and waited while the phone rang out.

"Yes."

Whitehouse immediately recognised Simpson's voice on the other end of the line. "You know who it is?" he said. Although he'd found no evidence to prove it he was certain that Simpson's phone was being monitored by either the Special Branch or Military Intelligence. In any case he wanted to keep his relationship with Simpson strictly their business.

"Go ahead, " Simpson's tone was as smooth as velvet.

"You told me to inform you if anything happened down here."

"I'm listening," there was a note of interest in Simpson's tone.

"It appears that our new Catholic constable has found a link between the two dead men," Whitehouse began. "Both the bastards spent time in Dungray during the early nineties."

"Why should that bother us?"

"They've latched on to Nichol. The sodding Taig dug up a fragment of a computer file on the Jamison business."

"I thought all traces of that affair had been erased." A profound feeling of unease swept through Simpson. That old pederast bastard Nichol had almost ruined them once before and the affair was going to come back to haunt them.

"Don't worry," Whitehouse interrupted Simpson's thoughts. "We destroyed the Jamison file years ago. There isn't one single scrap of paper left. But that doesn't mean that some bollocks didn't leave a short sodding description of the case on the computer by accident. I've read the file. It says bugger all. Nichol has nothing to do with the murder of either Patterson or Peacock and as soon as Wilson and his tame Taig find that out they'll piss off and leave him alone."

Simpson's mind was working at a mile a minute and all he could foresee was a disastrous event. Opening up the Nichol can of worms would inevitably lead back to his political masters who had worked so diligently to bury the affair. If that happened there would be hell to pay. Wilson was the key to the whole bloody thing and he was about the only person that they couldn't get to.

"Is there any way to get Wilson off the track?" Simpson asked hopefully.

"Wise up," Whitehouse laughed into the black mouthpiece. "You know Wilson as well as I do. If you try to throw him a shimmy, you'll only make him twice as anxious to get to the bottom of what happened to Jamison. Let him talk to the old fucker. Tell Nichol to keep his big trap shut and you're in the clear. The connection is slim so next week the sodding Taig'll be off on another lead."

"Holy Shit!" Simpson could feel a wave of panic pass through him. "This was your fucking baby, you stupid bollocks. You were supposed to bury that deeper than the holds of hell. The last thing in the world we needed right now was for that old chestnut to reappear." If Whitehouse had been in front of him he would have hit him. "Let me think for a second." The wheels inside his brain were moving so quickly that he couldn't concentrate properly. The possibility of the police opening up something so potentially damaging to his boss and their party had thrown him into a blind panic. "I want to know exactly what's goin' down and when. If he's goin' to interview Nichol I want to know the when and the where."

Whitehouse could hear the fear in Simpson's voice and it threw him. Simpson didn't scare easily. "Don't worry I'll keep on top of it," he said.

"You bloody better," Simpson said. "You've fucked up enough already by not covering up the traces. Don't balls this one up."

The line clicked and Whitehouse was left listening to outer space. He slammed the receiver back on to its cradle and kicked the ball of wet paper on the floor of the cabin. It was all that bloody woman's fault. If she hadn't been nosing around on the computer, the Nichol business would never have come to light. As soon as they could get Wilson out of the way, she was going to find herself back on the beat whatever the new policy on Catholics was. George Whitehouse was going to take care of that personally.

He stood in the phone box for several moments weighing up the situation. Simpson's reaction had surprised him. Maybe there was more to this than met the eye. Perhaps he should take advice from elsewhere. The Master of the Lodge should know about the latest developments. He picked up the phone and dialled the number of PSNI Headquarters in Castlereagh. "I'd like to speak to DCC Jennings," he said as soon as the operator came on the line.

Simpson walked to the sideboard in his living room and took out a bottle of Bushmills whiskey. He poured himself a large shot and then slumped into an armchair. Yesterday his main purpose in life was to keep a lid on Protestant retaliation for three murders. A full-scale return to violence might cause the Brits to cut the Province loose. The great British public would probably clap until their hands fell off if that came about. The threat from Nichol was much greater. Nichol could undermine the Ulster Democratic Front. He took a long slug of the amber liquid. There was a big difference between keeping the lid on sectarian retaliation and having the Nichol affair blow up in their faces. He drained the glass. He'd never understood why they hadn't let Nichol take the fall for the Jamison business. There would have been political fall-out. But they would have managed to survive it. The situation was quite different now. If it ever came out that a major Protestant political grouping had suppressed evidence and instigated a cover-up of a murder just to protect their political reputations, the Party would be finished and they might all go to jail. He didn't need to be a rocket scientist to realise that this thing was too big for him. It was going to require major muscle to keep the lid on whatever Wilson managed to come up with and he just didn't possess that kind of juice. He stood up, walked reluctantly to the telephone and dialled a number.

"It's Richie. Is he there?" Simpson asked when the telephone at the other was answered.

"Yes, Richie," the deep bass voice of Billy Carlile came on the phone.

"We've got a major problem," Simpson began. "I've just had that idiot Whitehouse on the line. Somehow the investigation into the two men murdered in West Belfast this week has got around to Robert Nichol."

"What!" the air exploded across the telephone line. "How the hell did that happen?"

"It turns out that the two murdered men were residents at Dungray in the early nineties. Some smart arsed policeman came up with Nichol's name and they think he might be able to help them with their enquiries."

"The stupid meddlers," the anger was evident in Carlile's voice. "That business was dead and buried. We had assurances."

"Whitehouse or somebody else on the inside screwed up. Some fool didn't wipe the computer file. There was a reference to Nichol in some note about the Jamison murder."

"I don't believe this is happening" Carlile said. "We need this problem like we need a hole in the head. The British are about to drop the boom on us and something comes up that could remove us from the political scene altogether. This has all the ingredients of a disaster. We've got to talk face to face. If we don't do something about this right away it could get out of hand. Meet me at my office in fifteen minutes."

Simpson replaced the phone. Fuck, fuck, fuck, he shouted. The whole bloody house of cards was going to come tumbling down because some son of a bitch had topped a couple of orphans. Why couldn't the bastard have picked on some other section of the population? Why in God's name hadn't they thrown Nichol to the wolves when they'd had the chance? He ran the palm of his hand over his stomach trying to dispel the pang of fear which gnawed at his entrails.

CHAPTER 26

A pall of dark grey rain completely obscured the Black Mountains as Detective Constable Moira McElvaney piloted the police car north on the Crumlin Road towards the Woodvale area of Belfast. The regular beat of the windscreen wipers revealed the labyrinth of narrow streets which extended away on both sides of the city's main artery. The entrance to each road was decorated with faded paintings of the province's flag or a hooded figure holding a Kalashnikov aloft and standing over the legend 'UVF'. The peace line, a wall of concrete and steel cladding which snaked its way through gardens and across roads creating a physical separation between Ulster's two communities, could be seen barring the exits of some of the streets on their left. A convoy of British Army armoured vehicles covered in brown/green camouflage paint rumbled out of the rain towards the two policemen like a line of Neolithic beetles. The heads of two soldiers wearing visored helmets protruded from steel turrets in the roof of each vehicle. Neither Moira nor Wilson remarked on the cavalcade. The scene of rumbling personnel carriers and visor wearing soldiers would have had science fiction connotations of a futuristic authoritarian state on the British mainland. In Northern Ireland it didn't even merit a mention.

Wilson sat in the passenger seat lost in thought. He felt old and tired. Twenty years of living with the stench of human degradation and decomposition was beginning to take its toll. How could one police a situation where the dismembered body of a young man can be found and the case dropped within a week? Where was the justice for the dead man? And what bastard had removed the file from the archives condemning the dead youth to eternal injustice? Enough was enough. He glanced across at McElvaney. The detective constable was young and obviously stubborn. He envied her. He remembered being young and stubborn himself but somehow his youth had been dissipated in the fruitless pursuit of justice while his toughness had increased to the point where he felt himself incapable of normal human emotions.

"Turn left in here," Wilson said automatically.

Moira glanced at the street sign indicating the entrance to Glenside Park. Beneath the street sign was a white sprayed `Fuck the Pope' and beneath that `No surrender' in alternate red, white and blue letters. The houses in Glenside Park were just one grade upmarket from the red brick terraced dwellings which lined the Crumlin Road. Small gardens separated the houses from the footpath. She drove slowly along the street while Wilson searched for the house number.

"That's it," Wilson pointed to a slightly run-down house twenty feet further down the road. "It would be just our luck if Nichol wasn't at home."

She stopped the car directly in front of the house that Wilson had indicated. As Wilson climbed out of the car he thought he saw a movement at the corner of the lace curtain covering the ground floor window. It appeared that somebody was home. The yellow pebble dash of the top half of the front wall of the house had been stained dark grey by a stream of rain water which emanated from a hole in the centre of the gutter. Nichol evidently wasn't the do-it-yourself type. He pushed open the iron gate and made his way up the short path to the door of the house. Moira joined him in the covered porch.

"It rained forty days and forty nights in the Bible but it looks like we might break that record," she said as she slipped under the cover of the porch.

Wilson pushed the bell and the two police officers turned to face the door.

Nothing happened. Wilson pushed a second time maintaining pressure on the bell for several seconds.

"It looks like we're out of luck," Moira said.

"I noticed the curtains moving after we pulled up outside. Somebody's home alright." Wilson pushed the bell for the third time keeping the pressure on the buzzer. He released the bell when he heard scuffling noises coming from the interior.

"Who the hell is makin' all that bloody racket?" a croaking voice called from inside.

"Detective Chief Inspector Ian Wilson of the PSNI," Wilson answered. "And Detective Constable McElvaney," he added as an after-thought.

"Push your warrant card through the letter box," the voice from inside the house said.

Wilson removed his warrant card from his inside pocket and pushed it through the letterbox.

After several seconds, the two police officers heard the lock of the front door being worked and the door opened slowly.

"You can't be too careful," the man who opened the door handed Wilson back his warrant card. "Many a man has ended up dead by being too hasty in opening his own door."

Wilson judged Robert Nichol to be in his sixties and a well preserved sixties at that. His angular parchment coloured face was topped by a neatly combed quiff of steely grey hair and a pair of flinty light blue eyes surveyed the two PSNI officers. Nichol wore a stylish checked sports-coat and grey flannel pants. A strong smell of perfume assailed Wilson nostrils. He had never met the man in the flesh before but he had seen him numerous times on television

234

and at one point Nichol's picture had appeared regularly in the newspapers. As far as he could see Nichol hadn't changed all that much since he had helped Billy Carlile found the Ulster Democratic Front. Nichol and Carlile had been the twin architects of the politics of hate. They had created a political entity that catered to the basest instincts of their constituency. They stood against Popery, Catholic priests and the surrender of their British identity. It was clear that a lot of Protestants agreed with them by putting the 'X' against Carlile's name at the ballot box. Wilson couldn't remember how or why Nichol had faded from the scene. At one time Nichol and Carlile had been as inseparable as Siamese twins. But nowadays when people thought of the UDF they thought only of Carlile.

"Are you Robert Nichol?" Wilson asked noticing that Nichol leaned on a walking stick which he held in his right hand.

"I am indeed," Nichol said. "What can I do for you?"

"We're hoping that you can assist us with a murder investigation, Mr. Nichol," Wilson said. "I think it'd be better if we could speak to you inside."

Nichol moved aside slowly and let the two police officers enter the narrow hallway of his house.

"The living room is on the left," Nichol said pointing at an open doorway. "How in heavens name can I help you with a murder enquiry, Chief Inspector? I'm an old man who leads a very quiet life."

"That remains to be seen, sir." Wilson looked around the hallway before walking into the living room. The interior of the house was in direct contrast to the exterior. The mirror at the centre of the hallstand was gleaming. The brass hooks shined to the golden gloss. Whoever did the cleaning was fastidious. He wished his cleaning lady would take lessons from whoever did Nichol's house. The mania with cleanliness was also apparent in the small living room into which Nichol ushered them. The cloth-covered three-piece suite which dominated the room looked like it had just left the showroom. The only intrusion on the air of cleanliness was the pervasive smell of cat. Wilson sat on one of the armchairs and watched Nichol make his way slowly into the room and deposit himself in the other single armchair.

"Now, how can I help you, Chief Inspector?" Nichol asked.

McElvaney sat on the two-seater couch which stood between the two armchairs. She produced a notebook from her inside pocket and held it on her knees.

"Detective Constable McElvaney and myself are investigating three murders which took place earlier this week," Wilson began. "On the surface, the killings appear to have a sectarian motive. All three victims were Protestants. None of them appear to have any connection with the paramilitaries."

Nichol's face registered perplexity. "I'm afraid you've got the better of me, Chief Inspector," He sat with his two knees together, the walking stick was propped into the groove formed by the knees. "I've hardly been outside the house these past few weeks. The poor state of my health only allows me out on Sunday so that I might worship the Lord." He fiddled with his walking stick to emphasise the point.

"Bear with me a while please, sir," Wilson said. "The killings carry all the hallmarks of having been carried out by a professional. We want to know why these particular men were selected." He noticed a smile flit across Nichol's thin lips. "Of course, we're well aware that in the area of sectarian murder there doesn't necessarily have to be a motive. We have managed to find a connection between two of the victims. James Patterson and Stanley Peacock were both residents of Dungray Home for Boys during the period nineteen ninety to nineteen ninety-two. I understand that you were the warden of Dungray during that period."

"That I was, Inspector," Nichol shuffled and put both his hand on the top of his walking stick. "But I'm afraid the dead men's names mean nothing to me," he said. "May they rest in peace with the Lord. Patterson and Peacock you said?"

Wilson nodded in affirmation. He took two police photographs of Patterson and Peacock out of his pocket and passed them to Nichol.

"These are photographs of two of the men murdered this week, Patterson and Peacock," Wilson said. "Perhaps you don't remember the names but maybe the faces will strike a bell."

Nichol examined the photographs closely then shook his head. "No sorry, Chief Inspector. These photographs are of grown men. I might just be able to remember the boys if I had younger photos of them. These mean nothing to me." Nichol passed the photos back to McElvaney. "The Lord is sometimes cruel, Chief Inspector. He gives life and then he takes it away. We must learn to accept the Lord's will."

"Must we?" Wilson said. "You're quite sure you don't remember them at all?"

"Of course countless boys passed through Dungray during the time I was in charge there. You're talking about nearly twenty years ago." He closed his eyes as though lost in thought. "Patterson and Peacock. No, Inspector, I'm afraid I can't help you with that one." Nichol held his fingers interlinked. He looked into the distance. "I was doing the Lord's work in running that home. There are so many boys that need the comfort that only the Lord Jesus can provide."

Very impressive, Wilson thought as he watched Nichol's face turned towards heaven. He had never trusted zealots and he wasn't going to start now. Perhaps Nichol was trying to deflect them with his little piece of theatre. "We appreciate that, Mr. Nichol," he said. "I can assure you that they were there when we say they were and that you were in charge during that period."

"I'm sure you're right," Nichol was huddled over his walking stick again. The warrior of Christ had shrunk back into the old man. "It's just that my memory isn't all it used to be," he lifted his head and smiled at Wilson. "I can hardly remember what I did yesterday."

You should be on the stage, Wilson thought as he watched Nichol's performance. "The only factor that links Patterson and Peacock is Dungray. That's a fact. When we ran Dungray and murder through our computer we came up with another name. Ronald Jamison." Wilson noticed Nichol's light blue eyes flicker at the mention of Jamison's name. It was momentary and not one other feature on his face responded. "Jamison was also murdered. Maybe you remember him."

"That poor unfortunate creature," Nichol's eyes glossed over. "Jesus called him unto Him. He's standing at Christ's side in Paradise." He looked towards the ceiling of the room as though expecting to see reflected in the white plaster the images of the murdered boy and his Maker.

"You remember the case?" Wilson asked.

"How could I forget, Chief Inspector," Nichol let his gaze descend slowly. "I've had my fair share of successes helping young men to find their way in the world. But sometimes I have failed some of those who were in my charge. I failed young Jamison and that weighs heavily on my conscience. My only consolation is that he is with Christ."

"Nobody was ever found for the murder," Wilson said. "The case seemed to die very quickly."

"The poor boy left Dungray and fell in with bad company," Nichol's knuckles showed livid white above his cane. "I hold myself responsible for letting him leave the home," Nichol shook his grey mane. "I wish to God the police had found the evil person who snuffed out his life. Maybe then I could live easier with my guilt."

Wilson watched Nichol lean over his cane again a look of abject sorrow on his lined face. It wasn't right, he thought. Something was wrong but he couldn't yet put his finger on it. He remembered Patterson's notebook. "Was Jamison homosexual?"

"Perish the thought," Nichol said keeping his head bent. "My boys were all pure, clean living Christians. It was never a question at the time."

"I understand that you were involved in paramilitary activities in the mid-eighties.' Wilson said.

"Oh dear no, Inspector," Nichol raised his head and smiled condescendingly as though Wilson had made a silly joke. "We did have a Protestant prayer group for young men but in no way could it be called a paramilitary organisation. Just a group of young men committing themselves to the work of the Lord."

That's a crock of shit, Wilson thought. He considered pursuing this line of questioning but couldn't see where it would get him. What the hell connection could there be between the vicious murder of a young man fifteen years previously and the executions of the past week? "I think we've taken up enough off your time. Thanks for your assistance." Wilson said.

"I'm afraid I wasn't much help," Nichol said starting to rise from his armchair.

"Stay where you are, sir," Wilson said moving towards the living-room door. "The Detective Constable and myself can see ourselves out."

Nichol slumped back into the chair. "Thank you, Chief Inspector. If I can be of any further assistance don't hesitate to call on me."

"Thank you, Sir," Wilson said, "I'll do that."

The two detectives left the living room and let themselves out through the front door. The earlier light rain had cleared. Wilson stood outside the house staring at the grey clouds zipping across the sky. Three young men who had been residents of an orphans' home had died violently. One over twenty years ago and two within the past few days. Even in Belfast that was too much of a coincidence.

"Our enquiries don't appear to be getting us anywhere," Moira said as her chief settled into the seat beside her.

"If you want to become an ace detective, you're going to have to listen and look a little more carefully" Wilson said looking at her. Moira's normally wild red hair had been plastered to the top of her head by the rain. "Nichol recognised the two names all right. He put on a pretty good act as a poor infirm old man but I think he's a lot bloody smarter than you might give him credit for. He didn't expect us to bring up the Jamison business. I wonder if he knows why the file disappeared."

She started the car and began moving back towards the Crumlin Road.

"Nichol is an ex-politician," Wilson continued. "That means he's a practised liar. I have a strange feeling that we've just been handed a crock of shit. But it's a crock that will probably hold up. Did you notice anything?"

"Nothing much except he seemed pretty particular about his appearance," She turned onto the Crumlin Road and piloted the car back in the direction of Tennent Street. "I'm always a bit suspicious about guys who run football teams or act as councillors for young boys. My Dad reckoned that a lot of them were a bit queer."

"Maybe your Dad should have been a policeman himself." Wilson said. "So you think our friend Nichol is a homosexual?"

"I wouldn't be surprised."

"Neither would I, McElvaney ace of detectives. Neither would I."

As soon as the two detectives had closed the door, Robert Nichol stood up and walked slowly to the window. He pulled aside the curtain and watched them make their way towards their car.

"Rotten bastards," Nichol said under his breath. "Dredging up that filthy little bollocks Jamison after all these years." The dirty little boy had deserved to die. He had cheated shamelessly on him flaunting his new role as a rent boy for all and sundry. He could just about remember the rage he had felt at the time. It had surged through his body and had turned him into a wild animal whose anger could only be satisfied by the letting of blood. Sweat began to break out on his forehead as he re-lived the moment he had ended Jamison's life. He ran his hand through his steel grey hair. Billy had saved his bacon on the Jamison business but the price had been high. He'd been forced, very reluctantly, to step aside and leave Billy in sole control of the Ulster Democratic Front. The party he had helped found was like a baby to him and Billy had demanded that he hand over that baby because of one little transgression which was easily swept under the carpet. And he had reluctantly agreed. He thought that he would never hear the name Jamison again. He shuddered as he thought what might happen if the police opened up that particular can of worms. He didn't think that there was a statute of limitation on murder. He could go to jail for the rest of his life but he would not be alone.

He returned to his chair and flopped into it. Patterson and Peacock, how well he remembered those two boys. He had a mental picture of both Patterson and Peacock as fresh-faced ten year olds. Jesus had called both of them just as he had called Jamison. Except for them he had used an assassin as an intermediary. He had seen a report of Patterson's death on the television and had read about it in the newspapers. The details had been skimpy but it appeared to be a normal sectarian killing. Then a day later Stanley Peacock had been murdered and he had felt a profound feeling of disquiet. He sighed for his former charges. They'd been such beautiful boys. What a pity that they had grown up. And yet he had denied them to Wilson. His feelings of self-preservation had told him that it would be very dangerous for him to admit that he knew them well as boys in Dungray. Surely the Lord was not going to let them punish him after all this time.

"Detective Chief Inspector Wilson," he said quietly to himself. Where had he heard that name before? Although he had been forced out of Ulster's political life he still kept in touch with all his old friends. There was something about DCI Wilson that he should know but he was damned if he could remember what it was. He smiled to himself. There was no need to worry. Jamison was simply a putrid corpse who had momentarily surfaced to bother him. He could be just as easily buried again. There was no evidence linking him to the youth. Not a shred had been kept. He was completely safe. The Lord still had work for Robert Nichol to do. Wilson could yap about his feet like a dog but he could not hurt him. However, a few phone calls would not go amiss. Those who Nichol had served in the past would have to be reminded of their obligations to him. The evil policeman would have to be restrained before he did any lasting damage to God's servant.

CHAPTER 27

Wilson's sense of apprehension, which had been rising since the first moment he had laid eyes on Patterson's corpse, had reached mountainous proportions. As the investigation evolved, the cocktail was becoming more explosive. Three men had been murdered in cold blood apparently by a professional. The only connection between two of those men led to a bizarre unsolved homosexual murder where the file had mysteriously gone missing. The latest piece of the jigsaw, Nichol and his shadowy paramilitary past, only added to Wilson's mounting apprehension. Wilson was an old time policeman. He liked solving crimes and he liked putting the culprits behind bars where they belonged. During his twenty year career in the police force he had come to hate one word - political. Crimes that were 'political' were ten times harder to solve. 'Political' prisoners made a laugh of the penal system and 'political' murderers where released to walk the streets after serving only a fraction of their sentences. Evidence against 'political' criminals conveniently disappeared. Colleagues could not be trusted as shadowy individuals who operated with carte blanche from their political masters manipulated the investigation. He was beginning to get the feeling that the Patterson and Peacock murders could turn out to be 'political' and if that was the case he was in deep trouble. Jennings would jump gleefully on his inability to solve the crimes and attempt to force his retirement.

As soon as they had returned to Tennent Street, directly after their interview with Nichol, Wilson had instructed the young constable to dig up everything the PSNI had on Nichol. The file on the Jamison murder might no longer exist but there should be sufficient material in the archives to get a fix on the ex-warden of Dungray. He had also put in a call to one of his contacts in the 'Belfast Telegraph' and a file on Nichol would soon be dispatched to Tennent Street. Something very rotten was going on and experience told him that the man who slipped the string on the sack would have to jump out of the way pretty damn quick if he was to avoid the shit.

"DI Wilson," Jennings' Secretary said formally as Wilson entered Jennings' outer office. "The DCC is waiting for you." She immediately pressed a button on her secretarial set. "DI Wilson is here," she announced.

Wilson walked to the office door and opened it. He'd expected the call from the DCC's office since he'd arrived back from interviewing Nichol.

Jennings was seated in his elevated position behind his desk. Wilson's eyes were again drawn to the prominently positioned photograph of a smiling Jennings shaking hands with Billy Carlile, Mr. Politics of Ulster. Knowing the `great man' wouldn't do Jennings any harm in his quest for the job of Chief Constable of the PSNI. Carlile was well known for supporting his own men.

"What's this I hear about you broadening the Patterson and Peacock investigation?" Jennings said sharply looking up from the papers on his desk.

"You're very well informed," Wilson said. He wondered who Jennings' informant was. "DC McElvaney found a link between the two men. It's a bit of a shot in the dark but both just happened to be residents in Dungray Home for Boys at the same time."

Jennings shuffled uneasily in his chair.

Jesus Christ, Wilson thought. Why the hell is everybody suddenly on edge? Whitehouse he understood. But the DCC was another matter. The shit was getting very close to the fan.

"That's not all," Wilson said watching the DCC closely. "McElvaney's a bit of a computer buff. She's also keen, hard-working and perseverant. I'm beginning to think that she'll make a hell of a good detective. She found the connection by slaveing all night over a hot machine. During her investigation, two strange things happened. Firstly, she tried to access the file of Robert Nichol who was the director of the orphanage during the period both Patterson and Peacock stayed there. The file is restricted and none of our passwords will open it."

Jennings nervously shuffled the papers before him on the desk.

"You may remember Nichol because he was active in Loyalist politics in the early seventies then dropped out of sight," Wilson continued. "Secondly, it appears that Nichol was questioned in a murder case. The body of another ex-resident of Dungray named Jamison was found dismembered and distributed throughout various parts of North Belfast. DC McElvaney tried to locate the file on this case in our archives but it seems to have gone for a walk. And nobody knows where it's gone to."

"I understand you've been to see Nichol," Jennings said.

Wilson noticed that the DCC had dropped his affected English accent. The effort of keeping it up and keeping his nerve at the same time was obviously too much for him. That was bloody fast he thought to himself. Nichol must have been on the phone as soon as they had left his house. "Yes, I interviewed him," Wilson said.

Jennings sat stiffly in his chair. His hands were pressed together in his praying mantis pose. "I have to say, Inspector, that I don't like the direction this investigation is taking," Jennings said slowly as though dwelling on every word. "Do you have any concrete evidence linking Nichol with either the Patterson or Peacock killings?"

"Not directly," Wilson replied. "But I suspect that he knows something about the two men which could help us in our enquiries."

"That's not good enough," Jennings said.

"No, what's not good enough is that this man's computer file is restricted which is impeding our investigations and that the file pertaining to a serious crime has apparently been purposely removed from our archives. That's what's not good enough."

"This may be the last opportunity I have to tell you that you are currently talking with a superior officer," Jennings' normally pallid face was streaked with red. "Therefore you will treat me with respect and you certainly will not tell me what is and what is not good enough. Do you understand?"

"Yes sir,"

"Good," Jennings relaxed slightly. "The reason Nichol's security file is restricted is that he was involved in our intelligence gathering operations the details of which are still highly confidential and sensitive."

"I'm sorry sir but I don't like the sound of this at all," Wilson said. "Are you telling me that Robert Nichol is effectively off limits?"

"What I'm saying," Jennings leaned forward across his desk, "is that Robert Nichol was part of an intelligence operation which I cannot discuss with you. If you have concrete evidence linking him to the murder of either Patterson or Peacock, you may pursue the matter. If not, he's to be left alone. His security file stays locked. Understood?"

"Perfectly," Wilson said trying to suppress his anger. "And the missing murder file on Jamison?"

"I shall issue an instruction to archives to carry out the most thorough search and to report their findings to me. Have I made myself perfectly clear?"

Wilson stood up. "Perfectly, Sir," he laid on the sarcasm.

"Then you may leave."

Wilson strode towards the door and pulled it open. He marched out banging the door behind him.

The Secretary jumped at the sound and returned to her typing.

What in God's name had he done? Wilson asked himself as he closed the door to the outer office. He'd already slipped the string to the sack and he was being advised to jump back before the shit began to fly. It remained to be seen whether he had sufficient brains to accept what might turn out to be good advice.

DCC Jennings cracked his knuckles and ran through the possibilities in his mind. He perceived Ian Wilson as a definite threat to his ambition of one day reaching the highest level in the Force. Somehow he would have to get the bastard off this particular case. Wilson was the anomaly that the Force could well do without. If only the man would retire, he could promote Whitehouse and then he could sleep easily at night knowing that somebody was covering his back. Maybe Billy could help. Jennings looked at his watch - it was almost five o'clock. Billy would be in the offices of the Ulster Democratic Front. Jennings picked up his private phone and began to dial.

CHAPTER 28

Billy Carlile and Richie Simpson sat across from each other in Carlile's office in the headquarters of the Ulster Democratic Front in Sandy Row just outside the centre of Belfast. The office was sparsely furnished being dominated by a large antique desk surrounded by four wooden straight-backed chairs.

Simpson finished relating the substance of his telephone conversation with Whitehouse.

"I knew that business would come back to haunt us," Carlile said smashing a thin bony fist into the solid oak desk. The six foot long surface was his workplace and was strewn with papers relating to his work as a Member of Parliament. "The question is what are we going to do about it?"

"According to Whitehouse there's no problem for the moment but who's to say that things will stay that way." Simpson had seen the brooding look on Carlile's face before and it generally boded ill for somebody. "I said at the time that we should have let the bastard swing."

"You're the last person in the world that I need telling me `I told you so'," Carlile's face reddened. He looked at his lieutenant who he had dragged from the hands of the paramilitaries and made into a semi-politician. Simpson was smooth enough to utter a 'sound bite' on the evening news without using the words 'fucker' or 'Taig'. But that was where it stopped. He had long ago realised that the UDF was a personal vehicle and that while minnows like Simpson might well like to jump aboard, the vehicle would scarcely outlive his own death. But that wasn't going to be his problem. He was interested in the present. The future could take care of itself. If Nichol threatened his vehicle, then Nichol had better watch out.

"There were reasons at the time as to why we covered up for that pederast," he said his lip curling as he pronounced the final word. "The people who drop their money onto the collection plate might not have been so happy to contribute if they knew that one of the leaders of the organisation had sexual feelings for every young boy under his control. That man was insatiable. All that 'Lord's work this' and the 'Lord's work that' counted for nothing. I took the damn man at his word. Then he goes and gets himself involved with a young man who ends up chopped to pieces. No, Richie, Nichol was a bigger liability than either of us realised. Throwing him over-board was the only thing we could have done. It was him or us and we made the right decision. As long as the cover-up is tight there's no way Wilson can drag up the past." he stared at Simpson the question unasked but hanging in the air.

"Of course the cover-up was tight," Simpson had taken care of it himself with the active assistance of Whitehouse and some of the other boys at Tennent Street. "There's nothing in existence to link Nichol with Jamison. Relax. Like Whitehouse says, so far we don't really have a problem."

Carlile lifted his eyes up to heaven. "Richie, sometimes your lack of intelligence boggles even my mind. We got Nichol out of the limelight but we couldn't turn him into a heterosexual overnight. The man may be laying low but he hasn't changed his spots. If Nichol cracks, then sooner or later it's going to come out that I was involved in helping to place a known homosexual in charge of running an orphanage we controlled. How do you think the devout Protestant people of Ulster are going to see that?"

"It'll never happen," Simpson said.

251

"Never happen my behind," Carlile said. "If Wilson gets his hooks into him, that's what's goin' to happen. Whether we like it or not."

Simpson was about to reply when the telephone on the desk between the two men rang. Carlile nodded and Simpson picked up the phone.

"It's Jennings for you," Simpson said handing over the phone to his mentor.

"Yes, Roy," Carlile said affably.

The leader of the UDF listened carefully to Jennings' report of his meeting with Wilson and the progress on the Patterson and Peacock murders. He let the Deputy Chief Constable tell his story with the minimum of interruptions.

"Don't worry, Roy," Carlile said when Jennings had finished. "We're well aware of the gravity of the situation and we'll take the necessary steps to get the thing sorted out. You and I should meet soon. I heard that the traitor in Downing Street wants to name a new Chief Constable. I think your name should be thrown into the hat." 'Keep them in your debt and you'll keep them in your pocket' was part of his political creed. He could almost feel Jennings' pleasure at the suggestion exuding across the phone line. When Jennings had expressed his gratitude, Carlile rang off and slammed the phone down.

"It's started," he said hunching his thin shoulders. "They're starting to run for the hills. Oh they're not saying that they're going to defect but that's what they'll do when the boom comes down. They're Lundys every man jack of them. That, of course, was our most senior police contact beginning to get the wind up. And he's only the tip of the iceberg. If he folds and Whitehouse follows him then there'll be no telling where it'll end." But he could guess that it might end with him in court on charges of perverting the course of justice. That would be the end of Billy Carlile MP,

MEP. That would be the end of the UDU and the final stop on the 'gravy-train' would have been reached. He was too old to go to jail and he had had money for too long to give it up without a fight. "We're going to have to do something and fast."

"As I see it, Simpson said. "There are two options. Firstly, we can cause a diversion. Get the paramilitaries to launch a sectarian murder campaign so vicious that it'll swamp the murders that Wilson is investigating right now. There are enough psychopaths running around in the UVF and the UFF to make that a reasonable option. The question is what do we offer in return. What do we have that the paramilitaries might want to have? Nothing."

"What's the second option?" Carlile asked.

"We could take care of Nichol ourselves."

"You mean, of course, that he's getting on a bit and that the Grim Reaper could be induced to arrive a day or two early," Carlile said choosing his words carefully.

Simpson nodded. He stared at Carlile fancying that he could see the wheels whirling inside his head. There was nothing more dangerous in the world than a cornered politician.

"That would be a great pity," Carlile said. "Robert Nichol served the cause of Ulster loyally. His loss would be a severe blow and we would labour long and hard to survive it. I suppose I can leave the arrangements to you?" Carlile turned and looked through the window of his office out across the rooftops of Sandy Row. "The end justifies the means," he said in a soft whisper.

As usual, Simpson thought. He stood up to leave and saw that Carlile had disappeared into another world. If there had been a bowl of water handy Carlile would probably have washed his hands. He moved slowly to the door of the office. All his life he'd wanted to be a politician.

To that end he had followed the great man around like a faithful puppy learning every facet of the visceral politics of Ulster. He had joined the UDU to get away from being a killer. He realised that he had not succeeded.

"What a fucking mess," Carlile said to himself after the door to his office closed. "Thirty years building up a political organisation from the backstreets of Belfast to the farmlands of Fermanagh and the whole edifice could come crashing down just because of Robbie Nichol." Carlile turned and glanced at the photo montage on the wall behind him. He'd been a leading figure in Northern Irish politics for what was almost a lifetime. He had come to prominence as a street politician after the political fabric of the Province had collapsed under the weight of the violence of the 'Troubles'. While the Unionist political elite had grown further from their constituency among the rank and file Protestants, Billy Carlile had taken their places by concentrating on grassroots Unionist values. The civil rights disturbances of 1969 had changed the face of Ulster politics forever and had signalled the death knell of rule by the patricians. The era of the terrorist had arrived. And Carlile had been one of the first to recognise the emerging Protestant paramilitary structures as a future power base. He had quit the party of the patricians and had a popular political organisation which for a long time did not attempt to hide its association with the Protestant 'hardmen' who were then establishing themselves in the Loyalist ghettos. The same party leaders who turned their backs on him had been only too willing to crawl back in order to use his contacts in East and West Belfast to raise a secret Protestant militia. He had cleverly resurrected the idea of Sir Edward Carson, Ulster's first Prime Minister, by recreating the local militia staffed mainly by experienced ex-soldiers. The patricians in the Unionist Party had initially clapped him on the back. They thought that his newly created `force' would be instrumental in protecting their farms and their big houses. After the new militia started to cull the Taigs, the Unionist leaders weren't so sure that they should be associated with sectarian murderers. It offended the sensibilities which had been developed on the playing fields of Eton. Carlile moved on to the second phase of his operation. While maintaining his contacts with the 'hard men', his public utterances took on a less radical tone. He distanced himself from the new criminal element which had taken over the organisations he had helped found. His anti-Catholic invective was reserved for closed meeting. He had succeeded in becoming a mainstream politician by grabbing the `middle ground' between the paramilitaries and the retreating patricians. The vehicle he had used to accomplish this feat was the Ulster Democratic Front. The new party embraced the most fundamental type of Loyalist Protestantism and overnight raised him from a controlled Unionist politician into a populist demagogue. He stood at the pinnacle of his powers being recognised by the majority of civilian Protestants and their militant brothers as the epitome of a recalcitrant Ulster. The namby-pambies of the Unionist Party might hand over Ulster to the Papists but he would go to his grave crying 'No Surrender'. This philosophy ensured that he was elected in whichever political contest he entered and he was currently a member of both the British and European Parliaments. The wall of Carlile's office in Sandy Row were covered with photographs of him in the company of the `good and the great' of world politics. In common with the godfathers who ran the Protestant areas, his commitment to the Protestant people of Ulster had not been without its reward.

His flinty grey eyes looked straight ahead. "No Robbie, you'll not bring me down with you," he said softly.

CHAPTER 29

It was almost time for Case to go to work again and it was feeling good. He climbed quietly out of his landlady's bed making sure not to wake the old bag in the process. Betty Maguire had proved as saucy as she had pretended. They had spent the day between screwing and pouring copious amounts of vodka down Mrs. M's throat. The more she drank the more performance she demanded from him and he had satisfied all her little fetishes. Eventually fully sated by sex and vodka the slut had fallen asleep. She wasn't the oldest women he had ever screwed. That distinction belonged to one of the old slags his mother hung around with. He was barely twelve years old when she had pulled him on top of her drunken body and helped him inside her. That type of experience wasn't to be found on the pages of the 'Joys of Sex'. He didn't mind giving it to the old biddies. What he did mind was listening to the drunken life stories. Mrs. Maguire had fairly bent his ear while he'd been pokin' her. He had a friend to the death. He could count on Mrs. M. no matter what. That might be useful over the next few days. He pulled on his trousers and left her bedroom closing the door noiselessly behind him. Moving along the narrow corridor, he entered his own room and locked the door. There was a certain thrill to be had from living right in the centre of his killing ground. Out there on the streets, the police were probably turning the place inside out looking for him and all the while he's sitting right in the middle of them givin' them the finger. The fuzz were so fucking dumb that he could have knocked off half the population of Belfast before the bastards would catch on to him. He looked at his watch. It was six-thirty five. Outside it was already dark. He pulled back the dirty curtains and watched a veil of black clouds from the direction of the Black Mountains roll over Belfast like a dark blanket. If he'd have ordered the weather he couldn't have made a better job of it. He prised up the loose floorboard and lifted out the steel suitcase which contained his weapons. Taking care to follow the opening sequence exactly, he composed the combination and flicked the switches which released the lid of the case. He removed the Browning and a clip of ammunition. He had planned to-night's killing as to be a door step job, a classic IRA assassination. Taking up the classical firing position he pointed the Browning at the cracked mirror on the tallboy. A thrill ran through him. This was the very last sight on earth that to-night's victim would have. He felt the surge of power.

He slowly came out of the firing position and sat on the bed methodically braking down and cleaning the individual parts of the Browning. Lovingly he brushed the dark matt metal of the gun's barrel with the soft cleaning cloth. He stroked the metal as he would a woman's breasts. It was his only true friend. A friend who never disappointed him. Every person in the world that he had trusted had finally betrayed him. That's the way it happened with all of them. His mother used to be his friend but then she tried to turn him in. Norma was his friend until he caught her fucking the black man. The officers in the Regiment were his friends until he was court marshalled. Well fuck 'em. He didn't need anyone except Mr. Browning as his friend. He finished cleaning the gun and re-assembled it. He slipped the weapon and the 13 round ammunition clip into the pocket of his reefer jacket. A two page dossier on his next victim sat on the bed beside him. He picked up the closely typed pages. The title page bore the legend `British Army Intelligence' and beneath it `A report into the activities of Leslie Bingham'. A large red `CONFIDENTIAL' had been stamped across each of the pages. Having friends in high places was the only way to go. It was a pity that all Leslie Bingham had in high places were enemies.

CHAPTER 30

`The Crown' was one of Wilson's favourite haunts. Maybe he was caught in a time warp but he felt comfortable in surroundings which had been maintained exactly as they had been constructed in 1848. There wasn't a piece of laminated plastic in sight and the gaslights produced the kind of ambience which the mock Victorian pubs spent thousands of pounds trying to recreate. He sat in one of the free wooden pews directly beneath an ornate window dating from the construction of the pub. The 'Crown' could make the weather, Belfast, the `troubles' and murder seem a million miles away.

When Kate McCann entered the lounge the eyes of every man in the room swivelled to take in the sight. She was wearing a back jacket and skirt combination over a white blouse which set off perfectly her blond hair and her sallow complexion. Wilson felt his heart rate increase as she made her way towards the table at which he was seated. She stood before him for a full minute before taking the seat directly across from him.

Before either of them could speak a waiter appeared at her side. "Double vodka and tonic," she said stifling his 'Good Evening'.

"Well Ian," she said leaning forward slightly. "I'm here because I found your telephone message intriguing. It sounded rather pathetic and since I have never associated you with being pathetic I thought I should at least see the changes which time has ravaged on you."

"You look fabulous, Kate," he said admiringly. "As usual. And I deserve whatever invective you want to hand out."

The waiter returned and placed a glass containing a double vodka and a small bottle of tonic on the table.

Kate poured some tonic into the glass without taking her eyes off Wilson. "You haven't changed, Ian. You're still the same prick that cast me adrift five years ago. Five years older and yes a little more pathetic but I bet you're still spinning lines aimed at getting into the pants of some young copper."

"You're half right," Wilson said. "I am certainly more pathetic but it has been a hell of a long time since I coaxed any woman to have sex with me."

"And that reputation of yours?"

"A man can live on his reputation for a hell of a long time. Things didn't finish right between you and me. I was wrong to end it the way I did but at that point the guilt was more than I could handle. I know I didn't give Susan the cancer but back then I knew that I had brought plenty of grief into her life. I needed to make up for that by staying with her when she needed me most."

"How gallant," she stared straight at him. "I had a career in Belfast and you took that away from me. You can't imagine how annoyed I was to learn that my psyche was so fragile that a rejection from someone like you could send me into a spiral of depression."

"I'm sorry. It wasn't intentional."

"So I suppose I was just collateral damage.' Anger flared in her eyes.

"No, I should have talked to you but the whole business with Susan and the doctors, the meetings to discuss possible treatments, the disintegration I witnessed in her every day allied to the shit this job throws up left me in a very bad place. I wasn't thinking straight. The days were a blur. After Susan died it took me weeks to get back to myself and by then you were long gone and I heard that you'd been taken on by one of the major chambers in

London. I was history and you had a new life in front of you."

She finished her vodka and tonic and looked towards the bar. The waiter was staring directly at her. She signalled for a refill.

"So that was why you didn't bother to follow me," she said. "The great love that you professed for me while I was in your bed had evaporated and you were happy to see the back of me. My departure didn't strike you as having anything to do with you. I was simply pursuing my dream of working in London. Even a mediocre detective might have put two and two together and come up with four."

The waiter placed a fresh glass containing a double vodka in front of Kate and then left.

"Don't be under any misapprehension, Ian," she said while pouring the tonic into the glass of vodka. "I haven't come here this evening to conduct a post-mortem on our dead relationship."

"Is our relationship dead?" Wilson leaned towards her.

She hesitated for a moment. "It would appear so," she said after some reflection.

"I don't really think you mean that. OK I didn't follow you and maybe I should have but I honestly thought that I was doing you a favour. You're a Queen's Council, Kate. I'm nothing but a copper with a faded rugby career. I'm going nowhere. I'll retire as a DCI. What the hell use am I to someone like you?"

"That was for me to decide. Where did you get my mobile number?"

"I snaffled your card off Jennings' desk."

She smiled. "I may be able to forgive you in time, Ian, but I will never forget."

"That will do for me," Wilson returned her smile and touched her hand. "Damn it all. Kate, but I missed you. Give me a second chance and you won't regret it. "

"We're not there yet, Ian. "

"Shall we begin with dinner?"

" I've got to be the biggest fool in Belfast on two accounts. Firstly, I'm trying to get this idea of a Truth and Reconciliation Commission going and secondly I'm going to have dinner with you.

CHAPTER 31

It was almost half past seven when Case crossed Carlisle Circus and made his way along the east side of the Antrim Road. Winter was descending rapidly on Belfast and as he passed each junction the bitter North East wind that whipped across Belfast Lough cut him like a knife. He ignored his cold fingers and dug his hands deeper into his reefer jacket. The Regiment had trained him to operate whatever the conditions. Heat, cold, rain, all that mattered was getting the job done. The thousands of pounds which the British taxpayer had invested in his training had not gone to waste. All his senses were attuned to the task at hand. His eyes continually scanned the deserted streets. He had already encountered two PSNI Landrover patrols on the short half mile walk from his lodgings in Fortingale Street. That was two too many as far as he was concerned. Maybe it was just his imagination but he thought that there were more coppers on the streets than usual. It was only to be expected that the buggers would be on the look out for him. He smiled to himself. Stupid bleedin' bastards. This was going to be a quick in and out job. The boys in blue wouldn't even realise that he'd come and gone. Leslie Bingham could count himself already dead. He glanced at his watch again. The sod was probably sitting before his telly watching the latest episode of `Coronation Street' without knowing it was going to be the last episode he'd see. He made his way quietly through the narrow streets keeping as close as possible to the houses. The smell of the salt air from the Lough mixed with spilled oil from the docks tickled his nostrils as he turned into Upper Meadow Street. A blast of cold wind from the East hit him as he turned the corner. What a fucking dump, he thought as he plodded along. Cold and wet and fucking miserable. And the locals killed each other because of this shit hole. Mad fucking Paddies. The sooner the Brits pulled out the better. Leave the buggers to slaughter each other. That's what the bastards needed.

Meadow Street was typical of the back streets of East Belfast. The housing stock dated from the end of the nineteenth century and consisted of grimy red bricked terraced houses. He checked the house numbers as he walked slowly along the deserted street. Bingham's looked exactly like all the others. A light was burning in the ground floor window and he could see the blue/red reflection of the coloured television through the net curtains. True to form he thought as he lifted the Browning out of his inside pocket and checked that the safety was off. He screwed on the silencer and stood directly before the door. Taking a deep breath he pressed the buzzer.

A sound of movement came from inside the living room. Case heard the steps approaching the front door and braced himself.

"Yes," Leslie Bingham's face was as blank as a sheet of plain white paper as he opened the door.

Case stood back removing the Browning from his pocket as he did so. He stared into Bingham's face for identification purposes while at the same time raising the gun. The man at the door was the person whose picture was in the file back at the bedsit. He fired the gun three times in rapid succession, the silencer muffling the sound. The top of Bingham's head disintegrated showering fragments of bone and brain along the hall until they splashed against the door at the far end. Bingham's body jerked before falling back into the hall of the house. Case knew his victim had died instantly but he quickly stepped inside and fired one further shot, placing it exactly between Bingham's eyes. He turned and started walking back the way he had come.

None of 'em expect it, Case thought, and smiled to himself. There was no challenge in taking out bozos who couldn't put up a fight. This was money for old rope. He remembered the border engagements between the SAS and the South Armagh Brigade of the IRA. There was a bunch of tough bastards. They never asked for quarter and they didn't expect it. The only prisoners that were taken were the dead ones. He'd never felt more alive than he had when he was in the middle of a fire-fight with the Provos. Best high in the fucking world. It certainly beat the hell out of standin' on some Joe Bloggs' doorstep and blowing the fucker's brains out. You could get brassed off with this job. If it wasn't for all the lovely lolly it was earning. Just one more, he thought as he walked calmly away. One more unknown civilian blown away and then off to the Costa.

The street was still deserted and he had almost reached the end of Meadow Street when he heard an ear piercing scream. Somebody's brain had finally found the gear and Bingham's body had been discovered. It was time to get out of there. The thought of running never entered Case's mind. He had taken part in enough assassinations to know that the first thing that attracted the attention of the police was some silly bugger hoofing it at top speed in the opposite direction from the action. Stay cool, he told himself. He was simply a punter headin' for the nearest boozer for a drink with his mates. He turned left at the top of Meadow Street and could see Girwood Park directly in front of him. In the distance was the grey forbidding shape of Crumlin Road Jail. He crossed the Antrim Road and started towards the entrance of the park.

"Don't move."

Case was startled. He looked around and saw two police constables standing beyond the entrance to the park. The man who had spoken wore a black padded flak jacket over his black police raincoat and held a machine gun cradled in the crook of his arm. A PSNI Landrover was parked twenty yards further along the road. He knew that he'd blown it. If he'd been concentrating he would have noticed the bastards before he walked out into the open.

"Yes, you," the constable said bringing his machine gun to the ready.

Fuck, Case muttered under his breath. No point in tryin' to blast his way out.

"What's a matter. officer," Case said in his broadest Cockney accent. He put both hands in the air.

The two constables looked at one another.

Case smiled inwardly. He knew that his accent would throw the men off guard.

"You don't have to put your hands up," the older constable said moving forward. "Sir," he added as an afterthought

"Fanks, officer," Case said dropping his hands. He was `sir', which meant the imminent danger had passed. He never ceased to marvel at how the Paddies started to bow and scrape as soon as they heard a good old Brit accent. God save the fucking British Empire.

"I'd like to see some identification, sir," the police officer said politely as he approached.

Case looked at the policeman. The copper was thirty pounds overweight and the straps of the bullet-proof vest were stretched to their limit. At close range he would probably have just enough time to nail the two bastards. But what was the point. Two dead coppers could screw-up the rest of his mission. That would piss off his bosses in London. That meant he wouldn't be used in the future. He wondered if either of the two men standing before him would ever know how close they came to death. The main thing was to keep them away from the Browning. That meant he wasn't going to be searched. Some of these bastards weren't as dumb as they looked. Some were even smart enough to put two and two together and come up with four. It was time to play an ace.

"Will this do, me old cock," Case said keeping his Cockney accent as thick as possible. He fished around in his coat pocket and pulled out the card which identified him as a member of British Military Intelligence. He handed the card to the police officer.

The constable let his machine gun hang on its strap while he took the card from Case's hand.

Case watched the expression on the man's face as he looked first at the card and then at him. He was hard put not to break out laughing in the constable's face. That put an end to your gallop, old son, he thought. There was no way he was going to be searched now. He'd been told only to use the card as a last resort. This was a last resort.

The fat constable looked at the card a second time.

"I don' suppose you'd like to tell me what you're doing here, Mr. Gardiner?" the constable asked, a new tone of respect noticeable in his voice. He handed Case back the card.

"Now you know better than that, officer," Case slipped the card nonchalantly into his pocket. "What's the flap?"

The police officer stared at Case. "We just got a report of a shooting incident in one of the adjacent streets. Some poor bastard was shot on his doorstep."

"Fuckin' IRA," Case said and spat into the gutter. "I'd love to run across one of the bastards. They should be strung up by the balls."

"We've got the area surrounded. Maybe this time we'll get our hands on the bastards." Constable Stanley McColgan had always gone by his instincts and he didn't like the man standing before him. Gardiner was young and fit and looked just like what you'd expect an undercover man from Military Intelligence to look like. In fact Gardiner looked just like every other British soldier in the Province. McColgan hesitated. Something told him that he should call this one in but standing orders were to keep out of these people's way. The Military Intelligence card looked genuine enough and the bloke was definitely a Brit. The thought of searching Gardiner flitted through McColgan's mind. Why should these people be above the law? Maybe for once he should disobey an order. But what if Gardiner complained to his superiors about being searched? McColgan would get a sharp kick in the balls from his own boss. It wasn't worth it. There were so many undercover people running around the Province it was a wonder they didn't get in each other's way. Standing orders were standing orders and Stanley McColgan was one for sticking to the letter of the law.

"I'd get out of here sharp if I was you," McColgan said. "Or you're goin' to be flashin' that card all night."

The two constables walked back in the direction of their Landrover.

That old bastard isn't as stupid as he looks, Case thought as he watched the two men re-join their vehicle. He saw the fat constable throw a final glance over his shoulder at him. Maybe it hadn't been such a good idea not to kill the two coppers. He quickly replayed in his mind the scene between himself and the policeman searching for some mistake he'd made which made the copper suspicious. There was nothing he could remember. Still he'd take even money that the old cop would spout off to somebody before the evening was out. What if he does? He said to himself. It would take some kind of evil genius to put together a report that a phoney Military Intelligence agent named Bryan Gardiner was in the area where a shooting took place linking him to the murder of Bingham. He glanced at his watch. It was already past eight o'clock and he had some important phone calls to make.

"Police confidential," the first voice on the PSNI confidential number was invariable female, soft and warm.

"Just before nine o'clock this evening, an active service unit of the Irish Republican Army executed Leslie Bingham for crimes against the Republican people of Belfast." Case's Belfast accent would have passed muster in even the most critical public houses on the Falls or Shankill Roads.

"Would you repeat that please?" the woman said.

Case carefully repeated the message.

"May I have your name please," the woman's voice was complete without emotion. Case wondered if she spent her day talking to murderers.

Case took the Sim card out of his mobile phone and tossed it in the gutter. A light mist was enveloping Belfast and the large imposing Victorian jail across the road. He looked at the red bricked facade. It looked like something out of those corny Hammer House of Horror films. Nobody was ever going to put him into one of them places. The bastard of an officer who'd put him in the cooler had paid. Two days after his discharge came through he broke into his house and raped his wife. I'll bet the bastard is more careful who he shops these days. With a bit of luck he's tryin' to deal with a little bastard he'd left behind him.

He walked off into the mist heading for Fortingale Street. He'd call London later and report his success.

CHAPTER 32

Wilson was in mid-sentence when his mobile phone rang. He reached into his pocket and switched the unit off.

"Blast that bloody thing," he said removing his hand from his pocket and resuming eating.

"Aren't you going to answer it?" Kate asked. She was surprised and more than a little annoyed with herself at how quickly they had fallen back into the old routine. If it wasn't for the pain he had caused her by his rejection she might have imagined that London had been a dream. Maybe it was the human condition to let bygones be bygones. She had known from the moment that she had met him that he was the 'one'. There had been plenty of men before him but she had never felt the depth of emotion for them that she had felt for him. Sometimes she wanted to kick herself for feeling the way she did. She had graduated top of her class at Queen's University which proved that she wasn't exactly dumb but how could she correlate her intelligence with her need to be loved by Ian Wilson.

"Don't you start behaving like a school-teacher," he forked some sweet and sour pork into his mouth and washed it down with a glass of Cote du Rhone Villages. He was feeling good for the first time in months. For once the mellowness wasn't associated with large quantities of booze. He was simply happy to be in the company of the woman he had been willing to leave Susan for. Why did the bloody mobile have to ring just now? Over the past two hours he had managed to forget Tennent Street, Ulster, killings. Couldn't the bastards have given him at least one evening of total relaxation? What were his needs against the reason his mobile had rung. In all likelihood somewhere in his area a human being had probably just died violently.

"You know that you really want to respond to the call," she looked at him reprovingly. "I've been around you enough to understand your code of loyalty to the job. What are you waiting for? Answer the bloody thing."

He looked at her. The drinks in the 'Crown' and the wine had added colour to her face. What a stupid bloody fool he'd been. What sort of idiocy had made him inflict his own guilt trip on the woman he had professed to love? Somehow he was going to make it up to her.

"They'll start getting frantic if you don't call in soon," she said breaking his train of thought. "It may be nothing. Why don't you find out?"

He stood up. "I suppose I'd better because I'm not going to be allowed to sit here all night enjoying myself without you reminding me of my duty to the good people of Ulster."

She watched him as he reluctantly pulled the mobile out of his pocket and switched it on again. He always reminded her of one of those big ageing bears on a natural history television programme. The ambling creature was still strong enough to lash and maim those around him who threatened him but the realisation was beginning to dawn on him that with his strength rapidly disappearing his days were numbered. She had never before noticed the crows feet which extended from the corner of his eyes. The skin on his face looked soft and puffy. Maybe he was suffering from burnout. If he was, he wouldn't be the first police officer to hit that particular wall. Nobody knew better than her the legion of enemies he had amassed during his years on the Force. The wolves scented blood and they were gathering to pull him to pieces. Maybe he would be smart enough to give them all the finger and get out completely. No matter how hard she wished for it she knew that it would never happen. He was like one of those heavy dray horses who when set free immediately look for a carriage to be hooked up to. He'd been born to be a copper. In any other job he would have shrivelled up and died.

His mobile started ringing as soon as he switched it on. He listened without speaking and then said Ok before cutting the communication.

"Jesus Christ but there's no rest for the wicked," he said pushing his unfinished meal away. "It looks like our friend with the nine millimetre has been out and about again. Somebody just murdered some poor bastard over beside the New Lodge. The brass want me to drop whatever I'm doing and get over there straight away."

"If that's the case don't let me keep you," she felt like screaming. "Just find the bastard and shove the result up Jennings and the rest of them. We can always pick up where we left off." She tried to keep the disappointment out of her voice but she wasn't' quite sure how well she was succeeding.

"You can be sure of it," he hated the job at moments like this. "Look, maybe I could call around later this evening."

"Remember what I said in the 'Crown'," she said fighting with her desire to say 'why not'. "We can't start from where we left off. Let's take it easy for a while. You get yourself off and find that bloody murderer. I'll settle things here."

He stood looking down at her. "I'm glad we got together again."

She thought before replying. " We're not there yet, Ian. You're just lucky I took pity on you, ye big oaf."

He leaned over quickly and kissed her hard on the lips. "I'll give you a call in the morning," he said when they both reluctantly broke off the kiss.

He squeezed her hand and then made for the door.

"Shit!" Wilson punched the steering wheel of the Toyota as he took his place behind the wheel. Why couldn't the bastard have taken a holiday to-night? He was feeling more emotions than he felt was good for him. Sure he wanted to catch the bastard with the nine millimetre but he also felt that if Kate and he had been permitted to spend the evening together they would inevitably have ended up in bed. He hadn't had sex since his wife died. That was bloody ironic because he had put it about enough when she was alive. He felt the need to make love to a woman stronger than he had ever felt it before. He took one last look at the exterior of the restaurant and started the car. He drove from Donegal Square up Royal Avenue and on into York Street. The wall of the dockyards ran parallel with his route as he drove towards the address on Meadow Street which had been the scene of the latest murder. Even from the scant details he had received on the phone, he had no doubt that the killing in Meadow Street was the work of the same man who had killed Patterson and Peacock. Ballistics would set a seal on it but in his mind it was already a sure thing. The ballistics tests were only a formality. This latest killing might be the straw that would break the camel's back. Four murders in the space of a few days would have the Protestant psychopaths champing at the bit. Blood would have blood as Mr. Shakespeare wrote on one occasion. But why was it happening now? Who could be crazy enough to start a sectarian war when the mood of the people was for peace? Maybe he'd already had his chance to find out and failed. The pressure to get him off the case would mount. And always in the background were the shadow men. The puppet masters who saw themselves as the defenders of the realm and who would stoop to any kind of dirty ploy to attain their aims. He crossed the Westlink motorway and continued on past the York Dock before turning into Duncairn Gardens. He wondered whether he'd already had too much of Belfast. Sometimes Jennings' threat of a beat in South Armagh actually appeared attractive beside ten more years on the city streets. Maybe he'd be able to have some class of a life with Kate if he could only get away from the mean streets. He looked out at the rows of dirty terraced houses. Belfast was the best candidate for urban renewal he'd ever seen. Maybe if they tore down the ghettos the sectarian divide might also disappear. Was there some sociological reason why the areas of greatest sectarian conflict were also the most run-down and dirty? On the Falls and in the Shankill, it was simply different coloured rats in the same sewer tearing at each other while in middle class areas life went on as usual. There was no sectarian strife in Malwood Park. No graffiti of hooded terrorists decorated the walls in Malone, Dunmurray or Hollywood. None of his yuppie neighbours feared the knock on the door which was the prelude to a sectarian murder. They sat safely in their middle class homes while the rats in the Shankill and the Falls devoured each other.

The yellow strands of crime scene tape restricting access to the murder spot that had been set up across the junction of Lepper Street and Duncairn Gardens. Wilson pulled the Toyota into the side of the road and got out. A light hazy rain swirled around in the grey light cast by the street lamps. A single young constable stood guarding the orange and red luminous tape. With his laminated black body armour slung outside his regulation raincoat, Wilson thought that he didn't so much resemble a policeman as a creature from one of George Lucas' space movies. The street was deserted except for the constable. He flashed his warrant card at the young policeman and made his way up the twenty yards of Lepper Street which separated Duncairn Gardens from Meadow Street. The scene he encountered when he turned into Meadow Street was so usual as to be boring. A bank of arc lights shot streams of cream coloured light into the hall-way of a house thirty yards in front of him. An ambulance and two police cars were parked in front of the house and he noticed the technical people's van ten yards further on. He walked slowly towards the garishly lit scene. He was ten yards from the house when Whitehouse exited from the front door and stepped onto the path.

"You're just in time," Whitehouse opened his white overall and stuffed his notebook into the side pocket of his coat. "We were about to move the stiff," he stood back to reveal the corpse lying on his back in the centre of the hallway.

"You've too much delicacy for this job," Wilson said pushing past his sergeant. "Don't you ever think that somebody might be listening."

"The deceased's name is Leslie Bingham," Whitehouse glanced at his notebook. "We're runnin' him through the computer. I'd bet a month's pay the slug checks out with Patterson and Peacock. The fuckin' bastard is going' after Prods. It's got to be Cahill or one of his crew."

And I'd bet a month's pay that Leslie Bingham turns out to be an ex-inmate of Dungray, Wilson thought to himself. "Any family?" he asked moving to the body.

"Wife and one kid," Whitehouse replied. "Usual story. Knock on the door. Bang, bang. The wife can't think of any reason why it should have been him. She was still hysterical when I got here. I only managed to get a few words out of her before the medics sedated her."

Wilson looked at what was left of Bingham. The shots had all been aimed at his head and it didn't look like any of them had missed. The side walls of the hallway were sprayed with flecks of dark red cranial blood and the door at the end of the corridor was splattered with a tapestry of red blood interspersed with grey tissue which he recognised as brain. The pattern reminded him of the red splattered cards in a Rorschach test. Bingham had been dead well before he hit the ground.

"Where's the wife and kid now?" Wilson asked automatically.

"Next-door neighbours," Whitehouse replied. "She's probably out cold by now from the size of the injection they gave her."

"What else do you have?" Wilson asked.

"Sweet FA. Three slugs dug out of the wall. Nobody seen leaving the scene. Just a matter of waitin' for the sodding phone call."

"Is he connected?"

"Ask your Taig friend, McElvaney. She's probably the one runnin' him through the computer."

"I thought I told you about the 'Taig' shit. Drop it. What else do you have? Anybody see the bastard?"

"Wise up," Whitehouse replied. "Nobody will admit to seein' anything. Right. The wife thought he was away a bit long so she went to investigate. That's the way she found him. The bastard must have used a silencer. The television was on. We haven't completed the `house to house' yet but my guess is that like the rest of them we won't turn up a hair. The lab boys should be here shortly."

"When can we expect something from ballistics?"

"Do we really need to go down that road? We'll get the slugs over there as soon as we can and put an urgent on them. They might have something for us tomorrow. If we're

277

lucky. They can't tell us anymore than we sodding well know, can they? It's the same gun and the same bastard and he's laughin' at us."

Wilson stood over the stricken man.

"As they say in darts," Whitehouse said. "Nice grouping."

The sight was grisly. Seeing the inside of a man's head scattered about a confined space was apt to turn the stomach of even the most battle-hardened copper. Wilson wondered how Bingham's wife had reacted to the sight. At least he was dead, his wife would carry the mental images of this night with her for the rest of her life. He wondered who the killer had really hurt the most. Mrs. Bingham was just another victim of Northern Ireland's reign of violence. It was hard to disagree with the logic that said the dead were the lucky ones. Whitehouse was right. They didn't need the results of the ballistics tests to know that he was looking at the handy work of the `professional'. There was a surgical precision about the killing which showed that the assassin's hand hadn't even so much as slightly wavered when he'd fired. The bastard who did this was a cold bloody fish, he thought. It took nerves of steel and skill to shoot with such calm assurance. The murderer was bloody good at his job.

Wilson made his way to the front door and pulled in a breath of cold fresh air. Outside a police van was disgorging the lab team already wearing their white plastic overalls.

Whitehouse's radio crackled. He listened to the radio for a few moments and then turned to face Wilson. "True to form. Claimed by the IRA."

Yes, Wilson thought, true to form but why didn't he buy it. It'd be so easy to lay it at the feet of the terrorists. Another unsolvable crime until somebody in the cells at Castlereagh or Kilburn broke down and admitted it. He sucked in a deep breath trying to clear his mind. These political crimes were a bloody labyrinth. When you thought you could see the light at the end of the tunnel it usually turned out to be a train heading in your direction. His stomach rumbled and he got the taste of sweet and sour bile in his mouth. He was beginning to feel like a man on a precipice. One false move and he would tumble into the abyss. And he probably wouldn't be alone.

"They can take him away now," he said and walked towards the nearest police car. He waved to the head of the forensics team. "

He pulled the mobile phone from his pocket and called the Station. "Get me McElvaney," Wilson said tersely into the phone.

"Evening, boss," Moira's voice sounded tired. Join the club, Wilson thought. A couple of days in Tennent Street had put a dent in her youthful zest.

"Not a very good evening, I'm afraid, Moira," Wilson tried to put an enthusiasm he didn't feel into his own tone. "Anything on this Bingham character?"

"Do you have any specific question you want to ask, boss?"

"Don't pull my bloody chain, Moira, I'm not in the mood. What do you have?"

"He was in Dungray the same time as the others," she paused to let the information sink in.

"I had a bet with myself on that one. I won. Anything else."

"Not a sausage," she said. "But it's early days. I just did the most obvious check. If we have four victims three of whom were inmates of Dungray at the same time, shouldn't that mean something." She left the obvious conclusion to her chief.

Wilson held the phone without speaking. Dungray had to be the key to this whole affair. And his connection with Dungray was Robert Nichol. So whether God almighty Jennings liked it or not he was going to squeeze Nichol until the bastard squealed. They were all connected somehow: Jamison's death, the missing file, the block on Nichol's file and the four murders. All would lead back to the spider or spiders sitting at the centre of the web pulling the strings. And when he nabbed the spider, he would have the murderer as well.

"Thanks Moira," Wilson felt the young woman needed a lift. "You've done a terrific job so far. Away off home with you and have a rest. I'm goin' to need you in top form early tomorrow morning."

"Goodnight, boss," she replied and the phone went dead.

Wilson handed the microphone back to the officer in the car and moved back towards the house. Bingham's body had been removed from the hallway and dark red blood stains splattered the area around the chalk mark on the floor which indicated where Bingham's body had lain. He searched among his emotions for the revulsion he should have felt at the scene. There was none. He had seen it all so many times before. The only emotion he felt was anger.

He turned to face Whitehouse. "Time to call it a night, George." Wilson left the hallway and stood on the footpath. There was nothing more either of them could usefully do. A solitary police Landrover that stood outside the house the only remaining evidence that a crime had been committed there.

"Fuck it," Whitehouse said and pulled the hall-door shut behind him. "Another body and we're nowhere nearer to nailin' the bastard."

"Excuse me, sir."

Wilson turned and noticed that one of the constables had detached himself from the Landrover and stood before the two detectives.

"Yes Constable," Wilson said. The man who had addressed him was about fifty years of age. He smelled a veteran who had the desire to live long enough to collect his pension. He looked into the man's face and recognition dawned on him. "It's Stanley McColgan isn't it?"

"You've got a good memory, sir," McColgan beamed.

"I never forget a good man, Stanley. What can I do for you?"

"It may be nothing," McColgan began hesitantly. "But right after the murder we stopped a man over by Girwood Park." McColgan paused as though deciding whether to proceed. "As soon as I started to question him, the bloke pulled out a Military Intelligence ID card."

"What!" Wilson said. "Was it genuine?"

"It looked genuine enough." McColgan saw the consternation on Wilson's face and knew in that instant that he had screwed up mightily. "But something about the bastard's been bothering me since. I know I should have pulled him but we're not supposed to stop them guys."

All Wilson's faculties were now trained on the constable. "You weren't to know. Tell me, Stanley, what did the man look like?"

"He was wearin' a black reefer jacket. I'd guess his height at about six feet. Weighed maybe eleven stone. His hair was plastered to the top of his head so I couldn't tell the colour but it was cut short in a sort of military fashion. That's another reason why I thought he might be genuine. Jesus it's hard to remember what he looked like. He was clean shaven with rugged features. His eyes seemed to look straight through me. They sent a bloody chill up my spine." McColgan remembered the feeling and didn't appreciate it.

"The bastard was bad news. I remember the name on the ID. card. It was Bryan Gardiner."

"What about his accent?"

"Cockney. I don't know if it was genuine but I'd bet my life he was a Brit alright."

"Did you search him?" Wilson asked.

McColgan pulled his cap tighter on his head. "No, Sir, I didn't."

Wilson knew that there was no point berating the older man for his error. "What makes you think he wasn't the real thing?"

"I can't put my finger on it but there was something about the bastard that didn't smell right. He looked and sounded the part and the card he produced was genuine enough but thirty years on the job tells me he was as phoney as a two pound note. If it wasn't for the standin' order sayin' not to screw M.I. up, I would have taken the bugger along."

"Would you recognise him if you saw him again?" Wilson asked hopefully.

"I think so. You get your hands on him and I'll finger him."

"Thanks Stanley, you've been a great help. One of my boys will contact you to-morrow and we'll take a detailed statement."

McColgan turned to leave and then turned back to face Wilson. "I know I screwed up, Chief Inspector, but the way things are I might have been in a bigger mess if I'd pulled him and he'd been genuine."

"I understand that, Stanley. You did the right thing." Wilson watched as McColgan made his way to the waiting police car. Both McColgan and he knew that there had been a screw up. There was no point in making a big deal of it.

"Is that it for to-night?" Whitehouse asked.

"What's that George?" Wilson's mind was miles away. Another piece had been added to the jigsaw but instead of assisting a solution it simply muddied the waters even more.

"I'd like to get out of here if that's OK with you," Whitehouse said.

"Off home with you," Wilson said. "There's nothing more we can do here this evening. I want you round here first thing in the morning to interview the widow."

Whitehouse was trying to make sense of the night's events. He shuffled away towards the Antrim Road taking the path used earlier by Case. Jesus Christ, he thought, how the hell was Military Intelligence involved in leaving four Prods dead? Were the Brits tryin' to start a war? This was a vital piece of information which would have to be passed on double quick. He paused when he reached the Antrim Road. He looked back and saw that there was nobody behind him. He pulled his mobile phone from his pocket. Simpson would want to know about the man with the Military Intelligence ID card.

Wilson punched his right fist into his open left palm without even feeling the blow. Like Whitehouse he was trying to make sense of what he had learned. It was very possible that the man McColgan had stopped was the man they were looking for. If that was so, they had just missed the only break they'd had in the case to date. But how and why did the murderer have access to what appeared to be a genuine MI ID card? And who the hell was he working for? There were a lot more questions than answers so far. McElvaney and the `magic machine' at the office would check `Gardiner' out. The result would be that no such person ever existed and that no M.I. card had ever been issued in that name. Even the `magic machine' could be presented with a blank wall. This case was turning him into a clairvoyant. He cursed having let McElvaney go for the night and started walking back through the rain towards his car. The closer he got to the killer and the motive for the murders the more muddy the water was becoming. Getting out of this one was going to take tact and diplomacy. Two qualities for which he'd never been well-known. Box clever, Ian me auld son, he said to himself as he slipped under the yellow crime scene tape.

CHAPTER 33

Robert Nichol pressed a button on the remote control and the channel changed on the television. Nichol stared at the screen. Two women comedians tried to outdo each other in being crude. "Lord God," Nichol said softly and shook his head as another stream of profanity burst upon his ears. To his mind women talking about their bodily functions was the height of toilet humour. This is what we've come to by throwing away Christian values, he thought. There was a time in the recent past when a woman didn't use words which were more common on building sites. Now anything went. God would certainly exact a great punishment from these women for their sins. Nichol pressed the buttons again flicking through the stations looking for a news programme. He was still unsure of the content of what he had picked up from the end of the previous BBC News programme. Could it really be true that the Leslie Bingham of Meadow Street who had been murdered by the IRA was the same person as the wee boy who had been in his charge all those years ago at Dungray? May God have mercy on his immortal soul if it was. And may the Republican bastards who killed him rot in hell. The news of Bingham's death had brought pain tinged with such wonderful memories. They had all been there in the golden years of Dungray. Leslie had been such a beautiful little boy. Just like Jimmy Patterson and Stan Peacock. And that deceitful little bastard Jamison. All his beautiful boys were being killed off. He hadn't meant to kill Jamison. The threat of exposure had driven him mad. The devil had temporarily entered his body and had made him do dreadful things. All his life he had fought against invasions of his body by the satanic powers. Nobody had blamed him for killing the little ingrate. Even God had forgiven him. All that was over now. He hadn't had to go to prison or anything like that. Billy had organised it so that nobody had to go to jail. He had been able to go on almost as before. His eyes stared at the screen of the television but they saw in his mind's eye the parade of young men he had inducted into the ranks of the `Save Ulster' volunteers. That had been his finest hour. A group of fine upstanding young Protestant men had been established to fight for their God and their Province. The devil had entered his body many times during those years. The heady mix of religious fundamentalism and patriotism made the young men's sexual juices flow. The devil in Robert Nichol had taken full advantage of every possibility open to him. Those had been the halcyon days: his beautiful boys at the home and a steady supply of dedicated youths through `Save Ulster'.

Nichol moved his position in the chair and a pain shot through his hip. The operation hadn't been a total success. He would pray to God and they would try again. For the present he would be grateful for small mercies. His lifestyle of twenty years ago if followed to-day would undoubtedly have led to his death in this age of Aids. What a pity that Jimmy and Stan and Leslie had to die so young. Nichol suddenly felt cold and he raked the fire into life. A ghost had passed over his grave. He gripped his Bible in his hand and his small eyes darted around the room searching in the shadows. His beautiful boys were being removed one by one. "My soul is clean," he whispered under his breath. "Dear God, my soul is clean."

Case whistled as he ambled along the road from his digs. The job was going according to plan. No sweat. A few more days in dreary old Belfast and then a couple of months in the sun. He never used a mobile for his contacts with London. Not since the 'Tampon' tapes anyway. But it was a hell of a job finding a public telephone box in the era of the mobile phone. He pulled open the door of the phone box and went inside. He carefully stacked four fifty pence pieces on the phone and then dialled the number. The phone gave two rings and was then picked up.

"Yes," the voice on the other end said.

"Mr. Bingham's package arrived this evening," Case said using the code he'd been given.

"That is excellent news," the voice appeared pleased. "So far you've performed excellently, Mr. Case. We are more than happy with your work. However, there has been a rather unexpected hitch. I'm afraid you will have to deliver two more packages than we anticipated. Some rather important ones."

"The more packages that get delivered the higher the cost," Case said smelling a sizeable bonus to his already substantial fee. He'd manage at least a year in the sun out of this job.

"That is completely understood," the voice said smoothly. "We think that seven and a half thousand per package would be a fair figure."

"That seems about right by me," Case was surprised by the level of payment but there was no way he was going to show it. "Who do I deliver to?"

"I've arranged for the details of the recipients of the packages to be available at the dead letter drop we agreed before your departure. Delivery must be made immediately"

"That's not the way I work," Case said. Rush jobs generally ended in fuck-ups.

"We're sure that you're equal to the task."

"If I can't make it to-night, what about to-morrow?" Case asked.

"The financial arrangements are consequent on delivery to-night, "the voice said firmly. "Perhaps the packages should have Czechoslovak stamps."

"I'll do my best," Case said thinking of the extra fifteen thousand pounds.

"Good man. I knew we could count on you. Report to-morrow."

The line went dead on Case. Had he held the apparatus to his ear for just a fraction of a second more he would have heard the click as the voice activated tape recorder on the phone at the other end switched itself off.

Simpson walked purposefully towards the small terraced house in Ligoniel. He'd taken the precaution of parking his car several streets away. The cold wind swirled around him. It was a blast that foretold a hard winter. He put his hand in his pocket and felt the jagged edges of the Walther P38. The gun was the kind of museum piece that Nichol might be expected to have locked away. He turned into Glenside Park and walked quickly to the door of Nichol's house. He knew the house well. Many years before he'd been one of those Protestant youths who had been fired by Nichol's brand of patriotism and Protestant fundamentalism. He'd been one of the first recruits of 'SAVE ULSTER'. He'd sat at the feet of the master and dedicated himself to do whatever was necessary to preserve a Protestant Ulster. And because of that he'd been one of the first to discover Nichol's 'weakness'. Robert Nichol didn't give a shit about Ulster. All he wanted was a supply of young boys to feed his desires.

The old bastard was still awake, Simpson thought when he saw the light burning in the downstairs lounge. He suddenly wanted to be somewhere else. If there'd been more time, he would have organised it differently. He should have gone to Rice and had one of the UVF psychos finish Nichol. But that would have put him in Rice's pocket for the rest of his life. The IRA might have done the job for him but they had no interest in killing Nichol. He was more of a liability to the Protestant cause alive than dead. It wouldn't be the first time that the other side had helped out with one of the Prods pressing problems. Killing Nichol didn't bother him. It was twelve years since he had been blooded by the UVF and ever since then he'd been respected as a `hard man'. He also had a personal score to settle with the old bastard.

He knocked on the door. The sound of the television ended abruptly and he noticed from the corner of his eye a movement in the curtain of the lounge window. You didn't get old in the Northern Ireland political game by not being careful. Nichol had spent more than half his life on IRA death lists and they still hadn't managed to nail him. He heard a shuffling noise from inside and then a series of locks being opened.

"Richie," the door opened just wide enough to admit Simpson. "Get yourself inside."

Nichol shuffled out of the younger man's way. "You can't be too careful," he said re-locking the door.

Simpson heard a series of bolts sliding into place. The house was like a bloody fortress. It had been at least two years since he had seen Nichol. He was taken aback at how well the old pederast continued to keep himself.

Nichol's lips were lightly rouged and he could see the traces of the cosmetics which covered the old man's face.

"Hello, Bob," Simpson waited until the door had been locked before he spoke. "I was in the neighbourhood and I thought I'd drop in."

Nichol raised his eyes. "Long time no see, Richie," Nichol walked slowly ahead of Simpson. "Come into the lounge. Can I get you a wee drink?"

"No thanks," Simpson dropped into an ancient over-stuffed cloth covered armchair.

"You were in the neighbourhood, you say," Nichol sat down opposite the young man. He felt apprehensive but didn't know why.

"How are you, Bob?" Simpson asked.

"The good Lord is still taking care of me," Nichol leaned on his walking stick accentuating its presence. "I don't think the hip operation was a success so I might have to go in again soon. You're looking good. Life in the Ulster Democratic Front agrees with ye. You say that you were in the neighbourhood but I fancy you want me to do something for you or Billy. Would I be right?" He smiled his most disarming smile. He had always known that sooner or later they would come crawling back looking for his help.

You're right, only we'd like you to drop dead, Simpson thought instantly.

"I hear the police paid you a visit to-day," Simpson leaned back in the chair. "We're gettin' the willies that somebody might start diggin' around in the Jamison business. It seems that we didn't cover your tracks as well as we might have."

Nichol hid his disappointment and looked into Simpson's thin face trying to divine the 'real' purpose of his visit. There was no immediate danger. Billy didn't send the likes of Simpson out to murder people but what his guest reported back could seal his fate.

"My soul is clean," Nichol said clasping his hands over his chest. "I sinned but the Lord God has forgiven me. There's nothing that man born of woman can do to me now. My sin was absolved years ago."

"You're not on the pulpit now, Bob. This is Richie. You can cut the bullshit."

"Do you remember the early days of the `Save Ulster' group?" Nichol said.

Bad tactic, Simpson thought as he nodded. It was the last thing he needed to be reminded of right now.

"We sat around in this very room formulating the plans which were going to keep Ulster British. Those were heady days Richie, weren't they?"

Were they? Simpson nodded again. He could smell the cheap Eau de Cologne that Nichol was wearing. He should have known. But he'd been young and he'd been wrapped up in the whole 'Save Ulster' business. He didn't know his arse from his elbow but Nichol was going to teach him. What a bloody fool he'd been. Taken in by one of the oldest tricks in the book. Nichol had used his powers of speech to whip up the young volunteers. But what he really wanted was fresh young arses.

"You know I helped Billy set up the Ulster Democratic Union," Nichol said.

Simpson nodded slowly.

"Of course you do," Nichol smiled at the recollection. "Sure weren't you there yourself with us." He pulled his chair closer to Simpson. "By God we showed the Brits who wielded the political power in this Province."

Keep talking, Simpson thought. Keep reminding me. You're only makin' it easier for me to do what has to be done.

"That little ingrate Jamison nearly ruined everything for us," Nichol continued. "God forgave me and thank God that Billy cleared all that business up. I have nothing to fear. All the evidence was destroyed. The policemen who came here to-day were only groping in the dark. They know nothing."

Maybe not now, Simpson thought, but they suspect and that might be enough to bring the whole house of cards tumbling down. Billy had been right. Nichol was living in his glorious past and if somebody was willing to listen long enough to his ramblings, all kinds of secrets might come out.

"Billy's worried," Simpson said simply.

"Sure there's nothing to worry about," Nichol forced a smile. His apprehension had returned with the realisation that Simpson would do whatever was necessary to protect the UDF. If that meant he had to die, then Simpson certainly wouldn't flinch from the act.

Simpson stood up slowly. "Ever since you screwed up with Jamison you've represented a major threat to the UDF." He walked across the narrow lounge and stood beside Nichol. "Against the advice of everybody else, Billy stood by you. The police're goin' to try and re-open the whole business. It's time you paid Billy back."

Nichol turned and looked up at Simpson. "You're not serious," he reached out his hand and touched Simpson on the leg. "You and I were very close once."

"Get your hands off me," Simpson said sharply. The smell of Nichol's Eau de Cologne swam in his nostrils. That smell forced to the surface the memories he had suppressed for many years back. I should have killed the bastard years ago, he thought looking at Nichol's shrinking figure.

"You wouldn't would you, Richie?" Tears forced their way along Nichol's cheeks. "Jesus doesn't want you to do this."

"This time God wants you to die," Simpson removed the Walther from his coat pocket. "We'd prefer if it looked like you did it yourself. There'll be fewer questions. Just put your fingers around the butt and I'll do the rest. Jesus is calling you."

Nichol looked at the small revolver. It was the time of retribution. He was being called by God to pay for all the dreadful sins he had committed during his life. The youthful faces of Jimmy, Stanley and Leslie swam before his eyes as he extended his right hand towards Simpson. Such beautiful boys to have died so young. Nichol felt he was swimming in a dream and that he was being asked to make a magnificent gesture. The Lord wanted him to die. He would be a wonderful martyr. He would follow the beautiful boys and stand before God for the part he had played in their deaths. He felt the matte plastic grip of the revolver against the palm of his hand and he closed his fingers around it. Dear God forgive me for all the wrong I've done during my life. He felt Simpson rotating his hand but he kept staring steadfastly before him at a picture of Jesus on the opposite wall. Such beautiful boys, he thought as the gun exploded beside his ear.

The noise of the shot reverberated around the tiny sitting room. Nichol's body slid slowly over the arm of the armchair and Simpson let the gun fall naturally onto the floor. He bent quickly and felt for a pulse. Nothing. It was time to get out. Shots were nothing new in Ligoniel and he had no fear of being stopped in such a staunchly Protestant area. He took one more look at Nichol's dead body and left the room.

CHAPTER 34

Case paced anxiously around his room. After phoning London he'd gone straight to the dead letter box and retrieved the papers which had been sent by his boss. If he'd known the contents, he would have asked the bastard in London for double. Taking out a couple of stupid stiffs who didn't suspect a thing was one job, but taking out two policemen on one night was a totally different kettle of fish. He looked at the dossiers one more time. A fucking detective chief inspector and a sergeant. The files were copies of the original personnel dossiers on the two men. What chance did these poor bastards stand against the kind of juice that could lift their confidential files at will? If they hadn't been lining his pockets, he could have felt sorry for the poor sods. The bastard in London was right. This wasn't a walk up and shoot situation. Both men would probably be armed and on their guard. There was no way he was going to expose himself to grief when he was this close to getting the job done. This was a job for Mr. Semtex just as London had suggested. It was a stroke of luck that he'd come well prepared. The Czechoslovak explosive had become the trademark of the Provisional IRA and topping the two coppers with it would place the crime squarely at the door of the Irish terrorist organisation. He picked a piece of the putty-like explosive from his suitcase and moulded it in his hands. It was going to be a long night but a profitable one. He packed the Semtex and two detonators into a small hold-all. The two bastards lived at opposite ends of Belfast. Transport was unavoidable and he didn't like that. Rush jobs are fuck-up jobs. That was the credo of the Regiment. He looked around the cramped bed-sit. Not to worry. If anyone could handle it, he could. It was nearly over and the fifteen thousand pounds would be the icing on the cake. He picked up the hold-all and went out into the Belfast night for the second time that evening.

It was after eleven o'clock when Wilson turned the Toyota off the Lisburn Road and onto Balmoral Avenue. He turned right into Harberton Road and followed the road around to the right skirting the dark shape of the Balmoral Golf Course. This wasn't the shortest route to his house but occasionally he needed to pass through a setting of suburban bliss to contrast with the perennial bleakness of the Shankill. He looked at the lines of neat designer houses set back into their own grounds. There was no sign here of the other Belfast. It hadn't been thought necessary for the government to run a `peace wall' through Malone to separate the Catholic doctors from their Protestant dentist neighbours. He turned left onto the Upper Malone Road and passed the expansive Malone playing fields. There were no such recreational areas in the Shankill or the Falls. The plebes played in their adjoining streets continuing the traditions of their segregated parents.

Wilson was mentally and physically exhausted. He could still see Bingham's mutilated body as vividly as if it were plastered to his windscreen. The crummy little terraced house in East Belfast would never be the same again. In the near future workman would come and fill in the holes made by the bullets that had killed Bingham. The blood would finally be erased after the ninth or tenth washing of the walls. But the scene of the murder would always remain fresh in the minds of those who had seen it. Bingham's death would be used by the local rabble-rousers to whip up hatred against the Catholic community and would serve to swell the ranks of the local UVF. Join us and we'll protect you. And the fools would swallow it and join up. There would be no end to it. He turned right into Malton Drive and then took the second left into Malwood Park. He was almost home.

Wilson brought the car to a stop fifty yards from his house. A Peugeot 305 was parked close to his driveway, much too close to his driveway. From his position he could see a single shadowy figure in the driver's seat. He looked around the deserted road searching the dark spots for a second shadow. This was the type of scene every police officer dreaded. Since its inception, every member of the Force had lived in fear of the assassin's bullet. Every time one of their number was callously murdered the message was hammered home: next time if you're not careful, it'll be your name that'll be pinned up on the notice board. He turned off the motor and extinguished the car's headlights. One advantage of living in Malwood Park was that strangers stood out a mile. If the car had been a Mercedes or a Jaguar, he might have assumed that his neighbours were entertaining. But a Peugeot 305 was a dead give-away. It could only mean one thing. Somebody was waiting for him. Well perhaps they would get more than they bargained for. He put his hand under his coat and loosened his Baretta from its holster. Through the steamed-up windows he could see the figure in the Peugeot sitting perfectly still. He slid slowly out of the driver's seat trying to stay as close as possible to the ground. The car door opened and he slipped onto the wet pavement. He made his way slowly forward crawling on hands and knees. The person in the Peugeot was a fuzzy image through the steamed-up rear window. He was twenty yards from the Peugeot when he slipped his hand under his coat and removed his revolver. He began to suck in deep breaths steeling himself for action. He crawled the last few yards until he reached the back of the car. It would all happen very quickly. He ran through his sequence of actions before taking the safety off the gun. Breathing deeply one last time, he flung himself around to the driver's side of the car and wrenched the door open.

"Don't move a muscle or I'll blow your fuckin' head off," Wilson stuck the gun at where he anticipated the driver's temple would be.

Kate McCann sat glaring directly in front of her. He thought that she was about to burst into tears.

"Oh Jesus!" he said lowering the gun. "I'm sorry Kate. I thought somebody was lying in wait for me."

"It's OK. It's OK," she drew in a large breath and held it in her lungs. "Oh God. Give me a minute to get my senses back. I decided to follow up on your invitation," the words came in gasps. "We've wasted enough time. What I didn't expect was to have the life half scared out of me." Although she tried to control herself, there was still a slight catch in her voice.

"There's a funny side to this," he said returning his gun to its holster and holding the car door open. "I've just ruined my best trousers crawling through the gutter. Let's get inside so I can slip into something more comfortable." He shook his wet legs and then handed her a door key. "You go inside. I'm just going to put the car in the drive."

Kate got out of the car and carefully locked the door. The die was cast. After he'd left the restaurant she sat for half-an-hour thinking about their situation. The time for foolish pride was over. She wanted him badly and she could think of no good reason why she had refused his offer of meeting her later. She walked up the driveway and slipped the key into the front door. Her hand hesitated before turning the key. This was Susan's house. The home of the woman that she had both envied and pitied. She turned the key but couldn't push the door in. There was a sense of violation that she couldn't overcome.

"Quick," He took her hand from the key and pushed the door in. "If I don't get out of these wet clothes I'll get my death of cold. The drinks are in the living-room. I'll have a very large Jameson."

He was bounding up the stairs before she could reply. She walked into the hall and quietly closed the door behind her. The hall was tastefully furnished with antiques. Everything screamed Susan at her. It was a woman's house. There was nothing here of Ian's. She walked into the living-room and switched on the light. Again as she glanced around the room she felt Susan's presence in every stick of furniture. Her eyes were drawn to the glass cabinet containing his sporting trophies which adorned one of the walls. Another of Susan's marks. Had it been placed there out of love for her husband or out of pride at his achievements? It really didn't matter. It was there and it showed that Susan had cared. Her heart was beating normally now. She moved to the drinks cabinet and poured them both a stiff whiskey. There was no point in holding back, she thought as she poured the drinks. They both knew that she was staying the night. The old mistress of the house would be well and truly laid to rest.

"A penny for them," he said from the doorway. He was wearing a terry cloth dressing gown that had seen better days.

"I was just thinking about the number of times I wondered what your house looked like." She crossed to him and handed him his drink.

"And what do you think?" he asked.

"It's not your house," she said sipping the whiskey. "It's your wife's. God I feel like I'm violating her by coming here this evening. I thought that in the time that you've been here alone you would have put your own personality on the place. But you haven't. She's still here. She's in every stick of furniture. I can feel her presence everywhere."

Wilson heard the sound of melancholy in her voice. He took a deep draught of the whiskey. "I needed that. It's been a bloody terrible evening. Horrible bloody murder. Killed in his own home. His wife found him with his brains scattered all over the hall. Sometimes I wonder if there'll ever be an end to the shit."

"When this shit ends," She said quietly. "People will still be killing each other. Only if Jennings has his way somebody other than you will be investigating the who and the why. That's why we need the Truth and Reconciliation Commission. Only when people face up to the terrible things they did will we be able to move ahead. The only problem is that nobody seems interested in either truth or reconciliation. Television programmes won't solve the problem. We need to get it all out in the open." She went to the sofa and sat down.

"I hate to burst your bubble but it's never going to happen," he said moving to her side and standing over her. "There are too many people who don't want what really happened to come out. The creatures under the rocks that you're trying to turn over are a hell of a lot more dangerous than you think. But enough of shop talk. Why did you come?"

"Like I said we've lost enough time. If we're going to put things together, then we should start as soon as possible."

He put his two huge hands down and gently pulled her to her feet. They kissed both tasting the whiskey on the other's mouth. She could feel his erection beneath the thin dressing gown. His hand ran over her body as they pressed their lips together. She pulled herself back still aware of Susan's presence in the house.

"It's OK," he said following her face with his and planting kisses on her cheeks and neck. His hands were on her bottom pulling her close against him.

"I know," she said and moved her lips to his again.

They held each other prolonging the kiss as long as they could. When they stopped he took her hand and led her from the living-room into the hall.

She stopped for a moment at the foot of the stairs. "Not in her room, Ian. Not in her bed."

"No," he bent and kissed her on the forehead. "Not in her bed."

CHAPTER 35

Case's watch showed five past eleven when he hailed a black taxi at the junction were the Woodvale Road becomes the Shankill Road. The night was dark and cold and the streets were deserted. The taxi pulled in to the curb where he stood and the driver carefully inspected his prospective fare before winding down the side window.

"Where to?" the driver leaned across towards Case.

Good bloody question, Case thought. He hadn't yet decided which order to do the bastards in. The inspector lived in the Malone area while the sergeant lived just off the Donegal Road.

"The Upper Malone Road," Case said deciding quickly. The Belfast accent was perfect as usual. He opened the back door of the taxi, tossed the hold-all containing the Semtex and the detonators onto the floor and sat on the red leather seat.

The taxi driver slipped the lever on his meter, pulled away from the footpath and moved away down the Shankill Road.

"It's goin' to be a bitch of a winter," the driver said looking at his passenger through the rear mirror.

Case didn't reply. Taking the taxi had been a risk. Ideally he would have preferred to stay away from any situation where he could be examined and later described. What he didn't need was a talkative taxi driver. So far his stay in Belfast had been totally anonymous. Finding a bedsit with Mrs. Maguire had been a stroke of luck. She was always so spaced out on vodka that the police would probably get a description of her dead husband.

"God cursed us by givin' us nine months of winter and three months of spring."

Case looked up and saw the driver's eyes examining him in the rear mirror. This was Belfast. Everybody was interested in everybody else and that was particularly true of taxi drivers. He knew enough about the geography of Belfast to realise that he didn't look like the type who'd ordinarily be travelling to the Malone Road.

"It's not the type of night I'd want to be draggin'" myself out on," Case said laying on his Belfast accent with a trowel. "I just got a call from the big fellah in the job. He's gummed up his fuckin' plumbin' and muggins has to drop everything and go and fit it. The way things are I had to throw a few tools in my bag and haul me arse out," he nodded at the hold-all on the floor of the taxi. "At least he's goin' to pay for the cost of the taxi."

The driver slipped smoothly onto the Westlink and began to head south.

"All the capitalist bastards are the same," the driver glanced into the rearview mirror. "They'll drag the working man out at any time of the night that suits them. We had unions to stop the bastards from exploitin' us. But that bitch Thatcher put an end to them." There was something about the bloke in the back of the car that bothered him. Something was nagging at his brain but he was damned if he could remember what it was. It was best to play it cool until it came back to him.

"Too fuckin' true, comrade" Case settled himself in the back seat and hoped the driver's curiosity had been satisfied.

The Westlink was empty. The taxi passed Celtic Park and Andersonstown and joined the M1 motorway. The driver spat out through the window as they passed Celtic Park.

"Look at that shit hole," the driver nodded in the direction of Andersonstown. "The Taigs are breedin' like rats over there. The bastards think they're goin' to breed us out of our country."

"Don't worry. The boys'll get rid of the extra ones. Another couple of nights like Graysteel will put things straight." Case knew how to play the Northern Ireland game. He knew that a taxi plying for trade on the Shankill couldn't be driven by anything other than a member of the UVF or the UDA. The terrorist `godfathers' had long ago grabbed control of the profitable Belfast taxi business.

"The more of the bastards we get the better." The driver nodded to his right and Case looked out the window to see the dark shape of Miltown Cemetery just off the side of the road.

"Ay, too true," Case said with conviction.

The driver glanced in the rear-view mirror again. It was comin' back to him. He remembered what was buggin' him about his `fare'. The man sitting on the back seat was a dead ringer for the bloke Ivan McIlroy was on the lookout for. Ivan had told all the drivers on the Shankill that there'd be a couple of extra quid for whoever could point him in the direction of the bloke who was sitting in the back of his taxi. As long as he could hold his cool, to-night was going to be his lucky night. He could already feel the twenty quid nestling in his pant's pocket. The taxi passed the sign for the Balmoral exit and the driver started to indicate. How the hell was he going to keep tabs on this bloke until he could get word to Ivan? If the boys were lookin' for this guy it was odds on that he was connected. He'd heard about the barney in the 'Black Bear' and there was no way he was going to tackle the bloke who'd put four of the mob into hospital. He remembered the bit about the severed fingers and he shivered. His mind was working overtime on how he was going to earn the twenty quid. Safely.

They were travelling along Stockman's Lane.

"What part of the Upper Malone are you goin' to?" the driver asked conversationally.

"Drop me at the Special School. I'll walk from there."

"Sure I might as well drop you where you're goin'. It's a wild night to be out walkin'."

Case didn't reply. He had been aware for some time of the driver's staring at him in the rear-view mirror. His little alarm bell was ringing again. There had to be a reason why the driver was so interested in him? What was it? What mistake had he made? Christ but he was gettin' jumpy. Maybe he was suffering from what the sailors called `channel fever'. The job was nearly over and he was starting to get skittish. He took a deep breath. Professionals sometimes screwed up when they began to get too anxious about finishing a job. Maybe he should have let this one go but fifteen thousand pounds extra was something that could not be easily passed up. Case pulled in another deep breath. Fuck the taxi driver anyway.

The taxi went into the tunnel which ran under the Lisburn Road and continued along Balmoral Avenue before turning into the Malone Road. The driver was sweating heavily. They were only half a mile from the Special School. The trip was almost over and he still hadn't come up with an idea for hanging on to his passenger. So near and still so far. The twenty quid was no longer nestling in his pocket when he swung right at the Malone Playing Fields and pulled in to the side of the road three hundred yards along the Upper Malone Road opposite the Special School.

The taxi driver turned off the meter and craned around to face his `fare'. "That'll be six pounds fifty, comrade." He examined Case's face closely as he took the money from his hand. It was bloody lucky that he had decided not to bother tackling him. He'd seen enough `hard men' around the Shankill to recognise the look. The `Black

Bear' mob must have been mad or pissed or both to have taken this guy on.

Case lifted the hold-all from the floor of the cab and opened the back door.

"Maybe you'd like me to hang around?" the driver put on his most friendly voice. "There's not much business to-night and you'll have a hell of a job pickin' up a taxi here at this time of night."

"Thanks," Case slammed the back door of the taxi. His hand slipped into his pocket and closed around the handgrip of the Browning. Just one more fucking word from you and you're a dead man, he thought looking at the driver. "Ye know the way these bastards are, I might be hours yet. The fucker'll most likely run me home to save the taxi fare."

This was the end of the road for the taxi driver. He'd pushed about as far as it was safe. Any further and he'd be lucky to end up like the mob from the 'Black Bear'. Most likely the medics wouldn't be able to put him back together again. It wasn't worth gettin' killed for twenty lousy quid. He smiled wanly, nodded and started away from the footpath. As he drove down the Upper Malone Road, he glanced into the rear mirror and saw his fare standing immobile were he had dropped him. He turned onto the Finaghy Road. He could always relay the message to Ivan on the cab radio. Then some greedy bugger would try to rip off some of the twenty. As soon as he was out of sight he'd get on the mobile. He refused to give up the hope that he'd get the payoff. He'd found the man Ivan was looking for. That ought to be worth something.

Case watched the taxi disappear into the hazy darkness. The bastard behind the wheel would never know how close he'd come to dying. First right and then fourth left, he said to himself, moving off in the direction the taxi had taken. He had three knacks in life, he could mimic accents, memorise a map after one look and kill people. There wasn't much of a need for people like him. But when there was he could make quick easy money. As far as he was concerned there was nothing wrong with that equation. He'd memorised the route to the houses of the two coppers. He would have preferred if this gig hadn't been necessary. But he wasn't about to look a gift-horse in the mouth. He would never have taken a contract to waste a copper on the mainland. It was too bloody dangerous to off a copper. But in Ulster who gave a shit. He reached the first corner and looked up at the plaque attached to the wall. Piece of piss, he thought to himself, turning into Malton Drive. This was going to be the easiest fifteen thousand pounds he'd ever earned. Every available policeman in Belfast was running around the Shankill and East Belfast looking for an IRA hit squad and here was he in the middle of `toffee nose land' where there wasn't a copper in sight. Piece of piss, he repeated to himself. Nice houses, he thought, as he walked past the rows of well kept bungalows and mock Georgian two storied dwellings. This was the other Belfast. The place where people could sleep safely in their cosy beds at night. He was about to change that. The Chief Constable's phone would be ringing off the hook to-morrow when the good citizens realised that they were as vulnerable as their poor cousins.

He checked the roads off to the left. Marwood Park was the next. The place was almost pitch black. A blagger's wet dream. This was just too easy. He had plenty of time to finish his business and move on to his second client. Money for old rope. The only thing that could fuck him was if his mark wasn't home. Still he had plenty of time. Two in one night. Bang, he said softly to himself feeling the power surge through him. He looked at the house numbers. They were consecutive. He stopped at the corner of the deserted street and counted off the houses. His eyes stopped when he reached the house he was looking for. Not bad for a copper, he thought as he examined Wilson's house. The place was in complete darkness but there were two cars parked outside. First stroke of luck. The mark was in. A Peugeot 305 was parked on the road directly outside his mark's house and a Toyota Corolla was parked in the driveway. The copper certainly knew how to pick a house but his taste in cars was shit.

Case moved quietly along the street trying to keep in the shadows as much as possible. He thought it unlikely that any of the local `hurrah Henrys' would be up and about past midnight. They'd need their beauty sleep so that they could get an early start making money. His sergeant in the Paras had drilled him on the importance of being safe rather than being sorry. He waited ten minutes standing in the shadows directly across from the house. When he had assured himself that he hadn't been observed, he crossed the road and quickly slid under Wilson's Toyota. He removed a pencil light from his coat pocket and put it in his mouth. He pulled himself into a position just under the driver's seat and opened his hold-all. The Semtex was in two small two kilo blocks. He took out one of the blocks and began to mould the dark grey putty-like material. Trust the Czechs to come up with a little baby like this. Just one kilo of Semtex would blow the Toyota and its occupant to smithereens. He pressed the explosive into a crevasse between the chassis and the floor under the driver's seat. He practised laying this type of charge hundreds of times. The explosion would be concentrated right under the driver's seat. He smiled to himself. The bastard wouldn't know what hit him. He wouldn't stand a chance. The first fucking Paddy in outer space. He removed the detonator from the hold all and buried it in the Semtex. His deft fingers led the wires up through the engine housing and under the bonnet of the car. Without moving from underneath the car, he slipped the wires onto the contacts of the starting motor. As soon as the wires were securely fastened, he lay back and examined his handiwork. Perfect. His instructor would have been proud. He grabbed the hold-all and slid out from under the car. Without hesitating, he walked out of Wilson's driveway and back down Malton Drive. He glanced at his watch. It was only twelve thirty. He walked out onto the Upper Malone Road. If the other copper was at home that would really make his night.

CHAPTER 36

The shadows of the deserted car park behind the pub on the Ormeau Road concealed Simpson perfectly from any nosy passer-by. It was one o'clock in the morning and the pub had long since disgorged its final customers. The building stood in complete darkness. A shiver passed through him. The bastards were running late. He heard the sound of a powerful engine and moved out of the shadows as a Sherpa van wheeled into the parking lot and made at speed for where he was standing. The van-driver braked hard as he approached him and the rear of the van swung around. The back doors swung open and Simpson dived inside. He threw himself on the floor and felt the course blanket being thrown over his head. The door of the van closed as soon as he was inside and the vehicle accelerated out of the car park. He lay quietly on the floor as the van raced through the darkened streets of Belfast. His heart pounded but he knew better than to take the blanket off himself. When it was safe his handler would let him know.

After a drive of about five minutes the van began to slow down. Simpson felt the blanket being removed from his head.

"Richie, my boy," Simpson's handler smiled as he dumped the blanket over a settee which stood against one side of the van. "Sorry for the urgent arrangements."

"You guys are going to get me killed," Simpson said looking around the rear of the van. He had been in many such vehicles since he'd been 'touting' for the British Secret Service. The van had been fitted out specially to receive people like him. A strong light had been set into the roof and illuminated a table and chairs as well as the settee. This was how the Forces Research Unit of the British Army liked to conduct its business.

"Let's not exaggerate," the handler said sitting on one of the wooden chairs. "We need to talk." He produced a small bottle of Bushmills from his pocket and offered it to Simpson.

Simpson took the bottle and drank greedily from it. "What do you want?" he asked passing the bottle back.

The handler screwed the lid on the bottle and replaced it in his pocket. "Information," he said quietly. "I need to know what you know, Richie. I need to know what's happening."

"We're all caught up with these murders," Simpson wished that the Brit would pass the bottle back his way. "Billy's in a flap because the PSNI boys want to open up Nichol's file."

"Why does that put Billy in a flap?"

The van turned a corner and both men braced themselves against the table which was secured to the floor of the van.

"Give me a fucking break. You people know more about that than we do. Billy's afraid that some honest policeman will find out what really happened all them years ago in Dungray. But weren't you boys at the heart of it?"

The handler remained silent while Simpson said a silent prayer for the re-appearance of the Bushmills. The events of the evening had given him a thirst.

"Billy thinks that the murders are linked to what happened in Dungray but he hasn't got a clue who's behind it."

"And do you, Richie?"

"Not a fucking idea. Billy was wonderin' whether Nichol might be the boy behind it."

"And was he?" the handler's voice was as smooth as silk.

"I don't think so," Simpson was beginning to sweat. He had a psychological problem every time he met his handler. A little voice inside him told him that this man, whose name he didn't even know, knew his innermost secrets. He'd been trained like some sort of performing dog to completely unburden himself to whoever was his handler at the time. Bouncing around in the rear of the Sherpa van Simpson was wracked with guilt. Not guilt at what he had done but guilt because he hadn't yet told his handler about it.

"I offed Nichol this evening," the words spilled from his lips.

"Billy really is in a flap," the handler said coolly. "I assume that he ordered you to do it."

"That he did. He was afraid that the old bastard was goin' to crack and send him down the crapper." Simpson ran his fingers through his hair feeling its wetness. "I tried to make it look like suicide. I gave it to him in the head. The gun's lying beside him."

"Not to worry, Richie. We're not too bothered that Nichol is out of the way. We'll make sure that the Plod keep away from you. We wouldn't want such a valuable asset to be destroyed over somebody like Nichol. What about the other murders? Who do you think is behind them?"

"I told you," Simpson was bathed in relief. They were going to make sure that he'd never be got for Nichol. "We don't have a clue. It's got to be something to do with Dungray but that's all we know. Willie Rice and the boys are lookin' for the bastard. I wouldn't like to be in his shoes if they get their hands on him."

"Are you sure you've told me everything?" the handler's voice had not changed in pitch since he'd begun to interrogate Simpson.

"Are you jokin' me? What the hell do you think I might have kept back.'

"Good boy, Richie," the handler put his hand inside his jacket and removed a wad of five pound notes. He slid them across the table to Simpson. "Two hundred pounds as usual."

Simpson picked up the notes and put them into his pocket.

"And Richie," the handler said his tone hardening. "I want to know the very instant something breaks on these murders. For instance I want to know immediately if Rice gets a line on who's behind the killings or on the murderer himself."

Simpson nodded.

"And Richie, it's important. Do I make myself understood?"

"When I know, you'll know. Alright"

"Good boy," the handler stood and lifted the blanket from the settee. "You know the drill," he said turning to face Simpson.

"I do surely." Simpson left the seat and lay down on the floor of the van directly in front of the doors. The blanket fell over his head. He lay there in silence wondering how many different touts would be touched for information. Maybe Billy himself was a tout for the Brits. It wouldn't surprise him. The van drove on before coming to an abrupt stop. The doors opened quickly and Simpson was rolled into a dark corner of the car park from which he had been picked up. The Sherpa had disappeared before he had picked himself up.

CHAPTER 37

Roy Jennings shifted uncomfortably in his chair. He was taking a considerable risk in coming personally to Billy Carlile's office at the Ulster Democratic Front headquarters. Anybody seeing him arriving at or leaving this office after midnight wouldn't need an abacus to put two and two together. But the apparent suicide of Robert Nichol made a meeting with Ulster's mover and shaker indispensable.

"This thing is going too far, Billy," Jennings said settling himself again in the chair. "That bastard Wilson is trying to turn over our neatly arranged apple cart. He and his team are like a group of pigs poking around in a trough of rubbish. Sooner or later they're going to uncover all the filth we've so carefully buried." He pursed his thin lips. "We should have forced Wilson out years ago."

"I suppose there's no chance we could replace him with Whitehouse on this one," Carlile said.

"Out of the question, I'm afraid. All we'd need would be another one of those bloody investigations by some smart copper from Cumberland or some other English backwater. It wouldn't take some smarmer two days to crack George. There's too short a connection between George's brain and his mouth."

"Then we'll just have to ride out the storm. We've done it before."

Jennings was disconcerted by the sight of the man who sat across the desk from him. Carlile's face looked paler than usual and folds of loose flesh hung from his pallid cheeks. He didn't look like a man who was going to be able to tough it out for much longer. The politics of Ulster were beginning to take their toll on the leader of the UDF. Jennings pursed his lips and wondered how many dark secrets were locked away in Carlile's head.

"You've no idea who's behind the latest killings in East Belfast?" Jennings asked.

Carlile opened his hands. "I have no idea in the wide world."

Carlile's face showed no emotion but Jennings couldn't shake the feeling that he was being lied to. For over ten years Jennings had been allied to this powerful politician and that allegiance had paid off handsomely. He was only one step from the top of the career ladder and Carlile would be a vital element if he was to capture the job he had sought since his first day as a recruit. No matter how Carlile was involved, Jennings couldn't desert him now.

"If by chance you did know anything, there's still time for us to fix things," Jennings knew that he was fishing in very deep waters.

"Please believe me, Roy," Carlile's face flushed momentarily. "I'm as anxious as you to find the people doing these murders." He stared into the Deputy Chief Constable's eyes. "Sooner or later the boys on the Shankill are going to get annoyed watching your lads chasing around after their tails. Then they're going to take things into their own hands. That won't improve our negotiating position with a Prime Minister who's intent on getting out of Ulster as soon as possible. If we want to win this one, we're going to have to convince the Brits that the IRA are the only terrorists."

"We can't let that happen," Jennings said. An all out war between the UVF and the IRA in West Belfast might seriously disrupt his carefully constructed career. "We have to put a lid on this business for once and for all."

Carlile stared straight ahead. "We may not be able to stop it. Controlling the new breed at the top of the UVF is like trying to hold onto a team of runaway horses. All those people want is murder and mayhem and the more of it the better. They don't have once ounce of political savvy. All they see is the Brits ready to jettison Ulster and the Papists being put in control. I suppose that we're responsible in our own way for creating the monster. I'm getting more than a little annoyed myself standing up for Rice and his people. There isn't an ounce of difference between them and the IRA. They're a shower of murdering scum."

"Since when have you been singing this new tune?" Jennings asked.

"I'm tired, Roy," Carlile said. "Tired of standing before a television camera ranting about the IRA and in the same breath trying to explain the 'frustrations' of the Protestant community. What the hell difference is there between murderers? The IRA justifies their murders by shouting about 'the cause'. The UVF excuses their murders by complaining about their 'frustration'."

"You need a holiday is all," Jennings said. Carlile looked beat. His time was coming to a close and Jennings would have to make the push for the big job shortly if he was going to be paid back for all the times he'd helped Carlile out. If only they could get over the current crisis. A cold shiver ran down Jennings' spine. The message from the men in his office that afternoon had been crystal clear. Military Intelligence and MI5 had a very specific interest in the murders which had taken place during the past week. Jennings' wasn't to know what that interest was but he was to keep both MI5 and MI informed of every step in the investigation. And nobody outside the four people attending the meeting in his office was to know anything about the involvement of the British Secret Service in the affair. That made Jennings very nervous. He wanted to discuss this event with Carlile but he wasn't about to fly in the face of MI5.

"I'd better be going," Jennings' nervousness was getting the better of him. He pushed his chair back and stood up. "I'll do my best to keep Wilson away from the UDF but you've got to keep a lid on things in West Belfast."

"We're sitting on a powder keg, Roy," Carlile sat back in his chair "One false move and the whole thing goes up. You, me, everybody connected with us will be caught in the blast. Wilson didn't get anything out of Nichol. You can take my word on that. We must keep our nerve and look out for one another. Do you understand me, Roy."

Jennings nodded.

"Sleep well, Roy." Billy Carlile forced a smile but he felt that his tame policeman would have difficulty in complying.

As soon as Jennings left the room, Carlile closed his eyes. Lord but he was tired. He had hoped to die before all the evil they had set in motion during the nineteen seventies came home to roost. He and his party colleagues had purposely created the political vacuum into which the terrorists of both camps had gratefully jumped. Giving up their own responsibility as politicians was a ploy they had used to force the Brits back onside. In fact, they had handed over the city of Belfast and perhaps the whole Province of Ulster to the most evil beast they could have imagined. He had been foolish enough to think that it was controllable but he had been wrong. They had opened Pandora's box and they were going to have to pay. His own responsibility in the Province's history was beginning to weigh on him. He'd been able to justify the excesses of his co-religionists with the rallying cry of 'No Surrender' but how could any cry explain away the depravity of Lennie Murphy and the butchers. The business with Nichol might wipe away whatever political reputation he had left. He didn't regret the decision to save Nichol's bacon. If they'd let Nichol

317

swing then he and the party would have swung with him. He ran his hand over his bald pate. He was as bad as the scum in the UVF. He'd ordered Nichol's death to save his own political reputation.

"To what depths descended," he said under his breath as he pushed himself slowly out of his chair. "To what depths descended."

CHAPTER 38

Wilson stretched out his arm in the bed and ran his fingers across the smooth skin of Kate's shoulders. She slept with her back to him her curly blond hair silhouetted against the whiteness of the pillow. He turned and pressed himself into her buttocks. She felt warm and smooth. He let his hand run over her breasts and then down her buttocks to the softness between her legs. She moved into his hand and pushed her buttocks against his erect penis. He slipped into her and they made love gently until he could contain himself no longer and he ejaculated. Their lovemaking the previous night had been tireless. Better than either of them could ever remember. Both seemed to be searching for some higher level of release from the coupling of their bodies. There were important demons to exorcise. He had been totally sated. He held her and kissed her bare shoulders.

"I didn't think that you had anything left after last night," she mumbled and curled into sleep again. "Working with that attractive female constable must have given you some added zest. Did you try to bed her yet?"

"She could be my daughter," he laughed but realised that given half a chance he might have attempted to bed her during the past week. "I'm a clapped out old copper. You're the only one who can raise me to action."

He slipped out of the bed taking care not to disturb her. It was a strange feeling sleeping with a woman after such a long period of abstinence. He crossed to the bathroom and stood in the shower cubicle. Where do we go from here? he thought as he turned on the water and stood under the hot stream. He knew that he had been wrong to shut Kate out during all those long months of loneliness. But what could he offer her? He was an ageing copper who had reached his zenith in the Force ten years earlier. If he was lucky he would be allowed to reach retirement with the exalted rank of DCI. There was the distinct possibility that he would fall into one of the traps his colleagues occasionally laid for him and that he would wind up pounding the beat again. What future was that to offer anyone? Perhaps he should have listened to Susan. Would it really have been so difficult for him to have become a Lodge member and used his fleeting fame to push himself up the ladder? A picture of Jennings flitted across his mind. Hell no, he thought. At least he was able to look at himself in the mirror every morning. But maybe she was right about getting out. Perhaps it was time to plan for the day when he could hand his warrant card in and give the job the two fingered salute. The water streamed over him and he began to soap himself. Was this really the first day of his new life? he asked himself as the water poured over him. Could an old dog get sense and maybe learn a few new tricks. It had never happened in his experience. He'd just have to wait and see.

Sergeant George Whitehouse poured the hot water into the cup and stirred until the instant coffee was totally dissolved. He bit into the stale cheese sandwich and then tossed the remnants into the rubbish bin. The food in the station canteen had to be better than this crap. He could have breakfast later. His wife was off looking after her demented parents in Londonderry and he was left to fend for himself. That's the way his marriage had been. Every time her parents whistled she was off to them on the first train and to hell with him. This morning George had a hell of a headache. Add to that the fact that he'd woken early and couldn't get back to sleep and you had one very sore bear. Every time that his wife was away he piled on the booze. Their only child had pissed off to London as soon as she'd finished her A-levels and they were lucky if she dropped by once a year to see if they were still alive. He sipped the coffee and wondered what Wilson would have in store for him to-day. It had better be something light. That McElvaney woman was wheedling her way in pretty well. The Chief was a sucker for a pretty face. He wondered whether he'd already scored with her. Rumour had it that Wilson had screwed every female officer in the Station. The bastard would get up on the crack of dawn. He picked up the cup of coffee and made his way into the lounge. He pressed the remote control to bring the television to life. Wilson might be a bit of a lad with the women but he was a damn good copper. The problem was he was too good. Real life isn't like the cinema. Real life was about sucking up to the brass to get ahead. You never saw the TV cops licking their bosses asses but that was the only road up in the modern police force. Wilson licked no one's ass. That was why they couldn't trust him. Some day they'd get rid of him and that would be his chance to move up. Until then he was going to do everything he was told to do.

He looked at his watch. It was almost time for the news. He flicked the remote to the BBC.

"The body of Robert Nichol the former politician and civil servant was found at his home early this morning. Mr Nichol died from a gunshot wound."

He almost dropped the coffee cup as he bent quickly and increased the volume.

"Mr Nichol, who was active in the politics of the Province during the early nineteen seventies, had recently suffered a serious illness. The police do not suspect foul play." The newsreader moved on to the next story.

They finally got to Nichol, he thought to himself. It had been alright to disappear the file but someone had decided that Robbie Nichol had become hot again. He wondered what Wilson will make of that one.

He knocked off the television and returned to the kitchen. He threw the remains of his coffee into the sink and quickly rinsed the empty cup. It was time to get to the Station. He closed the door of his small semi-detached in Rosemary Street.

The Ford was parked exactly where he'd left it the previous evening. When he tied one on he was sometimes surprised to find the car in front of his house the following morning. That car probably knew it's way home. He walked briskly towards the car and opened the driver's door. He smiled to himself. The police did not suspect foul play in the Nichol death. That was a bloody joke. Once Wilson got his teeth into that one there'd be hell to pay. He took his place behind the wheel and slipped the key into the ignition. The key made a slight clicking sound before it engaged the starting motor. The world disintegrated around him. His eardrum blew out and the force of the explosion tore his body open. The pain was excruciating but short lived. He was dead before the fire had started to consume what the explosion had left of his corpse.

Wilson raised the volume of his radio when he heard Nichol's name being mentioned. He listened carefully to the news report and then slammed his fist into the kitchen table. The place settings, which he had carefully laid for Kate and himself, jumped with the impact of the blow. Nichol was dead and their chances of getting a lead on the motive for the killings had disappeared with him. They had been so close. And why now? If only they'd had the chance to interrogate Nichol further. The bastard would have cracked. He was sure of it. He smiled when he heard the final phrase about the police not suspecting foul play. That was a piece of horseshit. Someone somewhere was running scared. Moira and the magic box was beginning to prise up a stone and all the little beasties underneath were beginning to tear at each other afraid of being caught in the light. Nichol had become exposed and represented a threat to the status quo. Therefore, he'd had to die. Suicide my arse, he thought.

He became aware of the noise of bacon sizzling on the pan over the gas fire.

"Shit!," he looked down at four pieces of very well done bacon. He'd wanted everything to be perfect.

"I like my bacon well done," she stood in the doorway watching him. "There's no need to get all temperamental about your cooking."

He stood watching her for a moment. "It was supposed to be perfect." His case had just been blown by Nichol's death but he still managed to smile.

"It is," she walked forward and kissed him. "Christ, I must look a mess." She sat down at the table.

He stared at her. "You're the most perfect mess I've ever seen." He recovered the charred bacon from the pan and put it on the plates beside the poached eggs and the fried tomato. He put one of the plates in front of her and took the other place at the table. "I made coffee and tea."

"Covering all bets." She covered his hand with hers. "I'm glad I came here last night."

"So am I," he said. "And I'm sorry for being such a bloody fool."

"It was understandable," she said biting on a piece of toast. "I have great difficulty seeing a great big hulk like you moping around being sorry for himself out of a misplaced sense of guilt."

"I don't think that guilt has anything to do with size," he said beginning to eat.

"With me size is everything," she smiled and looked at him.

A smile flitted across his lips.

"Come on, lighten up," she said.

"What happens next?"

"Who the hell cares? Let's just take it one step at a time." She forked some egg into her mouth.

"And the future?" he asked.

"To hell with the future," she said. "Living in Ulster makes one very aware that living is a day by day experience. Even when Susan was alive I never asked you to leave her. That was your idea. Since we're together again there are no pre-conditions. We give it a try and we see how things go. Have your breakfast like a good man."

"My appetite's a wee bit off," he said.

"Something to do with me?" The smile faded from her face.

"No. I just heard on the news that Robert Nichol topped himself."

"So what," she relaxed and continued to eat her breakfast. "He won't be missed. I never had much time for any of those fundamentalist bible thumpers."

"McElvaney and myself interviewed Nichol yesterday on the Patterson and Peacock murders. It turns out that both Patterson and Peacock were resident at Dungray when Nichol was in charge there."

Kate immediately stopped eating. "That's just too much of a coincidence. I've got the most awful feeling about this business. Ian, you've got to be extra careful. I don't trust Jennings. Actually the only person I really trust is you."

"You think that Jennings had something to do with Nichol taking his own life? That's a bit far fetched even for here."

"I'd put nothing beyond that bastard," she stood up and moved behind him cradling his head in her arms. "Promise me that you'll take extra care from now on."

He kissed her hands. "I promise. Nichol was on edge when we spoke to him yesterday. Maybe our visit pushed him over the edge."

"That doesn't sound like the Robert Nichol I remember," she planted a kiss on the top of his head. "It's about time I was out of here. You won't believe this but I have an interview this morning for a place in chambers."

"What's the expression for barristers. Is it break a leg?" He looked at his watch. "Jesus, is that the time. I should have been at the office half an hour ago myself. You've only been here overnight and already you're distracting me." He stood up and held her in his arms. "Thanks," he said kissing her.

The ringing of a mobile telephone split the air.

"Not now," he said.

"Go on answer it," she said straightening her clothes. "We can distract each other to-night."

"That's a promise," he said heading for the phone.

She watched him walking away from her. Maybe it was her imagination but he seemed to have regained some of his bounce. He looked more like the old Ian Wilson. You stupid bloody woman, she thought to herself. She was old enough not to try and deceive herself. They were good for one another and she would try to keep their relationship on the rails but she had no illusions. Ian Wilson was a maverick. Anything could happen with him and to make matters worse it probably would. But what the hell. At least she would enjoy the ride.

"Yes," he said into the phone.

"I've got some bad news inspector," the Station Sergeant's voice was sombre. "We've had a report that a car has been blown up in Rosemary Street. It was a Ford registered to George Whitehouse." The Duty Sergeant hesitated. "We've recovered a badly burned body at the scene which we are assuming are George's remains. I'm sorry, sir. All the lads are."

"Oh Jesus, no." the words exploded from his mouth. He pulled in a deep breath to quell his rising panic. What the hell was going on? George Whitehouse blown to pieces. What possible reason could there be for killing George? His mind raced. He could visualise George as he had last seen him. He'd get whoever did it. Whether they were inside or outside the PSNI he would get them and he would nail their skins to the wall. "Are you positive it's him??" he asked when he found his voice.

"As much as we can be at this point in time. Poor bastard didn't stand a chance. The fucker who set the explosives knew what he was about. George took the full blast."

Jesus Christ, he thought, another name on the wall. Another copper killed for doing his duty. He wasn't convinced that George was one hundred per cent behind him. He was too close to the hierarchy for Wilson's liking. But why the hell take him out? Life sucked.

He stood for a moment silently holding the apparatus to his ear and imagining what had become of the man who had been his assistant for the past five years. He'd seen the results of bomb assassinations. At that moment they would be scraping what was left of Detective Sergeant George Whitehouse into a plastic bag. No need to call the wife and ask her to identify his remains. Lumps of raw flesh are anonymous.

"The Army have Rosemary Street sealed off in case there're any other booby traps around," the Desk-Sergeant paused. "He was one of your boys, how do you want to handle it?"

"I'm on my way," he said mechanically. He knew they were rattling somebody's cage but he had never realised that this would be the consequence.

"Not yet please, Sir," the Desk-Sergeant cut across his thoughts. "The Army Bomb Disposal Unit has asked us to warn all the Station personnel to watch out for devices. Don't open any parcels and give your car a good goin' over before you drive it. You know the drill. Just don't ignore it."

"Yes, Sergeant," Wilson said wearily, "I know the drill." He prepared to cut the communication.

"And, Sir."

Wilson returned the receiver to his ear.

"We're all bloody sick about this," the Sergeant said and hung up.

"Bollocks," he shouted as he put the phone down. "Jesus Christ but I hate this bloody life."

"What is it?" she watched Wilson's anguish from the doorway.

He turned around and faced her. His face was as white as a ghost's. "George Whitehouse was blown up by a bomb this morning."

"Oh my God," she moved quickly to him and cradled his head in her arms. "You poor man. When will it ever stop. But why him?"

"That's what I'm trying to get my head around. George was one of the boys. He licked up and kicked down just like he was supposed to. And he knew where the skeletons were buried but I'm sure he'd never say. Then again maybe it was working with me that got him killed."

"Don't be so damned silly," she said. Ian took chances that other policemen didn't take. That could get his partner killed, she thought to herself. It wasn't a sentiment that she would ever burden him with. "Whoever killed him did it all on their own. Don't start taking blame for something you had nothing to do with."

"We'll soon know for sure," he moved to the hall door picked up a long rod with a mirror on the end and went outside.

"What do you mean?" she said following him.

"If it was only George then I know where to start looking for the bastards. If they tried to get me too, then there's something about the investigation that someone wants very badly to cover up." He walked to the Toyota and manoeuvred the mirror into position. He moved slowly from the rear towards the front on the driver's side. He saw it almost immediately. Since the early nineteen seventies, every police officer in Ulster received training in the procedure of checking for car bombs but that didn't always save them. The explosive was packed into a crevasse between the chassis and the floor. A handful of grease had been used to obscure it but he could clearly see the stubby end of the detonator sticking out of the moulded explosive. Explosives weren't his field but he'd bet a month's salary that it would be Semtex.

"I'm sorry George," he said softly continuing to examine the bomb.

"Well," she said.

"Get back to hell out of here," he said sharply. "Unless you want to find yourself in a thousand pieces." He carefully removed the mirror and moved on to Kate's Peugeot. He repeated the procedure but found nothing.

"I'm going to call this in," he moved off back towards the house. "I'd advise you to head off for the office by taxi.

Your car's going nowhere until that bomb's been made safe. Now we know for sure."

"For God's sake, Ian," she stood before him. "Don't jump out of one guilt trip and straight into another.

"Now I've bloody done it," he strode through the front door with Kate directly behind him. "I should have known when to leave well enough alone."

"It wasn't your fault," she said standing beside him while he dialled the Station on his mobile.

"Wasn't it?" It was all connected. Now he was sure that the murders were not random. Patterson, Peacock and Bingham had been marked for death and clinically executed. They had seen or heard something that they shouldn't have seen or heard while they were living at Dungray and for that they were being murdered. The IRA connection was simply a red herring to throw him off the track. He was going to find out why. Somebody was scared that they were getting close. Nichol had to be terminated and so did the investigating officers. As soon as Whitehouse and he were dead, the investigation could be handed over to somebody who would bury the affair as deeply as was required. George knew more than he had said and he had died because of it. He thought about the missing files and the way George had fidgeted in his office the previous day. Perhaps George had screwed up. Nichol was back in the frame and that wasn't appreciated. The cover-up hadn't been complete so now the body count had to rise. This time they'd gone too far. But who the hell were 'they'? What was so important that people had to die to protect the secret? He felt exposed and alone. The bomb under his car hadn't been a warning. It was meant to kill him. Time was running out for him. Not for the first time in this investigation, he felt a sense of foreboding. He had come to realise that he wasn't dealing with common criminals, he was dealing with subversion within the system. The mindless goons of the IRA and the UVF hadn't put this thing together. If it were possible to gather all the members of both organisations in one room, they wouldn't constitute one brain.

"You'd better get back to the city," he said turning to Kate. "The Bomb Disposal Squad will be here within fifteen minutes. I can already tell you what they're going to find. The explosive is Semtex, Czech made and the favourite of the IRA. Gustav Havel once said that the Czechs have sent enough Semtex to Northern Ireland to blow the whole Province up ten times over. So that's going to be a major dead-end. I'll also bet that the detonator is also the type favoured by the IRA. That piece of information will lead nowhere as well. Every bomber has his own peculiarities, like the way he sets the detonator or ties up the wires. It's like a finger print. The boys in the Bomb Squad can tell the signature of every sometime bomber in the Province. I bet they come up with a new boy on these bombs. In other words, it'll all lead to a dead end. A quick investigation will consign George's death and the attempt on me to the rubbish bin. Case unsolvable."

"What will you do now?"

"I'll have to warn the neighbours. We wouldn't want some innocent stock broker or banker to collect my little package. They've never been comfortable living beside a copper but this'll put the tin hat on it. I wouldn't be surprised if some of the more nervous get up a petition to get rid of me. I want the bastard who did this no matter what side of the fence he's on."

"I'm sorry," she said holding his arm. She wanted to hold him tight and kiss him. She wanted to believe that she could erase the pain he was feeling but she knew that she couldn't.

"I know," he forced a smile. "It's a hell of a way to finish a date. We'll talk later."

Reluctantly, she released her hold on his arm and moved down the driveway. The street was quiet and still. There was no hint on the surface of the death and destruction lurking beneath Wilson's car. God but she hated this Province. What evil creature had created the situation where human beings living in close proximity to each other harboured such hated that they rejoiced in killing their supposed enemies?

She walked slowly down the street away from his house. Ian could be dead now, she thought. He should be dead. Only her arrival last night had thwarted the bomber. Somebody wanted the man she loved dead and perhaps they would not stop until they had succeeded. A tear formed at the corner of her eye. Please God, she thought, please let him find the bastard before there's any more killing.

CHAPTER 39

It was ten o'clock in the morning and Willie Rice was suffering from the effects of a monumental hang-over. He looked at the cup of black coffee on the table in front of him and his stomach turned.

"It's nothing definite," Ivan McIlroy had seen his chief in this condition before and wished he were somewhere else. Willie had lately added a liking for cocaine to his fondness for Napoleon brandy. Coming down from the combination made him one mean bastard to deal with. "One of the black cab men reported liftin' a guy that could have been our friend from the `Black Bear'.

"I want the bastard," Rice winced as a dart of pain shot through the top of his head.

"The pick up was from just beyond the Shankill Graveyard," McIlroy moved Rice's coffee cup and opened a street plan of Belfast on the kitchen table between them. "That means that he probably lives somewhere between the Woodvale Road in the West and Tennent Street in the East," he drew two red lines down the streets he had named. "And between Azamor Street in the South and Sydney Street in the North," he drew a heavy line down the streets on the plan.

Rice looked at the plan through the fog which clouded his eyes. He knew that he needed to think but his faculties were in such disarray that no act of will on his part could succeed in pulling them together. McIlroy had drawn a square with a side of approximately half a mile. It lay smack in the centre of the area controlled by Rice.

"Cover the area house-by-house. Anyone who looks like our man get's lifted and brought to the Riverside Club." Another bolt of pain shot across Rice's eyes. "Tell our blokes that if they miss him I'll flay their skins off."

McIlroy folded the map. He had no doubt that Rice would burn some arses if the bastard from the 'Black Bear' wasn't found. "You heard the news about Robert Nichol?"

Rice had only just crawled from his bed. "No," he sipped at the hot coffee.

"Topped himself," McIlroy slipped the map into his side pocket.

"In a pig's arse, he did," Rice's hand shook and he spilled some coffee on the table. "That old bastard wasn't the type to top himself. Somebody offed him and they want to make it look like suicide. Jesus Christ! I wish I hadn't taken such a load on last night. My head is fuckin' splitting. There's something very wrong going on here. The Shankill has been littered with bodies this week and then Nichol gets himself topped. I don't like it. Somebody is screwin' around with us. Maybe it is the Provies?"

"No way. They're not about to screw things up by gettin' into a gang war," McIlroy didn't like his chief's mood. In this frame of mind, Rice was downright dangerous. "We've got arrangements with them."

"I wouldn't trust that fucker Cahill as far as I could throw him." Rice walked over to a wall cabinet, took out a pill bottle, shook three tablets into his mouth and swallowed them. "Maybe we'll have to take the old fart out."

"The man's dyin', Willie. What would be the point of takin' him out now?" McIlroy could see that assassinating Cahill would be seen by the other side as an outright declaration of war.

"I'm gettin' pissed off sittin' here and doin' nothing when I can feel it in my bones that something's goin' down." The tablets were beginning to deaden the pain in his head. "Get on to George Whitehouse at Tennent Street and find out whether the bollocks knows anything."

Rice sipped on his coffee while McIlroy removed a mobile phone from his pocket and dialled a number. Something was stinking to high heaven. It had taken him ten years to consolidate his power in East Belfast and to build up a profitable operation. No business operated in East or Central Belfast without paying their tribute to Willie Rice. Shit he'd even taken on accountants to set the levies on businesses. Nobody was going to take that away from him without a fight. Despite the pills the drums were still playing away in his head. Sometimes instinctive action was called for and Rice's instincts were already screaming for retaliation.

"Jesus," McIlroy wore a puzzled look as he put away his phone.

"What the fuck is up now?" Rice asked.

"Some arsehole blew up Whitehouse's car and tried to do the same to Wilson." McIlroy sat across from his boss.

"It's got to be the Provies," another bolt of pain seared through Rice's skull. "It's Cahill's last fling before they box him."

"That's not all," McIlroy continued. "'Our boy' was at the scene of the hit last night. One of the coppers on duty stopped a Brit heading away from the scene."

"Who do you mean 'our boy'?" Rice asked sharply.

"The description fits the boy from the 'Black Bear' to a tee," McIlroy leaned across the table. "And get this, he produced a Military Intelligence ID card when the fuzz stopped him."

"Holy Shit!" Rice's head began to swim. This was stretching coincidence too far. "I don't like it, Ivan. There's an operation on for sure. But what are they after. A couple of Prods are murdered. Some of our men at the 'Black Bear' are roughed up and Nichol 'tops' himself. I can see the fuckin' dots but I just can't connect them."

"It could be anything. The Brits are bloody devious when it comes to the `dirty tricks'. They wouldn't be trying to set the Provies and ourselves at each others throats?"

Rice thought of his gut reaction of several minutes ago. "Could be. Did you tell our contacts what we know?"

"I did in my arse. It might not be too smart to find this boy if he really is military. Maybe we should just keep our noses out of it until the killing stops."

Rice knew that would be the logical thing to do. Over the years, he and his colleagues had built up a nice little empire but he didn't think for one minute that they were immune. The British Government and the police tolerated them. Letting the paramilitaries skim a little out of the system didn't hurt anybody, so they were allowed to operate within limits. Murdering a British agent could bring the whole house of cards down around their ears.

"I still want to know where he is but tell the boys to leave him alone." The pounding in Rice's temples was beginning to subside. The gutter rat in him smelled an opportunity to squeeze a little more out of the Brits. "Knowing where we can put our hand on this bollocks might turn out to be an ace in the hole."

CHAPTER 40

Wilson acknowledged the nod from the Desk-Sergeant as he strode through the hall-way of Tennent Street police station. The atmosphere in the station was tense. Every policeman felt touched by the death of a colleague. Especially a well-respected local colleague. He made straight for the Squad Room tossing his coat onto the battered coat-rack in his office as he passed. His total complement of staff were present. Taylor, Graham, McIver and Davidson stood up as soon as they saw him enter. Moira remained at the back of the group.

"Sorry, boss," they intoned in order. "We're going to miss old George."

"We're going to get the bastard that did this," Wilson said staring directly at his team. "And when we do we're going to make sure that he pays for everyone he's killed. All bets are off on this one. Pull in anyone you think can help. We're going to turn this town upside down if we have to but we're going to shake this bastard off his branch. Killing George was the worst mistake this guy could have made."

"Don't worry. We'll get him Boss," Taylor said and the other detectives nodded their heads in agreement.

"What's the news from George's place?"

"The car was totally destroyed," McIver said retaking his seat. "It burst into flames after the explosion and torched what was left of him." McIver saw the look of horror on Wilson's face. "He was dead before the flames started," he added quickly. "The bomb disposal people are examining the bomb that was under your car at the moment but we won't know for certain until later this morning whether the two bombs were set by the same person."

"I'll bet a month's pay they were," Wilson could feel his energy returning with his indignation. "And I'll bet the bomb boys have never dealt with the son of a bitch before. It was my bloody fault. I rattled a cage and the animal inside went a bit berserk. We were supposed to think that Patterson, Peacock and possibly Bingham were random sectarian killings." He looked over at Moira. "But our new colleague is one of those keen obstinate coppers who can't let go once they get on the scent. Turning up the link with Dungray and Nichol was the vital discovery. We were gettin' too close to what had to remain hidden. I should have bloody seen it. McElvaney is a novice but I'm supposed to be the old pro. Our visit to Nichol signed his death warrant. He'd kept his trap shut fifteen years ago but someone didn't trust him to go all the way." He felt a shiver run down his spine. His intuition told him he was on the verge of opening the biggest can of worms that anyone in the Province could ever imagine. Who was at the centre of the web which had killed four innocent men, then Nichol and George Whitehouse? The killing wasn't going to stop until that person or persons felt completely safe. That meant that he would have to watch his back. He was definitely in the loose-end category. "I want all of you to drop what your doing and review the files on the Patterson, Peacock and Bingham murders. Moira, get on the computer and find me every man jack who was at Dungray at the same time as Patterson, Peacock and Bingham. Eric, you get on to the lab boys. I want every scrap of physical evidence for the four murders re-examined for a connection." He turned towards Graham. "Harry, I want you to get over to `A' Division and see what they've got on Nichol's suicide. I want to know everything no matter how unconnected it seems." He strode towards the door. "And Harry."

"Yes, boss," Graham replied.

"Pass the word. Anyone caught fucking around with this investigation is going to pay a heavy price. I'm off to Castlereagh to stir some shit."

Jennings' Secretary was seated behind her desk when Wilson walked in the door.

"I want to see him, now," he said.

"I'm sorry but you'll have to make an appointment." She looked directly into his strained face. Her hand moved towards the telephone.

Wilson ignored her and opened the door to Jennings' office without knocking.

Jennings' phone was ringing as he looked up from his desk. He picked up the receiver and said OK.

"What the hell is the meaning of this, DCI Wilson?" Jennings' replaced the receiver and turned to face his visitor. "Nobody but nobody just barges into my office like this."

"You can stuff your procedures up your arse," Wilson leaned his bulk across the desk separating the two men. "One of my detectives was blown to shit this morning."

"I can understand your indignation and anger at DS Whitehouse's death but it doesn't give you the right to invade my office in this manner. I greatly regret George's death and, in fact, I've just been on the phone expressing my condolences to his widow. I assume you've had the good grace to do the same."

Wilson tapped his forehead. "I'm about up to here with your shit. You don't give a fiddlers for George Whitehouse or any other constable on this Force. You'd sit on a mountain of corpses as long as it got you where you want to go. Yesterday you refused me access to Nichol's file. To-day both Nichol and Whitehouse are dead." He leaned across the desk until his face was only inches from Jennings'. "Does that strike you as coincidental?"

Jennings didn't waver under Wilson's physical pressure. "You've been a policeman long enough to know that anything is possible."

"You don't think that it's strange that just one day after we interview Nichol that both he and one of the investigating officers are murdered. And it would have been both investigating officers if everything had gone to plan. Maybe you can answers me this. Why was Nichol so bloody important that a police interview with him leads to both his and George's death?"

"I've heard about your lucky escape," Jennings pushed his swivel chair back from the desk. "Nichol's death is not being regarded as suspicious. It's a clear case of suicide. He was found in his living-room with the gun still in his hand. Perhaps you should examine your own conscience about the role your visit may have played in unhinging the poor man's mind."

"Bullshit. I don't care if somebody took a video of him shooting himself. I don't buy it. That boy was buried up to his armpits in something dirty. He was murdered because his accomplices thought he might crack. What about the missing file on the Jamison murder? Somebody removed that file and that somebody is probably still around here somewhere. I want access to Nichol's computer file."

"I'm afraid that's impossible," Jennings said.

Wilson walked around Jennings' desk catching his foot on the raised platform on which Jennings' chair was set. He grabbed his superior's collar and pulled him out of his chair. "You are fucking unbelievable. Dead bodies are turning up with monotonous regularity. Someone has blown up one police officer and attempted to blow up another and you persist in impeding this investigation. Watch my lips. I want access to that file, now."

"You are one step away from being suspended," Jennings' bravado was belied by eyes that bulged with fear.

Wilson wondered who Jennings was afraid of, him or somebody else? He drew back his right fist. "Now."

"I said I can't give it to you," there was a catch in Jennings' voice. He added quickly. "It is a question of national security. Nichol was mixed up with Military Intelligence in the mid nineteen seventies. He was being used by them for some of their intelligence operations. Even I'm not privy to all the details but you'll certainly never get access to Nichol's file."

Military Intelligence were involved after all. Everyone in Ulster knew about the `dirty tricks' campaign. During the nineteen eighties and nineties some smart alicks at the Forces Research Unit had got out of hand and set up public figures. Sometimes their methods weren't so subtle or their bedfellows so palatable. But how did Nichol fit in? The man had been some kind of second division politician and raving Protestant fundamentalist preacher. Maybe that was his introduction to the world of military intelligence. But he was also the warden of a boy's home and a leading suspect in a bizarre homosexual murder. Robert Nichol was ideal material for a `dirty tricks' operation. He thought back to the previous night and the man called Gardiner who he had stopped at Girwood Park. The bastard may well have been the genuine article but now they would never know. If he really was M.I., he wouldn't be left in their hands for more time than it took to get a car around to Tennent Street to get him out. It was entirely possible that the `professional' they'd been looking for was a member of some obscure branch of the British Secret Service. But why did the Secret Service need to murder nobodies like Patterson, Peacock and Bingham? A wave of despondency washed over him. Where could he go from here? Jennings had a self-satisfied look on his face. He couldn't shake the feeling that the smirking bastard was part of the whole rotten scheme of things.

Wilson grabbed the two arms of the Deputy Chief Constable's chair and bent down to face him. "You can tell your contacts at Military Intelligence that they had better not be involved in either the East Belfast murders or in George's murder. You can also tell them that no matter what barriers they put in the way I'm going to get to the bottom of this business irrespective of what kind of worms get dredged up." He stood back and started to cross the office towards the door.

Jennings straightened his tunic and looked at the departing back of his detective inspector. "For your sake, I'm going to forget what has happened between us in this office this morning. DS Whitehouse's death has obviously been a great shock to you. Otherwise your behaviour towards a senior officer would be unpardonable. But I warn you Chief Inspector, one more act of insubordination and you'll be pounding a beat in Crossmaglen."

Wilson looked over his shoulder and then left the room without speaking.

Jennings watched the door close. Wilson posed the single greatest threat to his ambition of becoming the chief constable of the PSNI. Why hadn't the bloody bomb killed the awkward bastard? Jennings put his head in his hands. Nichol dead and Whitehouse murdered in the same twenty four hour period as the fourth victim of Wilson's `professional'. `C' Division was becoming awash with dead bodies. The sins they had committed in the Province's name were returning to haunt them. Jennings picked up the telephone and dialled Carlile's number. Only Billy would know what to do in these circumstances.

Wilson exited Jennings' office and paused for a moment beside the Secretary's desk. A light plinked on the telephone handset on her desk indicating that Jennings was on the phone. I wonder who you've rushed to for succour, Wilson thought as he moved towards the door of the outer office.

CHAPTER 41

Case woke later than usual. It had been after two o'clock in the morning when he'd finally hit the sack. Placing the bombs had been a piece of cake but he had decided to walk the two miles between Wilson's house in Malwood Park and Whitehouse's place in Rosemary Street. The taxi driver had spooked him. Everybody expected to be examined in Belfast but the taxi driver's interest had been more than passing. He got out of bed reluctantly and immediately began to go through his early morning exercise routine. Keeping fit had become a religion with Case. Even when he wasn't on a job, he kept his daily exercise pattern. The bruise on his side no longer bothered him. He began to do sit-ups. The first hundred were easy but after that he'd have to sweat. As he pumped himself up and down, he wondered about the results of last night's work. "Bang," he said through clenched lips as he pushed towards a hundred and thirty. Things were going pretty smoothly, he decided. Three of his four targets were already dead and there was the bonus of the two policemen. Shit! He should have listened to the news. It was beyond the hundred and fiftieth sit up that he began to feel the strain. He pushed against the tightness in his stomach. One hundred and sixty. At one hundred and seventy he allowed himself to come to rest with his back on the floor. He remembered the two UVF stiffs who had approached him in the `Black Bear'. The older one had a gut that would have done credit to a woman nine months pregnant. You could always tell a Paddy terrorist by the size of his belly.

Case stretched his arm up to his locker and switched on the small clock radio he had bought as soon as he'd moved in with Mrs. Maguire. The radio was set to a local station and the sweet voice of Van Morrison filled the air above his head. He rolled over and started the next part of his work-out. He pushed up on his knuckles the way he'd learned in his unarmed combat classes. He would never be able to thank the British government enough for all the time and effort they put into turning him into a killer. The music faded and a jingle led into a news bulletin.

"Two men have been murdered in Belfast during the past twenty-four hours," the newsreader's voice sounded young. "Last night in East Belfast, Leslie Bingham, a building worker was shot on the steps of his house in Meadow Street. Police said that Mr Bingham had no connection with either the security forces or the paramilitaries and suspect that the motive for the murder was solely sectarian."

Case grunted as he pushed himself beyond the thirty press-up mark.

"Early this morning," the newsreader continued, "a car bomb killed a PSNI constable. Detective Sergeant George Whitehouse died when an explosion, thought to have be caused by the Czech made explosive Semtex, ripped through his car. No group has claimed responsibility for the killing but the police say that the use of Semtex points to a splinter Republican group as the possible culprits."

Case heaved himself past the fiftieth press-up and collapsed on the floor.

"A similar explosive device was found under another officer's car in the Malone area of the city and the police have removed the device for a forensic examination."

"Bollocks!" he said as he lay on the floor, I only got one of the bastards, he thought. He pushed himself off the floor and sat cross-legged beside his bed. It was a bad omen. The reason clients employed Joe Case was because they were sure that the job was going to be done properly. He

344

stood up and began to go through a series of bending and stretching exercises designed to improve his suppleness. Somehow the copper had discovered the bomb. His bonus stood at seven thousand five hundred and the second victim had been alerted. Hitting the copper wouldn't be so easy now. He finished his exercises and crossed his bedroom to the off-white sink. He looked at himself in the chipped mirror. Rivulets of sweat ran from the edge of his cropped hair across his brow and down onto his face and neck. His muscles glistened under the sheen of the sweat. He turned on the tap and sloshed cold water onto his face and his torso. Exercising generally made him feel good but this morning there was something nagging at the back of his mind. The nosy taxi-driver and the botched attempt on the copper could be the start of things going wrong. He should never have taken the contracts on the two coppers. It was too rushed.

There was a soft knock on the door. He tensed.

"Are you awake, Joe?" Betty Maguire tried to make her voice sound deep and sexy.

Case opened the door and put his head out to face his landlady. He nearly laughed. The old bag had tarted herself up. She'd managed to get the hair right but her hand hadn't been steady enough to apply the lipstick. The top of her upper lip and chin had been liberally covered with the garish red colour. For a second she reminded him of his mother, the dirty old slut. "What can I do for you, Mrs M?" he forced a smile.

"I thought we might spend a little time together," the leer on Betty Maguire's face left no doubt as to what she had in mind.

Oh fuckin' hell, he thought, looking into her cow-like face, she's in love. "Not to-day, Mrs M, I'm a bit busy, see."

In just two more days, I'll never have to look at her stupid Paddy face again, he thought.

"You seemed happy enough with me before," Betty Maguire put on her petulant pout. She wasn't giving up so easily.

"That was before," he said harshly, "now why don't you piss off like a good woman."

Mrs Maguire hunched her shoulders. "Maybe I'll piss off and go searchin' for them two boys who came around here this mornin' askin' questions about somebody who could very well be you."

He was instantly alert. Surely he hadn't left any traces. "What two boys were they, Mrs M?"

"Two local boys who are connected, if you know what I mean."

He knew well what Betty Maguire meant. It was the men from the 'Black Bear' looking for a bit of revenge. Maybe he'd gone a bit over the top takin' that guys fingers off. He didn't need the aggro now but that's the way the cards had been dealt.

"They wanted to know whether there were any strangers about," Mrs Maguire continued without prompting. "Sure we had a great chat there on the front step. They're lookin' for a fellah who bears a remarkable resemblance to you. It seems this fellah roughed up four of their men in a fight a few nights ago. They think he's livin' around here and they were canvasin' the whole street."

So the fight at the Black Bear had been his undoing. All he needed was a couple of UVF thugs on his tail. It was too close to the end of the job for this type of complication. His earlier apprehension had been justified. It was easy to explain the taxi-driver's interest now. The taxis were owned and run by the paramilitaries so they obviously formed the front line of the information gathering crew. He'd have to move out of here quickly but where would he go. Everything had been so well planned and all of a sudden the plan was in crap.

"You know me Mrs. M. I wouldn't hurt a fly. I hope you didn't shop me." he said innocently.

"You can rest easy, Joe," Betty Maguire pushed in the door of his bedroom, "I told them nothing about you." She walked into the room and looked appreciatively at his bare torso. "The fellah they described seemed a little like you but there's no way I'd hand you over to people like that. Those boys would murder you as quick as they'd look at you."

A smile spread over his face. All wasn't lost. He wouldn't have to move because the bastards still didn't know where he was. Maybe, just maybe, he could still get his business done and get out of Belfast in one piece. His only real problem stood directly in front of him. The old bag had become a liability. If he had a future in the killing business, Mrs. Maguire would have to die.

"I think you probably did the right thing, Mrs M," he moved to the battered tallboy and pulled a shirt out of the drawer. "I'm grateful to you."

"You're not putting on your shirt are you?" Betty Maguire put on her best coquette look. "You haven't shown me yet just how grateful you are."

"Not yet," he dropped the shirt back into the drawer and removed his combat knife in the same swift movement. He crossed the gap between himself and Betty Maguire and threw his arms around her. She turned her badly painted mouth up towards his. "You're a darlin' girl, Betty," he said sliding the razor sharp knife through her clothing and past her ribs into her heart. He held her tightly as the smile faded from her painted face. Her body spasmed and then went limp.

He pulled out the knife and let her body slide onto the ground. As a professional, he hated mindless killing but Betty Maguire's big mouth was going to get him killed if he hadn't stilled it. A pool of bright red blood stained the worn carpet at his feet. There was no need to clean up the mess. The body wouldn't be found for days. He pulled the eiderdown off the bed and wrapped it around the still warm body. Then he lifted up the bundle and carried it into the empty room beside his own. Living in the same house as a corpse meant nothing to him. He'd spent two days sitting in a dug-out on in Bosnia with two Serbs whose throats he'd cut from ear to ear. He didn't believe in the afterlife or ghosts. In his book, when you were dead you stayed dead.

He slipped out of his blood-stained boxer shorts and tossed them on the floor close to the spot where Betty Maguire had lain. He carefully cleaned his body with a wet sponge and towelled himself vigorously when he had finished. Even with Betty Maguire dead his days in Belfast were numbered. He smiled to himself. The PSNI and the thugs of the UVF were both out to get him and he was going to outwit the whole bloody lot of them. He extended the index finger of his right hand, cocked his thumb and pointed at the mirror above the sink. Bam, bam, 'Rambo' Case.

CHAPTER 42

Wilson arrived outside the offices of the Ulster Democratic Front in Sandy Row at exactly ten minutes past eleven. The Toyota had been cleared by the bomb squad and he had been returned to Malwood Park to collect it. On the journey back to the centre of Belfast, he ran over the events of the past few days in his head. Five murders had been committed without a single clue as to who the perpetrator or perpetrators might be. The motive was still unclear although he was now certain that it had something to do with Dungray Home for Boys and Robert Nichol. Whoever had placed the bombs knew where he and Whitehouse lived as well as the cars they drove. That information was strictly on a need-to-know basis. Maybe they had been followed over the past few days? If they had it had been a very professional job. The bastard who had set the bombs had known exactly where to find them. As he had suspected, the bomb boys were unable to recognise the bomb as being set by one of their regulars. He thought about the `professional'. There was no reason why the man shouldn't be as well versed in explosives as he was in guns. But why turn his attention to Whitehouse and himself when they weren't even close to finding him?

He switched off the motor and slammed his hand into the steering column. The frustration was getting to him. Unless he collared the killer soon both he, and by extension Kate, would be in grave danger. He didn't care much for his own miserable hide but George Whitehouse was the last person who was going to die because of his stupidity.

The offices of the Ulster Democratic Front were housed in a building which had formerly consisted of a ground floor shop with accommodation on the two floors above. He entered the front door and found that the shop had been transformed into a large reception area. He looked around the tastefully decorated room. The receptionist sat at a desk to the left of the door, a picture of the founder of the UDF glaring across her shoulder. At the other side of the room, two large men in almost identical blue suits sat on a couch. Carlile's minders looked up from their newspapers and examined him.

"I've a meeting with Mr Carlile at eleven fifteen," Wilson said standing before the secretary's desk.

"Chief Inspector Wilson?" the secretary asked.

Wilson nodded. "The very same."

"He's expecting you. His office is on the first floor at the rear of the building." She turned her head in the direction of a white staircase at the rear of the room.

"Thanks." He moved towards the staircase expecting one of the minders to intercept him on route and frisk him. The two men remained seated and simply watched his progress towards the staircase.

"Chief Inspector Wilson," Carlile stood on the first floor landing with his hand extended. "It's always a pleasure to meet with the brave constables of the PSNI. One of your colleagues was murdered by a terrorist bomb this morning. I cannot tell you how sorry I am. I've already sent a message of condolence to the poor man's wife."

Wilson didn't respond but simply shook Carlile's hand and followed him towards the rear of the building. As he walked behind the founder of the UDF, he thought that the years had not been kind to Carlile. The two men were almost the same height but Carlile's tall thin body was beginning to hunch and Wilson had noticed brown flecked pouches of skin hanging on what had been twenty years before the striking face of Protestant resistance.

"Please sit down, Inspector." Carlile took his place behind the desk in what had once been a back bedroom in the original house.

Wilson saw spats of rainwater begin to run down the only window in the room which overlooked a small concrete yard at the rear of the house. A tall barbed wire fence surmounting the outside walls of the yard was visible through the rain splattered pane of glass. He looked away from the window and sat in the chair which Carlile had indicated.

"Well, Chief Inspector, we're always pleased to receive a visit from the members of our security forces."

Wilson looked directly at Carlile. As in Jennings office, the wall behind him was covered in photos depicting the leader of the UDF in proximity to the great and the good. Pride of place on the wall went to a photo of Carlile in close conversation with President Clinton. Ranged around the centre-piece were photos of the leader of the UDF with lesser but nonetheless important beings. The message was clear. The man seated across from him represented about as much influence as could be wielded in the province of Ulster.

"I'm afraid my visit is of an official nature," Wilson said crossing his legs.

"I've never liked the air of formality that accompanies an official police visit," Carlile said punching a button on his desk. "I don't suppose you'd have any objection to one of my assistants attending the interview. Very often there's a degree of disagreement later about what exactly was said during one of these official visits."

Wilson shook his head. "I have no objection." He was never happy dealing with members of the political fraternity. Divining the truth from the statements of the criminal classes was a cake walk in comparison with the politicians who had raised lying to an art form.

"Send Richie up," Carlile said into an intercom on his desk. "Well, Chief Inspector, should we commence."

Wilson leaned forward in his chair. "I'm investigating a series of murders in Belfast over the past week."

One of the men who had been seated downstairs entered the room.

"This is Richie Simpson," Carlile said introducing the new arrival.

"I've heard of him," Wilson didn't offer his hand. What he'd heard about Simpson hadn't been good. He was a known ex-hard man who'd seen the error of his ways and nowadays believed in the political process as a way to preserve Protestant Ulster. Bullshit, he thought, once a terrorist always a terrorist. Simpson slouched into a chair beside his mentor. Wilson took an instant dislike to the man.

"You were saying, Chief Inspector," Carlile continued. "You are investigating these heinous sectarian murders."

"Yes, and in the course of my inquiries I had reason to speak with Robert Nichol."

"Ah, yes, poor Robert," Carlile interrupted a little too quickly "A brave servant of the people of Ulster. His tragic death will be felt by us all. I personally was very close to Robert and I've accepted to give the eulogy at his funeral."

"There are a couple of peculiar coincidences connecting Robert Nichol to our current investigation."

Carlile leaned across the desk. "You mean you suspected Robert Nichol of murder. You cannot be serious, Detective Inspector."

"I didn't say that he was suspected of murder. What I would say is that I believe that he had information which could have been vital in helping us solve these murders."

"Now that the poor man has taken his own life it's unlikely you'll ever get that vital information. It's the curse of this Province that the police always seem to be hamstrung in their efforts to bring the murderer to justice. If I or my associates can help," Carlile turned and looked at Simpson, "we surely will."

"I was hoping you'd say that, sir. You see all the murdered men were residents of the Dungray Home for Boys during the period when Nichol was the warden. As I've already said, I interviewed him only yesterday and I felt, rightly or wrongly, that he was withholding information. By an amazing coincidence, he takes his own life on the evening after we interview him. By another coincidence, the other investigating officer on the cases, DS Whitehouse, was blown to pieces and an attempt was made on my life."

"Will this madness never stop," Carlile sat bolt upright in his chair. "I heard the reports on the radio but I had no idea that the officer in question was you. You're a very lucky man indeed, Inspector."

Wilson smiled in admiration. Carlile was one of the best 'handlers' that he'd ever seen. His concern actually appeared genuine.

"We've looked into the files at Headquarters and quite honestly there isn't much information on Mr Nichol's activities while he was at Dungray. I understand that you and he were quite close at the time and I wonder whether you could give me any details which could help me."

Carlile let himself slide back in his chair. The question was how much information to give the man from Tennent Street. He had heard quite a lot about Ian Wilson and what he had heard was borne out by his first impressions. Wilson was a tough honest copper and nobody's fool. Once he got the bit between his teeth it would be a hard ride for everybody concerned. He would have to tread carefully the narrow bridge between appearing to help the man and yet making sure that the water remained as muddied as possible. It would be no easy feat.

"I'm trying to think how I might be of assistance to you," Carlile began warily. "Robert was a fundamentalist Protestant like myself and had already established some sort of loose Protestant association of young men before I decided to found the UDF. I knew him, of course, as a fellow politician, although he was strictly second rate."

Wilson was left to draw the obvious inference.

Carlile continued. "Then Robert tired of politics and seemed to drop out of sight. I've only had sporadic contact with him since then."

"Would his virtual retirement from politics have had anything to do with his being implicated in a homosexual murder of one of the boys in his home?"

Carlile winced involuntarily. "I am not aware that he had been implicated in any such affair."

Wilson let Carlile's response stand although he felt the man was lying through his teeth. "Do you have any idea why his file is restricted for security reasons?"

Carlile was beginning to see the danger in Wilson continuing to probe in the direction of links between the UDF and Nichol. It was time to toss the Chief Inspector a bone. "You understand, Chief Inspector, that a man in my position gets to hear a great many things about the more dubious happenings in this Province." Carlile was encouraged by Wilson's nod. "In Robert's case there was a great deal of gossip. For example, it was widely believed in the nineties that there was a strong connection between Robert and a `dirty tricks' group within Military Intelligence."

"Can you be more explicit?" Wilson asked. That was two mentions in one day of the connection between the recently deceased Robert Nichol and Military Intelligence. He could almost feel himself being led along by the nose. He had already decided that he was going to play along. The phrase 'dead men tell no tales' ran through his mind.

"I don't know all the details," Carlile pressed his two skeletal hands together in front of his face. "It appears that a group of intelligence personnel decided to implement a rather unofficial programme of discrediting major political figures. Myself included I should hasten to add. Some of their ruses were relatively crude, such as setting up bogus bank accounts in the name of a public figure and effecting payments to that account which would be consistent with bribery. That was what happened in my case. Where the targets were more partial to sins of the flesh, their pleasures were catered for and were then documented in great detail. In effect, Military Intelligence set up an unofficial blackmail operation."

"And Nichol was part of this `dirty tricks' sex network?" Wilson asked his mind racing because of the information he'd just received.

"That was what was rumoured at the time. I'm afraid Robert's sexual preferences ran to his own sex. We shouldn't malign the dead but I suppose nothing can hurt him now. I must warn you, Inspector, that what I am telling you cannot be proven. The tracks of this operation have been well and truly covered."

But it was so bloody plausible, Wilson thought. If Military Intelligence was tying up some loose ends, that would explain everything. It would also close the door on his investigation. This was the broadest hint he had yet received. In Ulster British Military Intelligence was taboo. Case closed. Time to go home.

"Is there anybody I could contact who could give me concrete details of what you've just told me?" Wilson asked with obvious excitement in his voice.

Carlile started to laugh. "The only man who could have helped you is lying dead in a mortuary at this moment. Don't you remember the number of coincidental deaths of people involved in the Kennedy assassination? These people are trained to cover their tracks. Everything that you've heard in this room will remain in the realm of rumour and gossip. That is unless someone from the inside comes forward and exposes the whole rotten scheme. For my own part, I can tell you no more."

"I can't tell you how much you've helped me," Wilson stood to leave. He had no idea how he was going to proceed but at least the fuzz which had been clouding his brain was beginning to lift. He could see an embryo of a motive developing. He had no doubt that the man McColgan had stopped near Girwood Park was the murderer and that he was possibly connected to Military Intelligence. He was being skilfully led into a cul-de-sac where he would be conveniently parked until 'they' decided what to do with him. He wondered which rural enclave was going to get the benefit of his services. And just how long he was going to be permitted to live by the maggots under the rock he'd turned over? If he exposed them, he was facing a lifetime of looking over his shoulder.

The leader of the UDF made no move to stand up and Wilson leaned across the desk to shake his bony hand. "The best of luck, Chief Inspector, I hope you get your murderer," Carlile said as he shook his hand. He motioned to Simpson to stay where he was.

Carlile watched Wilson's back disappear down the stairs.

"Why the hell did you tell him all that?" Simpson asked.

Carlile put a finger against his thin lips. He waited about one minute and then pushed a button on the intercom. "Is he gone?"

"Yes," the secretary replied.

The leader of the UDF sat back in his chair a wide smile creasing the white flesh which stretched across his cheeks. "The reason I imparted a morsel of information to DCI Wilson, Richie, is that I was working on the principal that you don't get something without giving something up. Our main fear was that Wilson would start probing around into our involvement in covering up Nichol's little incident with Jamison. I've managed to point him at a maze from which there is no exit. The sex ring which was set up by Military Intelligence with Robert's help is as real as the nose on your face but delving into it is going to be the most frustrating experience of the DCI's career. With Robert dead the only weak link in the chain has ceased to exist. The ranks will close behind one another and Wilson will find himself running around in circles. Nobody on the Army side is going to admit that Military Intelligence used a boy's home as a brothel for homosexual politicians and civil servants they wanted to set up."

"But if Wilson gets frustrated trying to nail M.I., maybe he'll turn his attention back to us."

"Our only weak link died with Robert as well," Carlile sat forward and looked into his lieutenant's face. "But just for good measure we're going to cement our relationship with the Chief Inspector. We're going to give him the murderer of those men in East Belfast and that's where you come in. I want you to get to Rice. If the killer is in Belfast, Rice will eventually find him. Promise him anything because I want to be the one that hands DCI Wilson his man on a silver platter and I want to do it to-day."

"But what if Rice can't find him?" Simpson asked.

"If the stakes are high enough? Rice will produce the goods," Carlile said confidently, "I leave it in your capable hands, Richie, but I want to hand him over to-day." The leader of the UDF shuffled a wad of papers on his desk signifying that the interview was over.

CHAPTER 43

Wilson's mood was black as he drove through the rain soaked streets towards Tennent Street. He finally knew where his case was going. Nowhere. What a bloody idiot he'd been. It had been staring him in the face since he had looked down on Patterson's blood soaked corpse and he had still failed to see it. He pictured George's round peasant face. Why had George been murdered? He could see that someone might want him off the case but why take out George. The only conclusion he could draw was that George knew something that shouldn't see the light of day. If that hypothesis was true, what the hell could that have been and what was so secret that George wouldn't spill it. The rotten bastards, he said softly to himself. Patterson, Peacock, Bingham, Nichol and George: they were all expendable. He'd been expendable too except blind luck in the form of Kate had intervened. They were all pawns in a game in which they hadn't even realised that they were players. Some bastard as yet unknown was issuing death sentences on people he didn't care about. The man carrying out those sentences was probably also a pawn playing out the part which had been allotted to him. Whether he was murdering for money or King and Country didn't matter to Wilson. He was going to have the bastard. He'd been right all along. From the moment he'd seen Patterson's body, he'd known instinctively that they weren't dealing with one of the usual Belfast triggers. He had the outline of the motive for the murders, the existence of the `professional' was effectively established. But he was no nearer to putting his hands on the bastard or his unseen handlers. Please God, he thought, if you have any pity in you at all, let me get this bastard. He'd open the swine up like a fresh oyster and lay bare the maggots who killed with such ease. 'Gardiner' was still out there somewhere flashing his Military Intelligence card every time he was near exposure. That bloody card made him 'official' and untouchable. I'll have you, you smug bastard, he thought. And all the bosses in London won't be able to pull you out of my hands when I do nab you. He'd have McColgan in as soon as he reached Tennent Street and get a sketch made of the bastard. If he was still in Belfast, he'd get him. Or maybe putting the murderer's face on the front page of the Belfast Telegraph would only serve to have him whipped back to whatever hidey hole they'd dragged him from. A wave of despair washed over him. Maybe the game was over and the killer had already gone to ground. Unlikely, his instincts screamed. The fact that George had withheld something of importance from him bothered him. Wilson was first and foremost a copper. Nothing interfered with the investigation. Whatever was turned up, however embarrassing to the hierarchy was put on the table. George obviously wasn't made like that. He'd done the favours and licked the arses and he had paid the price. Whatever he knew was going to be interred with his corpse. Whoever was running the killer probably knew more about their investigation than they did themselves. It had to be that somebody within the organisation was tracking them and passing on the information. He found himself thinking about Roy Jennings. The sneaky little bastard would crawl up whatever arse was necessary to get to the top of the totem pole. His mind flipped through the other possibilities. It could be any one of the detectives in the Murder Squad. Northern Ireland was the quintessential totalitarian state. Nobody was quite sure who was in whose pocket. He would have to live with the conclusion that George had been murdered because he knew too much. That could mean that whatever was taking place wasn't over yet and someone didn't want PSNI paws stuck into their business. He began to relax. Things were probably coming to a head but he still had time. The question was how much. He turned off Sydney Street West into Tennent Street and parked in his usual spot inside the fortress. A blast of wind laden with rain blew across his face as he exited from the car. The rain felt cold and fresh. He lifted his head to the sky focusing on the remains of the observation tower which had once dominated the end of the street. I'm alive, he thought, when I should by rights be dead. George, or whatever was left of him, was lying on a slab in the city morgue while he was celebrating his escape. "If I get him," he said softly speaking to the sky. "No power on earth is going to take him away from me. That's a promise."

Ivan McIlroy slumped down into an easy chair in the living-room of Rice's terraced house in Woodvale Road. He was bone-tired. His eyes felt like two piss-holes in the snow and he was beginning to feel that he'd never sleep again. He'd been on the go ever since the taxi-driver had reported his suspicions about his passenger the previous evening.

"We've got three possibilities," McIlroy said taking the can of beer which Rice offered him. "Two are Brits on temporary jobs with Shorts. They're sharin' a digs on the Crumlin Road right on the edge of our search area."

Rice leaned forward as McIlroy took a slug from the can. He knew his lieutenant and he could tell Ivan had kept the best wine till last.

"The third one is a much more active possibility. While the boys were makin' enquiries in Fortingale Street, some of the residents told them there was a strange lad livin' in one of the houses. But when the boys called around there, the old doll who owns the place swore she doesn't keep lodgers." McIlroy took another slug from the can watching the look of anticipation on his boss's face. "The neighbours described someone who looks very like the boy we're lookin' for. He never seems to be around much during day-time. Keeps himself to himself sort of. Nobody knows whether he works or not. The only thing they're sure of is that there's somebody livin' there for the past week or ten days."

"Jesus Christ" Rice said. "Right under our fucking noses. This bloke has a set of balls whoever he is. How many people are in the house?" he asked sitting on the edge of his chair

"As far as we know just the owner-Mrs Maguire-and our boy," McIlroy drained the can, crushed it and threw it into a waste bin.

"What do you think, Ivan?" Rice could barely contain his excitement.

"I think it's him," McIlroy lay back in the chair. "What I can't make out is why the old doll didn't shop him to us."

"Fucking brilliant," Rice's mind was running through what needed to be done. "Did you leave anybody behind?"

"A neighbour is one of ours. I left two of the boys with him to keep an eye on the place. Nobody stirred out of there this morning so if it's our boy he's still inside. The neighbours have it that the Maguire woman is a dypso. She often doesn't surface for days on end."

"I know you're bolloxed but I want you to get down there. This is one fucker I don't want slippin' through the net. Have you got me now?"

McIlroy shook his head.

"Tell them boys to keep a bloody good eye on that place. You can rest up for a week when we put this business away. You've earned yourself two weeks in the Canaries with this one."

I'll believe it when I see, McIlroy thought and he smiled in appreciation. He'd heard promises like that from Rice plenty of times before.

"I want to be totally clued in. If that bastard moves a muscle out of there I want to know about it pronto. What are the blokes like that you left there?"

"Third division," McIlroy answered trying to stifle a yawn. "Alright for trampling the streets and throwin' a frightener into the Taigs but there's no way I'd put a gun in their hands. They'd more than likely blow their own fucking heads off."

"I want you to organise a stand-by unit. Pick the best lads that we've got and arm them to the teeth. We'll keep them holed up in the Riverside in case we need them. That bastard showed how dangerous he is at the `Black Bear'. You better put the local unit on the alert as well. We might need a couple of extra bodies urgently."

McIlroy moved slowly out of the chair. "That's a tall order," he said. "I'd better get on it right away." He started walking towards the front door, then stopped and looked back over his shoulder. "I hope all this effort is goin' to be worth it."

"Take it from me, Ivan," Rice said, "we're going to turn that boy in Fortingale Street into his weight in cash."

Wilson punched the `Leaning Towers of Pisa' stacks of files which covered his desk and sent them flying across the floor of his tiny office. Several other piles of documents on the desk tottered briefly before regaining their stability. Frustration was building to a crescendo. Since returning from Castlereagh to Tennent Street, he had been frustrated beyond all acceptable limits. One of his men had been slaughtered. A woman had been widowed and yet the security apparatus which had been set up to protect life in the Province was being used to frustrate his attempts to bring the murderer to justice. Jennings had been quick off the mark. No matter what favour he called in, the files on Dungray were not going to be opened. His contacts were all too busy to take a call from him. The whole business smelled like hell. He was creating enough of a stink himself to ensure that his transfer to parts unknown would be expedited. Despite his misgivings he had issued an APB for `Gardiner' and at that very moment McColgan's description of the man was being turned into a police sketch. If `Gardiner' was still in Northern Ireland, he would not get out easily. That was bullshit, he thought. Assuming `Gardiner' was genuinely a spook and working under orders from London, there was every possibility that he would get back safely to the mainland. An unmarked car would simply drive him to Aldergrove Airport and he would disappear off the face of the earth as far as the PSNI were concerned. Well this time it wasn't going to happen.

Harry Graham appeared at Wilson's door. He was holding a sheet of paper in his hand. "The artist has just finished," he said handing the paper to his boss. "McColgan claims it's a damn good likeness."

Wilson took the sketch from Graham's hand and looked at a very passable representation of Case. His first thought was that the picture looked like the face of a football hooligan. A thin layer of cropped hair stood on top of a sharp angular face. The cheekbones stood out of an otherwise unremarkable oval face. He stared into the dark eyes. "You bloody did it all right," he said softly as he held the black and white computer likeness before him. His instinct developed over twenty years in the job told him that this was the bastard who had already killed five people and who would kill again unless he stopped him.

"I want every copper in Belfast to have a copy of this sketch within the hour," Wilson said, still concentrating on the man's features. "If anyone knows or has seen this guy, I want to know about it immediately."

"It's already on the way, boss. We're running off the copies and we've got messengers waiting to rush them around the stations."

"Well done, Harry," Wilson tried to burn the murderer's features into his mind. "I want this one badly. He's a callous son-of-a-bitch and I want him nailed before he does any more mischief. Has anybody managed to dig up the names of any of the other occupants of Dungray during the period when Patterson, Peacock and Bingham were resident there?"

"Moira's working on it. There should be something shortly."

Wilson noticed that Graham had used her first name. That was a high level of acceptance. Moira McElvaney had made it into his squad.

"If the bastard is going to hit again, I want to know where it's going to be. And I want to be there waiting. In the meantime check every damn report that was made in the metropolitan area last night. Maybe our friend 'Gardiner' stumbled into another patrol."

"You'll get him, boss," Graham said looking directly at Wilson. "George could be an awkward bastard but he was one of us. We all want to get the bastard that did him." Graham turned and went into the Squad Room. "And if anyone can nail him it's you."

I wonder will we get you? Wilson thought looking at the sketch. And if we do, what will we do with you. He raised himself out of his chair, walked to the wall directly across from his desk and pinned the sketch to the wall. The face of Joe Case was looking directly at his seat. He retraced his steps walking over the files which littered the floor. He dropped his bulk into his swivel chair and the seat groaned as it took his weight. He lifted his eyes until he was looking directly at the sketch.

"A penny for your thoughts," Kate McCann stood at the door of his office.

"What are you doing here?" he turned to look at her. He felt his humour brighten as soon as he heard her voice.

"You mean people will talk," she tried to close the door behind her but the files covering the floor prevented her. She kicked the coloured cardboard containers blocking the door into the Squad Room and pulled the door shut. "There, we can talk in what passes in this place for complete privacy. And I don't give a damn about what people might say."

"Good for you," he said smiling at her. He looked beyond her and saw Moira staring into his room. There was a smile on her pretty face. "That's the bastard I'm looking for." He nodded at the sketch pinned to the wall.

Kate looked at the likeness of Case. "He's quite unremarkable really. A bully probably but not the kind of person you'd expect to be a murderer."

"Just some mother's little boy trying to make his way in the world," Wilson said sarcastically

"Do you think you'll get him?"

"Oh, we'll get him alright. The question is will we be able to hold him."

"What do you mean by that?"

He explained about `Gardiner' flashing an MI identity card the previous evening and about the possible motive for the murders provided by Carlile.

"I don't like it Ian. You're mixing with people who wouldn't hesitate to get rid of you. And I don't mean just out of Tennent Street."

"This is political. I can feel it in my bones. The question is whether I'll be allowed to continue with the investigation." He stared at the sketch on the wall. "The killer might already be out of Belfast. I might already have missed the boat on this one."

"Maybe it would be better for you if he was already gone. But that wouldn't really satisfy you. Would it?"

"I want him so badly it's an ache in my stomach. He's killed five people on my patch and nobody does that. I want him and I want to know why those five had to die."

"Now I'm really worried, Ian. You've got to be prepared to let this go. Have you faced up to the possibility that you won't be able to solve this one?"

"If I don't get him it won't be the first one to get away. But blowing up George and trying to kill me have made it personal. Maybe they, whoever they are, shouldn't have done that."

"I've still got some friends in London and the Head of Chambers there has some pretty important connections. Maybe I can find out something that'll help."

"It's a long shot but give it a try. I'm in the firing line but that's what they pay me for. I don't want you exposing yourself so whatever enquiries you make, be ultra discrete."

She smiled. "Your concern is touching. Maybe you do care a little."

He stood and moved close to her. "I care a whole bloody lot. Now that I've found you I don't want to lose you." He bent and kissed her aware of the eyes on them from the Squad Room. "One way or another this will be over soon and we can start building a life together."

She returned his kiss. "I can't wait."

"Now off with you," he said opening the door of his office. "I have a bastard to catch. I'll call later."

He watched her disappear through the doorway. She was one hell of a woman and he didn't really deserve her. He was buried in shit and she was the only person in the world that he truly trusted. Everybody needed someone like Kate in their lives. This time he was going to hold on to her. His eyes scanned his tiny office. Not much to show for twenty years service. If they'd told him the first day he'd joined the Force that this was the way he was going to end up, he might have had second thoughts. But that was long ago and far away. He'd had his chances to ingratiate himself with the brass and he hadn't taken them. His character wouldn't allow him to do it. He was going to stay a Detective Chief Inspector until the day he retired. Unless they decided to break him. He'd seen enough frame-ups in his life to know that if they really wanted him in uniform again that could be easily arranged. He was beginning to feel that his relationship with his current employer was terminal. The only question remaining was which particular straw would break either his or the Force's back.

CHAPTER 44

Case looked out of his bedroom window into the deserted rain soaked street below. His internal alarm bell had been ringing quietly away for some hours but he couldn't for the life of him put his finger on the source of the danger. Maybe topping the Maguire woman had set it off. But he doubted it. He pulled aside the dirty net curtain for the umpteenth time and looked down the road. Nothing. The filthy weather was even keeping the housewives away from their shopping and the unemployed men off the street. He turned from the window and moved to the hiding place he had made under the floorboards. The threadbare carpet which had earlier covered the floor was rolled up and stood in the corner of the room. A small amount of Betty Maguire's blood had soaked through the thin threads of the carpet and onto the wooden boards below. The dead woman in the next room was just one more reason for getting out of this God forsaken kip as soon as possible. By this time tomorrow, it would all be over and he'd be back in London collecting all that lovely lolly. The escape plan he'd prepared was simplicity itself. He would steal a car in Belfast and drive it South over any of the unapproved roads in South Armagh that he knew like the back of his hand. Then he'd dump the car in Dublin and hop the next ferry for Hollyhead. Then the train to London to collect his money. He could see the mounds of bank notes in his mind's eye. It was a pity about the hit on the second copper but maybe the scare that had been thrown into him had been what was required. He wondered whether he should try to charge for the attempt but decided it wouldn't be professional. In his business you only got paid if you succeeded.

Case bent down, loosened the floorboards and lifted the steel suitcase. He laid it on the bed and carefully composed the code numbers for the locks. The lid sprang open when he applied pressure to the clasps. One single dossier lay on top of his equipment. He had carefully burned the dossiers he'd received on Patterson, Peacock and Bingham as well as the information on the two coppers. His Military Intelligence ID had also gone up in smoke. It had a 'once only' use value. The copper he'd flashed it at would put two and two together sooner or later. Case looked at the Browning and the Uzi lying side by side in the specially fashioned case. By to-morrow morning, the suitcase and its contents would be lying in the mud at the bottom of the Lagan River. It was a pity that he had to ditch the weapons and the Semtex but these things were easily replaceable and the consequences of getting caught with them didn't justify the risk. He lifted out the final dossier, lay back on the bed and started reading.

Patrick McGinn was another `mister nobody' just like all the others. Case re-read the two typed pages which described the life of his next victim. He looked at the photograph pinned to the first page. It showed a thirty year old with lank fair hair, a round face and a weak chin. To-morrow McGinn would be dead and Case's contract would be completed. He took the street map of Belfast from the locker beside his bed. He'd already sussed out McGinn's house in Jellicoe Drive in the Skegioniell area of East Belfast. He traced his finger along the map on the route he had marked out between Fortingale Street and his destination.

The internal alarm bell was still buzzing away. Case dropped the type-written pages on the bed and crossed to the window. The street was still deserted and the rain beat against the mural of the hooded UVF man holding his Kalashnikov aloft. Case looked at his watch. It was two o'clock. He'd hit the streets at about eight and he'd be on his way to the Irish Republic by ten. The job was almost over. One more hit and he was home and dry.

CHAPTER 45

Simpson turned his car off the Shankill and along the Woodvale Road passing Woodvale Park on his left. Rice's house lay half a mile up the road. There had been something about Rice's voice on the phone. An excitement that Rice had been unable to conceal. Something had broken. But what? He thought back to the meeting with his British handler. If Rice and the boys ever found out that he was touting for the Brits then his life wouldn't be worth a spent match. And leaving it wouldn't be pleasant either. The UVF had its fair share of psychopaths who'd like nothing better than to make a tout's last few hours on earth the most painful of his life. He felt a pang of fear grip at his stomach. Everybody in Northern Ireland was aware of their own mortality but those who strode both sides of the fence were acutely aware that the next moment might be their last. All it needed was one tiny mistake. A careless remark. An otherwise innocent sighting somewhere he shouldn't be. He was caught between the Devil and the deep blue sea. And it was all about two measly hundred pounds a month. He must have been mad to have been sucked in by the Brits. They had him by the balls and they were going to squeeze until his eyes watered. He pulled the car in to the curb outside Rice's house and switched off the engine. Two men lounging across the street suddenly came to life. He quickly got out of the car and turned to face them. One of the men obviously recognised him because he tapped the other on the shoulder and they resumed their positions.

The door was opened almost as soon as Simpson rang the bell. Rice stood in the hall-way holding a spring loaded inner steel door ajar. A smile stretching nearly from ear to ear. Above the smile Simpson could see that Rice's eyes were as dark and as dead as always. "Come in, Richie," he opened the door fully to admit Simpson. "I appreciate you comin' over so quickly."

"The tone in your voice didn't leave me much option." Simpson stepped inside and the steel door clanged shut behind him. He wondered whether the villa in the Canaries was secured in the same manner as the house in the Woodvale Road. He doubted it.

Rice led the way into a small but comfortably furnished living room. A large flat screen TV in the corner of the room displayed a snooker match. "I didn't get a chance to see the last few frames last night," he said nodding at the TV set by way of explanation.

"So," Simpson said sitting in the chair which Rice indicated. "It seemed urgent."

"You'll be wantin' a drink?" Rice asked.

"A Black Bush would go down alright, I suppose." Simpson didn't appreciate the cat and mouse game but there wasn't much he could do about it.

Rice watched the snooker on the television as he moved to a small bar and poured two large whiskeys.

Rice handed Simpson his drink. "Slainte," he said raising his glass.

Both men drank deeply before Rice re-took his seat. The television still seemed to be his main pre-occupation. "I think we might be able to help you out after all," he said without taking his eyes off the screen.

"Does that mean you have a line on the fucker?" Simpson couldn't believe his ears. Carlile had the luck of the devil. They'd be able to hand the killer over to Wilson and the business with Nichol would be forgotten. But was Rice going to hand him the real killer or was he setting up a patsy.

Rice turned to him, the smile on his face widened and he nodded.

The look on Rice's face was unmistakable. He knew where the murderer was. "Well where the hell is he?" Simpson didn't try to hide the excitement in his voice.

"All in good time, Richie, all in good time. We've got the bastard covered. Anytime we want him we can pick the bugger up."

"Who is he?" Simpson was sitting on the edge of the armchair.

"How am I supposed to know? We haven't picked him up yet. We've only found him for you."

"How do you know he's our man?" Simpson asked.

"Do you want a written guarantee? He's your man. Take my word for it."

Simpson finished his whiskey. "Mind if I help myself," he said moving to the bar before Rice could reply.

"Be my guest," Rice watched him as he went to the bar and poured himself a large measure of Black Bush. He noticed that Richie's nerves were on edge. He looked like a man with a sea of troubles on his mind. Sammy Rice didn't like nervous people.

"So do we horse trade," Rice said when Simpson was in his seat again.

"That's what I'm here for," Simpson sucked greedily on his whiskey. The liquid was gradually removing the fear in his stomach.

"Me and the boys own a couple of buildin' firms. We've put in a tender for some local authority housin'. It wouldn't do us any harm I suppose if Billy put in a good word on our behalf."

"I suppose it wouldn't at that," Simpson said.

"Can I take it then that we're organised?"

374

"This kind of thing is tricky," Simpson couldn't believe how greedy the bastards were. Rice and his pals had certainly learned everything the Mafia had to teach. He wondered how much Rice and the other UVF leaders were about to rip off. The man had balls there was no doubting that. He was asking for a licence to print money at the expense of the British Government. "Billy would be taking a hell of a risk getting behind something like that. Surely there's something else he could do for you?"

"I thought you people wanted this fucker badly," there was a flash of anger in Rice's eyes. "Don't fuck about with me. I've got the bastard on tap and I can keep him that way. Or I can let him get on with reducin' the population of West Belfast and blowing up policemen."

"He was the one who planted the bombs?" Simpson said incredulously.

"Who the hell did you think did it? Santa Claus. One of our taxi driver's dropped the bastard close to Wilson's place in Malone last night." Rice stared into Simpson's eyes. "Either you have the authority to negotiate or you piss-off."

"I've got Billy's authority to make a deal."

"Then do we have a deal on the housing tender or not?"

"OK. We'll support you on the housing tender." What the hell, Simpson thought, it was no skin off their noses. Some of the councillors would rant and rave for a while but it would eventually become yesterday's news and the only people who would suffer would be the inhabitants of the jerry-built houses and the British tax-payer.

"That's my boy," the twinkle was back in Rice's eyes. He took the glass from Simpson's hand and refilled it with whiskey. "You know better than to renege on me." He handed Simpson the glass of whiskey. "Don't you, Richie?"

Simpson took the glass and swallowed some of the contents. "We'll keep our side of the bargain," he said.

"Good. You'll find your boy here." He handed Simpson a slip of paper with Case's address in Fortingale Street. "The old doll who owns the house is called Maguire."

Simpson stared at the slip of white paper. He could hear his handler's words ringing in his ears. The Brits wanted this guy as badly as Billy and the police did. What the hell was goin' on? Who the hell is this guy?

"That's right, Richie. The bastard has been living right in the centre of my territory. He must have balls as big as an elephant's. He's living within a mile of where we're sittin' right now."

"You're sure he's still there?" Simpson's voice was anxious.

"Nobody's stirred in that street since we've started watchin' the house. He's in there and we've got him."

Simpson's brain was racing. Both his masters needed to know the whereabouts and neither of them would appreciate the other knowing first. If he informed the Brits first they'd instruct him to keep his mouth shut until they did whatever they had in mind to the bloke. That scenario might drop Billy in even more shit with the police. He quickly made up his mind what had to be done.

"Mind if I make a call?" he asked.

"I was wonderin' when you were goin' to ask me that," Rice sipped his Black Bush. "Be my guest."

Simpson went to the hall, took out his mobile phone and dialled the headquarters of the UDF. He explained to Carlile the content of his conversation with Rice and gave him the address where the murderer could be found.

"You've done very well, Richie," Carlile said. "When this affair is out of the way we'll have to re-appraise your position within the organisation."

Where had Simpson heard that one before. "What about Wilson?" he asked.

The smooth burr came over the line. "You can leave Wilson to me. Well done, Richie."

The line went dead in Simpson's hand. He dropped the mobile into his pocket and returned to the sitting-room.

"Your boss happy then, is he?" Rice smiled wickedly. "Don't worry, Richie, when we take over this Province, the likes of Carlile will only be a memory and we'll find a place for you. Good men with a set of balls are always in demand."

Simpson said nothing.

"You don't like to think of us in charge here, do you?" Rice continued warming to his theme. "Nobody likes to think of the men with the guns headin' up the government." Rice walked to the bar and poured himself a shot of whiskey. "But look around you. Yesterday's terrorist is today's world leader. Look at your man Mandela. Ulster belongs to us. Not to the Taigs and not to the big farmers in the Unionist Party." Rice spat onto the ground. "We'll wipe them bastards out before we start on the Taigs. Fucking parasites. We know who we can count on. Don't we, Richie. After we take over, we can afford to turn ourselves into politicians. We'll be just like the blacks in Africa: bombers and terrorists one day, politicians the next. Mark my words, Richie, Carlile, the UDF, the Unionist Party and the Nationalists won't count for dog shit. If you ever want to throw your lot in with us, just give me a call. I mean it."

Simpson finished his whiskey and stood up. He looked at the smiling man who stood before him. If this was the future leader of Ulster, he wanted no part of it. Simpson smiled at the chief of the UVF thinking that he had to get out of there to make a second phone call. It was time to place the call to his MI5 handler. They were going to go apeshit when they heard that Billy already knew. But that was another day's work. The big trick was staying alive and that was something that you did one day at a time. "Thanks for the drink," he said handing Rice the empty glass. "I'll remember what you said."

CHAPTER 46

Wilson put down the phone, took a deep breath and leaned back in his battered swivel chair. Something primeval in him made him want to scream in triumph. He had the bastard. Carlile had come good and now, like hundreds of other citizens of Belfast, he owed him one. He never thought that someone like Carlile would drop a present into his lap. Why hadn't Carlile used the well tried route of the DCC? It didn't really matter. He sprang out of his chair with a burst of energy which he hadn't felt in years. The bastard had been living right in the centre of the Shankill all along. This one would need special care. Anyone capable of planning and executing a series of murders from the centre of the Protestant enclave was someone to be treated with extreme caution.

"Harry," Wilson screamed at the top of his voice.

"Yes, boss," Detective Constable Harry Graham stuck his head around the edge of the door. The rest of the Murder Squad looked up from their work. It was obvious to all that Wilson had hit high gear.

"We've got him, Harry," Wilson said, his voice betraying no emotion. "He's holed up in a Mrs. Maguire's house in Fortingale Street."

"Jesus Christ! How did you find him?" Graham said incredulously.

"An informant," Wilson said without feeling the need to give any further explanation. He pulled a street map of Belfast from his desk drawer. "I want half a dozen well armed detectives down there straight away. Without causing any alarm, they're to try and get the neighbours out. I don't want anyone near our man. If it's anyway possible I want the evacuation to be done discretely. One family at a time. Get on to operations. I want road blocks across the bottom of the Agnes Street, Conlig Street, The Old Lodge and Bristol Street. That place is to be sealed off tighter than a duck's arse. I want nobody going in and nobody going out without me knowing about it."

Graham was busy writing the instruction on a pad. "What about the Army, boss?"

"There's no need to call them in for one man. Anyway our boy isn't a terrorist, he's just a common murderer. Everyone's to be issued with a bullet-proof vest. Get on your bike, Harry. Get the rest of the squad to help you because I want everything in place within a half hour. Keep Moira out of the firing line. I don't want her killed on her first case."

"No problem, boss," Graham consulted his notebook. "What about upstairs?"

Wilson knew it was proper procedure to inform his superiors about a major operation. But in this case he concluded it might be better if Jennings was appraised when the operation had been successfully concluded. Jennings' involvement might only screw the operation up. "I'll organise the warrant," he told Graham. "You can organise everything else on my authority."

"I almost forgot, Skipper. Moira dug up the name of another bloke who was at Dungray at the same time as the others." He looked at his notebook. "It's a Patrick McGinn with an address in North East Belfast."

"Get someone over there and bring McGinn in."

"Jesus Christ!" Graham muttered as he left the office.

Wilson opened his desk drawer and removed his gun and a box of cartridges. He opened the base of the automatic and flicked out the magazine. It was full. He glanced over his shoulder into the squad-room and saw Harry Graham giving frantic orders to the other detectives. Eric Taylor and Ronald McIver put their coats on and, after looking in the direction of his office, rushed out the door. Moira McElvaney was standing still and looking bemused. Harry was keeping her out of the action and the look on her face said that she didn't like it.

"Boss," Moira strode towards Wilson's office.

"Sorry, Moira," Wilson pulled on his coat. "Somebody has to hold the fort."

"Bullshit," she said. "I'm holding the fort because I'm a woman. I was okay for dealing with Cahill and his men but now my sex is keeping me away from the action."

"Not true," Wilson said as he crossed the office. He had no time to debate. "Every other officer on the squad has experience in this type of action. You don't. End of story. Nothing to do with your sex, lots to do with you being the junior officer. Your time will come. Now stand by those phones and if someone from Headquarters tries to interfere, buy me some time. I'm out of here." He rushed away before Moira could challenge him.

They would be set up in Fortingale Street in five minutes and the evacuation of the houses beside Mrs. Maguire's would begin shortly after that. He took a deep breath and tried to compose himself. This was the lull before the storm. In half an hour, all the machinery would be in place and it would be his job to conclude the operation without anybody being killed. He wanted `Gardiner' badly and he wanted him alive. "You'll spill your guts to me," he said quietly. "And when you do I'll take everyone involved down with you."

Case sat bolt upright on the bed and looked at his watch. A film of sleep still clouded his vision and he had to blink several times before he could see the face of the watch clearly. It was three-thirty in the afternoon. His stomach rumbled and he remembered that he hadn't eaten since the previous evening. He swung his legs off the bed and stepped into his jeans which were lying on the floor beside him. A cup of tea and a sandwich would help to quash the eruption in his stomach. The internal alarm bell was still clamouring away without any apparent reason. He slipped on a black sweater and made his way downstairs to the back kitchen. He switched on the kettle and made himself a cup of tea and a ham sandwich. Just a few more hours and it would all be over.

A turn of the century Orange Hall stands on the corner where Agnes Street and Fortingale Street intersect. The large billboard outside the hall carried a rain soaked poster declaring `The Lord is My Shepherd I shall not want'. Across the road, the corner house facing the hall had a mural painted on its side depicting William of Orange astride his horse holding a sword in his hand. Underneath the painting was another legend `Remember 1698-NO SURRENDER'. Beside King William in black relief was a hooded figure holding a Kalashnikov aloft. The small group of people passing by in the rain paid scant attention to the police activity taking place behind the barriers which had been strung across the road at the rear of the hall. The citizens of Belfast had seen it all many times before.

Wilson's car drew up on the Agnes Street side of the hall and the DCI got out. A number of police Landrovers and PIGS, the PSNI armoured personnel carrier, were parked close by. They were drawn up in a neat semi-circle like a group of covered wagons anticipating an Indian attack. Police officers moved around the vehicles their dark blue rain coats puffed out by the padding of the obligatory flak jackets. Wilson walked towards the police vehicles. A PSNI constable detached himself from the other officers and came towards him.

"DCI Wilson?" the constable asked. He was young and fresh faced and Wilson noted the exaggerated tone of respect in his voice. He remembered what Moira had said about his reputation among the younger officers. The Heckler and Koch machine gun which hung from his shoulder seemed incongruous with his youth and innocence.

Wilson nodded.

"DC Graham's established a forward observation post in Bristol Street. Would you follow me, sir."

"It OK., Constable," Wilson replied. "I'll see myself there." He could sense the young man's disappointment. It wasn't his day to pander to other people's need to be part of the circus which was about to arrive in town.

Wilson walked towards Bristol Street and the young policeman returned to his colleagues. The street of terraced houses ahead of Wilson was narrow and deserted. A scene straight out of Victorian Britain. Wilson slid his hand into his pocket and ran his fingers along the metal of his revolver. He hoped to God there would be no killing although the possibility couldn't be ruled out. If the bastard was a professional, then there was an outside chance that he might recognise the hopelessness of the situation and give up peacefully. If, on the other hand, he was a rogue terrorist, anything could happen. A dark shape moved out of a side street sixty yards ahead and before he could recognise the police raincoat Wilson had already drawn his revolver. The policeman beckoned him forward. Wilson replaced the gun in his pocket and moved quickly down the street.

"DC Graham is expecting you, sir," the constable said as Wilson approached. "We're set up about forty yards from the house. DC Graham reckons we shouldn't go much closer."

Wilson turned the corner and saw Graham twenty yards ahead.

"Thank God you've arrived, boss," Graham said switching off his two-way radio. "The officer in charge of the uniforms is a real hero type. He's been pushing me to let him try rushing the place. Here you better put this on." Graham handed his superior a flak jacket and a luminous orange outer half jacket.

Wilson pulled the jackets on over his coat with difficulty. There was no way it was going to button so he left it flapping. "No way. We don't want anybody killed unnecessarily. I want that man inside the house alive. You make the hero, understand that. Did you get everybody out?"

"The street's clear for fifty yards on either side and the rest of the residents have been told to stay inside."

"Good work, Harry. Any movement from inside the house?" Wilson asked.

"Not a lot. We may have a problem."

"Spill it," Wilson said.

"According to the neighbours we should have two people in the house. The owner, Mrs. Maguire, and our boy."

"So?"

"We put the heat sensors on the house as soon as we arrived. They only show one heat source. Either Mrs. Maguire or our boy is not there."

Wilson was thinking what the DCC would say about the cost of this operation if it was unsuccessful. "There's no chance the sensors were faulty?"

"None," Graham said. "We have to suppose that the one source is our boy."

"Then where's the Maguire woman?"

Graham hunched his shoulders. "Let's think positively, boss. Let's assume that the heat source is our boy. Right now he's upstairs in the front bedroom."

"I hope for my sake that it is him. I wouldn't like to explain all this shit to Jennings. What about the roadblocks?"

"All in place," Graham replied. "If our man is in there then there's no way he's going to get out. And if he isn't there were goin' to look like an awful bunch of tools."

A uniformed inspector detached himself from a group of police officers and approached Wilson. "How do you want to play this?" he asked.

"Low key," Wilson replied, "I don't want any shooting if it can be avoided. If there is shooting, your men are to fire only on my orders. Understood."

The inspector nodded.

"Now get me a walkie-talkie and a loud-hailer," Wilson said. "I'm going to go down there and talk to the bugger."

CHAPTER 47

The sandwich and tea helped to quell the disturbance in Case's stomach but did nothing to dispel the feelings of anxiety which dominated him. He had left the residue of his snack on the kitchen table and had moved back to his room upstairs. For some reason he felt the need to be close to his shooters. As soon as he entered the front bedroom, he moved to the window overlooking the street and drew back the curtain. Nothing. What was it about this town that a street could be empty of people for almost one whole day. Then the penny dropped. That was the problem. This was a working class area of Belfast. No matter how bad the weather there were always kids on the street or old biddies going next door for a fag and a chat. But not to-day. Since early morning, there hadn't been a single person on the street. He tried to open the catch on the window. It wouldn't budge. The two pieces of metal were cemented by a large russet blob of rust. He pushed hard on the catch and the assembly came away in his hand, the catch separating completely from the two parts of the wooden window frame. The bottom half of the window initially resisted his efforts to push it up but it finally eased and he managed to open it wide enough to get his head outside. He put his head slowly through the gap left by the raised bottom panel. A gush of cold rain rapped against his face and caused his vision to blur. He tossed his head and looked quickly up and down the street. Nothing. He was pulling his head back into the room when a movement at an intersection twenty yards down the street caught his eye. He immediately recognised the muzzle of a rifle protruding from the wall. He quickly withdrew his head and turned to the bed where the steel suitcase remained open where he had left it. He picked out the Uzi and a handful of magazines. He slipped a magazine into the machine gun and made his way to the back bedroom. Betty Maguire's bleached white body lay on the ground where he had left it. She looked like a marble cast of his former landlady. A dark red patch covered the thin eiderdown and snaked into a pool of powdery dried blood which lay beside the body. He wondered who the hell was lurking outside? It had to be the police. But how the hell had they managed to get a line on him. He walked to the back window, pulled aside the curtain slowly and looked out across the back gardens of the houses on Fortingale Street. Each garden was directly connected to that of the house immediately backing on to it. Low wooden fences or hedges separated the small gardens from each other. If he had to make a run for it, this was the route he was going to have to take. He made his way to the front of the house cradling the Uzi in his arms.

A wicked rain laden wind whipped into Wilson's face as he turned the corner into Fortingale Street. He pushed closer to the wall as he walked slowly towards the Maguire house. Everything was in place. Sharpshooters had been stationed on the roofs of two houses at the end of the street and the back of the house was being covered from the windows of the houses directly behind it. Mr Gardiner was going nowhere. Wilson felt somewhat better about the operation knowing that there was someone in there. He'd been seen poking his head out through one of the upstairs windows. Maybe they should have taken their opportunity for a shot at him, but he wanted this one alive. He inched his way along the street glancing occasionally into the front room of the deserted houses. Stopping twenty yards from the house he took shelter in the recess of a doorway. His stomach gurgled as though he hadn't eaten in a day and he felt sweat running freely down his face and the back of his neck. This could very well be the big one. He could remember vividly the day the bomb had gone off beside him. He had hit the deck but not quite quickly enough. When he woke up in hospital he found that his only serious injury had been in his thigh. Half of his muscles had been removed and he would no longer run like a young gazelle around the rugby field. The news had shattered both him and his career. But he had learned to live with it. Now he was in the firing line again and if he was right about the man in the house then it could all end here for him. He looked down at the loud-hailer and noticed that the right hand was shaking. Steady on now, he thought to himself. It's nearly full time and we're just about to win the game. This wasn't the time to panic. With a little bit of luck everybody involved would still be breathing at tea-time. All that was needed was for him to talk the bastard out.

Case heard the steps approaching along the street. All his faculties were concentrated on his problem. They hadn't trained him to think in the Regiment. They'd trained him for action. He had made a quick assessment of the situation and had concluded that his chances of escape were slim. If the police had already surrounded the house, the odds were that they'd already put snipers in strategic positions. Things didn't look too healthy. The word in the Regiment had it that sieges usually ended badly unless there was a hostage handy. He started laughing. What a bloody idiot. He shouldn't have offed old Betty until he had no more use for her. But he didn't know this morning that by afternoon the house was going to be surrounded. He'd have to suss out what they wanted and try to negotiate the best possible deal for himself. They'd do him for Mrs. M's murder and the Browning would link him in to the other four killings. There was the Semtex to tie him in to the copper's death but that was only circumstantial evidence. At most, he'd be up for five murders. If he kept his mouth shut, then the boys in London just might pull his chestnuts out of the fire. Fat fucking chance. They'd run a mile from him. Chances were that they'd have him murdered before he'd get a chance to send them down the river. You're on your own in this one, Joe me old mate, he thought.

"Mr Gardiner, are you inside?" The tinny sound of the loud-hailer penetrated the front bedroom. "My name is Detective Chief Inspector Wilson of the Police Service of Northern Ireland. I have a warrant for your arrest in connection with the murders of James Patterson, Stanley Peacock, Leslie Bingham and Detective Sergeant George Whitehouse. We've got the building completely surrounded. We don't want anyone to get hurt anymore than you do so why don't you come out with your hands raised."

"Gardiner. Bollocks," Case said quietly as he moved to the half open window. The fat copper who'd stopped him after he'd done Bingham. I should have taken the two bastards out, he thought. Making sure not to expose any part of his body for a possible shot, he looked down into the street. He couldn't see the copper with the loud-hailer. The bastard was sheltering in a doorway just down the road. He pressed himself against the wall of the bedroom. If the place really was surrounded, there was very little chance of getting out.

"In a pig's arse I will," Case screamed through the open window mimicking the Belfast accent perfectly. "I've got the owner of the house tied up as a hostage. Get me a car and I'll let her go when I'm away."

Wilson was taken aback by the accent. McColgan had distinctly said that Gardiner had spoken with a Cockney accent. "Bring the woman out and let her talk to us through the window," Wilson pulled the walkie-talkie from his pocket. "Harry."

"Yes, boss," Graham's voice crackled over the radio.

"He says that he's got a hostage. Are you sure about the heat sensor?"

"Absolutely sure, boss."

"You better get the tear gas ready."

Case rushed into the back room and picked up Betty Maguire's body. He hauled her to her feet and carried the chalk white form into the front bedroom. "Come on, Betty you've one more little job to do for your Joey," he said tugging her into the front room. It was a long shot but it just might come off. He looked at Maguire's body. Nobody in their right mind was going to buy this.

"You out there," he shouted through the window, "I'm going to put her head out. Don't shoot." Case manoeuvred the body to the open window and dangled the head over the pavement. He tried to make the head turn and look down the street but failed. Then he abruptly pulled the body inside again.

Wilson watched the woman's head appear through the window. Her hands seemed to be held against her back and the head and neck were oddly stiff. The head quickly disappeared inside again.

"I didn't hear her speak," Wilson said into the loud-hailer. He felt that he could add Mrs. Maguire to the list of victims.

"She's too scared to speak," Case shouted letting the stiff slide onto the floor at his feet.

"The Maguire woman is dead, Harry," Wilson said quietly into the walkie-talkie.

He switched off the walkie-talkie and raised the loud hailer to his mouth. "I don't believe you've got anything to bargain with there. We've done a heat scan of the house and it shows only one heat source. Face facts, it's over. We've got the house surrounded and it's only a matter of time before you give yourself up. The sooner you do it the better it is for everybody. In ten minutes, we're going to start lobbing the tear gas." He set the loud-hailer on the ground and removed the pistol from his pocket.

"You do and you'll have a fuckin' war on your hands," Case could have kicked himself. Of course they would have done a heat scan of the house. "I've enough firepower in here to take plenty with me." He launched a kick at Betty Maguire's corpse. "You were no good, dead or alive," he said angry at himself for killing her before her usefulness had run out. He might live to regret that action. He had to think. He sucked in a deep breath and let it out slowly forcing himself to relax. There was only one possibility. He began dumping the few piece of furniture in the room onto the bed. Taking the suitcase from the bed, he moved to the door and carefully lit the edge of the bedspread with a lighter. The cloth caught fire immediately and within seconds the mattress was ablaze, smoke billowed from the darkened cloth and flames licked at the furniture piled on top of the bed.

Wilson saw the smoke pouring from the front window and knew immediately what had happened. He pulled the radio from his pocket. "Harry."

"Here, boss."

Wilson's breath came in short bursts. Adrenaline was coursing through his veins. "He's set the bloody house on fire. Give the order to toss the tear gas in. Concentrate on the ground floor windows. There's to be no shooting unless absolutely necessary and then only on my command." Wilson heard Harry Graham relay his orders. "He's going to try to make a break for it in the confusion. And for God's sake tell somebody to get the fire brigade."

Smoke and flames were beginning to pour out of the front window of the room where the fire had been started. The window pane shattered and sprayed tiny shards of glass across the road.

"Shit," Wilson said watching the flames. This was one mad bastard whoever he was. He was either going to die in a hail of bullets or he was going to fry.

Two police men wearing riot gear and bullet proof vests rushed past Wilson and fired tear gas canisters into the upper and lower stories of the house. The canisters left the muzzle of the launchers with a dull thudding sound and landed amid the inferno Case had created in Fortingale Street.

As soon as he heard the canisters landing, Wilson covered the twenty yards to the door of the blazing house.

Smoke was already drifting through the downstairs rooms as Case made his way along the hall towards the kitchen and the rear of the house. He heard the smashing of the glass and the thudding of the tear gas canisters as they hit the floor of the front room. It was only a matter of time before some fools in balaclavas would storm the house. He cradled the suitcase in his arm. Then there'd be shit to pay. He had only a few minutes to get out. The smoke from the fire was combining with the white plume of tear gas to form an acrid eye and throat stinging mixture. He stood behind the door between the kitchen and the back garden and prepared to go out.

Wilson put his full weight against the front door and it splintered in pieces. A stinging mixture of gases rushed through the opening into the street. He dashed into the hallway and threw himself on the ground in a firing position.. The hallway was empty but thick fumes swirled about the banister leading to the upstairs floor. Smoke poured down from the upper story and Wilson reckoned that there was no way their man was still up there. That left three possible rooms on the ground floor. He held his handkerchief to his mouth as he made his way towards the rear of the house.

Case exited from the rear of the house like a magician appearing suddenly on a stage in a puff of smoke. Before the snipers at the rear of the house could focus on the fleeing figure he had disappeared into the foliage between the two gardens. So far so good, he thought as he sat hunkered against the hedge. He pulled the Browning automatic out of the suitcase and stuck it in his waistband before stuffing three magazines into his pocket. It was time to get rid of the suitcase so he pushed it into the hedge. His shoes were already sinking into the soft ground beneath his feet and rain pelted into his face washing away the effects of the smoke and gas. This was shit or bust. He knew that what he was doing was crazy. But it was a hell of a way to go. It was like the last scene of `Butch Cassidy and the Sundance Kid'. Except that he didn't fancy the thought of dying in a blaze of glory. He pressed closer to the hedge and made his way slowly towards the rear of the small garden.

The smoke and the gas seared Wilson's eyes and tore at his throat. He heard the back door crash open and passed through the hallway and into the small kitchen. Smoke and gas was pouring out the back door and into the welcoming fresh air. A crash of timber collapsing came from upstairs as he moved slowly towards the open door. He hadn't heard any shooting so Gardiner must have made it out into the garden. There was no way the bastard could escape. Or was there? He lay flat on the ground and crawled the last few yards to the open doorway. He sucked at the fresh air which was entering the room at ground level. Smoke and gas billowed in the air above his head. His eyes ached from the effects of the gas and tears streamed down his cheeks. He blinked and tried to focus on the garden in from of him. The garden was small maybe fifteen feet wide by twenty feet long. The hedge separating the adjoining houses was wild and overgrown. He pulled the walkie-talkie from his pocket.

"Our boy is in the back garden," he coughed. "I'm coming out the back door. For Christ's sake nobody fire until I say so. He slipped the walkie-talkie back into his pocket and crawled carefully past the open doorway until his head was completely outside. He welcomed the rain beating on his scorched eyes. A movement in the hedge fifteen feet ahead of him caught his eye. He blinked and tried to focus on the spot where he had seen the movement. The hedge moved again.

All Case's concentration was aimed at reaching the end of the garden without mishap. It was a slim chance but at least there was one.

Wilson slipped noiselessly into the garden. His eyes still stung but he had enough vision to pick out the shadowy figure pressed against the hedge near the bottom of the garden. The man was turned away from him. He raised his gun to the ready position.

"Freeze," Wilson shouted.

Case heard the shout and remained dead still where he was. One shout, one copper, he thought to himself. He could take him out but that would give away his position. Then the snipers would do their job. He decided to wait for his chance. The longer you stayed alive the better the chance of escape.

Wilson steadied his gun hand and concentrated so hard on the figure at the bottom of the garden that he felt his eyes were standing out inches in front of his face. Away from the swirling smoke his vision had cleared sufficiently to recognise the man whose likeness he had pinned on his wall earlier in the day. "Stay exactly where you are. I don't want to shoot but if you don't toss your weapons aside I'm going to put one in you that won't kill you but it'll hurt like hell." He held his gun steadily before him.

Case remained crouched in the hedge. He recognised the voice. It was the copper who had spoken to him on the loud-hailer. There was something about the soft lilting Paddy accent that told him he shouldn't doubt that the copper was prepared to carry out his threat. It was decision time.

Wilson watched as Case tossed the Uzi onto the grass in the middle of the garden. "Now the pistol," he said sure that Gardiner would be carrying more than one gun.

Case laughed deep in his throat. This copper was good. He reached into his waistband and pulled out the Browning. The grip felt good in his hand. This was his last chance. Whatever way he looked at it the odds were against him in a gun battle. It was time to let it go. He tossed the gun on the ground beside the Uzi.

"O.K." Wilson said without relaxing his grip on his gun. "Stand up slowly and turn around."

Case stood up and turned to face Wilson.

"Move away from the weapons," Wilson edged down one side of the garden and indicated to Case to move away from the Uzi and the Browning and back towards the house. Smoke continued to billow from the open back door and Wilson could hear the sound of a siren in the distance. He pulled the radio out of his pocket. "Harry, we're in the back garden. I've got him." Wilson slipped the radio back into his pocket and looked at his prisoner. He could hear the sound of a helicopter approaching. Probably one of the Army's reconnaissance choppers attracted by the plumes of smoke rising from the house. He looked up as a Westland Scout with Army markings skimmed over the roof-tops and hovered over his head. A man dressed in a black boiler suit and wearing a black balaclava sat in the rear seat of the helicopter cradling a rifle in his arms. As Wilson watched, the man lifted the rifle deliberately and pointed at the garden.

"No." the scream seemed to come from somewhere else but Wilson recognised it as his own voice. It was so harsh that it hurt his throat.

Two shots rang out almost instantaneously. Wilson whirled and saw his prisoner collapse onto the ground, half of his head blown away.

"Bastards," Wilson screamed and turned back to the helicopter. The pilot was already putting the machine into a turn and accelerating away from the scene. He emptied his pistol after the fleeing machine but knew that it was only a pointless gesture. He walked to the fallen body of the killer. The contents of the man's skull lay splattered across the wet grass. "I wanted him alive, you filthy bastards," Wilson screamed in frustration.

"Jesus Christ!" Harry Graham stood at the back door. "What the fucking hell happened, boss?"

"You wouldn't believe it even if I told you, Harry," Wilson put his revolver into his pocket. "Pick up the Uzi and the Browning," he nodded towards the two weapons. "The Browning will match the killings of Patterson, Peacock and Bingham." Wilson looked around the garden and noticed the steel suitcase in the hedge. He pulled the case out and passed it carefully to Graham. "Take this box of tricks to forensics and have it examined."

The fire in the house had died down but smoke continued to billow out through the broken windows.

"Is this our boy?" Graham asked nodding at Case's body.

"That's him alright."

"Who shot him?"

"Some bloke in a helicopter," Wilson answered simply.

"What do you mean, boss?" Graham asked puzzled.

"Just that. A bloke in a helicopter shot him and we're never going to find out who it was or why." A terrible tiredness spread over Wilson. "I'm going back to Tennent Street. You clear up here, Harry."

CHAPTER 48

It was all fucked up, Wilson thought, as he sat in his cubby hole of an office. He'd bought a half bottle of Jameson on his way back to the office. He needed something to kill the pain and the whiskey had seemed like a good idea. But when he had tried to drink it neat he had almost screamed with the pain. He got himself a coffee and laced it with the whiskey. The combination warmed his throat and chest as he drank from his cracked office cup. His whole life had changed in the past twenty-four hours. Nothing would ever be the same again. He should have known. Somehow he didn't really care whether he remained a policeman or not. He sipped his coffee. His body slumped in his chair. Six months on some sun drenched beach was what he needed. That might just be about enough to put his body back but his soul was damaged irreparably He'd been right. Police work in Northern Ireland just wasn't possible. He'd solved a crime and yet he hadn't solved it. The murder of Gardiner would never be solved. It was a certainty that Gardiner wasn't even his real name. Nobody would claim the body. There would be an autopsy and he would be cremated. They would take his fingerprints but there would be no matches. Everything would be cleaned up nice and neat. The files would be impeccable. The procedures would be followed to the letter. After all why not. He would be a hero. The murderer had been located and a potential flair up of hostilities between the paramilitaries had been averted. A multitude of excuses would be prepared: one of the snipers had become nervous and fired off a couple of loose shots, a ricochet had hit the prisoner, etcetera, etcetera. The bottom line was that nobody was going to admit that some SAS type sitting in the back seat of a Westland Scout had blown the bastard's head off. That scenario must have been a figment of his overactive imagination. And yet he could still see in his mind's eye the black clad figure raising the rifle. Getting at the truth of the matter was out of the question. When Nichol died, he took whatever he'd known with him to the grave. Since Gardiner or whatever his name was had joined him on the slab, the reasons behind the murders would in all probability never be discovered. Somebody somewhere must be very happy with the result of to-day's job of work because he certainly wasn't.

He poured another shot of whiskey into the coffee and sipped the mixture. The pain in his throat was beginning to fade and the liquid slipped down easily. He looked at the wall opposite where the likeness of the murderer's face still stared back at him. He felt no sorrow for the man. He just wished he'd had the opportunity to try and unlock the secrets that were hidden behind those dark eyes. He looked around the rest of his office: his home for the past ten years.

He heard a noise at the door and looked up. Moira McElvaney stood in the doorway.

"You look terrible, Boss," she forced a smile.

"It goes with the territory. You heard about the fiasco?"

She nodded.

"I really wanted that bastard alive. Now we'll never know what was behind the killings. He'll be branded a lone wolf. A serial killer with no motive. Another file left hanging."

"We located Patrick McGinn and brought him in. He's in one of the interview rooms."

Wilson had forgotten about McGinn. "Let's go see Mr. McGinn," Wilson stood up slowly and followed Moira out of the office.

The Patrick McGinn that sat at a small wooden table in the interview room was a small balding thirty something who would weigh in at 50 kilos sopping wet. Wilson assumed that the stunting had been the result of insufficient food in childhood. He introduced both himself and Moira before sitting down.

"Mr. McGinn," he said sitting down. "Can I call you Patrick?"

Moira took the seat beside her boss facing McGinn.

"Why not," McGinn wrung his hands nervously. "Are you the one who had me brought here?"

"I'm sorry if we interfered with your day, Patrick. We brought you here because we felt that there was a threat to your life."

Sweat instantly broke out on McGinn's bald pate.

"We think that threat no longer exists," Wilson added quickly. " Do the names James Patterson, Stanley Peacock and Leslie Bingham mean anything to you?"

McGinn's face contorted. "I knew them a long time ago. We were in a children's home together. I haven't seen them in twenty years."

"Are you aware that all three men were murdered this week?"

"No." There was genuine shock on McGinn's face.

"You didn't read about it or hear the news on the radio?" Wilson asked.

"I'm severely dyslexic and I avoid the news. It's all bad anyway."

"Can you think of any reason why someone should want to murder these three men?"

"Not offhand. Like I said I haven't seen them since we were kids."

"Did you also know a Ronald Jamison?"

McGinn swallowed hard and then dropped his head into his hands. "Yes," he said so quietly that it was almost a whisper. "He was at the home as well."

"Ronald Jamison was murdered. You knew that?"

"Yes," again the whispered reply.

"Do you know who killed him?"

McGinn lifted his head slowly. His face was the picture of sadness. "No, but we assumed it was Nichol or one of his friends. But we were kids what the hell did we know."

"You said Nichol or his friends. Who were these 'friends'?"

Tears rolled slowly out of McGinn's eyes. "Robert Nichol was a pederast. All the people you mentioned were abused by Nichol and the men he brought to the home. Some were local but a lot of them had English accents." Tears streamed down his cheeks. "They had sex with us. Sometimes we were forced to give them oral sex other times they buggered us."

Wilson looked across at Moira and saw that her eyes were glassy. "I know this must be extremely painful for you, Mr. McGinn. Do you have any idea of the identities of the men Nichol brought to the Home?"

"No. But they were important people. People Nichol wanted to do favours for."

"Why didn't you tell someone?"

"We saw what happened to Ronald Jamison. He was a spikey wee bastard. Said he was goin' to shop the whole bunch of them. Then he disappeared and wound up dead. I put the whole business out of my mind for the past twenty years. Sometimes I can convince myself that it was all a dream and that it never really happened. But I sometimes wake in the middle of the night and the memories make me sweat even on cold nights."

"We think that Patterson, Peacock and Bingham were killed because of what happened in Dungray," Wilson said. "The man responsible for their deaths was shot dead earlier to-day. We are convinced that your life was in danger because of something you saw or heard during the abuse you suffered in Dungray. Are you sure you have no idea of why these men were murdered?"

McGinn dried his face with the sleeve of his jacket. "Like I said my coping mechanism was to convince myself that it never happened. Maybe it didn't. But I don't remember anything that could have gotten them boys killed."

Wilson was wondering where he could go next with the interview when Harry Graham stuck his head in the door.

"Boss, important," he said simply.

Wilson rose slowly. "You've been very helpful, Mr. McGinn. DC McElvaney will arrange for a police car to drive you home." He shook hands with McGinn and left the room.

Harry Graham was waiting directly outside the room. His face, already long and angular, appeared to be dropping to his waist.

"What happened, Harry," Wilson said on seeing Harry's depressed demeanour. "Somebody kill your dog?"

" No, Boss," Graham said quietly. "I just don't want to be the one to bring you this news."

"Get it out, Harry, and quick."

'There's been a fuck-up. After you left Fortingale Road, we had the usual parade of crime scene investigators, the Coroner, a couple of shooting scene investigators. The place was like a three-ringed circus. Anyway, after the coroner finished with the body, two ambulance attendants arrived to take it away. They bagged the corpse and loaded

402

it in an ambulance to take it to the Royal Infirmary. Ten minutes later another ambulance crew arrived to do the same job. I assumed there'd been a screw up and sent the second crew away. Bottom line is that the first crew never made it to the Royal. The ambulance was stolen and has been found burned out. There was no body inside. The corpse has disappeared."

"You are fucking joking me, Harry," Wilson shouted. "Tell me that you are fucking joking me or I promise you that you'll be pounding a beat to-morrow."

"Sorry, Boss. How was I supposed to know? The crew were kosher. Proper uniforms, proper ambulance, the lot. You might have done the same."

Wilson fought to contain his anger. Harry was right. They had been playing with the big boys and they had been gazumped. They'd lost the body and with it their only chance of finding out who exactly the murderer had been. The bastard had killed at least five men and one woman and could have been involved in the 'suicide' of Robert Nichol and they would never know who he had been

He put his hand on Graham's shoulder. "It's OK, Harry. Forget what I said. It could have happened to anybody."

He moved off in the direction of his office. He'd always considered Tennent Street to be his womb. Now he felt threatened by it. Those who really pulled the strings could invade his womb. He felt totally exposed for the first time in his life. There was nobody to trust. He was alone and he had failed.

The mood in the Squad-room was sombre. His team sat dejected at their desks. Wilson closed the door of his office, removed a bottle of Jameson from his desk and poured himself a very large measure.

Moira opened his door. "Better save it for later," she said. "The Deputy Chief Constable wants you at his office. The Duty Sergeant was afraid to tell you in person. Apparently you're looking for a head to bite off."

Wilson took a sip of the whiskey before putting the glass on his desk. "Don't go away. I'll be back for you." he said to the glass. "Well let's not disappoint the DCC." He opened his desk and removed the copy book which he had taken from Patterson's flat.

"What's that?" she asked.

"A little present for the DCC," he said shoving the copybook into his pocket.

CHAPTER 49

"Ah! Detective Inspector Wilson," Jennings came forward from his desk. As Wilson entered his office. "May I introduce you to Chief Constable Sir Thomas McKannan." Jennings was a model of obsequiousness.

The Chief Constable of the PSNI stood and extended his hand to Wilson. He was tall and grey-haired and dressed in his blue uniform. He exuded 'gravitas'. "Pleased to meet you Detective Chief Inspector."

The handshake was firm. "Likewise," Wilson said.

"Our two friends here are from the Home Office," Jennings said without offering their names. Both of them remained seated and neither made any move to shake hands.

Wilson stared at the man and woman from the 'Home Office'. They looked straight through him. The man was the elder and had an unremarkable rotund face topped off by a bald pate. Strands of wispy grey hair were just visible hanging down the back of his neck. His grey eyes looked out from beyond the thick lenses of horn-rimmed glasses. He hadn't bothered to remove a well worn Barbour wax jacket. His younger companion was dressed in a dark polo-neck jumper beneath a black leather blouson and black trousers. She was as plain as her dress sense. She returned his stare through bottle-top glasses. If these two were with the Home Office, Wilson was a monkey's uncle. Wilson knew a spook when he saw one. A smile played on his lips. He was about to be sold a barrel of shit.

"Firstly let me say how sorry I am about the death of your colleague DS Whitehouse," the Chief Constable began. "He wasn't the first man to give up his life for the Force and he certainly won't be the last. He will of course be buried with full honours."

"Of course. He was a brave man," Wilson hated himself for uttering such a cliché. He knew it sounded trite but his emotions were so strung out that he could think of nothing else.

"Please sit down," Sir Thomas indicated the chair beside his.

Wilson sat beside the Chief Constable and directly across the desk from Jennings. The spooks were seated to the side. They were there not as the principles but as the chorus to Wilson's Greek tragedy.

"And I understand it congratulations are also in order," Sir Thomas replaced his sombre look by his pleased look.

Score one for Saatchi and Saatchi, Wilson thought. The Chief Constable had handled the change of mood like the true professional he was.

"You apprehended the fellow who's been murdering people in West Belfast." Although McKannan was born and raised in County Antrim, like Jennings he had deduced at an early age that the possession of a British accent was an added advantage. He had therefore cultivated an Oxford accent long before he had been sent to serve in the Metropolitan Police. The accent only served to irritate Wilson.

"Only briefly," Wilson replied staring at the two 'Home Office' officials. The Chief Constable and his Deputy tried to ignore the remark. He didn't care. "I mean I only apprehended the man for a short period." Like five seconds, he thought.

Sir Thomas looked at Jennings.

"I've been looking back on your file, Ian," Jennings began flicking through a blue folder on the desk before him.

Wilson did not miss the significance of the use of his Christian name.

"Do you recognise this document?" he pushed a typed sheet across the desk towards Wilson.

"It is a copy of the Official Secrets Act."

"Signed by whom?"

"By me." Even his signature on the document looked younger and stronger than its current variant.

"You do, of course, understand the consequences for yourself were you to contravene any of the sections of the Act."

"I think that I do."

"Good," Jennings continued preening himself. He was the star turn on the stage. "Then I have to inform you that everything associated with the events of this afternoon are covered by the Official Secrets Act. The murders of Patterson, Peacock and Bingham are closed."

"And DS Whitehouse's murder?"

Jennings and the Chief Constable shifted uneasily in their chairs. The two officials from the 'Home Office' didn't bat an eyelid. Dead Plods in Northern Ireland were a dime a dozen.

"I think that in the fullness of time the man shot in Fortingale Street this evening will be proved to be DS Whitehouse's murderer," Jennings said grasping the nettle. His initiative would certainly not be forgotten by his superior who was already casting a benign smile in his direction.

"So it's all neat and tidy," Wilson said looking at his superior officers. "Five men and one woman murdered and the murderer apprehended and then disappeared. No nasty questions to answer. No court case. The lone assassin theory vindicated. A thoroughly satisfying conclusion. The widow Whitehouse will be pleased."

For the first time since he entered the room Wilson noticed the older 'Home Office' man flinch. He'd touched a raw nerve. His remark wasn't in the script and he was deviating from the part of the hapless copper which had been so carefully constructed for him. He hadn't landed the collar. So he could be blamed if the shit began to fly.

"I think I've put the whole thing together," Wilson said removing Patterson's copybook from his pocket. He noticed that he had the undivided attention of every man in the room. "I suppose I should have seen it much sooner it was so bloody obvious. But sometimes you can miss something that's staring you in the face." He tossed the copybook across the table towards Jennings. "I should have guessed what was on when I found that copybook at Patterson's."

Jennings held the battered copybook by the edges of his fingers. He prised open the first page and looked at the sketches. Wilson watched as the DCC's face turned into a scowl. Jennings held the copybook in a position where the two 'Home Office' officials could see it clearly.

"If I'd been awake when I saw that book for the first time," Wilson said. "I might have saved poor old George's life. That was the key. That's what it was all about. Dungray, Nichol the pederast, the boys that someone wanted dead. An ancient screwed-up intelligence operation. A sex ring to trap a person or persons unknown. Except that that person or persons no longer has all their screws in place and wanted the pawns in the operation removed." He looked at the faces of the two from the 'Home Office'. "I suppose that we'll never get to the bottom of why six people had to die?"

The question hung in the air unanswered.

Jennings pulled himself up to his full height. "Neither I nor the Chief Constable appreciate your tone.

The murders have been solved. The responsible is dead and the matter has been closed."

"I'm afraid we've seriously underestimated you, Detective Chief Inspector," the older 'Home Office' man spoke. The accent was Oxbridge overlaid with a military clipping of the words. "This is as far as you go. You've done a commendable job in tracking the killer down and I'm sure we're all very grateful to you. You've also managed to avoid a resumption of hostilities. All in all, a job well done."

"It's nice to be appreciated," Wilson said angrily. "All's well that ends well."

The senior spook removed a paper from the inside pocket of his barbour jacket and pushed it across the desk towards Wilson. "Do you know what that is?"

Wilson ignored the sheet of white folded paper.

"It is a Public Interest Immunity Certificate. It has been signed at the highest possible level. It means the case is closed, Inspector. Permanently. The murderer has been found by the ever-attentive police. I understand that a search of what was left of his lodgings has turned up nothing. He had no possessions with which to identify him. His body has been stolen and will in all probability never be found. He's a dead end. The trail stops there. I can of course understand your sense of frustration but I would caution you to accept the situation as you find it. Any other course of action on your part could have serious repercussions for your career."

"Maybe I'm not so sure that I want to continue to be a policeman."

"Then that would be a pity," the Chief Spook said. "Perhaps you should discuss this with your lady friend. As a QC she should be able to give you valuable advice."

So they knew about Kate and him. They would have a complete dossier on him. His affairs. His betrayal of his wife. It would all be used to discredit him if he went any further. Wilson could feel the anger boiling up inside him. They had him where they wanted him and he was beginning to realise it.

"I dare say that some snotty rag might run the risk of publishing your sordid little story but we still control enough of the press to make sure that the great unwashed British public give as much credence to your utterances as they do to those of foreign politicians. Think about it for a second. You're a disaffected man, Chief Inspector. You haven't been promoted in the past ten years and you resent it. In a station of over one hundred people you don't have one person that you can call a friend. And then there is the question of your sexual peccadilloes. That could see you out of the Force without a pension. You cheated on your wife even when she was dying horribly. What will Joe Public think of that?" The 'Home Office' man's tone never changed by as much as a decibel. There was neither anger nor jubilation in it. He removed a batch of photographs from a briefcase at his feet and tossed them on the table in front of Wilson.

The Detective Chief Inspector picked slowly through the ten or so black and white photos.

"You have some very peculiar drinking companions," the 'Home Office' man continued indicating some photos of Wilson, McElvaney and Cahill in the Republican Club." I wonder what could we make of that little gathering and your current dalliance of course." He indicated a photo of Wilson and Kate McCann making love which had undoubtedly been taken by a hidden camera in his house. "If you are unwise enough to pursue this matter, we'll break both you and your lady friend. I wonder will her obvious affection for you survive that."

Wilson fought to control his anger. He wanted to jump on the supercilious bastard and tear his living heart out. He took a deep breath and tossed the photographs of Kate and himself back on the pile. "You're nothing but scum. Do you know that. How the hell do you people live with yourselves?" He turned and looked at Jennings and the Chief Constable. "And you'd let them get away with this shit?"

The look on both men's faces answered the question for him.

"I can understand your indignation," the Chief Spook said. "But it's over."

"I just go back to my little office and forget that all this happened."

"Just so. You're a good policeman. It would be a pity to lose such a good officer."

Wilson looked at the photos spread on the table and then at the DCC. Jennings' lips moved slightly.

"Don't say anything, Sir," Wilson said. "Or I'll smash your bloody head to pieces. I'll see you at the funeral along with all the other hypocrites." He turned and left the room.

CHAPTER 50

They sat at a table in the corner of the lounge at the 'Crown'. Wilson was on his fifth whiskey and Kate held his hand while she stared into his eyes. The news from Kate's former boss at the Chambers in London hadn't been good but had confirmed what Wilson already knew. The 'powers that be' wanted the whole matter of the Belfast murders swept under the carpet. Kate's boss had been unequivocal, the matter should be dropped immediately.

"It can't end like this," Wilson said for what seemed like the fifth time.

"You've got to let it go, Ian," she said. "It's over. You can't bring back George and the man who killed him is dead."

"But there's someone behind this whole mess and that's the one I want," Wilson was beginning to slur.

"You can't go there. One thing I've learned in the course of my career is that justice is a somewhat elusive concept. Sometimes the guilty go free even after lengthy due process."

"But that doesn't make it right," Wilson lifted his hand to signal to the waiter but Kate caught it and returned it to the table between them. "That smarmy bastard Jennings and his spooky friends will have won."

Kate could see his eyes become glassy and his head began to droop. Life was cruel if someone with the integrity of Ian Wilson could be crushed at the whim of some faceless bureaucrat. But that was the way things were whether they liked it or not. The five people who had lost their lives for no good reason were only a drop in the ocean of deaths for no good cause. The men who wielded power at the centre would retire with their pensions and tend their rose gardens. Jennings would use his acquiescence to curry favour with those who could help him progress his career. His integrity level was zero but that was his trump card. Meanwhile their eyes and ears would be upon Ian and people like him. She glanced around the lounge. Nobody appeared to be taking a blind bit of notice of her and Ian. But that could be very far from the truth.

She ran her hand along his face. She felt a patch of wet where a tear had slipped from his eye. "Time we were away," she said tossing back the remnants of her drink. "A taxi home this evening I think. We wouldn't want to give Mr. Jennings and his friends the chance to cashier you. You'll stay with me to-night."

"Kate you are much too good to me," Wilson stood up heavily. He lifted his glass. "May God in his mercy be kind to Belfast," he announced to the room.

EPILOGUE

Sir Jeffrey Huntly OBE, MP sat between two plain clothes police officers in the back of a black BMW sedan as they passed through the gates of New Scotland Yard. He was sweating profusely and had been since he had been approached by the two officers at his office at the Houses of Parliament. Huntly was frogmarched between the two officers to an unmarked office on the third floor of the building which housed the Metropolitan Police. One of the police officers knocked on the door, opened it and ushered Huntly inside before withdrawing.

Huntly, his heart pounding like a drum, looked around the room. Three men stared back at him. An older man sat at the only desk in the room while a second much younger man stood at the edge of the desk. The both had hard craggy faces and carried themselves like military officers. The third man sat at the back of the room away from the two others. He was the only one that Huntly recognised and he was surprised to see the Prime Minister's Principle Private Secretary looking at him.

"Sit down," the man behind the desk ordered.

"I am a Member of Parliament not a dog that you can order around," Huntly fought to get a grip on his racing mind. He didn't like this situation and he particularly didn't like the fact that these people felt they could piss on him. He glanced at the Principle Private Secretary. "I shall complain to the PM about your insolence."

The man behind the desk smiled. "Please do so. The PM told me that if I wished to drop you off the top of this building I could do so. I suggest that you sit down and speak when you are spoken to."

Huntly was aware that neither of the two men facing him had introduced themselves and that fact bothered him greatly.

"You've been a rather naughty boy," the man behind the desk began when Huntly sat down. "We've been aware of your little scheme in Belfast for some time but we had difficulty tracking your man Case down. Oh, by the way, there was a shoot out in Belfast today and Case ended up being shot dead."

Huntly's face collapsed. His mouth was flapping open and shut but no sound was coming from it. He appeared to age by ten years in the past minute.

"I see the penny has dropped," the man at the desk said. "You now realise that you are here because you are responsible for launching a scheme which has led to the death of at least five people. If you were to go to court, you would spend the rest of your miserable life in jail." He stopped speaking and stared at Huntly. " We have had a certain amount of difficulty with your motivation but we think we've got there finally. You can interrupt me if I've got something wrong. We've interviewed some of your former colleagues who also enjoyed what was available in Dungrey and they have been delighted to put everything down on tape. It appears that the MP was considering you for the post of Secretary of State for Northern Ireland." Huntly was nodding his head. "As a back bencher you were pretty anonymous but as Secretary of State your face would be all over the newspapers and the television. Somebody might remember. So you decided to eradicate those you had already abused as children. A sort of double whammy for the poor unfortunates. You must have been out of your mind to send someone like Case to do your dirty work. The man was a psychopath. If it was up to me alone I would have you before the courts and you would never see the light of day again."

Huntly buried his head in his hands. "I couldn't risk accusations for something I did more than twenty years ago. I didn't want to end up like Savile and those aging TV people being paraded in front of the press and dragged before the courts. I can see now that I was unhinged but it looked like the only way out at the time."

"Case is dead and will never be seen again," the man behind the desk said. "Now all we have to do is deal with you." He turned and looked at the PM's Principle Private Secretary who rose and stepped forward. Without speaking he removed a sheet of A4 paper from his document case, placed in from of the man at the desk and retook his seat. "The PM's office has been kind enough to draft your resignation from Parliament," the man at the desk said. He tossed a pen on top of the sheet of paper. "Sign it."

"And if I don't," Huntly said.

"You really don't want to go there."

Huntly picked up the pen and started to read the letter.

"I didn't say read it, I said sign it."

There was so much menace in the tone that Huntly immediately complied and tossed both the resignation letter and the pen back on the desk.

The young man standing at the edge of the desk picked up the resignation letter and handed it to the PM's Principle Private Secretary who placed it in his document case. Then he stood up and left the room without speaking.

"Good," the man behind the desk said. "I assume that you have some patch of land somewhere out of the way in Cornwall or Skye or some other Godforsaken place that you can disappear to. We should be very mad indeed were we ever to hear from you again. The two gentlemen who accompanied you here are waiting outside. They will escort you from the building where you will obtain a taxi. Your office at the House has already been cleared and the boxes sent to your residence. And I think that concludes out business." He nodded at the young man who moved behind Huntly and raised him from the chair.

Huntly's body had taken on a whole new shape since he had entered the room. The confidence and the stature were gone and replaced with a bent back and a hangdog demeanour. The man had been broken in fifteen minutes. Huntly shuffled to the door and the young man ushered him out.

The man behind the desk opened a drawer and removed a bottle of Laphroaigh and two glasses. He poured a generous measure into each glass. "Your people did well, Peter," he said.

The younger man took the glass, toasted and took a large swallow. "We used a lot of resources on that idiot. I would have preferred to have followed the PM's advice and drop him off the roof."

"The PM never said that," the older man said. "I was interpreting." He smiled. "As a professional I think that copper in Belfast did a pretty reasonable job. Pity we're going to have to keep an eye on him."

"And Huntly?" the younger man asked.

"Now it's your turn to interpret, Peter," the older man said draining his glass.

Made in the USA
San Bernardino, CA
12 August 2015